Reading Reality

E. THOMAS FINAN

Reading Reality

NINETEENTH-CENTURY AMERICAN EXPERIMENTS IN THE REAL

UNIVERSITY OF VIRGINIA PRESS
Charlottesville and London

University of Virginia Press

Printed in the United States of America on acid-free paper

First published 2021

1 3 5 7 9 8 6 4 2

Library of Congress Cataloging-in-Publication Data
Names: Finan, E. Thomas, author.
Title: Reading reality : nineteenth-century American experiments in the real / E. Thomas Finan.
Description: Charlottesville : University of Virginia Press, 2021. | Includes bibliographical references and index.
Identifiers: LCCN 2020033424 (print) | LCCN 2020033425 (ebook) | ISBN 9780813945590 (hardcover) | ISBN 9780813945606 (paperback) | ISBN 9780813945613 (ebook)
Subjects: LCSH: American literature—19th century—History and criticism. | Realism in literature. | Reality in literature. | Emerson, Ralph Waldo, 1803–1882—Criticism and interpretation. | Whitman, Walt, 1819–1892—Criticism and interpretation. | Dickinson, Emily, 1830–1886—Criticism and interpretation.
Classification: LCC PS217.R4 F56 2021 (print) | LCC PS217.R4 (ebook) | DDC 810.9/12—dc23
LC record available at https://lccn.loc.gov/2020033424
LC ebook record available at https://lccn.loc.gov/2020033425

Cover art: The Voyage of Life: Youth, Thomas Cole, 1842, oil on canvas (Ailsa Mellon Bruce Fund, National Gallery of Art, Washington); manuscript page from *The Wide World*, Ralph Waldo Emerson, 1820 (MS Am 1280H [2], Ralph Waldo Emerson Memorial Association deposit, Houghton Library, Harvard University)

The very language we speak, thinks for us, by the subtle distinctions which already are marked for us by its words.

—Emerson

Let fame, that all hunt after in their lives,
Live registered upon our brazen tombs,
And then grace us in the disgrace of death;
When, spite of cormorant devouring time,
Th'endeavour of this present breath may buy
That honour which shall bate his scythe's keen edge,
And make us heirs of all eternity.

—Ferdinand, King of Navarre

Contents

Acknowledgments

I am fortunate to have taught at Boston University's College of General Studies during the composition of this book. Dean Natalie McKnight and her predecessor Linda Wells have provided great personal and scholarly support, for which I am very thankful. Adam Sweeting and Meg Tyler served at various times as chair of the Humanities Division at the College. Their support, encouragement, and advice have been great gifts. My colleagues at CGS have exemplified the spirit of intellectual cooperation that is at the heart of the College's mission. I am particularly grateful for the financial support provided by the College and Dean McKnight for the permissions and indexing costs of the book. Under the auspices of Boston University's Center for Interdisciplinary Teaching & Learning at the College of General Studies, Bruce Dennis provided helpful research assistance in the later phase of this project. I am very grateful for a publication award from the Boston University Center for the Humanities to support this project.

Portions of this book were delivered at conferences sponsored by the American Comparative Literature Association; the American Literature Association; the Association of Literary Scholars, Critics, and Writers; and the Thoreau Society. A portion of this book was also delivered as a talk at Boston University through the Faculty Research and Scholarship Committee at the College of General Studies. I am grateful to the organizers of these events for the opportunity to present and to the audiences for their useful comments, questions, and suggestions.

A variety of friends and colleagues (two not mutually exclusive categories) read portions or earlier versions of this manuscript: Cheryl Boots, Charles Capper, David Mikics, Cristanne Miller, Allen Speight, Adam Sweeting, and Meg Tyler. I am also grateful for discussions about this project with Marshall

Brown, David Dowling, Leslie Eckel, Lucas Fain, Paul Franz, Robert Habich, Daniel Karlin, Wendy Martin, Pat McCarthy, Anita Patterson, John Paul Russo, David Sloane, and others. Kevin P. Van Anglen has been an invaluable scholarly resource, and his comments on drafts for this project have improved it immensely. This book grew out of a dissertation for which Rosanna Warren served as the principal advisor; her incisive commentary, intellectual generosity, and continued support have made this and so much else possible.

At the University of Virginia Press, Eric Brandt proved indispensable in helping this volume through the publication process. Charlie Bailey, Helen Chandler, Morgan Myers, and the rest of the press staff also helped shepherd this book through its production. Leslie Tingle's editorial eye did much to improve the text. The anonymous readers commissioned by the press showed great critical care and intellectual charity, and their remarks greatly improved the manuscript.

Research for this book has been assisted by the holdings of Mugar Memorial Library at Boston University; the Houghton Library at Harvard University; the Thomas P. O'Neill Jr. Library at Boston College; and the American Antiquarian Society.

My parents and brother have provided support that goes far beyond this book. In the closing days of this project, my wife and I welcomed our first child into the world. To Jenny and Cecilia—for being and for coming to be.

Reading Reality

Introduction

An essay in the April 1833 issue of the *New-England Magazine* declares that poetry "is all reality; it deals in reality, and reality alone."[1] The author of this mostly forgotten essay is unknown, but its claim represents a wider nineteenth-century interest in the connection between poetry and reality. In one of his early poetry notebooks, Walt Whitman writes, "I am the poet of reality," and Ralph Waldo Emerson finds in his 1875 essay "Poetry and Imagination" that poetry "is the speech of man after the real, and not after the apparent."[2] Exploring this connection between poetry and reality affords insights into the intellectual debates and literary strategies of nineteenth-century Americans, particularly in the middle third of that century. It also provides a window into the broader enterprise of reading—what is gained and what is at issue in the experiential encounter with a text.

Many of the authors both inside and outside the conventional literary canon of the antebellum United States were deeply interested in some sense of a metaphysical reality and often saw literature as a place for interrogating experience in the hope of finding reality. The shift from antebellum *ideal* to the post–Civil War *real* (and Realism) is a standard in American literary studies and a staple of undergraduate surveys.[3] But American writers prior to the Civil War also laid claim to their own sense of the "real" and often foregrounded the real in their discussions of the literary enterprise, especially poetry.

Attending to this alternative sense of the real involves a reorientation of some of our standard connotations of the real. Across many spectrums of discourse, the term "real" has acquired the following associations: material, physical, particular, concrete, hard, practical, and true. Contemporary discourse often conflates the real and the physical. So we might reference a "real table." Contemporary uses of the term at times also often prioritize the everyday or the ordinary: the "real world" is contrasted with the fantasy imaginings of children, for example. This exposition is more a general contour than a totalizing list of all resonances of the real, and how the real came to acquire these resonances would be another book entirely.

While that tradition of the real had considerable influence on Realists after the Civil War and could also be found in American writing prior to the Civil War, many American writers in the first two-thirds of the nineteenth century drew from a tradition that assigns the following resonances to the real: metaphysical, interrogative, initiating, spiritual, introspection-inspiring, transformative, and true. These senses reach back many years and can be found in some of the earliest uses of the word "real." Moreover, they tap into intellectual debates that have been ongoing since the dawn of philosophy in the Socratic tradition. Rather than simply identifying the real and the everyday, many nineteenth-century Americans also embrace the senses of the real as what is sincere, as spiritual testimony, as what *is* rather than what appears to be, and as some metaphysical truth. Antebellum Americans in part participate in a Platonic tradition of the real that locates reality beyond the physical world, but their interest in the extra-actual real does not mean a rejection of the physical world. Instead, it involves a dialogue with the incidents of the physical world, as immediate appearances are tried by the experiencing individual. For many antebellum figures, the real is not simply the physical and might be found beyond it. This real might be the reality of God or of some idea or of immediate personal testimony. Antebellum authors often conflate—rather than contrast—the "ideal" and the "real" (and "idealism" and "realism"). In complement to the blending of the real and the ideal, antebellum writers sometimes distinguish between the "actual" and the "real": what is actually present in the world of the flesh may be less real than some personal response or some grand idea. These conceptual emphases have a Platonic heritage, but they are also influenced by, among other sources, the works of Immanuel Kant and transatlantic responses to them.

I will at times refer to this tradition as being one of the "experiential real."[4] In invoking this tradition, I do not mean to say that it offers a singular metaphysical account of "reality." Instead, it is informed by a variety of accounts of reality that use experience as a venue for finding the real. For this tradition, atoms alone do not define the real, but the process of finding reality demands a trial of the appearances of life. "Experience" derives from the Latin *experientia* (trial), so the phrase "experiential real" foregrounds that task of trial. This task of trial is important for the literary techniques and aims of antebellum Americans, but it also affords a vehicle for examining the stakes of reading. In the wake of reparative reading, distant reading, and postcritical reading, scholars have turned with renewed interest to the ways that literary reading involves a trial of particularity. Investigating the intellectual context and literary practices of antebellum Americans reveals an interest in grounding literary provocations in the quest for reality, and exploring this literary dynamic can cast light on the broader way in which literature can prompt us toward some realization—that is, the way it can prompt us to alter our account of real existence through our encounter with the particulars of a text.

Antebellum interest in some metaphysical reality is not an entirely alien topic to critical narratives of this period; indeed, the aspiration to glean a deeper spiritual meaning in the physical world has long been recognized as a major theme for American writing in the nineteenth century and beyond. Nineteenth-century Americans inherited a Christian tradition that stressed a craving for God and spiritual values beyond the things of this world. New Englanders in particular grew up in the distant shadow of the Puritan tradition of typology, which attempted to read the events of the physical world for a sign of God's will.[5] Other traditions both old and new contributed to this quest for a reality beyond the material. Platonism and its offshoots (including the seventeenth-century Neoplatonists who proved influential for many New Englanders) called for a perception of real ideas through the physical objects of the world. Many seventeenth-century British writers—such as Thomas Browne—who proved so fascinating to their nineteenth-century successors had deep philosophical and literary commitments to the testing of appearances in order to find some realer truth. In response to the philosophical challenges posed by John Locke and David Hume, German idealists dwelt on the way that the subjectivity of the human mind can condition what we take to be the material. Samuel Taylor Coleridge and other British Romantics served as conduits for these philosophical ideas in the United States.

In part because of its philosophical influences, transcendentalism has long been associated with this endeavor of seeing a visionary reality. Ralph Waldo Emerson, Henry David Thoreau, George Ripley, Frederic Henry Hedge, and others often called for some recognition of a reality beyond the physical world. But this interest was not confined to the transcendentalists. Nathaniel Hawthorne's works are haunted by the effort to interpret the concrete and everyday in light of a greater metaphysical reality; spiritual interpretation and its challenges weave throughout his tales and romances. In *Moby-Dick* Herman Melville writes an epic of the (perhaps frustrated) struggle to reach beyond the physical in order to grasp some reality of meaning. Emily Dickinson's poetry so often starts from some immediate event and then turns to reflect on what lies beyond the physical.

The field of Americanist criticism has long acknowledged the significance of the tradition of interrogating the actual. Indeed, early histories of the antebellum era, written long before the establishment of American literature as an academic field, drew attention to this tradition. For instance, Octavius Brooks Frothingham's history of transcendentalism, *Transcendentalism in New England* (1876), highlighted it. Interrogating the actual has permeated American academic accounts of the antebellum period from F. O. Matthiessen's *American Renaissance* and Charles Feidelson's *Symbolism and American Literature* onward. In recent decades this approach has been supplemented by increasing interest in the historicization of American literature; expanding the literary canon; recasting literature through the lenses of race, sexuality, class, and gender; and situating the United States in a broader global environment. All these approaches have brought considerable things of interest to light. Some have rebuked the transcendentalist hypothesis by insisting that we return to material circumstances and even to the material itself (as the field of material studies suggests). Others have returned to this transcendentalist hypothesis by suggesting the potential complications of transcendence for the literary enterprise. For instance, Elisa New's *The Line's Eye* expresses some reservations about the effort to render the world transparent—to "see through" it to gain some deeper knowledge.

Scholars of nineteenth-century literature have long recognized that "reality" and "real" can be contested literary terms. What counts as real might respond to various technological changes, economic pressures, or social expectations. Donald Pizer has found that debates about "social reality" were "conducted principally within an arena deeply colored by controversial and polemicized social and cultural issues" and says that authors, in deciding how to represent what and whom, must ask themselves what kind of society they wish for America and how "realism and naturalism contribute to the achievement of that society."[6] In her critique of the denigration of "sentimental" writing, Jane P. Tompkins finds that later critics' condemnations of sentimentality arise from the fact that "the reality *they* perceive is organized according to a different set of conventions for constituting experience."[7] Moreover, writers might invoke the real or realism in order to claim a certain cultural place for their work. Amy Kaplan explores some of these cultural pressures in *The Social Construction of American Realism,* and Michael Davitt Bell's attention to the "problem" of American realism notes intersections of claims about realism with questions of gender, class, and the literary marketplace. As Bell puts it, to "proclaim oneself a realist or naturalist in this context was most fundamentally to claim for literature the status of a 'real'—that is, socially normal—activity."[8]

References to some reality beyond the physical have circulated throughout Americanist criticism. Recently, Nancy Glazener has drawn attention to that "ideality, which combined various hopeful beliefs about humans' nature and capacities with the vaguely Platonic sense that the truest reality existed in a dimension beyond the reach of science."[9] In her reimagining of the role of Realism in poetry in the later part of the nineteenth century, Elizabeth Renker finds that the "materialist premises" of postbellum Realism seek to "overturn a longstanding prior use of the term 'reality'—that is, in its Platonic sense of idealist truth opposed to 'appearance.'"[10] There is a long critical history for such diagnoses about some "idealistic" form of reality. For example, Matthiessen contends that "integral to Emerson's idealism" is the seventeenth-century Platonist Ralph Cudworth's belief in there being "as much reality in fancy and consciousness as there is in local motions."[11] Daniel Walker Howe writes that the "Transcendentalist artist interpreted the ideal realities behind . . . physical superficialities."[12] In her discussion of Emerson and philosophy, Barbara Packer finds that such idealism can convince the individual of the existence of "spiritual realities."[13]

Digging into the precise operations of the terms "real" and "reality" in American literature prior to the Civil War (and even after the war) reveals additional complexities. In much of the argument of this book, I will examine one angle of reality—the experiential one. The experiential real demands a continued return to experience, which preserves the incidental qualities of the particular even as it situates this particular in a broader narrative. This narrative of the real can connect the transcendental and the empirical. As will be developed in the succeeding chapters, a narrative exploring the experiential challenge to the actual is not completely removed from the political questions that have animated much recent scholarship; the dynamics of the experiential real have a bearing on questions of pluralism and political incompleteness, for instance. Rather than "seeing through" the particular by abnegating it (and thereby glimpsing some abstract ideal), the tradition of the experiential real instead seeks a double mode of vision, in which the particularity of an object is recognized by seeing it in light of a broader vision.

This awakening return to particularity signifies a shift away from the notion of representation and toward the project of provocation. Though not uniformly, the theme of representation threads throughout many critical discussions of Realism. For instance, Tompkins differentiates "three distinct levels of apprehension: 'reality itself' as it appears to people at a given time; what people will accept as an 'accurate description' of reality; and novels and stories which, because they correspond to such descriptions, therefore seem true."[14] Tompkins here foregrounds "description" and "correspondence"—what we find to be an "accurate description" of reality is one we will accept as realistic. Renker offers the following as the initial trait for many of the poems in her postbellum Realist archive: "Realist poems represent (or sometimes propose) a domain they construe as the real or reality, with all the attendant complications, both literary and ontological, that these projects entail."[15] While there may be disputes about what counts as real and what representation entails, that theme of representation connects many literary approaches to the real.

Many works seen in this tradition of the experiential real might include certain claims about spiritual reality and might try to represent that spiritual reality on the page. But they also take on a provocative task, seeking to find realization in the experience of certain moments of vision. Achieving the "real" for this tradition is about the encounter with the particular in conversation with a broader vista. As will be explored in the first chapter, many accounts of reading in the nineteenth century stressed the idea of reading as an experience—as a dynamic exercise that prompts new visions and personal changes. This dynamic approach to reading has implications for grasping the real in reading; it is not enough simply to read accounts of some grand truth, but a work might be structured so as to provoke a revolution in understanding. It is in that revolutionary pivot that realization can be found.

In the turn toward provocation, this alternative tradition of the real also addresses some contemporary prevailing questions within literary studies. One thread of this study involves the intellectual-historical elements of the tradition of the experiential real, but another thread instead deals with a methodological narrative: the role of experience for the act of literary reading. The themes of incompleteness and interrogation found within the tradition of the experiential real have a bearing on the broader practice of literary reading. After all, the relationship between the details of experience and the hope of visionary transparency is one of the major questions of the methodology of literary criticism. In a time when methodologies of reading proliferate—distant and close, theoretical and formalist—a reflection on the tradition of the real as seen in the nineteenth century can help advance a narrative of literary reading that combines experiential attention with theoretical vision.

The tradition of the experiential real might be amenable to a phenomenologically inflected approach to reading (an approach to which proponents of postcritical reading such as Rita Felski have been sympathetic). The experiential real demands the interrogation of the phenomena of everyday experience in the hopes of glimpsing some greater reality. Writers working within this tradition often make a work of literature itself a venue for phenomenal trial: following out the course of a literary work might bring us to conceptual challenges, psychological reorientations, and existential disruptions. A work of literature itself is part of existence, and it prompts us toward a further accounting of existence. A full-spectrum approach to a literary text—one that grapples with both formal traits and theoretical traces—reveals the ways in which this text offers realizing provocation.

The "real" is a loaded term for antebellum discussions of literature, and the first chapter sets out to discuss the weight it bears in different contexts. It digs through the philological-conceptual sedimentary layers of the real in order to explore the significance of "real" and "reality" for Americans in the first two-thirds of the nineteenth century. Some early nineteenth-century writers criticized literature for not being "real" enough, but by the mid-1830s, a number of American writers replied to this criticism by developing an alternative sense of the real and by locating that sense of the real in literature. Moreover, they often emphasized the experiential element of reading—offering it as a mode for exploration and reflection.

The broad outlines of this alternative tradition of the experiential real provide an infrastructure for discussing the works of Ralph Waldo Emerson, Walt Whitman, and Emily Dickinson in chapters 2, 3, and 4, respectively. I do not propose that these three writers constitute a unified poetic school. While they are all informed by antebellum traditions of the real, they respond to the enticements of these traditions differently. I focus on these writers as much for their differences as for their commonalities; they can provide a prism for separating and thereby clarifying various aspects of the real in nineteenth-century America as well as the project of experiential reading. Emerson again and again presents the poet as a realizer, and he often conceives of the poet as seeing through the actual (or the material) in order to glimpse the real. However, a tension lurks in the act of seeing through: the trace of the actual persists even in the enterprise of poetic vision. The play between transcendence and trace permeates his approach to knowledge as well as a number of his poems and essays. Whitman's verse emphasizes the importance of the reality of witness. The enterprise of *Leaves of Grass* involves the quest for realizing witness, which at once insists on distinction between self and other and suggests a unification that blurs distinction. The experiential real reveals the way that Whitman's poetry preserves the particular even as he promotes a visionary politics. Emily Dickinson does not seem to embrace as clearly as Emerson or Whitman the notion of poet as realizer, but her work provides another opportunity for the examination of the intersection of the stakes of reading and reality. When they do mention the real, her poems often emphasize the disruptive aspects of realization. Chapter 5 reflects on the interrogation of particularity in the name of the real and applies the tactics of this interrogation to a range of writers from the nineteenth and twentieth centuries. This final chapter also discusses how the interrogation of particularity recasts contemporary debates about reading.

This attention to the alternative sense of the real in the antebellum period allows for a recovery of a certain strand of American intellectual history and aesthetic practice. While Elizabeth Renker in particular has done valuable work to reorient the role of poetry in the age of post–Civil War Realism, it is also worthwhile to excavate what the real means for the literary enterprise prior to the Civil War.[16] Just as the experiential real affords a vehicle for understanding the literary dynamics of influential American writers, it also presents a way of accounting for some of the distinctive traits of the literary experience. In a time of critical foment about methodologies of reading, the tradition of the experiential real reminds us of the vastness and possibility of the literary encounter.

As outlined in the following chapter, one of the canonical distinctions regarding the real is the contrast between appearance and being, and individuals often appeal to the term to maintain this distinction: those things that *seem* without *being* are often classified as unreal. Thus, calls for access to some reality often function as calls for the interrogation of appearance—only by interrogating appearance can one see what truly counts as real. What this interrogation consists of can, of course, be quite broad; it might be inner reflection, intellectual analysis, or scientific experimentation, for instance. American antebellum writers often stress the importance of literature as a vehicle for this interrogation.

The tension between appearance and reality—between seeming and being—becomes a great source of energy for nineteenth-century writers. It helps explain the restless dynamic of the works of Emerson, Whitman, Dickinson, and others: the desire always to test, the impulse always to press on, and the embrace of open-ended particularity. If that instant of reality is the ring of truth in the flux of appearances, every appearance provides an opportunity for trial. A thoroughgoing application of the principle of the trial of appearance suggests that not only physical objects might be tried: so too might concepts, cultural categories, words, and any received cognitive ordering. After all, these concepts, categories, and so forth also appear (albeit not in a physical way). A seemingly abstract idea has its own surface, which can be as imprisoning as any material one. There is the risk that in taking up an abstract idea—say, Beauty or Democracy or Freedom or Reality—one puts that idea on a shelf, where it remains mute, reserved, and utterly solid. For the tradition of the experiential real, it is not enough merely to invoke immortal, uncontained beauty.[17] That surface appearance, however grand it may sound, need be no better than the buzz and din of stock markets, walnuts, and rubber tires. Of course, that "no better than" might cut another way: stock markets, walnuts, and rubber tires can themselves be the opportunity for the vision of a further real. Merely fleeing from the physical to the abstract does not offer much of a salvation for those who would pursue the experiential real. The surfaces of the abstract can also leave one with a barren appearance.

This need for the continued trial of experience ensures that the enterprise of the experiential real does not simply become the effacement of the particular in the pursuit of radical abstraction. The tradition of the experiential real affords a way of marrying an attention to experiential detail with a broader intellectual vision. The way that the experiential real involves the continued trial of the particulars of experience creates a space for a narrative that combines the desire to see through experience with continued attention to the details of that experience. The status of the particular has long been a topic of concern for accounts of nineteenth-century American literature. For a number of writers in the later Realist or early modernist eras, the presumption was that, all too often, antebellum writers "saw through" the things of the world in a way that caused them to abandon the incidents of real living in the pursuit of some fantastic ideal.[18] Partly in response to this presumption of abstraction, some later scholars have emphasized antebellum writers' deep engagement with—rather than indifference to—the affairs and materials of this world.

This concern about abstraction persists in American literary studies, as contemporary narratives of transparency demonstrate. Many scholars have focused on the capacity of transparency to obviate difference—to nullify the seen-through in an instant of imperialistic projection. For example, both Elisa New and Branka Arsić argue for attention to immediate surface in nineteenth-century literature while also critiquing (or at least expressing anxiety about) the methodology of transparency. New in *The Line's Eye* and Arsić in *On Leaving* lay out two distinct ocular dualities that are reflective of contemporary scholarly concern: vision and sight, and gaze and glance, respectively.

For New, the incidents of actual experience fade before the zealous sun of the visionary, so "the visionary finds only Israel or Babylon, Promised Land, Manifest Destiny, or a receding Frontier (plantations of power abounding, but no place and no satisfactory calling)." Visionary transparency "distends and defers."[19] New also finds that "transparency will ever romanticize shallow projection as natural genius."[20] In contrast to imperial vision, New celebrates the possibilities of an American poetic sight. Rather than indulging in the gaudy transparency of vision, sight turns to the concrete incidents of lived experience, so, in place of the grand projective ideals of Frontier and Promised Land, we can have "birds and pasturage and work."[21] The "more watchful eye" of experiential sight will "cultivate more dynamic relations" by accepting the fraught complexities of the experiential.[22]

In her account of Emersonian perceptual methods, Branka Arsić draws from the work of visual theorist Norman Bryson, who outlines two methods of seeing: gaze and glance.

> As Norman Bryson explains: "Both in English and in French, vision is portrayed under two aspects: one vigilant, masterful, 'spiritual,' and the other

> subversive, random, disorderly." Emerson's "trained" eye, which fixes the mobile, manifests the force of gaze since, according to Bryson, gaze precisely "attempts to extract the enduring form from fleeing process; its epithets tend toward a certain violence (penetrating, piercing, fixing), and its overall purpose seems to be the discovery of a second (re-)surface standing behind the first, the mask of appearances." Gaze is fixed and fixes in order to see the "depth," thus disregarding the surface. In negating the truth of the immediately visible, corporeal, and changeable, the gaze idealizes (or, as Emerson would say, "detaches" and "magnifies by detaching"). Taking its distance from the immediate, the gaze becomes a sort of ocular skepticism, aloof and distant from the world.[23]

Arsić contrasts this "alienating idealization" to the practice of the glance, which is "entrusted to the sensual" and which "spreads over a surface and follows its motions, which is why it is always distracted." The glance "subverts the major values of Western logos—such as depth, stability, or form."[24]

Even if "vision" and "sight" are not entirely analogous to "gaze" and "glance," there are parallels between the two dualisms. Both New and Arsić appeal to one mode of vision (or gazing) that nullifies the incidents of experience in favor of some idealistic purity. Their narratives of "vision" and "gaze" also have resonances of transparency. New contrasts experiential poetics (and sight) to the "poetics of American transparency," and visionary transparency seems a projective, potentially imperialistic, enterprise.[25] Arsić emphasizes the tropes of penetration in Bryson's articulation of "gaze"—"penetrating, piercing, fixing," and so on—and alleges that such a gaze "disregard[s] the surface" in order to find the depths that lie beneath. In both cases the act of going through disregards the surface. Meanwhile, the experiential turn of New's "sight" suggests a roving, ever-provisional encounter with the heterogeneous incidents of life, a tendency very much in line with Arsić's portrayal of "glance." Whereas gaze dismisses surface in the lust for depth, glance lingers on that ever-fluctuating surface.

The literary dynamics of the experiential real, however, offer an alternative narrative of transparency, one that finds an alliance—rather than enmity—between transparency and attention to surface detail. Lee Rust Brown poses a critical opening for this alternative narrative in *The Emerson Museum* when he writes that one "of transparency's 'beautiful laws' is that, when the eye sees *through* something, it secretly insists on what it seems to have denied."[26] The hidden insistence of transparency—its emphasis on the gone-through surface in the act of seeing—opens up the possibility of a narrative of transparency that affirms disruption and difference. Rather than being a one-way street of visionary tyranny, this mode of transparency instead allows a dialogue. The medium is not completely left behind. The very form that allows one to see *through* remains in some way even as it is, in another way, gone beyond.[27]

This dialectical play offers an example of the unsettledness of such appeals to the real, and disruption often plays a role in the tradition of the experiential real. In *The Light of Common Day,* Edwin H. Cady sketches out the case for realism as "a theory of Common Vision."[28] Cady's notion of realism depends on the socialization of reality—that which we can verify through our conversations becomes real. As Cady puts it, "We check the content and qualities of our experience with the experience of others to see whether ours is 'real' or not."[29] In their revision of particularity in pursuit of the real, antebellum Americans often stress an *uncommon* vision, a sight of personal and social disruption. They explore moments of aperture, when a new vision of the real comes to disrupt old conceptions of themselves.[30]

The mode of heterogeneous transparency provides a device for conceptualizing some of the dynamics of the experiential real. For antebellum Americans, the quest for the real entails going through the incidents of the actual. The enterprise of going through demands attention to the surfaces of the concrete, but it does not stop with them. The realizing eye does not ignore and is not oblivious to the incidents of the actual world. Instead, it goes through them, rendering them, in a way, transparent. In part because of the resistances of transparency (the way that transparency rebukes the obviation of what is seen through), transparency provides a helpful trope for examining some of the transformations we see in the works of Emerson, Whitman, Dickinson, and others. Just as looking through at once insists on and transcends the transparent form and just as the quest for some extra-actual "real" at once insists on and goes beyond the actual, so too do the works of these writers manifest a tension between transcending a given figure and insisting on this figure.

The play between transcendence and immanence in the enterprise of transparency recasts the status of the particular in antebellum writing. The vision of the real demands an accounting of particular, actualistic details. Far from being annihilated in the instant of real vision, the details persist as a gateway. Returning to the incidents of the particular can disrupt rote attitudes in order to inspire us to some further real insight, and the quest for such reality demands the perpetual trial of the particular incidents of the actual world. Efforts at provocation in pursuit of realization are double-edged: the quest for the real can cause a revision of the particular even as our encounters with the particular can in turn revise our broader view of the world.

This theme of interrogating appearance makes this issue of the real relevant to both critical accounts of nineteenth-century American literature and contemporary scholarly debates about reading. If uses of the term "real" often demand the resituation of appearance within some greater account of reality, that "real" can have multiple implications for the act of reading. Literary works can shift our understandings of the appearances of the world or our greater understanding of reality as a whole; moreover, our experiential encounters with individual parts of a text involve a constant dialogue with our understanding of that literary work as a whole. The transformation of surface involved in the tradition of the experiential real has implications for the act of literary interpretation. The enterprise of "close reading," after all, demands the interrogation of the surface details of a text in order to connect these details to broader traits. Just as the seen-through is not entirely effaced for the vision of realizing transparency, literary interpretation—in close reading and other modes—looks through without nullifying the details of a text. Indeed, returning to these details affords a rejuvenation of broader interpretive narratives.

American literary studies have been invigorated by a meditation on the stakes of a close attention to literary details.[31] However, the fate of reading has implications that go far beyond Americanist literary studies, and the tradition of the experiential real can help mount a defense of experiential reading in a methodologically pluralist context. Even the project of "distant reading," as espoused by Franco Moretti, draws on experiential capital. Moretti has argued that literary studies might profit from going beyond the extended literary interpretation of a relatively narrow number of texts to mount instead a computational survey of select details (such as title lengths) of a vast sea of texts. The claims advanced on behalf of such a method of reading include that it can offer a more comprehensive picture of the literature of a given era, that the typologies of graphs and maps cast light on the greater forces influencing the construction of literature, and that this method allows literary studies to harness the strengths of scientific methodologies.[32]

The practice of "distant reading" has uncovered numerous intriguing results both in comparative and American literary studies, and I have no intention here of dismissing such computational methods of reading.[33]

However, the process of distant reading in part depends on the use of categories and terminologies derived from the direct encounter with a text. For instance, Moretti's famous essay "The Slaughterhouse of Literature" has a revealing evolutionary discussion of the role of clues in detective fiction in the late nineteenth century.[34] The formalization of the literary "clue," though, depends on the particular navigation of a text. Someone who had never encountered detective narratives would be unable to formulate a distant-reading diagnostic about the use of clues in detective fiction.[35] This might seem a trivial point (and nowhere does Moretti call for us to stop reading individual texts), but it underlines a deeper methodological truth: the diagnostic variables of computational reading depend on, and are renewed by, the thoughtful engagement with individual texts. Thus, distant reading's computation relies on the experiential encounter with individual works. To surrender the enterprise of individual interpretation is, then, to foreclose the horizons of future computational analysis, as such analysis would grow out of the findings and fashionings of reading-informed literary criticism.[36]

Attending to the real in antebellum American literature reveals the enduring importance of close attention to literary texts as part of the enterprise of sketching out literary history. The recovery of this alternative tradition relies, first, upon examining in detail the particular texts of the time. This examination may use some of the tools of data analysis (such as the searchable database), but it puts these tools to the service of an in-depth investigation of particular uses of the real. Moreover, the recovery of the experiential real also demands the close interpretation of literary texts; one of the major contentions of this study is that the antebellum approach to the real depends on the cultivation of certain literary dynamics, which discursive commentary on individual texts reveals. Personal meditation on these texts and not computational analysis (at least by any computer that currently exists) allows us to grasp the contours of this real for American literature.

Thus, if we want to recover and understand the experiential real, we need to continue the project of experiential reading. The alternative tradition of the real exemplifies a broader truth about the fact that some traditions and some traits of literary history might be invisible to the eyes of computational reading. If, then, we want to gain a full perspective of literary history, we cannot afford to sacrifice experiential reading. Again, I do not mean here to suggest that advocates of distant reading are necessarily calling for the end of close reading ("distant" could be a supplement for the "close"), but it nevertheless remains the case that sustained reflection on an individual text can still teach us much. The narrative of the real explored here outlines certain literary resistances to computational analysis.

This literary resistance to computational analysis ties into a broader contemporary question about the fate of reading in literary studies. In recent years some scholars have argued for an expansion of the methodological and affective valences for literary reading. Eve Kosofsky Sedgwick has explored the potential of "reparative reading," a mode of reading that accepts the possibility of surprise.[37] More recently, Rita Felski in *The Limits of Critique* calls for a mode of "postcritical reading," in which the methodology of "suspicious" critique would be supplemented by a broader range of readerly modes (such as recognition and enchantment). Both Sedgwick and Felski have emphasized a spirit of reading that creates an opening for the experience of surprise, a feeling that can frustrate a programmatic reading of a work of literature. The importance of surprising disruption is itself found within the tradition of the experiential real; that task of interrogating appearance urges us in the continued direction of (surprising) openness. The constant negotiation between the particular and an account of reality means continued readjustment and the possibility of surprising reversal. This has parallels with the act of reading. The experience of reading a work—that encounter with its particular textures—opens up new insights and interpretive possibilities.[38]

Though I will return to Felski in chapter 5, it is worthwhile to say a few more things about that encounter with the text and its stakes for reading (suspicious or otherwise). Felski finds that "suspicious reading" is fixated on certain metaphors, such as "digging down" into certain metaphors in order to reveal their hidden meaning or "denaturalization" in order to reveal the implicit (ideological, sociological, etc.) context in which a work operates.[39] This study is not devoid of some of this rhetorical iconography. Indeed, much of the first chapter involves digging into the meaning of the real over time as a way of tracing a broader intellectual horizon. But the tradition of the experiential real also has resonances with some of the claims that Felski makes on behalf of a more expansive, postcritical mode of reading. She writes that a "work of art is a potential source of knowledge rather than just an object of knowledge—one whose cognitive impact and implications are tied up with its affective reach."[40] Moreover, the "act of reading" involves "fresh ways of organizing perception, different patterns and models, rhythms of rapprochement and distancing, relaxation and suspense, movement and hesitation. We give form to our existence through the diverse ways in which we inhabit, inflect, and appropriate the artistic forms we encounter."[41]

The enterprise of the experiential real charted out in the pages to come is in many ways in harmony with these claims. For this project, the act of reading is the act of provoking the reader into speculation, introspection, and wonder. A Dickinson poem or an Emerson essay prompts the reader to reconsider his or her experiences. That reconsideration may indeed involve "fresh ways of organizing perception" and other opportunities for renewal. It is in this dialogue between reader and work that new understandings of the self and the world around the self arise. Moreover, this dialogue encompasses a wide affective range. It is not merely about rational analysis or the rigors of deconstruction. Instead, it might occasion moments of joy—of whirligig enthusiasm—of heartache and heartglow. It is in part through exploring that affective gamut that we can gain a glimpse of how these works *really* operate.

The writers examined in this study offer certain narratives of the real and use certain techniques in pursuit of it, but the broader experiential real in which they participate is not limited to nineteenth-century America. Instead, it illuminates the way in which the reading of literary works can prompt us to look at the world and ourselves with a sharper and more open eye. Exploring the experiential real helps rehabilitate a mode of looking that combines visionary aspiration with attention to the disruptive details of everyday life. This tradition also casts light on the relationship of literary reading and writing to reality: far from being an escape from reality, the encounter with literary works can, ultimately, help us gain a renewed understanding of and enchantment with the real. In the pages ahead I attend to the course of readings with not only suspicion but also care and wonder.

· ONE ·

Real Excavations

In the early nineteenth century, concerns about literature's moral value saturate critical debates about it, and the faithfulness of literature to "reality" serves as an important criterion for reflections on literary morality. "Real," "reality," and "real life" circulate throughout discussions of the worth of literature in the early part of the nineteenth century. During this period works of literature—especially, but not only, the novel—are criticized as lacking reality, and the gulf separating literature from the "real world" often serves as a reason for finding literature to be morally suspect. Terence Martin has argued at some length that this skepticism about the literary enterprise can be partly attributed to the prevalence within American education of Scottish Common Sense teachings, which, he finds, prioritize the actual and concrete at the expense of the possible.[1]

Americans in the early nineteenth century could be strident and censorious in their criticism of various literary forms, but this response can be traced to an awareness of how powerful literature can be. In his inaugural address as Alford Professor of Natural Religion, Moral Philosophy, and Civil Polity at Harvard in 1817, Levi Frisbie says that the "compositions in poetry and prose, which constitute the literature of a nation, the essay, the drama, the novel, it cannot be doubted, have a most extensive and powerful operation upon the moral feelings and character of the age."[2] Because of the "magic of fiction and poetry," Frisbie urges particular probity in considering the worth of literature. Literature can do much good, but it could also do much harm. Frisbie notes with "peculiar pleasure the sentence of just indignation, which the Edinburgh tribunal has pronounced upon Moore, Swift, Goethe, and in general the German sentimentalists." Frisbie elaborates on the influence of Byron. He appreciates the power of "the author of Childe

Harold"—the intensity of emotion and the instants of the sublime—but ultimately finds that Byron "leaves an impression unfavourable to a healthful state of thought and feeling, peculiarly dangerous to the finest minds and most susceptible hearts."[3] The intensity of Byron leads, Frisbie warns, to alienation from society and the world at large.

Frisbie approvingly cites the literary judgment of the "Edinburgh tribunal." The remarks of James Gray, a clergyman and graduate of the University of Glasgow, to the "Philadelphia Academy for the Instruction of Young Ladies" (1810) demonstrate a Scottish-American critical fusion.[4] Celebrating the education of young women, Gray offers some further thoughts on the improvement of young minds and souls, and much of his commentary focuses on the risks and possibilities of reading. He hopes that the reading habits of young people will center on "biography, history, and works of religion and morals" in addition to sacred scripture.[5] He then turns to a far more suspect genre: the novel. It would be a mistake, I think, to equate Gray's censure of the novel with a criticism of poetry as such; criticizing novelistic fiction is not the same as criticizing verse compositions, and the criticism of the novel taps into a broader skepticism of the novel as a literary form in the eighteenth century. However, Gray's criticism of the novel does turn on a particular notion of the real and the way that the real may or may not be registered in literature.

Throughout his remarks on the novel, Gray criticizes the form for creating a literary environment that is separate—and potentially a distraction—from reality and the real world. He finds that there is a great appetite for novels, but these works fail to teach "young people the knowledge of human nature" and risk corrupting the sensibilities of their readers. Both these failures occur due to the novel's separation from reality. Gray readily grants that the novel does offer examples of human behavior, but the unreality of these behaviors (as demonstrated by fictional characters) vitiates the notion of learning about the real world from a novel. At best, the novel offers an exceedingly flawed reflection of real human life. Even those "few rare men . . . who have achieved great things in characteristic moral painting" still "have not come up to nature." The novel may show some "extravagance of vice which does not occur in real life" in villains or "virtues that have never been practiced" in heroes. Such vice "can never answer the purpose of deterring us from vitious indulgence," and fictional portrayals of virtue "can scarcely become examples."[6] Thus, Gray argues that "no persons are more apt to err and blunder, when introduced on the stage of real life than those whose imaginations have been deeply impressed with the characters of fictitious composition." The distortions of fiction—its deviation from the real facts of the world—offer a flawed picture of life. Likewise, the great feelings that reading fiction inspires are "a species of artificial stimulant," which may "indispose us to the practical exercise of sympathy in real life."[7] Again and again, Gray opposes the novel to the real.

Terence Martin has argued that "the crux of the matter" for this discussion of the novel is "Gray's definition of reality"; he finds that the "inherent metaphysical assumption underlying these words is that true reality is limited to the actual."[8] While Gray does seem to emphasize the reality of the actual, his discussion of "reality" also stresses the social (or the interpersonal) as having particular access to the truths of human nature. Gray considers the novel as a possible, flawed rival to history: "However narrow the circle of individual feeling and experience may be, it comprises almost the whole of what any person knows of this subject: and no extent of genius and learning can supply the want of a practical acquaintance with society. The only accession which our experimental knowledge on this subject admits, is derived from authentic history."[9] The fantasies of the novel cannot substitute for the "practical acquaintance with society" or (a possible surrogate for this acquaintance) the reality of history. We are hemmed in by our own subjectivities, and the intercourse of society offers one of the few authentic ways to expand that ring of awareness. Gray claims that to "study human nature you must mix with mankind: it is in the drawingroom, not in the library, in the forum, not in the cloister, that the nature of man can be learned, because it is in the former places, not in the latter, that it is displayed in its true colours and proportions."[10] Martin suggests that the drawing room and forum might be considered real from Gray's perspective, while the library and cloister are artificial, but it is also worth noting that the former two locations function for Gray as explicitly social while the latter two are places of lonely remove.[11] The "forum" also suggests a place of public, secular republicanism, perhaps responding to the tradition of claiming the United States as a successor to the Roman republic, while the "cloister" provides an image of Catholic religious practices and alludes to the iconography of the Gothic. It is in the realm of public sociality that one learns about "human nature"—not in the locked-away realm of literary reading or isolated Romantic/Gothic reflection.

Martin's analysis of this passage finds that Gray's critique may apply to literary genres other than the novel, such as poetry, and his finding is certainly understandable. If the novel's literary picture is flawed, so too might be poetry's portrayal of human nature and feelings. The novel's "artificial stimulant" may be more than matched by the stimulating effects of poetry. Think of Anne Elliot's warning to Captain Benwick in Jane Austen's *Persuasion* (published late in 1817): that she hoped he did not "always read only poetry" since "she thought it was the misfortune of poetry, to be seldom safely enjoyed by those who enjoyed it completely; and that the strong feelings which alone could estimate it truly, were the very feelings which ought to taste it but sparingly."[12] The dangers that Gray finds in the novel could also be found in other literary forms, and Gray's attention to this danger focuses especially on the lack of reality in such literary forms. The real life of the public world—the realm of interpersonal exchanges—stands in sharp contrast to the falsities found within the pages of nonfactual and nonreligious books.[13] At best, novel-reading can provide a way of habituating young people to reading in general, Gray says, but he hopes that the reading of such novels will remain a diversion of immaturity. As the young mind grows and "as the grand prospects of society expand to its view, it becomes incapable of being roused to action by any thing but what is real."[14]

Decades after Gray's address to the young ladies, a skepticism about the reality of literature persists, as the following item from the *Boston Olive Branch* from late July 1850 (titled "Poetry and Reality") demonstrates: "Beware of the woman who professes to love you, while she goes with hands unwashed, a hole in her stocking, and sits all day reading a yellow novel.—A kiss from her pretty lips will not make your shirt; neither will her strong profession of attachment cook a good meal. Such a girl will not answer for a sterling man. She may understand the poetry of life; but after all the stern reality is what you must recall."[15] This item contrasts the "poetry of life" with "reality" and connects this discussion of the real with narratives of gender: those real tasks of a woman involve the practical skills of shirt-making and meal-cooking. The woman who understands only the "poetry of life" according to this narrative seems impractical and morally suspect (spending all her time reading yellow novels). This combination suggests a continuing association of literary unreality and moral danger.

There are a few possible responses to skepticism about the reality of literature. One would be to endorse the notion that literary works are deficient in reality and thereby pose a threat to the minds (and perhaps souls) of readers. Another would be to concede the lack of reality in literary works but still hold that this lack need not render reading such works an entirely morally disastrous enterprise. In the *Port Folio* in 1807, Joseph Dennie seems to take such a position. He argues that reading novels and romances may be viewed as "an amusement the most dignified, the most worthy of the attention of a rational being," if such a being already has a thorough acquaintance with "the real nature and motives" of humans. For such a grounded individual, the reading of fiction is a potentially salubrious break from the rigors of the world: such an "employment of the Imagination is but a refreshing slumber to the Judgment."[16]

A third response would be to dispute the premise of the unreality of literature and argue instead that literature *does* involve reality: far from being a vacation from reality into fantasy, literature can provide a way of gaining access to the real. This third response suggests numerous possible strategies. One strategy would be to clothe a piece of fiction or a poem in the language and tropes of fact. This turn toward fact is a major conceit in many early American novels, which assert that they are telling something true: they are relating a real/true series of events. Emphasizing fact could push the novel closer to a kind of history. In her preface to *Charlotte Temple* (an eighteenth-century bestseller), Susanna Rowson writes that "this Tale of Truth" should be regarded "as not merely the effusion of Fancy, but as a reality." The author insists on the factual provenance of the novel: it was related "some little time since by an old lady who had personally known Charlotte, though she concealed the real names of the characters."[17]

Another strategy would be to dismiss the claims of material facts as having a sole purchase on reality. Just as there is more in heaven and Earth than dreamt of in Horatio's philosophy, so too could there be more to reality in literature than recounting historical happenings. In order to defend works of literature and of the imagination, writers could attempt to claim the real as their own turf. The real world is not simply the purview of the drawing room or the forum (*pace* Dr. Gray), but works of the imagination too can grant a view of reality. Such an effort will involve certain narratives of reality and of the purposes of literature, including claims for the act of reading as an enterprise of experiential reflection.

The Quarry of the Real

Understanding this process of defending literary reality first involves an excursion into the broader traditions of the real. The real involves a tangle of issues—many of them touching on the role of interrogating experience—and surveying the complexity of this word's use casts light on the abiding intellectual concerns involved in the real. In his survey of realism in *Keywords,* Raymond Williams draws attention to an overarching duality in uses of "real." One is the contrast between real and imaginary—that is between *existing* and *nonexisting.* The other is the contrast between real and apparent—that is, between *being* and *seeming.*[18] The first contrast is implicitly ontic: it addresses the question of what exists. The second contrast is implicitly epistemic: it addresses the question of how we know what exists. These contrasts cannot always be cleanly distinguished from each other. For instance, saying that something is only *apparent* can be an indirect way of saying that it doesn't really exist: "The mirage's splendid oasis was only apparent; it didn't actually exist."

Let us start with the language of existence: often, the term "real" can be used to denote what exists, and contentious metaphysical assumptions may be built into this. For instance, a strict materialist might argue that only particular material objects exist, that our own internal responses to these objects consist of patterns of brain waves, chemical signals, and so forth. Because consciousness derives from material processes according to this strict materialist viewpoint, our personal experiences, observations, and thoughts are a byproduct of those physical operations. For this materialist strawman, particular material objects are all that exists, and our interactions with a given material object generate second-order experiences, thoughts, and reactions. Those second-order responses derive from the operation of material qualities but do not have a being independent of them.[19]

The real has a long relationship to *thing*-ness. The third edition of the *Oxford English Dictionary* offers derivations of "real" from the Old French "*real, reel*" and the Latin "*realis.*" Although there seems to be a level of uncertainty about a number of the earlier uses of the word,[20] some of the earliest uses of the term "real" given by the *OED* relate to real property (see 7a and 7b). Perhaps as part of the history of the real as deriving from the Latin *res,*[21] there is a long association of the real and things. The *OED* offers definition 1a of the "real" as "actually existing physically as a thing," and definition 4a explains the term as "relating to, concerned with, things."

This tradition of associating the real with the material has a long pedigree. For instance, in the fourth book of his *Essay Concerning Human Understanding,* John Locke says that, since the "essences of things" are "only abstract ideas," they give "us no knowledge of real existence at all."[22] He offers three types of existence of which we have knowledge: ourselves, God, and other things. We gain the first through intuition and can arrive at the second through "demonstration." (Locke offers a series of arguments for the logical necessity of God.)[23] Sensation allows us to know the existence of other things: we continually encounter things that seem independent of us (from a candle flame to the sun), so sensation testifies to this external existence. As Locke explores elsewhere in his *Essay,* knowing that these individual things exist gives us at best only extremely limited knowledge about those things themselves, but sensation at least reveals that *something* exists.

In Locke's discussion of how we speak about or know that *something,* he continually associates the real with particularity. He defines the "real essence" of something as the "generally (in substances) unknown constitution of things, whereon their discoverable qualities depend." The "nominal essence" of things instead depends on "certain abstract ideas" that we have connected to a figure. For instance, he finds that the real essence of a ring is "the real constitution of its insensible parts, on which depend all those properties of colour, weight, fusibility, fixedness, &c." The nominal essence of this ring is instead "its colour, weight, fusibility, fixedness, &c."[24] Realness is here embedded in particularity for Locke—not in the abstract ideas used to classify particularity.

However, one might also pose certain metaphysical accounts of the real, which find that things beyond the physical world might have some particular claim to being real. For example, we might contrast the radical materialist account of the real with a broadly theistic narrative of existence. According to this theistic narrative, God ultimately exists. The material world is a product of God's will and depends on His assent. Particular objects are the creation of God and give evidence of His glory. One of our tasks is to try to know this ultimate divine reality through the signs and figures of the world. The Puritan enterprise of typology took this task of divine interpretation as a key premise. The things of this world seem—they offer signs and figures—but they only have a derivative category of being. Americans in the nineteenth century for the most part grew to maturity in the context of this theistic narrative (at times with Platonic accents). Even if they might use the word "real" to typify things or materiality, they might often believe that some divine power offered a more ultimate reality.

Neither "real" nor "reality" are Greek words, nor are there easy one-to-one cognates for them in Greek. Nevertheless, the narrative of being found in the Platonic tradition represents a significant influence for the use of the real, especially for Americans in the nineteenth century. According to many standard interpretations of Plato, the objects of the actual world stand as representatives or embodiments of certain ideas. These ideas stand beyond the world of generation and decay, but their participation in this world can be seen in the forms of the physical.[25] The Platonic tradition complicates the actual: the actual world is necessary for grasping something greater, but it is also gone beyond. In the *Phaedrus* Socrates offers an extended speech on love, memory, and the grasping of realities within the physical world. Physical objects inspire the memory of reality, Socrates says: the act of philosophical recollection is that process by which the soul recollects "the things . . . [it] saw when it was traveling with god, when it disregarded the things we now call real and lifted up its head to what is truly real instead."[26] The individual who uses such reminders of reality "stands outside human concerns and draws close to the divine."[27] Within this Platonic myth, the objects of the physical world seem important media for humans grasping greater realities, so the philosophical soul at once needs these physical things and must go beyond them.

In translating these lines from Plato, Alexander Nehamas and Paul Woodruff translate the Greek "τὸ ὂν ὄντως" as "what is truly real." A strict translation of "τὸ ὂν ὄντως" might be "the beingly being."[28] These two twentieth-century translators partake of a broader tradition of translators of Plato who use "real" as a word for marking *being* in Plato. Thomas Taylor, a translator of Plato much esteemed by Emerson, translated that passage in the following way: "This is a recollection of what our soul formerly saw with divinity . . . when she despised what we now consider as realities, and was supernally elevated to the contemplation of that which is true."[29] These things of the material world—which we "now consider as realities" (a phrasing that implies the provisionality of the materially real)—fall short of true being. Within this tradition of interpreting Plato, the physical objects of the world can be signs that we use to locate true being but are themselves distinct from full reality. Nineteenth-century Americans would be quite familiar with the narrative of the Platonic ideas as being more real than the physical. For instance, Thomas Reid, a writer often taught in nineteenth-century America, specifically argued against the notion (attributed to Plato) that the ideas were "more real" than the physical. He wrote that "we need not believe, with [Platonists], that ideas are eternal and self-existent, and that they have a more real existence than the things we see and feel."[30]

The term "reality" presents its own complications. One of the *OED*'s senses of "reality" reveals a telling duality: "Real existence; what is real rather than imagined or desired; the aggregate of real things or existences; that which underlies and is the truth of appearances or phenomena" (1). This listing of senses includes a set of meanings that overlap but are individually distinct. Reality could be "what is real," but it could also be the "aggregate of real things or existences." The latter sense almost suggests a collection of multiple individual reals (suggesting something like the "real" as particular). In a philosophically themed survey of the word "reality" in the *Dictionary of Untranslatables,* Jean-Francois Courtine claims that the original meaning of *realitas,* coined by the Scholastic thinker Duns Scotus, was the "essence, or rather the essentiality, of the *res* as such in abstraction from existence."[31] This sense of "realitas" as essence continues for centuries afterwards. For instance, according to Courtine, Leibniz's sense of "realitas" is in considerable harmony with Scotus's: "The content or tenor of what [consciousness] apprehends as quiddity, or essence."[32] By the 1700s "reality" has also gained the significance of something that exists outside of and independent of us, but the sense of "reality" as essence suggests the longstanding importance of metaphysical conceptions for narratives of reality.

The contrast between some metaphysical and some physical senses of "reality" is obviously one with high intellectual stakes, and these overarching philosophical concerns inform the intellectual-historical context for the nineteenth-century United States. As Joseph Urbas has recently argued, nineteenth-century Americans were engaged in a vigorous ontological debate. As Urbas puts it, the "key question for philosophy, then, was *being,*" a term with important implications for the real.[33] These ontological discussions have a significant bearing on American philosophy as well as theology. As Bruce Kuklick notes, theological concerns played a major role in America philosophy in the first half of the nineteenth century, especially in college settings.[34] Many nineteenth-century American writers are especially concerned with religious reality. For instance, in his introduction to selections from the work of the nineteenth-century French philosopher Victor Cousin, George Ripley finds that "contemplative individuals" strive for a "philosophical system which shall explain and legitimate" a "deep conviction of the reality of spiritual truth."[35] Partly in response to the philosophical challenges posed by Francis Bacon, John Locke, David Hume, and others, Americans from this period appeal to a wide variety of thinkers, including Plato, Immanuel Kant, and Victor Cousin.[36] At times, these discussions of the nonactual real are influenced by German idealism and the British Romantics who served Americans as conduits for idealism.

Transcendentalism obviously plays a significant role in this transmission of idealist philosophy. In an 1840 article Orestes Brownson suggests the importance of spiritual reality for transcendentalism: "The real aim of the Transcendentalist is to ascertain a solid ground for faith in the reality of the spiritual world."[37] In *Transcendentalism in New England,* the (erstwhile) transcendentalist Octavius Brooks Frothingham offers a stereotypically Platonic sense of the real: the "Transcendentalist believed in man's ability to apprehend absolute ideas of Truth, Justice, Rectitude, Goodness; he spoke of The Right, The True, The Beautiful, as eternal realities which he perceived."[38] Frothingham's narrative of transcendentalism thus raises the notion of seemingly abstract entities (such as "The True, The Beautiful") as some kind of "eternal realities" beyond this world of the flesh. An 1843 essay by Brownson touches on a similar theme in proclaiming that the "old [Scholastic] Realists were right, in affirming the reality of Ideas, kinds, genera."[39]

In addition to describing physical and spiritual entities, the real has also been used to typify personal feeling and thought, including in the antebellum era. For instance, in his 1826 sermon on I Thessalonians "Pray without ceasing" (5:17), Emerson says that every "thoughtful man has felt, that there was a more awful reality to thought and feeling, than to the infinite panorama of nature around him."[40] This early sermon suggests Emerson's broader concern with some kind of reality residing within the operations of the self (its thoughts and feelings).

This emphasis on reality as residing within the self may draw from the legacy of German idealism, but the real also has a long tradition in the English language as describing feelings. For example, the "real thing" can mean both the "thing itself, as contrasted with imitations and counterfeits" (definition 4c[a] in the second edition of the *OED*) and "true love as distinct from infatuation, flirtation, etc." (definition 4c[b] in the same edition).[41] Other senses of the real relating to feelings include "sincere, straightforward, honest" (11a); "true or loyal to another" (11b); and free "from nonsense, affectation or pretence; 'genuine'" (11c).

As Lionel Trilling has explored, "sincere" entered the English language in the sixteenth century (the same century when the sense of "real" as sincere gains increased prominence).[42] Trilling notes the continued modern salience of sincerity and authenticity, topics that the real addresses. The *OED*'s use of "genuine" in these "sincere" definitions of the real also draws attention to other qualities of the real in contemporary popular culture. In the early twenty-first century, "real" can still be a synonym for "genuine"—not posing craft but honest straightforwardness, not seeming niceness but raw directness. The specter of authenticity haunts contemporary culture, and "real" often becomes a loaded word in looking for authenticity.[43] When a long-running American cable television show says it aims to present what happens "when people stop being polite and start getting real," it reveals how much Americans in the early twenty-first century take seriously the notion of an opposition between some false social patina ("being polite") and true interaction ("getting real").[44]

While Trilling in part traces the rise of "sincerity" to the class foment of the late Renaissance, both the "real" and "sincere" also address persistent epistemic questions about the relationship between appearance and being. Here, Raymond Williams's distinction between "appearance" and "being" plays a role. We conventionally take a sincere individual to be one who does not put up a false front of appearance; his or her apparent feelings demonstrate his or her true feelings. More broadly, uses of the "real" often invoke the term to distinguish between some apparent seeming and some true existence.

Definition 10b of the *OED* speaks to this theme: "That is actually present or involved (as opposed to apparent, ostensible, etc.)." Citations for other definitions of "real" often entail some challenge to—or at least doubts about—appearance or the perceptive faculties. For example, almost all of the citations for the very first definition of "real"—"having an objective existence; actually existing physically as a thing" (1a)—express doubts about the truth of perception (particularly the truth of sight). One citation for this definition comes from Shakespeare's *All's Well That Ends Well:* "Is there no exorcist / Beguiles the truer office of mine eyes? / Is't reall that I see?" Hobbes's assertion in *Leviathan* that "some such apparitions were not Imaginary, but Reall" follows fifty years later, and Stephen Parkinson's claim in *A Treatise on Optics* that a "real visible object and its optical image differ" comes about two hundred years after Hobbes. Albeit in different ways, these three citations contrast the testimony of subjective observation and the facts of the objective world. In *All's Well That Ends Well,* the King of France wonders if perceived objects are real (if what he believes himself to see actually exists). Hobbes writes how Christ's disciples took spirits intervening for the sake of God not as imaginary appearances but as truly existing entities. Writing from the scientific sphere, Parkinson posits a distinction between the real object seen and its image. In each of these uses of the real, the writer or speaker uses "real" as a way of differentiating some appearance from some authentic existence.

The distinction between appearance and reality pervades antebellum discourse about the real. A passage from Thoreau's *Walden* is instructive here: "We think that that *is* which *appears* to be. If a man should walk through this town and see only the reality, where, think you, would the 'Mill-dam' go to? If he should give us an account of the realities he beheld there, we should not recognize the place in his description. Look at a meeting-house, or a court-house, or a jail, or a shop, or a dwelling-house, and say what that thing really is before a true gaze, and they would all go to pieces in your account of them."[45] This passage appeals to reality in order to challenge the seeming solidities of conventional materialities: the appearances of the material world may not themselves be the truest kind of being. Seeing "only the reality" could disrupt our apprehension of the "Mill-dam." This consideration of the distinction between that which *appears* to be and that which *is* also involves the role of narrative, as "saying what that thing really is before a true gaze" can lead to "them" to "go to pieces in your account of them."[46] Truly describing real being, then, involves a challenge to conventional discourse and conventional ways of apprehending the incidents of the material world. This sense of the "real" as socially disruptive contrasts with earlier accounts that stress the importance of social consensus for the real. Instead, the enterprise of *Walden* involves the cultivation of the "true gaze" in order to see really.

William Wells Brown's novel *Clotel* at times counters reality or the real to appearance, and this countering can emphasize the faulty appearance of the law. When the title character is purchased by Horatio Green, the two enter a common-law marriage: "The tenderness of Clotel's conscience, together with the care her mother had with her and the high value she placed upon virtue, required an outward marriage; though she well knew that a union with her proscribed race was unrecognised by law, and therefore the ceremony would give her no legal hold on Horatio's constancy. But her high poetic nature regarded reality rather than the semblance of things."[47] Here, a "poetic nature" is associated with an inclination toward "reality"—that is, a marriage in spirit, while the official recognition of the law would merely be the "semblance of things." However, there is a sharp irony in this appeal to reality: Green will eventually marry a "white" woman, who will in time demand that Clotel be sold to another (and that Green's child with Clotel become a servant in their house). The reality of their affection did not prove so enduring in the face of broader sociological forces.[48] Nevertheless, it suggests a distinction between reality and the socially recognized, a theme developed elsewhere in *Clotel.* When the escaped slave William finds himself in a free state, he contrasts names (a kind of linguistic appearance) with reality: "William found, after all, that liberty in the so-called Free States was more a name than a reality; that prejudice followed the coloured man into every place that he might enter."[49] This contrast between names and realities connects to the *OED*'s definition 9a of "real": that which is "actually and truly such as its name implies." A true name is real, while a false one is not.

A brief item in the August 25, 1849, edition of the *Literary American* examines the difference between appearance and reality for personal feeling: "APPEARANCES AND REALITIES.—How little do we know the real state of those we envy or compassionate. We are apt to think of their outward circumstances, not their inward feelings, when we speculate on their happiness or misery."[50] Like Thoreau's reflections in *Walden,* this item ponders the contrast between outer seeming and inner being. For the anonymous author of this item, the "real state" of those around us involves not their outer displays of wealth or poverty but their "inward feelings." The real here comprises feelings rather than outer circumstances.

One of the central journals of nineteenth-century Unitarianism (and, eventually, an organ for transcendentalism), the *Christian Examiner* offers a variety of examples of the real as testing appearance and as guaranteeing feeling or some kind of meaning. The author of the essay "Perversion of Scripture Language" (1825) speaks of using "conversion" and "convert . . . in their real meaning."[51] This sense of the real attends to the true meaning of a word (compared with some surface interpretation). In the same year an essay by future Harvard president James Walker argues that those enterprises in which one takes a "real and active interest" reveal the character of an individual.[52] For Walker, that real interest is both a deep interest and one that really reveals the character of the interested person. A letter from the minister Washington Gladden to Emily Dickinson later in the nineteenth century reveals another association of reality, truth, and being. Responding to Dickinson's questions about the afterlife, Gladden writes: "'Is immortality true?' I believe that it is true—the only reality—almost; a thousand times truer than mortality, which is but a semblance after all."[53] For Gladden, immortality is both true and, perhaps, "the only reality." Gladden's discussion of immortality also exhibits a distinction between appearance and reality in its contrast between the "only reality" of immortality and the "semblance" of mortality.

This metaphysical account of the "real"—asserting some reality beyond the material—influences the orientation of other terms in transatlantic nineteenth-century discourse. For instance, oppositions between realism and idealism may be troubled. In part cribbing from the German idealist Friedrich Schelling (himself influenced by Kant), Samuel Taylor Coleridge finds in the *Biographia Literaria* that a philosophical position is "only so far idealism, as it is at the same time, and on that very account, the truest and most binding realism."[54] Coleridge further presses the association between realism and idealism in claiming that "we are all collectively born idealists, and therefore and only therefore are we at the same time realists."[55] In *Aids to Reflection* (the first American edition of which was edited by University of Vermont president James Marsh and published in 1829), Coleridge proposes "subjective" and "objective" "as substitutes for *real* and *notional,* and to the exclusion of the *false antithesis* between *real* and *ideal.*"[56]

Furthermore, distinctions between the real and the actual (the latter of which often functions as a synonym for the physical) will sometimes be highlighted, especially for writers tapping into the Platonic tradition. Orestes Brownson's "The Community System," an essay on social reform in the February 1843 edition of the *United States Magazine and Democratic Review,* opens with an excursion into Platonic philosophy. Brownson invokes the Platonic notion of the ideal, providing the following gloss: "Ideal, not as opposed to substantive, to real, but as opposed to actual." He adds that "man's existence is, then, to be contemplated as Ideal and Actual."[57] Brownson thus undoes the opposition of "ideal" and "real." In his 1865 reflections on Thoreau, James Russell Lowell emphatically underlines the distinction between actuality and reality: "George Sand says neatly, that 'Art is not a study of positive reality,' (*actuality* were the fitter word,) 'but a seeking after ideal truth.'"[58] In replacing Sand's "reality" with "actuality," Lowell not only distinguishes the actual from the real but also undoes Sand's implicit opposition of "positive reality" and "ideal truth." Lowell also seems here to look favorably on literature as involving the ideal and—in contradistinction to Gray and others—the true.

Not only were these various senses of the "real" and "reality" implicit in antebellum American discourse; they were explicit, too, as the 1828 edition of Webster's *American Dictionary of the English Language* reveals. Here is the entry for "real" as an adjective (excluding the fifth entry, which involves the legal and religious uses of "real"):

> 1. Actually being or existing; not fictitious or imaginary; as, a description of *real* life. The author describes a *real* scene or transaction.
> 2. True; genuine; not artificial, counterfeit or factitious; as, *real* Madeira wine; *real* ginger.
> 3. True; genuine; not affected; not assumed. The woman appears in her *real* character.
> 4. Relating to things, not to persons; not personal.
>
> Many are perfect in men's humors, that are not greatly capable of the *real* part of business.
>
> [*Little used or obsolete.*][59] *Bacon.*

Consider also Webster's entry on "reality":

> [1.] Actual being or existence of any thing; truth; fact; in distinction from mere appearance.
>
> A man may fancy he understands a critic, when in *reality* he does not comprehend his meaning. *Addison.*
>
> 2. Something intrinsically important, not merely matter of show.
>
> And to *realities* yield all her shows. *Milton.*
>
> 3. In the *schools,* that may exist of itself, or which has a full and absolute being of itself, and is not considered as a part of any thing else. *Encyc.*

4. In *law*, immobility, or the fixed, permanent nature of property; as chattels which savor of the *realty*. [This word is so written in law, for *reality*.]

Blackstone.[60]

Though Webster often uses "actual" as a way of qualifying "real" ("actual being or existence"), these definitions do not rest content with mere material actuality. The first sense of "reality" even slides from the actual to the suggestion that appearance is in some kind of play; tellingly, the citation from Addison refers not to the reality of a material object but the reality of understanding. The "real" as sincere or genuine makes an appearance in Webster's dictionary (in the second and third definitions of "real"), as does a sense of a contrast between gaudy shows and the heart of being.

Webster's definitions of "realization" and "realize" foreground the stakes of existence for both terms. Realization is "the act of . . . making real" (definition 1), "the act of believing or considering as real" (definition 3), and "the act of bringing into being" (definition 4). Likewise, "realize" can mean "to bring into being" (definition 1) or to "impress on the mind as a reality; to believe, consider or treat as real" (definition 3). That latter definition stresses the role of subjective trial for realization (to "impress on the mind"), and the fourth definition further underlines that subjective element: "To bring home to one's own case or experience; to consider as one's own; to feel in all its force." To realize in this sense is to gain a deeper appreciation of (the existence of) something. One "feels it in all its force" and is thus awakened to the fullness of it. Literature can facilitate a trial of appearance in order to find the real, and it can also offer opportunities for realization—bringing new insights into being, making certain principles real to us, and heightening the force of ideas and experiences.

Real Foundations for Literature

As the critiques of Frisbie and others discussed earlier imply, the senses of "real" and "reality" formed key battle-lines in debates about literary value. Some of those in the Scottish Common Sense school asserted the "unreality" of literature, a point echoed by other critics of the literary enterprise.[61] Lord Kames's *Essays on the Principles of Morality and Natural Religion* is instructive here. Kames suggests that one of the aims of literature is to provoke feeling. However, he often contrasts the figments of literature with reality. For instance, he defines tragedy as "an imitation or representation of human characters and actions. It is a feigned history, which commonly makes a stronger impression than what is real."[62] The writer is able to keep viewers and readers "in continual suspense and agitation, beyond what commonly happens in real life." The fact that tragedy goes so far beyond the norms of real life is what can make it so effective for Kames.

However, alternative orientations for the real might make very different claims about the real and literature. For instance, those accounts of the real that stress the reality of some transcendental ideas or principles might instead offer literature as a central device for achieving that real. The January 1843 edition of the *United States Magazine and Democratic Review* features the fifth part of Orestes Brownson's "Synthetic Philosophy," which focuses on the "operations of the mind": perception, memory, and imagination. The essay as a whole enters into a dialogue with Scottish Common Sense writers, British empiricists, and German idealists, but the section on the imagination represents a particularly concentrated reply to and revision of standard literary terms for American critics in the early 1800s.

Throughout this essay Brownson attacks claims that imagination and poetic composition have little to do with reality. He says that "the bright world of Romance into which we rise from the dull Actual in all our moments of higher and intenser life" is not "all unreal."[63] The imagination plays a key role in nurturing that "higher and intenser life." Drawing from his Romantic predecessors, Brownson complicates the Hobbesian view of imagination as "decaying sense."[64] Instead, imagination's "essence consists rather in the degree of intenseness and energy with which" we perceive and feel. Those moments of "higher and intenser life," enjoyed by lovers and poets, are instants where "the soul penetrates beyond the Actual to the Ideal, which is the basis of all reality."[65] Rather than being opposed to the real, the ideal affords the basis for reality. That which lies beyond the immediacies of the physical world provides a grounding for it. As he writes elsewhere, figures of poetry clothe "real thoughts or actual apperceptions" and they "conceal under them an *objective* reality, no less than a subjective reality."[66] The seemingly fictitious surfaces of literature reveal realer depths. In contrast to Lord Kames, Brownson finds that reality is central to literature's effect, in part because literature stimulates an intensity that helps us rise to the true sphere of ideal (i.e., real) being.

Other writers argue for the importance of the real for literature. The essay "Poetry No Fiction," published in the April 1833 issue of the *New-England Magazine,* makes striking claims about the reality of poetry and literary art in general.[67] Like Brownson, the anonymous author of this essay (H.) complicates the role of the fictitious for literary creation. H. defends literary works against the following charges: "They have nothing to do with reality. They are fictitious. Can a rational mind be satisfied with such airy food?"[68] Replying to these objections, the essay's author argues for the reality of literature and the intellectual worth of poetry (that it is not "airy food" lacking real nutrients). The author claims at one point that poetry "is all reality; it deals in reality, and reality alone." H. adds that "no poetry was ever truly felt unless it contained something of reality."[69]

In this defense of the reality of poetry, the author emphasizes the reality of thought: the "feelings which are produced in the mind, the sympathies which are called forth, the pleasures, the elevation, the enlarging and purging of the soul, the infusion of high and holy thoughts, the inward glorying at what is holiest and best—these are real."[70] Rather than asserting that the real resides merely in the physical, the author instead stresses the reality of the individual's subjective experiences. Furthermore, this assertion of the reality of feelings also stresses the moral and spiritual improvement offered by poetry, as the soul is both purged of the inferior and lifted into the heights of holiness. The author spends a considerable part of this essay arguing that poetry is no less real and no less worthwhile than mathematics or philosophy. Waging war against a cultural suspicion of the value of the literary enterprise as anything more than a mere distraction, the author of this essay asserts that literature holds a spiritually empowering quality.

This essay is not entirely without internal tensions. Even if the author exalts literature, he still maintains a skepticism of fiction; H. persistently claims that poetry is not fiction or fictitious. Shakespearean creations such as Hamlet and Othello may be real, and what realizes them are the deeper truths they demonstrate.[71] Moreover, the author's picture of imagination is a complicated one. For H., imagination is not a radical, creative power. H. stresses that "imagination cannot create."[72] The imagination is instead a synthetic faculty, uniting disparate aspects of the world into another form. This synthesizing power of imagination helps establish the reality of poetry: since God creates and since imagination only synthesizes what God has made, the products of the imagination trace their roots to divine creation.

In addition to speaking to substantive accounts of some metaphysical or subjective real, literature can also become a vehicle for interrogating appearance. Contrasts of the real to the nonexistent differ markedly from those of the real to seeming in at least one key point: the nonexistent has no basis in being, but that which seems can (indirectly) reveal being. *Seeming* is the middle ground between the observer and the thing seen—the potential pathway between the observer and the (observed) being. This double-edged quality of *seeming* (that it can both obscure and illuminate) has a profound influence on many uses of the "real," both in the antebellum era and outside it. It can have especially high stakes for writers of literature, a field that depends on seeming.[73] Writers in the tradition of the experiential real will often use the seeming of literature as a vehicle to provoke readers into interrogating the seeming around them. That interrogation could take place in a variety of ways. It could mean reorienting standard assumptions about the world, reflecting on internal responses both to instants in that literary work and to elements of broader experience, exploring the consequences of ideas, and other readerly moves.

Many nineteenth-century writers approached reading as a place of trial—as a venue where the seeming of ideas, the world, and inherited cultural traditions could be tested. In the "Reading" chapter of *Walden,* Thoreau writes that "to read well, that is, to read true books in a true spirit, is a noble exercise"; such books must "be read as deliberately and reservedly as they were written."[74] Recalling that Thoreau says he went into the woods because he "wished to live deliberately" gives a particular charge to this argument for deliberate reading.[75] The project of "deliberate living" suffuses *Walden.* It demands the continued interrogation of experience, seeing everything from beanfields to books to the depths of a pond from surprising angles. As the course of *Walden* shows, such a project of deliberation is experimental and open-ended. Deliberate reading might make the same demands, calling on us to return anew to the surface of the text in order to see what new, surprising depths might lurk within.

In "The American Scholar," Emerson also homes in on ways of reading. A key portion of this address attends to the uses and abuses of books. According to this address, books are best used as devices to prompt us to deeper intellectual activity. Books, he writes, "are for nothing but to inspire. I had better never see a book than to be warped by its attraction clean out of my own orbit, and made a satellite instead of a system. The one thing in the world of value, is, the active soul,—the soul, free, sovereign, active. This every man is entitled to; this every man contains within him, although in almost all men, obstructed, and as yet unborn" (*CW* 1: 56). The essay "Books" echoes this claim about the transformative potential of reading: "I find certain books vital and spermatic, not leaving the reader what he was: he shuts the book a richer man" (*CW* 7: 99). The encounter with a book, then, can prompt a generative enrichment in the person from Emerson's perspective. Perhaps in some harmony with the Scottish school that suggested that reading was inferior to immediate experience, Emerson elsewhere in "The American Scholar" finds that books "are for the scholar's idle times. When he can read God directly, the hour is too precious to be wasted in other men's transcripts of their readings" (*CW* 1: 57). But this address nevertheless holds out for some form of "creative reading" and celebrates the transformative power of reading; some of this transformative power may come from the fact that reading itself is an experience, and its surface can be inspected as well as other modes of appearance.

In 1838 the "Editor's Table" section of the popular monthly magazine the *Lady's Book* (also known as *Godey's Lady's Book*) devotes two months to how to read.[76] In the March issue this section lays out the hope of a "*systematic course of reading.*" These comments on reading suggest that both novels and poetry can be abused, but this column also holds that imaginative literature can have an instructive influence on its reader. According to the editor, "The imagination needs to be awakened and properly cultivated; and the heart may be impressed with right feelings, and pure and elevated hopes and aims" through the instruction of the novel.[77] In April the column continues the survey of reading by specifically addressing methods of reading in a way that has striking resonances with "The American Scholar." It laments an excessive and passive reading that renders the reader a mere "book-worm" and argues that such a form of reading is one of the reasons why American literature has been so imitative of European models. Instead of such passive reading, the column advocates a form of "mental composition" that demands engaged reading. This mode of reading "make[s] frequent pauses, and trace[s] out the inference, and the particular bearing and tendency of detached portions of" a work. Upon finishing reading a work, such a mode considers a work's "scope," "moral tone," the "correctness" of its "sentiments," and its style. This mode of reflective reading "call[s] into vigorous action" the whole of a person's faculties.[78] This column portrays reading in its highest use as inherently a reflective exercise—examining parts of the work and setting this examination of the parts in conversation with the course of the work as a whole. That process of reflecting on the work in turn renews and enriches the self's inner resources.

Faced with a literary environment skeptical of literature's reality, antebellum writers sought to defend the reality of literature by differentiating that reality from the physical world. This defense is informed by philosophical narratives of the self that suggest the reality of the subject's experiences, but it also draws from a broader sense of the real as offering a testing of appearance. If challenging *what seems* in order to find *what is* serves an important purpose, there might be a renewed importance for literature as a vehicle for this testing of *what seems*. The extra-physical location of reality often plays a major role in the antebellum defense of the literary real, yet such literary defenses also often assert the importance of the writer engaging with details of the physical; if reality involves the testing of appearance, then appearance must be brought forward and interrogated.

This narrative of the real, then, demands not a flight from the incidents of experience but an intimate dialogue with them. This experiential account of literary reading offers a way for literature to provide a window on experience. A work might encourage us to see something in a new light. It might inspire in us a certain intensity of feeling or thought. It might offer an account that organizes the incidents of life, and our encounter with this account might prompt us to see the world around us with different eyes. Literature, then, might speak to the real not only by creating a catalogue of seeming facts; instead, it can urge us onward to test the textures of experience, to inspect *what seems* in order to see *what is*. Some American critics in the early nineteenth century warned that literature presented a set of falsehoods that could corrupt one's sensibility or lead to moral error, but an alternative narrative offers itself: that reading literary works offers a provocation that can lead to new realizations.

· TWO ·

The Drops of Summer Rain

The real permeates Ralph Waldo Emerson's writings about poetry. So often for Emerson, finding the real means gaining a certain view of experience, when the seemings of the world become transformed, revised, or vivified. Seen in light of reality, the appearances of life gain a new edge. Often, then, the quest for realization in Emerson involves successive moments of unrealization, as apprehensions formerly taken to be real are recognized as not final but initiatory—not ultimately real but only phenomenally apparent. Within much of his work, the quest for the real becomes a search for an initiating view: the ability to see one thing as leading toward some greater reality.

This attempt at renewed vision entails a recasting of particularity. In "Nominalist and Realist" Emerson writes that we are "amphibious creatures, weaponed for two elements, having two sets of faculties, the particular and the catholic" (*CW* 3: 135). "Nominalist and Realist" charts the tensions between these two faculties. The realist looks through particular instances in order to grasp general realities, and the nominalist instead examines the disruptive possibilities of attending to particulars. While this essay suggests the importance Emerson places on interrogating particulars in pursuit of the real, it also models one of the key strategies of this interrogation: the silhouetting of contraries. At the outset of this essay he explores the realist perspective and moves to the nominalist one later, but the conclusion of "Nominalist and Realist" finds that we must be both realist and nominalist. The conclusion performs this dual fate, expressing contrary impulses and finding that every person is both a partialist and a universalist (*CW* 3: 145). Both perspectives are distinguished and intermingled. Even as "Nominalist and Realist" speaks of the particular, the course of this essay interrogates particularity (in this case, the particularity of a given perspective) to reveal the incompleteness of each particular aspect. Emerson's narrative of the search for the real involves a thoroughgoing analysis of particular appearances, examining not only the particular appearances of physical objects but also the appearances of rhetorical tropes and conceptual methodologies.

Emerson's writings use the strategies of re-vision: piling up trope after trope, he invites us to read through these various tropes, at once distinguishing them and reaching through them to gain some further realization. Emerson's prose and verse perform the simultaneous knitting and unknitting of integration, as the course of "Nominalist and Realist" demonstrates. We are invited to revise our understanding of rhyme, the circle, or the American scholar through grasping different resonances of them. The figure (e.g., the American scholar) becomes a way of grouping together these sometimes seemingly disparate resonances, so the cumulative effect of any piece of Emerson's writing requires the noting of unifying forces. Yet this grouping of resonances also relies on the accumulation of difference: different figures, different implications, different emphases, different forms, and so forth. Thus, Emerson seeds his unities with disruptive heterogeneities.

Attention to the real in Emerson's theory and literary practice affords a way of reconciling two traditions in Emerson criticism: the aversive and the correspondent. Starting with the recovery of Emerson as a philosophical figure in last third of the twentieth century, the aversive school has emphasized Emerson as a figure of transition, resistance, and leaving. Stanley Cavell, Richard Poirier, Sharon Cameron, Branka Arsić, and others have championed various elements of the aversive tradition. Cavell's essays on Emerson stress his connections to the debates about philosophical skepticism and deconstruction. Richard Poirier notes that Emerson's language displays a "flexibility wherein meanings are emplaced only to be edged out by alternative ones."[1] In charting out the idea of impersonality for Emerson, Cameron emphasizes the process of personal divestment, as existential moment follows moment.[2] Branka Arsić's *On Leaving* explores the persistence of leaving for Emerson; this "leaving" touches on elements of personality, language, society, and other topics.

The correspondent tradition in Emerson studies has instead emphasized the abiding concern within Emerson for correspondences; connection—not resistance—has been the major theme in the correspondent tradition. In *Emerson's Angle of Vision,* Sherman Paul offers one of the most sustained expositions of correspondence for Emerson. For Paul, Emerson's "daily problem was to maintain a living connection between the horizontal-worldly and the vertical-otherworldly"—that is, to fuse attention to the daily details of experience with a "vertical" vision that joins the material and the spiritual.[3] Joseph Urbas has recently reinvigorated the correspondent tradition in *Emerson's Metaphysics,* which finds that ontology (not epistemology) is Emerson's central concern. Urbas argues that Emerson champions a "bipolarity" that seeks to maintain a space for both metaphysical permanence and experiential change.[4]

Emersonian aversion and correspondence are not inherently opposed; like other members of the correspondent tradition, Urbas makes a place for disruption, and the aversive tradition at times uses the drawing of connections as a vehicle for disruption. Attending to the real for Emerson as both a theoretical concept and an influence on literary practice suggests a way of reconciling both these traditions. Invoking some reality beyond the physical world, Emerson proclaims the importance of poets (and others) glimpsing this reality through the physical; this glimpsing requires using the particulars of the world as a setting for real connection and correspondence. However, that project of glimpsing the real demands a continually renewed vision, and that continual renewal in turn requires the prospect of continued disruption. Being alive to the particulars of experience—that is, seeing their reality—means being receptive to those particulars. Receptivity (a loaded word for George Kateb's interpretation of Emerson) in turn means an openness to revision and the drawing of new connections.[5] Seeing Emerson in light of the tradition of the experiential real offers a way of affirming simultaneously the disruptive potential of the particular and the hopes of a broader visionary view of reality.

Emerson's vision of the real involves some sense of reality that is beyond the physical, and he offers the poet as a figure who can provoke us to find that reality within everyday life. Just as this poetic provocation demands a return to the details and textures of experience, Emerson's style relies on the accumulation of tropes—on the insistence on particularity. The analysis in the pages ahead will often situate passages from Emerson in the context of the greater work in which they occur; partly because his essays depend on the accumulation of tropes, the full power of a given line often demands an accounting of the work as a whole. As Emerson calls for the integration of instants of experience into a greater whole, attending to the way that instants of his prose (that is, lines and phrases) fit into an essay as a whole can reveal great—albeit at times conflicted—rewards.

A Vision of the Real

In an 1826 sermon Emerson proposes that there is "a more awful reality to thought and feeling, than to the infinite panorama of nature around" us, and the insistence on some reality beyond the material can be found throughout his career.[6] He often associates some deeper reality with life, truth, causation, unity, and morality. Joseph Urbas draws attention to the way that Emerson and many of his contemporaries on both sides of the Atlantic tried to make a place for some metaphysical sense of being in the aftermath of both Lockean sensationism and Kantian idealism.[7] Plato has a particular bearing on Emerson's approach to metaphysics, though he is also informed by a diverse range of thinkers, from the Puritans to Victor Cousin.[8]

The "Introductory Lecture" to his 1841–42 lecture series, *Lectures on the Times,* demonstrates the range of Emerson's sense of the "real." Beneath the appearances of the world "lies that which is, that which lives, that which causes. This ever renewing generation of appearances rests on a reality, and a reality that is alive." He then says that this "reality, that causing force is moral. The Moral Sentiment is but its other name. It makes by its presence or absence right and wrong, beauty and ugliness, genius or depravation" (*CW* 1: 182). Within two paragraphs, Emerson makes this reality the foundation of appearance, a living force, the moral sentiment, and the endower of good traits (such as rightness, beauty, and genius). There is something Platonic about this narrative of reality; as the Socratic dialogues often give the ideas both existential and moral priority, Emerson here makes this undergirding reality both an existential cause and a source of moral purpose.

However, grasping this deeper reality entails returning to the immediate appearances of the world in a new way—not completely ignoring them. In this same lecture Emerson calls on his listeners to see the things of the world as depending on this reality:

> As the granite comes to the surface, and towers into the highest mountains, and, if we dig down, we find below it the superficial strata, so in all the details of our domestic or civil life, is hidden the elemental reality, which ever and anon comes to the surface, and forms the grand men, who are the leaders and examples, rather than the companions of the race. The granite is curiously concealed under a thousand formations and surfaces, under fertile soils, and grasses, and flowers, under well-manured, arable fields, and large towns and

cities, but it makes the foundations of these and it always indicates its presence by slight but sure signs. (*CW* 1: 182–83)[9]

As that granite lies underneath but also supports the surfaces of the material world, so too does that "elemental reality" await us beneath the surface of appearances. These appearances are necessary, however. The beginning of any quarry starts with those "superficial strata"; digging for the truth, we must start from someone's backyard, even if it's our own.

"Being and Seeming," one of Emerson's 1838 lectures (parts of which later appear in "Spiritual Laws" and "Experience"), highlights the importance of interrogating phenomenal surface in order to grasp the real. The lecture associates "being" with sincerity, solitude, empowerment, activity, and joy. "Seeming" is the province of falsity, society, weakness, enervation, and boredom. Emerson claims that if a person lived alone, "he could never act foolishly, never with affectation, but always he would be in earnest," so it "is with Society that Seeming comes in."[10] Being offers life, excitement, faith, and reality. Emerson wonders, "what is Genius but this very love of reality?" (*EL* 307). He urges his listeners to "trust *being* and let us seem no longer" (*EL* 301) and calls on the individual to "trust to Being" to triumph over the "extreme difficulties" of making oneself "thoroughly genuine" (*EL* 302).

This discussion of being finds the spiritual to be more real than the physical. Noting the presumption of many that "bread and flesh . . . are real" and that "thought and will . . . are less real," Emerson goes on to speak of the legacies of two men, one who considers himself "a practical man and so wedded to that which can be touched, smelled, and tasted" and one who is "entirely wrapt in his meditations on the Absolute Cause of all things." Emerson says that "eternal superiority belongs to the contemplative man over his more forcible and honored neighbor; that the former moves in a real world, the latter in a phenomenal" (*EL* 297). He adds that the activity of this "contemplative man" is "life, properly so called" (*EL* 297). Because the contemplative man meditates on that "Absolute Cause," he draws closer to real life.

Yet, for all this lecture's criticism of seeming, it also alludes to the way in which appearances testify to real truths. Emerson relates the theory that if a lawyer does not believe in the rightness of his case, the jury will be able to sense the falsity of his legal position (*EL* 300). He expands on this notion to claim "that which we do not believe, we cannot adequately say" (*EL* 300).

Though being and seeming are often opposed in this lecture, Emerson also sometimes allies them by making seeming a vehicle for viewing being; the lawyer's delivery reveals his intellectual uncertainty about the case. Society, the seeming realm of falsity, also reveals a kind of virtue, as the "existence of society indicates the presence of virtue in its upholders" (*EL* 305). He adds that "the actual fabric of Society [is] upheld by what real life it encloses" and that, since "we are interested only by reality," "to Seem you must Be" (*EL* 305–6). Phenomenal appearance requires some source of being, which we may be able to grasp through this appearance.

So we cannot entirely abandon seeming appearance. Our "love of reality" causes us not to turn our backs on appearance but to interrogate what seems. The interrogation articulates itself as a forward-looking move in Emerson's lecture. For "a true and ingenuous mind the appeal is always being made to the future" (*EL* 303), and "what is really good is ever a new creation" (*EL* 308). Openness to newness is one of the reasons why the genius maintains, for Emerson, a childlike quality (*EL* 303), by which the world is always fresh. He also here describes genius as "a spontaneous soul . . . which does not accept from others but speaks from its own insight" (*EL* 307–8).[11] Key to Emerson's discussion of reality and being in this lecture is why the love of being should also lead us toward a perpetual reaching beyond. Even as Emerson emphasizes the permanence of real things, he also stresses our subjective need for perpetual spontaneity in order to arrive at reality. We live within appearances, yet these appearances are not themselves the source of life. We must perpetually try these appearances to find a further insight into being.

Lee Rust Brown finds that Emerson terms many things "real"—"instinct, spontaneity, God, cause, source, self, life, youth, absolute or supreme nature, force, light." Brown claims that these distinct things all point to "the work of an inner drive" that leads us to "what Emerson calls 'reception,' which entails opening ourselves to things but with an eye first to what they provoke from our own secret resources."[12] In writing about the role of self-reliance for Emerson, George Kateb raises a similar point: the aim of Emersonian self-reliance is "to help us see. To see is to be receptive, to take things in as truly or honestly or accurately as one can."[13] Kateb situates this kind of self-reliant seeing in the rhetoric of retrospection, but it can also be seen in light of real relations.[14] The need for perpetual spontaneity in pursuit of the real can be seen as an iteration of that quest for reception. Appearance must be tried in order to unlock both ourselves and the world around us.

Some of the things that Brown says that Emerson describes as "real" might be described that way because they help us perceive reality. Spontaneity, for instance, allows us always to open ourselves up to instants of experience so that we can "take things in as truly or honestly or accurately" as we can.

Often portraying the poetic enterprise as the search for correspondent reality within the seeming of the world, Emerson's writings on poetry also speak of the need to try appearance in pursuit of being. Sherman Paul draws attention to the stakes of correspondence and reality when he finds that, for Emerson, correspondence is "the *perception* of the symbolic import of an object: a way to apprehend reality. To stand as realized symbols, objects had to recreate in others this perception of the reality behind things."[15] That task of perception is central for Emerson's discourse of poetry. Though "poet" comes from the Greek *poieo* (I make), he often defines the poet's task as an enterprise of perceiving rather than making. As he writes in a letter to Lydia Jackson prior to their marriage, Emerson finds himself a "poet in the sense of a perceiver & dear lover of the harmonies that are in the soul & in matter, & specially of the correspondences between these & those."[16] In *Nature* he claims that the "perception of real affinities between events, (that is to say, of *ideal* affinities, for those only are real,) enables the poet thus to make free with the most imposing forms and phenomena of the world, and to assert the predominance of the soul" (*CW* 1: 33).[17]

In both *Nature* and the letter to Lydia, poetic perception involves finding connections—whether harmonies, correspondences, or affinities. This task of drawing affinities might proceed in multiple ways. It might go forward by drawing a connection between some material fact and some spiritual tendency—for instance, finding in the lion a symbol of courage. But affinities could also be found between two seemingly concrete instances. For example, one might draw an affinity between a raging lion and a parent protecting a child. This affinity between lion and parent, while starting from the material, depends on the recognition of deeper connections. In a third way one could also (and Emerson often does) draw an affinity between two different ideas; that affinity would in turn reveal further significances for those ideas. In this case one could draw a connection between the admiration of beauty and of the good—both testify to the heart's desire for what ennobles it. In all three cases particular instances (whether material or conceptual particulars) afford a vehicle for grasping broader currents.

Two of Emerson's essays on poetry—1844's "The Poet" and 1875's "Poetry and Imagination"—reveal this abiding concern with vision and connection. "The Poet" exhibits the broader Emersonian tradition of the poet as a see-er. He defines the insight of the imagination, a key quality of the poet, as a "very high sort of seeing, which does not come by study, but by the intellect being where and what it sees, by sharing the path, or circuit of things through forms, and so making them translucid to others" (*CW* 3: 15). "The intellect being where and what it sees" suggests that, far from nullifying the immediacies of its encounters with the world, poetic vision demands an intimate involvement with them. Poetic vision may lead to the experience of fluidity (the "circuit of things through forms"), but it can also lead to the experience of integration. With a mode of heightened perception, the poet "re-attaches things to nature and the Whole" (*CW* 3: 11). In the face of worldly alienation and dislocation (the state of detachment from "the life of God" being what makes things seem ugly, Emerson tells us in this essay [*CW* 3: 11]), the poet offers holistic connections. So we have returned to the sense of harmonies sketched out to Lydia.

"Poetry and Imagination" reinforces many of the themes of "The Poet."[18] Emerson declares in this work that poetry "is the speech of man after the real, and not after the apparent" (*CW* 8: 10).[19] The poet may use appearances and be involved in them, but the aspiration is the real. The forging of connections plays a key role in this essay, too. Emerson writes that imagination is a "perception and affirming of a real relation between a thought and some material fact" (*CW* 8: 15). This "real relation" goes beyond the material elements of the world; it arises from a union of mind and matter. This essay distinguishes between common-sensical and imaginative perception: common sense "looks at things or visible Nature as real and final facts," but "poetry, or the imagination which dictates it, is a second sight, looking through these, and using them as types or words for thoughts which they signify" (*CW* 8: 9–10). Common sense may see the physical world as "real and final," but poetic vision instead "look[s] through" the things of the world, viewing them not as final but as initiatory, not as solid but as transparent. Poetic vision rebukes the purported reality of common sense (the world of things and material facts) in order to gain a glimpse of a further meaning.

Emerson, then, defines the poet's task as achieving some kind of perceptual vista, one in which the poet can "look through" the objects of the physical world for the view of some spiritual reality. This looking through, however, does not necessarily require the annihilation of the thing seen. He speaks of the poetic intellect "being where and what it sees," and the project of finding a real relation between the material particular and spirit means attending to that particular. Revealingly, Emerson also associates this realer vision with fluidity and liberation. "The Poet" presents poets as "liberating gods": "They are free, and they make free" (*CW* 3: 18). "Make free" occurs in both *Nature* and "The Poet," and there is a telling duality to this term; the poet can help free others by encouraging them to view the world in a new way and can also "make free" with the figures of the world by unlocking them from their standard associations, putting them in a new context.

Realizing vision's interrogation of immediate experience suggests one way that Emersonian realization resists the erasure of distinctness in experiential encounters. Shannon Mariotti has argued that prior to 1844, Emerson often indulged in what she terms "focal distancing," which "tends to devalue material particularity as superficial, to be looked past, progressed quickly beyond."[20] Mariotti finds that that Emerson's discussion of slavery represents a decisive shift in favor of confronting particularity. However, his earlier writings insist on a commitment to the experience of particularity; that "superficial" surface of seeming nevertheless remains an important vehicle for glimpsing some realer vision. This use of the particular—finding its real correspondence—does not ultimately nullify the details of that particular experience. Indeed, those very details serve as a path for charting that real relation. Sherman Paul's proposal that Emerson tried to "maintain a living connection between the horizontal-worldly and the vertical-otherworldly" insinuates the importance of some attention to the ordinary for Emerson. That "living connection" can only be afforded by a rigorous attention to the details of the daily world, which are continually coming to be and passing away. A passage from "The Poet" exhibits the ways that Emerson both theoretically and rhetorically insists on the importance of an enduring trace of the actual:

> And this is the reward: that the ideal shall be real to thee, and the impressions of the actual world shall fall like summer rain, copious, but not troublesome, to thy invulnerable essence. . . . Thou true land-lord! sea-lord! air-lord! Wherever snow falls, or water flows, or birds fly, wherever day and night meet in twilight, wherever the blue heaven is hung by clouds, or sown with stars,

wherever are forms with transparent boundaries, wherever are outlets into celestial space, wherever is danger, and awe, and love, there is Beauty, plenteous as rain, shed for thee, and though thou shouldst walk the world over, thou shalt not be able to find a condition inopportune or ignoble. (*CW* 3: 24)

Invoking some essence "invulnerable" to the "impressions of the actual world," this poetic apotheosis could in some ways be seen as an iteration of Sharon Cameron's narrative of the "impersonal," a process of "ravishment" through which "the person is annihilated in the impersonal."[21] Nevertheless, this celebration of poetic transformation retains a preoccupation with the terms and figures of concrete experience. The contours of Emerson's prose testify to the persistence of the actual: the impressions of the physical world remain embedded in this paragraph. Take this "summer rain." It may be tremulous, transparent, nurturing, and soft, but the figure of rain persists as a vehicle for communicating the effects (or the lack thereof) of the impressions of the actual upon the soul. Imagery of the rain returns at the end of the paragraph with that invocation of "Beauty, plenteous as rain."

As with other works in the tradition of the experiential real, this passage insists on heterogeneous transparency, in which the trace of the seen-through persists. The prefatory poem to "The Poet" complements Emerson's invocation of "forms with transparent boundaries." The "moody child" who is the subject of this opening verse has "joyful eyes" (2) that "[t]hrough man, and woman, and sea, and star, / Saw the dance of nature forward far" (7–8), and through "worlds, and races, and terms, and times, / Saw musical order, and pairing rhymes" (9–10).[22] "Through" embodies the complexities of Emerson's poetic transparency. "Through" could emphasize seeing past a given object, in which the particularities of the object are left behind or ignored in the apprehension of this "musical order." "Through" could also, however, be a required medium (entering a house through its only door, for instance). That sense of "through" emphasizes the importance of that which is gone through.

This moment from "The Poet" exhibits a tension between the persistence of the figures of the actual and the transcendence of these figures. Emerson's poem "Bacchus" supplements this essay's comments on poetic liberation. In "The Poet" Emerson speaks of the "new energy" gained by "abandonment to the nature of things" and celebrates "mind flow[ing] into and through things hardest and highest" (*CW* 3: 15–16). "Bacchus," too, rejoices in the ability to "open and flow" (50), and the poem as a whole expresses a yearning for a transfiguration of experience that allows for a new energy.

As Hyatt Waggoner notes, this poem can be seen in light of the desire for a "Transcendental communion with Reality."[23] The speaker of this poem calls for a wine that will transmute experience in order to give it the edge of reality. However, as the poem reveals, this transmuting does not require the nullification of experience. Instead, it calls for the reintegration of experience through those "winds of remembering" that blow with "ancient being" (47–48), and memory becomes a figure for this reintegration. Whereas Waggoner finds that the language of memory in this poem can be traced to the rite of Communion, memory and forgetting play deeper structural roles in Emerson's work as a whole.[24] For Emerson, memory and forgetting often function as key intellectual processes for the sense of self-integrity. He opens the essay "Experience" with the figure of that "Genius which . . . gives us the lethe to drink" (*CW* 3: 27), and, after the "slid[e] to confusion" in the poem "Uriel" (34), a "forgetting wind / Stole over the celestial kind, / And their lips the secret kept" (43–45). At times, forgetting functions in Emerson's work as an act of disintegration within consciousness.[25] The mind no longer apprehends connections between one thing (itself, an intellectual principle, a specific quality) and another. The risk of disintegration in "Experience" is, in part, initiated by this draught of Lethe. In Emerson's writing Lethe appears as a figure of the loss of integration. As he writes in his journals, the "Lethean stream . . . washes through us" and gives "sometimes a film or haze of unreality,"[26] and, after a moment of insight, "a Lethean stream washes through us and bereaves us of ourselves."[27]

In contrast to the "Lethean stream" of the journals, the wine of "Bacchus" offers an integration of self with world and self with itself. Instead of bereavement, we have renewal. This renewal affords the prospect of new integration, and this integration allows for the facts to be newly seen and rendered with a fresh vitality. The closing lines of this poem yearningly dwell on the prospect of integration:

> Pour, Bacchus! the remembering wine;
> Retrieve the loss of me and mine!
> Vine for vine be antidote,
> And the grape requite the lote!
> Haste to cure the old despair,—

Reason in Nature's lotus drenched,
The memory of ages quenched;
Give them again to shine;
Let wine repair what this undid;
And where the infection slid,
A dazzling memory revive;
Refresh the faded tints,
Recut the aged prints,
And write my old adventures with the pen
Which on the first day drew,
Upon the tablets blue,
The dancing Pleiads and eternal men. (51–67)

Invoking memory, the final stanza of the poem emphasizes "re": remembering, retrieve, repair, refresh, recut. This piling of resonances hints at a fusion of conceptual meanings. The "remembering" of the wine can also be a "retrieving" of the speaker's self and the "repair" of the seemingly broken world, which allows for a "refreshing" of the old colors and "recutting" of "aged prints." Building on the Platonic tradition of recollection, Emerson offers memory as a mode for the integration of the world, in which the various parts of time are joined together and related. In *Nature* Emerson declares that the solution to the "problem of restoring to the world original and eternal beauty" is the "redemption of the soul" and says that the "reason why the world lacks unity, and lies broken and in heaps, is, because man is disunited with himself" (*CW* 1: 43). "Bacchus," written approximately ten years (1846) after *Nature*'s publication, returns to this association of self-unification and the unification of the world. Like the closing of "The Poet," it insists on the textures of language and calls not for the hollowing out of experience but instead for the vision of it with a sharpened eye.

Provoking Vision

Such an eye situates the particulars of experience within a greater spiritual reality, and this sharpness of vision grants a renewed encounter with worldly particulars. *Nature*—one of his great experiments in vision—offers a vehicle for examining the stakes of transformative sight and the encounter with the particular.[28] Cornel West asserts that the "primary aim of Emerson's life and discourse is to provoke," to which one might add that Emerson aims to provoke in the name of a vision of the real.[29] He claims near the beginning of *Nature* that all "science has one aim, namely, to find a theory of nature" (*CW* 1: 8), and *Nature* offers a theory of nature in (at least) two senses. Both of these senses rely on some sense of provocation. In accord with our contemporary notion of "theory" as a set of organized principles, it offers numerous reflections on nature and puts them together in a (faux-)systematic fashion. In reading *Nature* we might take some of these theoretical claims in a provocative fashion—to use the concepts brought up as vehicles for a vision of certain deeper tendencies in the human condition. But *Nature* also offers another "theory of nature": a theory in the classical, Greek sense of a beholding.[30] *Nature* encourages an enterprise of beholding and a recovery of seeing in a more fully realized sense. By attending to the true meaning of facts and "behold[ing] the real higher law," we shall "come to look at the world with new eyes" (*CW* 1: 44).

Nature as a whole offers a guidebook of provocation for gaining those "new eyes." As Christopher Windolph notes, *Nature* is "a treatise that attempts not to convey facts, but to lead others in the path of perception."[31] Provoking that "path of perception" relies on particularity in a broad sense: particular sections, images, and phrases offer jumping-off points for the dialectical interrogation of experience. Embodying the course of provocation, the book moves from the retrospective (opening with "our age is retrospective") to the prospective (the final section, titled "Prospects"). The goal of prospects organizes the broader narrative arc of *Nature*. It provokes readers to see through the things of the world, and this provocation demands reading in an exemplary mode: that we take the parts of *Nature* not as final disquisitions upon various topics but as instances of broader tendencies.

Elizabeth Duquette has drawn attention to complexities of the example for nineteenth-century Americans and others. She finds that Frederick Douglass resists tendencies to reduce complexity to examples and warns about the moral dangers of reducing other people (including former slaves) to mere examples for others. Key for Duquette's analysis is a distinction between particular and general, or between the example and the abstract. She suggests that Douglass perceives a danger in "an exclusive focus on the particular example (or body), divorced from a nuanced understanding of the possibilities associated with abstraction."[32] In Duquette's account, Douglass is deeply concerned with the dialogue between example and abstraction. We are limited in our understanding of any given example; Douglass claims in "Self-Made Men" that "man is too closely related to the Infinite to be divided, weighed, measured and reduced to fixed standards, and thus adjusted to finite comprehension."[33] Douglass's claim offers one argument against reducing a person to an example, but one could make an Emersonian expansion of that proposition: because of our closeness to the infinite, our thoughts also cannot be corralled to a single fixed standard. Duquette explores the way that Emerson appropriates the lives of others into examples in *Representative Men,* but Emerson's work more broadly often emphasizes the restlessness of any example—of the way that examples do not reduce complexity but add to it.[34]

Emerson often turns seemingly abstract categories or concepts (such as philosophical idealism) into examples of broader tendencies. Making the abstract an example of a broader spiritual tendency represents another layer of the Emersonian endeavor to find correspondences. That process of exemplification finds affinities between seemingly distinct movements, but attention to the textures of these movements (and their principles) can also be a way of disrupting our prior understandings of the world. On one hand, that process of exemplification could be viewed as a way of reducing the complexity of a movement—rather than being distinct and particular, it becomes only an instance of the general. On the other, the fact that this exemplification is not total (a particular can become an example of other traits, too) suggests that the particular has more possibilities within.

Nature's strategy of provocation has profound implications for its broader rhetorical structure. Section provokes succeeding sections. So the first section, "Nature," introduces the topic of nature and calls for a more expansive understanding of the term. Later sections—"Commodity," "Beauty," "Language," and "Discipline"—offer concrete explanations of some of the uses of nature while also revising our understanding of their particular organizing terms. Having established these various uses, the narrative rounds on itself in a reconsideration of nature. "Idealism" becomes a road to the realization of "Spirit" in the second-to-last chapter. Significantly for Emerson's rhetorical purpose in *Nature,* "Spirit" is not the concluding chapter—"Prospects," an appeal for self-awakening, is. "Spirit" provides a possible intellectual horizon, but "Prospects" urges its readers out in the direction of that horizon.

The longest single section of the work, "Idealism," models the dynamic of provocation in *Nature.* Poetry plays a central role in this section, which also references the "real."[35] Rather than offering an epistemology (that is, a science of knowledge) in *Nature,* Emerson instead offers an *epistemuthos,* or a myth of knowledge. That myth of knowledge invites us to realize the things of the world as intimately connected to ourselves. In "Idealism" he explores how various aspects of life (perspective, poetry, philosophy, science, and religion) suggest to us the role of personal agency in shaping the perception of the world. This section embodies the way that Emerson can turn to the disruptive use of the particular—in this case, particular intellectual schools. This section is not—and does not aim to be—a philosophical history of "idealism" (whether German idealism or the idealism of Berkeley or of Plato), nor does it seek to be a rigorous analysis of approaches to the ideal. Instead, it strategically and at times subtly invokes the rhetoric of debates about idealism in order to find the freeing uses of nature.[36] It uses such philosophical controversies as representative of broader tendencies. Whether nature "enjoy[s] a substantial existence" or not, it is "alike useful and alike venerable" to him (*CW* 1: 29). Idealist philosophy is likewise useful for Emerson.

The course of "Idealism" starts with that "noble doubt" about whether "nature outwardly exists" (*CW* 1: 29). The exposition of this "doubt" holds resonances of Descartes, Hume, and the broader history of epistemology in Western philosophy from the seventeenth to the nineteenth centuries. Emerson reflects on his "utter impotence to test the authenticity of the report of [his] senses, to know whether the impressions they make on [him] correspond to outlying objects" (*CW* 1: 29). Perhaps anticipating the development of Pragmatism later in the nineteenth century, Emerson finds that how we resolve such debates about trying to "verify" the truth of seeming outer appearances matters less than that we learn from this "noble doubt" the greater practical lesson of seeing "nature as a phenomenon, not a substance; to attribute necessary existence to spirit; to esteem nature as an accident and as an effect" (*CW* 1: 30). The liberating strategies of "Idealism" depend on the power of "Reason," which he opposes to a more quotidian "understanding."[37] The "presence of Reason," Emerson says, "mars this faith" in the ultimateness of things, and the "first effort of thought tends to relax this despotism of the senses, which binds us to nature as if we were a part of it, and shows us nature aloof, and, as it were, afloat" (*CW* 1: 30). "Idealism" at once chronicles the disenchantment of the self with the immediacy of the world (as doubt causes the individual to step back from the seemingly pressing demands of the surfaces of life) and the truer enchantment of the world through using it as a vista for seeing reality. Barbara Packer notes that for Emerson, idealism can become the "midwife" rather than the "murderer" of faith: "The man who believes that the mind alone is real, matter only a phenomenon, is easier to convince of spiritual realities than the empiricist who continually demands sensible proofs."[38] In addition to that "spiritual" use, idealism can also cause the individual to return to the empirical with a more receptive eye.

"Idealism" has a use for this work insofar as it disrupts a naïve faith in the finality of material surfaces and urges one onward to the subjectively mediated and free. For example, Emerson claims that intellectual science "has been observed to beget invariably a doubt of the existence of matter," but this science also "fastens the attention upon immortal necessary uncreated natures, that is, upon Ideas" (*CW* 1: 34). Over the course of "Idealism," Emerson broadens idealism beyond an epistemological movement to a tendency of human existence of which various cultural institutions and intellectual paradigms are modes.[39] He claims that these modes of poetry and science and religion "all tend to affect our convictions of the reality of the external world" (*CW* 1: 35). Yet this change in conviction regarding the external world need not become a cause of alienation, as Hume and others may fear; instead, it can become a vehicle for internal revolution. Emerson outlines these modes of idealism in order to indicate "the ground which to attain is the object of human life, that is, of man's connexion with nature" (*CW* 1: 36). Beholding nature as "aloof" can be part of the effort to apprehend this "connexion." Emerson claims that "culture . . . brings the mind to call that apparent, which it uses to call real, and that real, which it uses to call visionary" (*CW* 1: 36). The course of idealism in *Nature* is one of reevaluating appearance and challenging material immediacies in order to apprehend some further beyond. This apprehension involves an evolving recognition of the real. Things formerly regarded as real become viewed as apparent, and those things that seemed "visionary" become newly seen as real. The tutelage of "Idealism" involves the loss of old notions of what counted as real and final in order to invite us into a further search for reality in new beginnings.

Nature, in particular "Idealism," calls for seeing through our immediate experiences in order to gain a view of deeper affinities and a deeper reality. As "Idealism" notes, this vision might be inherently disruptive, as we come to call *apparent* what we used to think of as *real,* and *real* what we used to think of as *visionary.* This emphasis on realizing vision as entailing some disorientation would seem congenial to the aversive tradition championed by Cavell, Cameron, and others. However, it is also worth noting that this very process of disorientation depends on the contours of the concrete particular. For Emerson, a recognition of particularity affords disruptive openness in a double-edged way: the particular encounter can help us gain a revised view of experience (and every particular object connects to the whole), and our own perception of experience is itself particular (and therefore open to revision).

His "Merlin" sequence exhibits both these elements of particularity. It discusses seeing through particulars in the pursuit of limitless extension and acknowledges the particularity of an individual instant of perception by recognizing that which lingers beyond even our furthest apprehension of things. In the "Merlin" sequence Emerson transmutes meter and rhyme—two principal terms for poetry—into figures that reveal the stakes of particularity. In "The Poet" Emerson says that "it is not metres, but a metre-making argument, that makes a poem" (*CW* 3: 6), and across his writings Emerson speaks of poetry as transcending the conventions of meter and rhyme.[40] Nevertheless, the figures of meter and rhyme—just like "idealism" in *Nature*—can be of use for the project of poetic provocation.

"Merlin I" emphasizes meter and rhythm, mentioning smiting and pounding throughout, as when the speaker claims that the true poet sings "aloud the tune whereto / Their pulses beat, / And march their feet" (45–47). "Beat" stresses rhythm, as does the march of "feet," which also alludes to the poetic "foot."[41] Saturated with imagery of pairing, "Merlin II" instead attends to rhyme. The two Merlin sections take differing approaches to the particular. "Merlin I" offers a rhetoric of freeing extension, as one figure becomes added to another in a process of infinite combination. The encounter with the particular becomes an avenue of endless extension. "Merlin II" attends to a whole surpassing the limits of a particular. The first considers the particular moving to comprehend the universal; the second considers the universal (and other particulars) standing in counter to a single particular. The first part is about the one embracing the other; the second puts forth the other as complementing the one.

Alluding to the role of stress in meter, the imagery of force saturates "Merlin I." The poem opens with a rejection of the "trivial harp" (1) and the "tinkle of piano strings" (6) in favor of a wilder force. Succeeding lines elaborate on the imagery of force and suggest the particular as a pathway to something greater:

> Merlin's blows are strokes of fate,
> Chiming with the forest tone,
> When boughs buffet boughs in the wood;
> Chiming with the gasp and moan
> Of the ice-imprisoned flood;
> With the pulse of manly hearts;
> With the voice of orators;
> With the din of city arts;
> With the cannonade of wars;
> With the marches of the brave;
> And prayers of might from martyrs' cave. (16–26)

This anaphoric series—"With the pulse of manly hearts; / With the voice of orators" and all the other sundry pounds of natural and human life—offers a catalogue of poetic forces that reach throughout the whole course of life. The compounding "with" allows the blows to knit together a range of particular circumstances: banging trees and the "ice-imprisoned flood," industrial manufacturers and soldiers' marches. In this poem the blows of the true poet reach through a dazzling range of circumstances. For Emerson's enterprise of realizing transparency, the particular testifies to the further, and the range of this anaphoric catalogue suggests how great this further might be.

Instead of the imagery of blows, the beginning of "Merlin II" invokes rhyme:

> The rhyme of the poet
> Modulates the king's affairs;
> Balance-loving Nature
> Made all things in pairs. (78–81)

Setting the "rhyme of the poet" alongside the assertion that "[b]alance-loving Nature" pairs all things, these lines suggest a correspondence between aural rhyme and a notion of existential pairing. In "The Poet" Emerson claims that a "rhyme in one of our sonnets should not be less pleasing than the iterated nodes of a sea-shell, or the resembling difference of a group of flowers" (*CW* 3: 15). He finds that "the pairing of the birds [to be] . . . an idyll" (*CW* 3: 15) and cites, in the essay's opening poem, a "pairing rhyme" (10). In "Merlin II" Emerson returns to the imagery of pairing, presenting the pairing of stars and the union of groom and bride. Rhyme has been expanded into a figure for a broader sense of complementarity.

Considering the balance of Nature, Emerson emphasizes a countering wholeness: a sense of a whole that comes from something meeting its other in the form of a corresponding half: "To every foot its antipode; / Each color with its counter glowed" (82–83). The structure of "Merlin II" relies on pairing. Images of the physical world stud the first stanza: the glowing colors, the matching of leaves, feet, and hands. The second stanza instead emphasizes the metaphysical. It speaks of thoughts going "hand in hand" (102), the wandering course of "solitary fancies" (107), and the pairing wings of justice. Concrete finds its abstract mate within the poem.[42]

After all this pairing, Emerson turns to the figure of Nemesis:

And Nemesis,
Who with even matches odd,
Who athwart space redresses
The partial wrong,
Fills the just period,
And finishes the song. (118–23)

As Nemesis reaches across long periods in order to offer a balance of nature, Emerson, in part, extends the lines between rhymes within this stanza. After the series of couplets leading to these lines, Emerson turns to a more extended rhyme scheme of abacbc. The lines of would-be couplets interweave. As Nemesis "[f]ills the just period," this "fills the just period" complements "Who with even matches odd"; "odd" waits until fulfilled by this "just period."

Emerson here portrays Nemesis as a figure that stands beyond even our furthest apprehensions and as a totem of complementary otherness, an eternal response to our own partiality. Nemesis challenges the comprehensiveness of one assimilation even as it invites us to a further assimilation. Nemesis "with even matches odd," but odd and even together comprise the number system. The prospect of realization in Emerson demands recognizing the limits of our old founding belief, and Nemesis stands as a figure for that recognition (and for what lies beyond our old limits).

The two parts thus embody a dialectic between unity and difference. "Merlin I" seems to hold out the hope of a stress that echoes across the whole of the world; this stress comes from an individual insistence, and this echoing responds to the various individual figures of the world. Individuality is asserted even as it is gone beyond in the blows of poetic stress. "Merlin II" offers a complex response to these tendencies. In an assertion of difference (rather than the unifying blows of "Merlin I"), it invokes a Nemesis that defies even the greatest unity. Nemesis stands as the perpetual response of Otherness to any One, no matter how far that One may seem to go. Yet this claim of Otherness is implicitly undermined if not nullified by the fact that the two extremes of One and Nemesis can be reconciled in the act of rhyme. The figure of rhyme asserts two extremes (the dual poles of a rhyme) and the unification of these extremes (the echo of one syllable with another). So "Merlin II" at once differentiates itself from "Merlin I" in its assertion of Nemesis and joins with "Merlin I" in the pairing act of rhyme.

Just as these two parts simultaneously invoke distinction and the obviation of that distinction, the structure of "Merlin" incorporates distinction and unification. The rhyme of "Merlin II" may seem the nemesis of the meter of "Merlin I," but, as meter joins with rhyme in the formation of these parts, "Merlin I" and "Merlin II" come together to forge "Merlin." Even the titles of the parts suggest the persistence of individuating trace: "Merlin / I" and "Merlin / II" leave ambiguous whether these are two different poems or two parts of the same poem.[43] The poem at once analyzes and synthesizes itself, and we can see this play both within its constituent parts and through the play of these constituent parts within the frame of the whole.

The course of "Merlin" offers another variant of the dialectic of the real for Emerson. At times, the quest for the real offers a vista for perpetual flow, as the things of this world are gone through in the pursuit of further realization. This emphasis on the things of the world acknowledges the status of particularity but seeks to use this particularity as a springboard for some compounding insight. However, the Nemesis of "Merlin II" reveals another aspect of realization for Emerson: the notion of some reality that exerts a tremendous force upon our lives but so often evades our direct apprehension. Emerson so often suggests that, however great our understanding, our realizations remain partial and limited, with some greater apprehension waiting just around the corner.

Even though much of Emerson's work praises the wonders of realization, we can also find instants where he casts "reality" as Nemesis—as something that resists our efforts to fully conceptualize it. We can perhaps see a hint of the figure of Nemesis in one of the most famous passages from Emerson's work:

> There are moods in which we court suffering, in that hope that here, at least, we shall find reality, sharp peaks and edges of truth. But it turns out to be scene-painting and counterfeit. The only thing grief has taught me, is to know how shallow it is. That, like all the rest, plays about the surface, and never introduces me into the reality, for contact with which, we would even pay the costly price of sons and lovers. Was it Boscovich who found that bodies never come in contact? Well, souls never touch their objects. An innavigable sea washes with silent waves between us and the things we aim at and converse with. Grief too will make us idealists. In the death of my son, now more than two years ago, I seem to have lost a beautiful estate,—no more. I cannot get it nearer to me. If tomorrow I should be informed of the bankruptcy of my principal debtors, the loss of my property would be a great inconvenience to me, perhaps, for many years; but it would leave me as it found me,—neither better nor worse. So it is with this calamity: it does not touch me: something which I fancied was a part of me, which could not be torn away without tearing me, nor enlarged without enriching me, falls off from me, and leaves no scar. It was caducous. I grieve that grief can teach me nothing, nor carry me one step into real nature. The Indian who was laid under a curse, that the wind should not blow on him, nor water flow to him, nor fire burn him, is a type of us all. The dearest events are summer-rain, and we the Para coats that shed every drop. Nothing is left to us now but death. We look to that with a grim satisfaction, saying, there at least is reality that will not dodge us. (*CW* 3: 29)

This passage from "Experience" occurs under the aegis of the lord of life "Illusion," so we might not need to view these words as Emerson's final statement on the role of grief.[44] Nevertheless, these lines are a stunning reversal of the celebration that concluded "The Poet" just a few pages earlier in *Essays: Second Series.* In "The Poet" one of the rewards of the poet was the fact that "the impressions of the actual world shall fall like summer rain, copious, but not troublesome to thy invulnerable essence." Now, the "dearest events are summer-rain, and we the Para coats that shed every drop." The "curse" of the Indian that "wind should not blow on him, nor water flow to him, nor fire burn him" contrasts with that promised reward of "The Poet": becoming that "true land-lord! sea-lord! air-lord!" who will find "Beauty, plenteous as rain," wherever "snow falls, or water flows, or birds fly." Rather than the integrating joy, we instead have alienated dispossession.

Like the ever-distant period of "Merlin II," the reality of this part of "Experience" is one that evades the grasp of the individual. It is tempting to view this passage as evidence of a shift in Emerson's thought—from freedom to fate, as Stephen Whicher put it long ago—but this notion of reality as Nemesis can be found throughout Emerson's writings and, to some extent, is a necessary implication of the hope of realizing renewal sketched out in his earlier work (such as *Nature*).[45] The possibility of the perpetual renewal of our viewpoints through particular encounters seems to imply the necessary limitations of any given viewpoint. Thus, there is always some vista of reality yet to be gained. In most of his writings, this limitation may not be as dire as it is in "Experience," but it nevertheless haunts his work. Indeed, as the next section explores, the implications of the perpetual possibilities of revision are a key subtext of the compositional strategies for his essays.

The Comedy and Tragedy of Transparency

As Emerson emphasizes the importance of the initiatory and transparent for grasping the real, his essays become a literary place for initiating inquiry. This provocation depends on the textures of language. Reflection on those textures—syntax, word choice, examples, and so forth—becomes a vehicle for the broader reflection on experience. That reflection in turn encourages drawing correspondences and interrogating the surface of appearance. Just as the particular details of experience afford a chance for a liberating apprehension of reality, the particular textures of language create a vehicle for cognitive play in pursuit of the real.

Early in his journals (in April 1835), Emerson hints at the way that the particulars of language can become a window for viewing broader forces:

"The Germans believe in [this] necessary Trinity of God,—the Infinite; the finite; & the passage from Inf. into Fin.; or, the Creation. It is typified in the act of thinking. Whilst we contemplate we are infinite; the thought we express is partial & finite; the expression is the third part & is equivalent to the act of creation."[46] According to this passage, while our contemplations may be infinite, the thoughts we express as a result of that contemplation are finite. Our conceptual categories are always limited in a certain way. However, our expression of these thoughts (the mode of language) allows for a bridge between finite thought and infinite contemplation.

Emerson's comments on the expressive potential of language can be extended and applied to the strategies of provocation in his work. The figurative textures of his work give a vehicle of seeming for the reader to interrogate. Emerson's essays talk about experience, but reading them is also an experience. In many of his essays he seems less to be trying to reason out a conclusion through a series of ironclad premises and more conducting a conceptual symphony, with a tendency toward discord and extreme swings reminiscent of Wagner. Context renders ambiguous forte declarations—the fodder for the greeting cards of the future. Queries peal out with the crystalline ring usually associated with immutable principles. Propositions are trumpeted forth only for their rivals also to resound.

Emerson's essays offer the prospect of transparency on the levels of sentences and paragraphs and on the level of the essay as a whole. Image succeeds image, and the connections between them are often implied rather than explained. Sometimes, this imagery leads to a gradual sense of accretion, as similar terms are lumped together to create a sense of polyphonic magnitude. At other points, one image will immediately reverse another. Sometimes, a seeming similarity will prove a surface for a deeper dissonance, as the following sentences from "Experience" demonstrate: "The outward trick of nature is too strong for us: *Pero si muove.* When, at night, I look at the moon and stars, I seem stationary, and they to hurry" (*CW* 3: 32). Galileo's (possibly apocryphal) "*Eppur si muove*" refers to the motion of the Earth around the Sun ("yet it does move"), so Emerson's "*Pero si muove*" and the following lines subtly revise Galileo; rather than the Earth moving around the Sun, Emerson conjures here the perspective of the earthbound individual for whom the moon and stars move, while the individual perspective on Earth seems stationary.

Emerson's essayistic style depends on the interpretative return to instances of particularity, in which particularity is reinscribed even as the particular is seen in light of a new whole. Just as Emerson's theory of poetry contrasts the vision of a "perfect whole" with the fluidity of human experience (parts of that whole), his essays rely on a continual exchange between the disruption of parts and the (fragmented) perception of the whole. George Kateb has argued that the Emersonian project of self-reliance depends on grasping "the world at large through honest perception completed or enhanced by retrospection."[47] The task of retrospection shapes the narrative course of an Emerson essay as a whole; retrospection allows for the synthesis of tropes across an essay, and that synthesis can make his essays at once delightful and disorienting. Retrospection places particular tropes and moments into dialogue, which enhances our perception of those tropes and of the world around us.

This process of retrospection allows for the preservation of particularity. Elisa New has suggested that Emerson's theory and practice might not always give the precise contours of the particular their due. Emerson's celebration of indeterminacy undermines his poems because "lyric poetry . . . is precisely a genre of determination," and his indifference to particularity can be seen in his lack of interest "in time, except as it is compensated by futurity, or—stilled geologically in 'fossil poetry'—as it repays our critical interest in archaeologies."[48] In Emerson's essays, however, it is precisely the archeological interrogation of fossils—those accumulated tropes—that creates intellectual energy and complexity. Moreover, those fossils depend on the determinations of language.

The aversive tradition emphasizes Emerson as a writer of fluidity. His stylistic transparency reinforces and complicates this narrative of fluidity. The secret insistences of transparency suggest that abandonment cannot be total. The polyphony of Emerson's prose depends on a resistance to total leaving. That very process of leaving—so eloquently explored by Richard Poirier, Branka Arsić, and others—demands that resistance. Leaving entails the dialogue between a former location and the transition from that location. That which is left insists on its presence as a not-quite-abandoned trace. The experience of "flexibility" in Emerson's prose, Poirier rightly notes, itself depends on keeping multiple senses together in one's mind, so that one meaning is not entirely displaced by a successor. If there were such radical displacement, we would have not flexibility but merely flickering rigidity. This stylistic reliance on memory—on preceding forms—thus offers a significant complication of the aversive tradition. For all his celebration of radical change, Emerson insists on the resistance to that change in the strategies of his essays. He invites us to draw correspondences between his aversive transformations.

"Circles" exemplifies the strategies of transparency for an Emerson essay. Throughout his discussions of the real, Emerson emphasizes the way in which the aspiration for the real is a yearning for the initiatory. Rather than viewing the things of the world as final, a realizing eye instead sees them as starting points; by going through, realizing vision grasps a further sense of being within the flux of appearance. "Circles" chronicles the stakes and methods of this quest for transparent vision. "Every ultimate fact is only the first of a new series" (*CW* 2: 181), this essay instructs us at one point, revealing how radical this desire for the initiatory can be. What seems ultimate in reality begins a path for further explorations. Moreover, "Circles" also chronicles the fate of literary reading for Emerson—the way in which the process of literary reading returns to the figures of particularity even as it ushers us toward some view of a further reality.

An early source for "Circles" can be seen in *Nature:* "Who looks upon a river in a meditative hour, and is not reminded of the flux of all things? Throw a stone into the stream, and the circles that propagate themselves are the beautiful type of all influence" (*CW* 1: 18). The figure of the propagating circles becomes a figure of flux, the rings of water pulsing outward from the thrown stone. That image of perpetually succeeding circles evolves into the opening passage of "Circles":

> The eye is the first circle; the horizon which it forms is the second; and throughout nature this primary figure is repeated without end. It is the highest emblem in the cipher of the world. St. Augustine described the nature of God as a circle whose centre was everywhere and its circumference nowhere. We are all our lifetime reading the copious sense of this first of forms. One moral we have already deduced in considering the circular or compensatory character of every human action. Another analogy we shall now trace; that every action admits of being outdone. Our life is an apprenticeship to the truth, that around every circle another can be drawn; that there is no end in nature, but every end is a beginning; that there is always another dawn risen on mid-noon, and under every deep a lower deep opens. (*CW* 2: 179)

The echoing rings of a stone in a stream have become the principle "that around every circle another can be drawn": a succession of rings has become a succession of tropes. In this exposition of (or lyric on) the circle, Emerson introduces physiological, theological, and philosophical tropes. Within one sentence we move from a circle as an initiating point in vision ("the eye is the first circle") to a circle as a limit of vision ("the horizon which it forms"). The circle can give us an image to comprehend God, or it can teach us about morality, or it can explain to us how each action might be exceeded. These images offer the reader specific vistas for the view of "this first of forms." This process of relation compounds the meanings of the circle and, in so doing, brings these various meanings into a new interpretive order.

In a process of polyphonic exemplification, Emerson offers various exemplary tropes for the circle. We can understand the significance of the circle through the appeal to St. Augustine's description of the nature of God or the notion of the seeing eye or the compensatory aspects of human life. As Emerson speaks of circles rippling out from a stone in water, this paragraph performs that succession of rings. The initiatory paragraph of "Circles" invokes the tactics of transparency by insisting on the play between the various rings. Throughout his essays, Emerson presents a string of images as a way of seeing through. The jumps between images, combined with their teasing associations, provoke and entice.

The unity of the circle serves as a way of introducing and associating this essay's various topics, yet this unity is also perhaps strained by the seeming looseness of association within "Circles." Indeed, it seems at times as though this essay leaves the circle behind in order to pursue idealism or surprise or the bitterness of age. But this leaving behind often serves as a kind of elaboration, because these other topics themselves rhetorically develop from the associations with the circle forged earlier in "Circles." The initiatory myth of the opening paragraph invites us to consider the circle not merely as a geometric form or as an image that can be applied to some other entity (e.g., the concept of the circularity of history, which explicitly references the visual shape of the circle) but as a totem for a broader play of concepts.[49]

The succeeding paragraphs of "Circles" expand on this play of concepts. In the second paragraph Emerson turns to the fact of the circle as "symboliz[ing] the moral fact of the Unattainable, the flying Perfect, around which the hands of man can never meet" (*CW* 2: 179). This analysis suggests that the circular pantheon initially proffered by Emerson provides some sense of that which cannot be reached, some limit that transcends human apprehension or achievement. Yet how is this transcendence experienced? The third paragraph offers a partial answer to this question: it speaks of the notion that there "are no fixtures in nature" (*CW* 2: 179). This paragraph turns to the nature of the transient, and the passing of objects and conceptual paradigms provides a temporal demonstration of transience. Great sculptures fall apart, and new innovations outmode even the latest cutting-edge technologies. (So, as Emerson notes, sail technology lost pride of place to steam, and steam in turn gave way to electricity and other forces.) The concrete demonstrations of human accomplishment are thus rendered provisional and temporary, flickering waves in the ocean of history that will soon enough lose their definition.

The fourth paragraph grounds these instances of accomplishment in something greater. Turning from products to producer, the fourth paragraph meditates on agency: "A little waving hand built this huge wall, and that which builds, is better than that which is built" (*CW* 2: 180). Emerson's consideration of agency includes the empowering aspects of individual perspective—a "rich estate appears to women a firm and lasting fact; to a merchant, one easily created out of any materials, and easily lost" (*CW* 2: 180). Even material facts—such as a plot of land—can, through the enterprise of personal interpretation, be transformed into different entities.

Thus far, then, the beginning of "Circles" offers a movement from one fact to a further grounding one. So the instances of creation are then traced to their creators. The fifth paragraph compounds this movement: we now move from the creator to the internal dynamics within this creator to the notion that the "life of man is a self-evolving circle" (*CW* 2: 180). What seemed final and grounding is gone through for further interrogation. The first paragraph of the essay performs imagistic transparency, and the later paragraphs extend this drive toward transparency, moving from one topic to the next in search of some kind of grounding. In this perpetual transition "Circles" undermines the seeming finality of any given moment: "Every ultimate fact is only the first of a new series." A circle ends where it begins, and the end of many of Emerson's essays is to find beginnings—in the world around us, in ourselves, and in the essay before us. This finding of beginnings demands looking through appearance. Joseph Urbas has argued that causation is one of Emerson's central questions, and finds that the ultimate causing source for Emerson is some deeper reality.[50] "Circles" performs that quest for a grounding cause, but it also suggests the endlessness of that quest: our apprehension of that cause itself needs to be interrogated.

"Circles" ends with a sense of radical out-doing. We seek with "insatiable desire," this essay says, "to forget ourselves . . . to lose our sempiternal memory, and to do something without knowing how or why; in short, to draw a new circle" (*CW* 2: 190). Emerson often presents the drawing of a new circle as representative of an escape from earlier limits, a sudden leap that utterly encompasses and goes beyond all that came before. This sense of escape suggests why Emerson turns at the end of "Circles" to the loss of "sempiternal memory"—after all, how often can memories seem to imprison us, can the trace of the past seem to fetter our wild ambitions? Bursting all bounds in a moment of recognition, the individual finally at last understands how things *really* are. Being has revealed itself in all its wonderful glory. Yet what once seemed comprehensive or fundamental can all too often later seem partial or secondary. So our instantaneous moment of forgetting ourselves in a sudden burst of spiritual influx becomes reduced to the following: it is, "in short, to draw a new circle." And one of the great teachings of "Circles" is that every circle can itself be superseded. After that high language of self-forgetting, we return to the stark casualness of "in short."

The end of this essay instructs us that the "way of life is wonderful: it is by abandonment" (*CW* 2: 190). The attention to abandonment, disruption, and leaving has provoked considerable interest in recent scholarly writings on Emerson. However, the process of "Circles" radically complicates that process of leaving. Arsić argues that "in journeying toward a new circle we don't retain the old one" and that "Emerson suggests that in contriving a new circle we let the previous one be."[51] At the end of "Circles," Emerson may indeed suggest the abolition of the past circle in the drawing of the new, but the compositional architecture of "Circles" implies the opposite: we are left at the end of this essay with all the accumulated resonances of the past (exemplary) circles of this essay. "Circles" may conclude with a fantasy of nullification, but that fantasy collides with the persistence of the previous tropes of the essay.

One paragraph near the end of "Circles" offers a telling addendum to the motif of fluidity within this essay. Emerson notes that "this incessant movement and progression . . . could never become sensible to us, but by contrast to some principle of fixture or stability in the soul" (*CW* 2: 188). Without some background of the stable, we would be insensible of the changing;

pure flux would be the same as pure stasis. The experience of flow seems to require some resistance to this flow, as transparency requires that some trace of the transparent object persists. A similar point applies to Emersonian stylistics. Preceding figures provide a crucial context for succeeding ones. An Emerson essay demands that we read forward and backward through each trope: that we connect each figure to figures later in the essay (that we be prospective) and to figures earlier in the essay (that we be retrospective). The incessant movement of Emerson's prose is registered through the persistence of tropes.

The conflicted status of persistence also has stakes for memory in Emerson's work. As noted earlier, Emerson often associates memory with the restoration and reinvigoration of the self, while at times connecting forgetting to a loss of reality. At the end of "Circles," however, he seems to associate forgetting with a kind of radical empowerment in the drawing of a new circle. The compositional dynamics of "Circles" afford one way of addressing this tension. These dynamics rely on memory in their dependence on the reader recollecting the persistence of tropes. Thus, even though the finale of "Circles" might exalt some kind of forgetting, the broader course of the essay insists that this forgetting is consigned to a single moment; the project of transparency demands the persistence of memory.

This play of tropes in Emerson's work bears on the fate of pluralism and connects to claims made by Elizabeth Duquette about the possible ways that examples can resist glib reduction to abstraction. In Emerson's work no one example gains totalizing mastery over another. Instead, these examples persist, distinct from—while in conversation with—each other. Maintaining this pluralistic exemplary demands the maintaining of distinctions, which are necessary preconditions for a conversation. "Circles" demonstrates how radically nonhierarchical this exemplary process can be. That "first of forms" becomes both an example of other tendencies and becomes exemplified through these tendencies. A circle may stand as an initiatory totem, but, over the course of "Circles," other things become totems for this circle. This two-way conversation suggests a nontotalizing aspect of Emersonian transparency: in looking through A to see B, we can also look back through B to see A. As a result of this dual looking, neither A nor B is absolutely effaced or rendered subservient to the other. When Emerson speaks of the circle as a "first of forms," he does not necessarily mean that this circle is first in the sense of providing a totalizing intellectual foundation for the various examples of circularity embodied in this essay; instead, he offers it here as textually first in the composition of the essay (it is the essay's title). But this compositional priority becomes a springboard for further considerations of the circle, and, as "Circles" demonstrates, our quest for theoretical foundations is an open-ended one for Emerson.

"Circles" dramatizes the tragedy (or, perhaps, comedy) of transparency. For all that "insatiable desire" to utterly abandon that which came before, the past—past events, past experience, past rhetorical figures—endures. The accumulation of resonances in Emerson's prose depends on this endurance. That delightful drawing of a new circle is the delight of at last finding a foundation of meaning. According to "Circles," life's lessons seem to suggest to us that these foundations are themselves the roofs of deeper temples of knowing, but we forget that truism in drawing those circles. So there is something essentially frustrated about this desire for a vision at last: no circle available to mortal eyes is finally comprehensive. That's the tragedy of "Circles" (and the shadow of the Nemesis of "Merlin"). But the denial of this comprehensiveness also implies that life's vistas are never finally closed to us. New ways of understanding for oneself are always open. That's perhaps the comedy. We yearn, seemingly triumph, and are frustrated, yet this frustration holds open the opportunity for further triumphs, as the satisfaction of this yearning for totalized knowledge would be our own defeat.

Initiatory Realizations

In one of his notebooks, Emerson translates the following passage from the introduction to Joseph von Hammer-Purgstall's edition and translation of the works of the Persian poet Hafez:

> Or, to borrow from the poet one of his finest pictures, his verses are costly pearls bored by a masterhand & ranged on the gold thread of gazelles, as ornaments for the hair the neck, & the hand of beauty & joy. Take them as such, ask not that the pearl band be a girdle of Venus, wherein still longings & burning desires, caresses, & sweet joys punishing jealousy, & soft words are woven by the hand of the graces into an beautiful whole; ask not that pearl on pearl as silver drops be melted together into a jewellers band of unbroken connexion.[52]

This passage could in many ways stand as a commentary on Emerson's own work, which combines flow (pearl succeeding pearl) and distinction (as the individual pearls of the band remain separate). To read an Emerson essay is to follow trope after trope, figure after figure, form after form. Following this band requires an eye for both unity (that is, correspondence) and discontinuity (or aversion). In *Nature* Emerson praises the poet for perceiving "real affinities," and the trial of an Emerson essay is the courting of affinities, which depend on simultaneously distinguishing and unifying the attuned.

Lee Rust Brown, George Kateb, and others have noted the importance of receptivity for Emerson's project, and the quest for the Emersonian real is in part the quest for reception—to awaken ourselves to experience anew. This enterprise of reception requires a continued negotiation between the concrete instances of experience and the narrative of reality within which they are seen. Glimpsing the deeper underlying causes of reality grants the ordinary surface of experience a new edge; opening oneself up to the particulars of experience can disrupt the patterns of the psyche in order to grasp that cause. And the reading of an essay becomes a tutelage in the process of reception. The conversation between tropes becomes a vehicle for moving from the (finite) trope to infinity: new connections and narratives of affinity can always be drawn. Our business is never complete (never, that is, perfect), Emerson so often proclaims, and our encounters with the things of the world are ever open to revision. Emerson's prose offers us a seemingly infinite series of sedimentary layers, a series we have to dig through phrase by phrase but are also invited to see through all at once (the moment we have finished a paragraph or essay or recall it to ourselves). Retrospection is crucial for the act of reading (and rereading) an Emerson essay, and that backward-looking path becomes an avenue to new understandings—of the essay, of some idea, and of ourselves.

Emerson calls for a deeper insight into reality, and his prose seeks to provoke this insight through its play of tropes. The particular is always provocative, and the goal of such Emersonian reading and thinking is to make ourselves aware of the provocations of the particular. This awareness preserves some trace of the particular (those drops of summer rain), but it also demands the effort to see that particular in the light of a greater reality. The dizzying spins and exultations of an Emerson essay hope to prompt in us the ability to become aware of the spiritual reality that teases us along railroad tracks, in bare commons, and between the pages of books.

· THREE ·
In and Out of the Game with Walt Whitman

Whitman is no stranger to the world of flesh and blood. He celebrates it, rebukes it, loves it, and transforms it. Making much of his praise of the ordinary, many critics have located Whitman as an anticipator of conventional Realism. In documenting Whitman's embrace of the real *qua* actual, critics have also drawn attention to the way in which the encounter with the materiality of the facts informs his poetic project. I have no interest at the moment in quarreling with the tradition of seeing Whitman as anticipating later Realism.[1] However, we can also read him within the traditions of the experiential real.

Early in his career as a poet, Whitman situates himself as a poet of reality, a project that demands attention to the physical, the spiritual, and the social. *Leaves of Grass* offers a multivalent account of reality. Part of this account is representational: the portrayal of diverse aspects of experience (from physical places to human connections to interior moments of wonder). However, it is not merely representational; individual poems and the book as a whole model a dynamic that prompts a broader interrogation of experience. The poems of *Leaves of Grass* create a space for interpersonal exchange, internal reflection, and the revision of particularity. Whitman writes in the preface to the 1855 edition that the "psalm" of the American republic "has vista," and the term "vista" typifies his quest for realization.[2] Vista combines a broadness of sight with an awareness of the particularity of a given view. Incorporating the tactics of realizing transparency, his poetry seeks vista within the particular (whether an object or personal perspective); it looks through the object or perspective to see a greater panorama. Finding vista involves situating that object or perspective in relation to other things.

Placing Whitman in the context of the experiential real (including the quest for realizing vista) addresses some fundamental concerns for Whitman scholarship in recent decades, especially the role of particularity. Attending to the narrative of the real in Whitman can help rescue his work from accusations that it embodies, in Philip Fisher's phrasing, "the aesthetics of abstraction."[3] In *Residues of Justice,* Wai Chee Dimock situates Whitman's work within the tradition of personal abstraction in liberalism; in the creation of an abstracted "democratic subject," Whitman strips the self bare of all its contingencies "until it is purified into no more than an idea, an empty form."[4]

The experiential real, however, affords a prism for seeing Whitman's work not as nullifying contingency but as haunted by it. Experiential details—core constituents of contingency—are not drained away but reaffirmed in the context of a greater reality. The enterprise of finding vista transforms the particular by seeing through it or placing it in a broader context, but it also affirms the determinateness of the particular by recognizing its individuality and its limits.[5] Whitman's effort to be a poet of reality often entails the celebration of human connection—not the evisceration of these bonds. As excerpts from Whitman's philosophical jottings indicate, he at times feared that the purportedly imperial self was actually not so far-seeing—that its view of what really constitutes the universal might be transformed by gaining another view. Perhaps in response to the anxiety about an unknowing parochialism, "Song of Myself" models the quest to accumulate determinate perspectives not to annihilate them but instead to test the reach of any viewpoint (a task that implicitly requires honoring the distinctiveness of this viewpoint).

Whitman's poetry offers a vista in another sense: it becomes a literary vista for its reader. The task of reading a Whitman poem—especially the more sprawling ones—involves toggling between specific instances and broader flow. That toggling affirms particularity while also demanding an accounting of this particularity within a wider context. The provocation of Whitman's poetry has a number of elements. It seeks to model the dynamism of the self. As George Kateb has noted, Whitman shows how attention to the conditions of others can in turn help us become aware of the dynamic potential of ourselves.[6] Through the vista of his ever-seeking poetical speaker, Whitman offers insights into a vast range of conditions.

The fact that the speaker claims to feel for them may become a vehicle for our own understanding of these conditions. The performative empathy of a poem such as "Song of Myself" becomes an enticement not only to empathy for others but also to the further exploration of one's self. What parallels can be drawn to that individual seen there? How would you—or *I*—feel in this condition? Where is the poet leading me, and why does my heart respond?

"Starting from Paumanok," the introductory poem to the 1860 edition of *Leaves of Grass,* underlines the projects of poetic communion and literary vista. "Haste, haste on with me" the conclusion of the poem cries (271), reinforcing one of its central modes (that of empathetic urgency). Earlier, the poem suggests a broader theme for Whitman's verse: "This then is life, / Here is what has come to the surface after so many throes and convulsions. / How curious! how real!" (18–20).[7] The curious and the real intertwine for Whitman's poetic vista. He means to provoke his reader's curiosity—to make the things of this world tantalizing and suggestive of a more sweeping order. The whirling panoramas of places and people in this poem (189–228 and 252–65) indicate the wider survey of *Leaves of Grass* as a whole.

"O camerado close!" the speaker exclaims near the end of "Starting from Paumanok," and Whitman continually invites his readers into empathetic identification with the speaker and others throughout his work. The particular plays a key role in this project of empathy. Martha Nussbaum has claimed that if "altruistic emotion is to have motivational power, it needs to hitch itself to the concrete."[8] The presentation of a particular case adds to the emotional intensity of any appeal to fellow feeling. The reader navigates between particular identifications and the image of a broader vista, and the project of empathy for Whitman involves a continued re-situation of the particular person within a fluid panorama. The constant negotiation encourages a kind of readerly sensitivity and expansiveness.

In exploring the dynamics of Whitman's poetry, I will often emphasize the language of incompleteness rather than abstraction. These connections are not total, and the given constellation of connections is not final (more could be made); the task of Whitmanian vista is to offer provocative examples of connection, not to lay out a comprehensive blueprint. Outlining Whitman's theory of poetry and the real sets up a discussion of how he seeks to test both the appearances of the outer world and the interior of the self.

Both enterprises of testing involve a recognition of contingency. Accounting for contingency, his poetry creates a place for interpersonal exchange and endless revision, which has implications for his poetic tactics and his broader political vision.

Claiming the Real

In his poetry and his reflections on his poetry, Whitman situates himself in the tradition of the experiential real. His grasping of his poetic register, when the whirlwind commences in earnest, occurs almost simultaneously with his reach for the real. In the pages of an early notebook,[9] Whitman writes:

> I am the poet of reality
> I say the earth is not an echo
> Nor man an apparition;
> But that all the things seen are real,
> The witness and albic dawn of things equally real
> I have split the earth and the hard coal and rocks and the solid bed of the sea
> And went down to reconnoitre there a long time,
> And bring back a report,
> And I understand that those are positive and dense every one
> And that what they seem to the child they are
> [And the world is no joke,
> Nor any part of it a sham][10]

This passage offers in embryonic form so many familiar themes and moments from "Song of Myself" and Whitman's verse more broadly. The statement "I am the poet of reality"[11] resonates with the following declaration in "Song of Myself": "I accept Reality and dare not question it" (483).[12] This invocation of reality entails a searching for foundations: the interrogation of the material grounding of the Earth becomes an emblem for something further. "All the things seen are real," the verse insists. The things of the world bear something of reality, and the witnessing, experimenting bard can locate this reality. Moreover, witness is itself "real" according to these lines. Whitman tellingly says that "what they seem to the child they are," which alludes to the leitmotif of incompleteness in his work. A child could represent incompleteness of both being (always growing into something new) and perception (always gaining new insights).

The verse expresses a craving that appearance is in some way anchored to being—that our experiences are not just figments. The "earth is not an echo," and man is not "an apparition." Whitman associates this reality of awareness with seriousness, asserting the world is not a "joke." In "A Psalm of Life," which was included in *Voices of the Night* in 1839, Longfellow offers a similar alliance of reality and seriousness:

Life is real! Life is earnest!
And the grave is not its goal;
Dust thou art, to dust returnest,
Was not spoken of the soul. (5–8)

The need to assert the reality of life shows Longfellow tapping into the tradition of the real that finds the real in more than the actual. "Life is real!" Longfellow implores, and those early lines from Whitman reveal a similar insistence.

An anxiety about the reality of appearance percolates throughout Whitman's verse. "Of the Terrible Doubt of Appearances" (originally published in the 1860 version of *Leaves of Grass*) reflects on the worry that appearances might deceive us: "Of the terrible doubt of appearances, / Of the uncertainty after all, that we may be deluded" (1–2).[13] The poem wonders, "May-be the things I perceive, the animals, plants, men, hills, shining and flowing waters, / The skies of day and night, colors, densities, forms, may-be these are (as doubtless they are) only apparitions, and the real something has yet to be known" (5–6). Contemplating the vast variety of phenomenal existence, the speaker comes to wonder whether or not he has encountered "the real something." The speaker finds that the company of "he whom [the speaker] love[s]" helps resolve that anxiety (11); love quiets epistemic doubt. This poem suggests that a feeling of human connection can help overcome (or at least keep at bay) radical skepticism about appearance. Throughout his verse, he appeals to human connection as a way of grounding a sense of the "real," and this quest for connection often serves as a vehicle for the affirmation—not the negation—of particularity.

In Whitman's work an anxiety about outer appearance can at times also become an anxiety about the self's own reality. In "When I Read the Book," the speaker wonders, "I myself I often think know little or nothing of my real life" (5).[14] "That Shadow My Likeness"—like "Of the Terrible Doubt of Appearances" originally published in the "Calamus" cluster in 1860—wonders about the reality of the self:

> That shadow my likeness that goes to and fro seeking a livelihood,
>   chattering, chaffering,
> How often I find myself standing and looking at it where it flits,
> How often I question and doubt whether that is really me;
> But among my lovers and caroling these songs,
> O I never doubt whether that is really me.[15]

Like "When I Read the Book," these lines express doubt about what constitutes the true reality of the self. As "Of the Terrible Doubt of Appearances" offers companionship as a remedy for anxiety about the epistemic status of the exterior world, the speaker of "That Shadow My Likeness" claims that "among [his] lovers and caroling these songs" he never doubts the reality of himself. "That Shadow My Likeness" suggests that fellowship and poetic composition provide a way of responding to anxiety about appearance. Throughout his work, Whitman meditates on the way that human connection can afford some trace of the real and how poetic vision allows access to reality.

A fear (or suspicion) that appearance may be false is not confined to his poetry. After a night on the town, the title character of *Franklin Evans* reflects on his encounters at a theater and a drinking establishment and says that the "occurrences of the night . . . taught me to question the reality of many things I afterward saw; and reflect that, though to appearance they were showy, they might prove, upon trial, as coarse as the eating-house waiter, or the blear-eyed actress."[16] As does Franklin Evans, Whitman at times uses the embellished language of showiness in order to suggest the limits of any appearance. In a notebook passage speaking of the busy-ness of Broadway, Whitman says to those "Phantoms" passing on the street, "Oft I doubt your reality whether you are real—I suspect all is but a pageant."[17] "Pageant" here implies emptiness and falseness—and a lack of reality.

If Whitman doubts the realities of some showy pageants, he also insists on the connection of his poetry to reality. In the 1855 preface to *Leaves of Grass,* he invokes the real multiple times. He writes that "the attributes of the poets of the kosmos concentre in the real body and soul."[18] The "real" of "real body and soul" may modify both "body" and "soul" and thus may assert the soul's reality, a possibility reinforced by the fact that "Song of the Rolling Earth" finds that "the soul is also real" (113).[19]

The preface also fuses the imagery of artistic representation and that of human connection. In a section discussing the role of artistic form, Whitman writes, "You shall stand by my side and look in the mirror with me."[20] He thus flips the mirror, the traditional (and favored Realist) artistic trope for the artist's reflection of the world, into an image of self-regard: the mirror may reflect nature, but it also reflects the view of the poet and the reader. The very moment of Realism becomes a moment of self-reflection, which allows not only the poet to examine himself but also his readers to examine themselves. In this image Whitman underlines the way in which the project of poetic vista becomes an opportunity for readerly introspection and for communion between reader and poet.

The 1860 poem "A Hand-Mirror" reinforces this transformation of the mirror:

> Hold it up sternly—see this it sends back, (who is it? is it you?)
> Outside fair costume, within ashes and filth,
> No more a flashing eye, no more a sonorous voice or springy step,
> Now some slave's eye, voice, hands, step,
> A drunkard's breath, unwholesome eater's face, venerealee's flesh,
> Lungs rotting away piecemeal, stomach sour and cankerous,
> Joints rheumatic, bowels clogged with abomination,
> Blood circulating dark and poisonous streams,
> Words babble, hearing and touch callous,
> No brain, no heart left, no magnetism of sex;
> Such from one look in this looking-glass ere you go hence,
> Such a result so soon—and from such a beginning!

"Who is it? is it you?" the poem asks in the opening line, revealing the way that this hand-mirror offers a challenge to immediate appearance and prompts an inquiry into identity. This mirror reveals what is beneath the "fair costume" and reveals some inner core of deprivation and misery. Whitman does not always offer such a grim mirror to his readers (though moments of vulnerability thread throughout his celebration of the self), but that project of mirroring involves that interrogation of immediate appearance across his poetry.

Whitman, then, claims the connection between his poetic project and reality, but he also expresses anxiety about knowing reality in two senses: wondering about the reality of himself (the "real I myself") and the reality of the phenomenal world around him. Seeming is thus doubly tested: What is the basis for the seeming of myself and of the world around me? "Of the Terrible Doubt of Appearances" and other poems suggest that human connection can be a remedy to doubts about reality, and Whitman more broadly appeals to connection as a way of situating phenomenal encounters in the context of a greater reality. This connection can be a bond between two people in an empathetic moment, but it can be broader, too.

The forcefields of affinities and oppositions, contrasts and similarities, alliances and enmities, and so forth generated around anything are part of reality. Whitman's poetry offers an accounting of these objects and their connections in multiple ways. It situates one entity in conversation with another through the catalogue format. It also comments on those connections (interpretation of, or reflection on, entities and experiences being a major mode in Whitman's poetry). The project of vista asserts the integrity of any particular object or phenomenal encounter but also its contingency and dependence on a vaster panorama, and situating that experience within a broader vista is part of recognizing its reality.

The project of realizing vista illuminates the controversy about the status of the particular in Whitman's work. One school of thought holds that Whitman's poetry can at times slight particularity, hollowing out the uniqueness of the individual in the giddy pursuit of unification (and, perhaps, self-assertion). Wai Chee Dimock is one of the most compelling proponents of this approach, and her discussion of particularity (or the lack thereof) in Whitman reveals some of the possible tensions in his poetry. Dimock finds that the following is one of the central questions in Whitman's work: "How can we reconcile the categoric conception of the self in democratic theory with our experiential sense of the self in human attachments, attachments that are, after all, not universal but highly particular, anchored to the self not in its commonality but in its distinctive features and substantive attributes—anchored, in short, not to what is 'me' but to what is 'mine'?"[21] She finds that Whitman, like other writers in the liberal tradition, tends to prioritize a self that is abstracted from particular connections.[22] This severing of the self from its connections leads, Dimock argues, to a variety of effects. She says that "Song of Myself" is "a poetry of sequence without sedimentation," marked by transposing "seriality into simultaneity."[23] In its courting of democratic integration and the (abstracted and categorical) democratic subject, "Song of Myself" drains the individual entries of its catalogues of binding significance. The transcendentally untroubled self is also sublimely isolated from the incidents of the world; "Song of Myself" churns through a sequence of images without ever being marked by the trace of sediment, and, in living in the present, it cuts "the weight of time" from past events, causing them to appear "contemporaneous with all events subsequent to them."[24]

While Dimock's attention to the dynamics of abstraction is instructive, Whitman's project of vista also shows some resistance to abstraction. Just as the process of leaving in Emerson often depends on a trace of the left behind, so too does the sequence of Whitman's verse rely on the enduring trace of sedimentation. The accumulative process of "Song of Myself" relies on the continued distinction of discrete entries within the poem. For this reason, I would like to extend W. C. Harris's claim that Whitman has an interest in "*pluralization* whereby integrity, identity, and differentiation are guaranteed."[25] This theme of pluralization applies both to Whitman's politics and to his poetics. In "Song of Myself" and elsewhere, he offers a poetry that affirms both identity and difference, both unity and diversity. Allen Grossman argues that, in part to address the dislocation of union in the United States in years before and after the Civil War, Whitman "devised a 'song' that would reconcile variety and order, equality and constitution, one and many without compromising either term."[26] In the preface to *Leaves of Grass,* Whitman writes of the hopes of gangs of kosmos and prophets who "shall find their inspiration in the real objects today, symptoms of the past and future."[27] Finding "symptoms of the past and future" in the present in some ways goes in the direction of simultaneity; past and future are seen through the present. But that hope also preserves the notion of seriality, just as the laid-out strips of a film reel can be simultaneously seen even as the sequencing of them honors the principle of seriality.

A few examples of Whitman's lists reveal some of the ways his poetry preserves particularity in the greater scope of a realizing vista. In *The List* Robert E. Belknap argues that in creating a list, "we transform chaos into cosmos,"[28] and Whitman, "a kosmos, of Manhattan the son" ("Song of

Myself" 497), uses the list as a way of rendering the cosmos of himself and the world. The transformation from "chaos into cosmos" involves the vision of a wider order in which those various objects participate. This transformation complicates the particular. As Belknap puts it, the catalogues of "Song of Myself" allow Whitman to "represent an 'ensemble' of particulars and emphasize both the total collective and the components that constitute it."[29] Speaking of Whitman's listing of various Americans in "Song of Myself" (see lines 263–353), Michael West notes that in Whitman's lists, "the poet's voice makes/reveals the type incarnate in the individual, so that the catalog seems both a list of people idealized into essences and a list of common nouns given the concrete particularity of proper names."[30] The duality posed here by West (idealized essences and concrete particulars) offers another iteration of the persistent tension between finitude and the perpetual for Whitman. The items in Whitman's lists are at once concrete things and avenues to go *through* the concrete into a more overarching whole. In their transformation "into cosmos," his lists invoke both concrete actualities and a broader whole in which these actualities participate. In offering an accumulative presentation of America, Whitman does not aim to embrace only those "seventy-five different Americans" but to present, through this list, some suggestion of the whole range of America.[31] As the catalog swings from baptized children to a sweating peddler to the president meeting with his ministers, it fuses immediacy of detail with the breadth of a panorama. Whitman's catalogues engage in a kind of silhouetting, as determinate entry enters into a dialectical relationship with the rest of the catalogue.

Whitman's lists are one of the most immediately intoxicating aspects of his poetry. Their capaciousness and seeming endlessness demonstrate his impulse to embrace experience and the world. The piling up of images in his lists strikes like an overwhelming tidal-wave: a rush that knows no limits and smashes any narrow walls that would hold it in. Yet tidal-waves, for all their force, obey the laws of physics, and we can note instances of order within Whitman's lists. That act of ordering provides one way of situating the entries of the catalogue into a vista. Order affords an articulation of relationships while also recognizing the distinctive traits of each particular item in the catalogue.

Consider the following three lines from the catalogue of activities in section 15 of "Song of Myself":

The young sister holds out the skein while the elder sister winds it off in a
ball, and stops now and then for the knots,
The one-year wife is recovering and happy having a week ago borne her
first child,
The clean-hair'd Yankee girl works with her sewing-machine or in the
factory or mill . . . (293–95)

This cluster attends to different opportunities for women in the nineteenth century. There are the prospects of familial work (the sisters with skeins), maternity (the one-year wife with her baby), and labor in industrial facilities (the Yankee girl). These lines provide a telling contrast between the work of the Yankee girl and the enterprises of the sisters and the new wife. The two sisters working with the skein and ball present an image that could reach back for centuries, as does the mother with her infant; the factory work of the Yankee girl is representative of burgeoning industrial modernity. Moreover, the presence of no other person (especially no other family member) is mentioned in the line about this "Yankee girl," suggesting also perhaps some of sociological effects of industrialization, such as the disruption of the family.[32] So this cluster alludes to the radical changes brought by industrialization for traditional societies. It also suggests the heterogeneity of American life at this time, as women partake of ancient and quite new endeavors. The structure of these lines allows a kind of generalization, in which these individuals pursuing these activities become representative of broader types.[33]

Whitman's lists, however, do not merely make individuals cutouts of different types. He will often emphasize the individual *qua* person, as well. For example, later in this catalogue, the following moment arises: "The bride unrumples her white dress, the minute-hand of the clock moves slowly" (303). This bride is in part representative of new wives, but Whitman heightens this catalogue entry by attending to the psychological details of this scene. He notes that the "minute-hand of the clock moves slowly." It is easy to be washed away with this flow of details, as the camera-lens of Whitman's verse jumps from one sight to the next, but this attention to the slow movement of the minute hand indicates the bride's expectation for her upcoming wedding. We can picture a woman smoothing her dress as she waits for her wedding to begin, her eye on the clock, which seems to drag out every second.[34] The few details of this line are evocative of a particular moment, and Whitman invites us here not merely to consider this woman as a type but also as this person *here* at *this* time with *these* particular experiences. Whitman's catalogues thus portray a *this*ness even as he casts each *this* as representative of broader types. They fuse an allusion to the unique with the suggestion of a panorama.

Within Whitman's catalogues, each entry implicitly enters into a dialogue with other entries. So the Yankee girl replies to the new mother, and the various locations and individuals in the extended catalogue (lines 717–97) of section 33 respond to each other. Establishing a dialogue between the various entries in the catalogue allows for a renewed understanding of each particular entry. The entry becomes situated within a broader web of other particulars, just as each particular figure is situated within a broader web of space and time. The particular mentions of particular individuals give the poem texture and sedimentation. The vista of a catalogue is heterogeneous, and that very heterogeneity is in part what allows that catalogue to provide vista. The heterogeneity affirms the distinct particularity of each individual item. While suggestions of order help associate these heterogeneous incidents, they also do not fully account for these incidents.

In his 1926 study of Whitman, John Bailey argues that in "When Lilacs Last in the Dooryard Bloom'd" and elsewhere, Whitman tries to flee the particular in the name of the universal: "All true poets live in the universal and escape to it, even from those actual and individual occurrences, personas and things which they realise so much more vividly than ordinary men. The particular is more real to them than to the rest of us, but it is also a part of a more real universal. And so Whitman turns from Lincoln's coffin to salute all other coffins, and from death as mere bereavement to something much larger, holier, and happier."[35] Yet there is a possible tension here. Bailey argues that the particular is "more real" to poets, and this accentuated sense of reality might come precisely from the effort to situate the particular in the context of a greater universal. Situating the particular in the vista of the universal might not be an "escape" from the particular but a compounding of it. Grasping the particular in light of that "more real universal" gives our experience of that particular more emotional heft and intellectual significance.

The course of "When Lilacs Last in the Dooryard Bloom'd" makes Lincoln's coffin the vista to the wider suffering of the Civil War. As with

Drum-Taps as a whole, the turn toward generality makes the particular experiences of suffering and trial all the more acute. Lincoln's Springfield-bound coffin emblematizes the death of a man, but it also prompts a reflection on the (at times, disorienting) grief at the deaths of hundreds of thousands of men and women. Far from escaping Lincoln's particular death, this vista renders that death even more bewildering and terrible. If, as Max Cavitch and Betsy Erkkila have argued, Whitman aims in *Drum-Taps* to foster reconciliation through a recognition of common pain, the distillation of the deaths of so many into the coffin wending its way back to Springfield performs the unification of collective suffering in a way that adds to the magnitude of any instance of individual suffering.[36] Hundreds of thousands of others died with Lincoln, so his death is of a piece with theirs even though it retains its own particular texture. *Drum-Taps* as a whole might be read as a catalogue of instances—of jubilation, struggle, suffering, and death. This catalogue preserves the distinct textures of particular moments, whether it be the sight of troop maneuvers in "Cavalry Crossing a Ford" or a family finding out about the fatal injury of a son in "Come up from the Fields Father." The particular instances of trauma retain their distinctiveness; they serve as pathways into the broader panorama of suffering, but they can only serve in this capacity as long as their particular qualities are recognized. The affirmation of particularity is a precondition for setting that particular in the context of a greater realizing vista.

Whitman's catalogues thus seek to realize their entries by situating them in a broader order, which gives these particulars significance and magnitude. In the "Merlin" poems Emerson recasts meter as a series of pounds that resound through the scope of the world; insistence on a particular (that stress) becomes an avenue to a broader cosmos. Whitman, too, places a precise stress on each particular object in order to glimpse a greater avenue of being.

The Vista of the Self

Some narratives that accuse Whitman of hollowing out particularity do not simply focus on encounters with exterior objects; they also claim that he espouses a kind of categoric self, which surrenders all particular conditions in pursuit of the all. So it is now worth turning to how the contingency of the self haunts Whitman's work, too. As he interrogates vista in the seen, he also interrogates it in the seeing eye. One of the ways that contingency haunts Whitman's work is in the gnawing anxiety about the provisionality of any viewpoint: that which seems to be universal—to see all—might actually be more parochial. As a worry about the reality of a person's self-perception simmers in many of his poems, Whitman's writing more broadly comes to wonder at the conditions of a given viewpoint.

The fragmentary "Sunday Evening Lectures" (see *Notebooks* 6: 2009–18) reveal Whitman's abiding interest in the limitation of a given viewpoint and how to preserve this viewpoint in conversation with a greater whole. Perhaps notes assembled for some hypothetical lecture series and of uncertain date (though at least portions of the material come from the early 1870s), the "Sunday Evening Lectures" attend to the development of Kantian and post-Kantian German idealism, particularly focusing on the "illustrious four" of Kant, Fichte, Schelling, and Hegel (*Notebooks* 6: 2016).[37]

Whitman proposes the following development: While Kant opened up new philosophical horizons, Fichte instead proposed a system dominated by the power of the "I." Whitman shows some sympathy with Fichte's assertion that "the whole universe, becomes in brief, the *I* as that is the only thinking subject, active principle and consciousness" (*Notebooks* 6: 2015). However, he also fears that Fichte's work demonstrates an "all-devouring egoism." These limitations are countered by Schelling, who supports the "objective" rather than Fichte's "subjectiveness" (*Notebooks* 6: 2015). For Whitman, Hegel realizes the potential of German idealism by combining the relative and the absolute. Whitman portrays Hegel as a Whitmanian figure: only he is "fit for America—is large enough and free enough" (*Notebooks* 6: 2011), and his philosophy "encloses" the work of Kant, Fichte, and Schelling (*Notebooks* 6: 2016).[38] Whitman celebrates Hegel's interest in a Spirit that suffuses all the happenings of the everyday world, which are themselves manifestations of a broader dynamic.

Whitman's discussion of these philosophers is preoccupied by the fate of particularity and the role of individual perspective. His concluding remarks underline this concern. He wonders whether "what we realize as truth in the objective and other Natural worlds is not the absolute but only the relative truth from our existing point of view." He restates this query: "That this is what we realize of the objective world by our present imperfect senses and cognizance and that what we thus realize would be entirely changed and perhaps overthrown and reversed if we were advanced to superior development and points of view" (*Notebooks* 6: 2017). Whitman also draws attention to what he takes to be a second outstanding question: whether the soul, even as it remains involved in particular conditions and under the "inherent and immutable laws of things," perhaps "far from ken or analysis . . . does not somehow, even now, by whatever laws and indirections, by its own laws, repel the inconsistent and gravitate forever toward the absolute, the supernatural, the eternal truth" (*Notebooks* 6: 2017–18).

These philosophical musings complement Whitman's abiding poetic concerns with perspective. The "Sunday Evening Lectures" reflect on "relative truth from our existing point of view" as an epistemic matter, and his poetry often considers the moments of access permitted by our "existing point of view." A line from "Of the Terrible Doubt of Appearances" (published in the 1860 edition of *Leaves of Grass*) mirrors the language of the "Sunday Evening Lectures" on the role of relative points of view: "May-be they only seem to me what they are (as doubtless they indeed but seem) as from my present point of view—And might prove (as of course they would) naught of what they appear, or naught any how, from entirely changed points of view" (9).[39] The parallels between this extended line and the concluding meditations of the "Sunday Evening Lectures" are striking. Phrases (such as "points of view") echo each other in these two distinct works, and both the "Lectures" and this poetic line reflect on the implications of the fact that our point of view may be limited. "Of the Terrible Doubt of Appearances" as a whole meditates on how appearances may deceive us, and that possibility of deceit implies that any given point of view may be limited. In both works appearance and points of view become things to be tried.

Whitman's poetics, then, are deeply concerned with the potentially unseen limits of any particular viewpoint. Perhaps as a way of addressing this concern, his poetry often attends to the experiences of others and emphasizes an expansionary tone. Those two tendencies are allied. In outlining his case for Whitman as an exponent of "democratic individualism," George Kateb argues that Whitman uses attention to the experiences of others as a way of understanding our own potential: "I am potentially all personalities and we equally are infinite potentialities."[40] Encounters with others awaken us to what we can be, so these encounters become a way of facilitating our awareness of our own self's range. This theme of awareness of others as leading to the expansion of oneself has been noted by other critics. For instance, Agnieszka Salska finds that "Song of Myself" consists of "sequence of 'movements' toward an ecstatic union": "Each ecstasy enlarges the protagonist's consciousness and so the scope of the poem. Each ecstasy pushes consciousness outward to encompass a circle larger than the one just completed."[41] There are clear resonances between Salska's exposition of the structure of "Song of Myself" and the myth of perpetual out-doing in Emerson's "Circles." The endless expansion of consciousness in "Song of Myself" involves taking on perspective after perspective, and, just as the traces of Emerson's circles persist even in their out-doing, so too does the trace of a shape of consciousness endure.

This persistence of trace has implications for the role of the particular in Whitman's realizing vista. The realization of witness demands that viewpoints be distinguished as individual even as they are joined in the greater expanding ring of the poem's performance of consciousness. "Song of Myself" may have impulses toward the universal, but it remains anchored in the experiences of the particular, which provide new spurs to the imagination at every turn.

"Song of Myself" offers a catalogue of points of view; there is an existential authenticity to those views but there may also be an incompleteness to them. These individual viewpoints become vistas on experience, and these viewpoints (with their details) cannot be wholly voided. They need to persist. "Song of Myself" embodies a profound tension in trying to cope with the relativity of viewpoints. It adds viewpoint to viewpoint in pursuit of giving a picture of a broader whole. But its own narrative of the whole may itself be relative and open to revision. That relativity may be one reason why Whitman so often emphasizes that poem as an ongoing process: it offers an endless succession of relative views in the hope of perpetual transformation toward some further apprehension. The "Sunday Evening Lectures" also, however, at least entertain the notion that our particular souls "gravitate forever toward the absolute, the supernatural, the eternal truth." This "gravitation" might indicate our own particular craving for "the absolute, the supernatural, the eternal truth." It might also be a sign of the fact that our own particular viewpoints reveal some trace of that grander absolute.

Whitman's remarks in the "Sunday Evening Lectures" suggest that we always see relatively, and "Song of Myself" can be read as an effort to provide that succession of viewpoints in order to gain a more expansive vista (even though that vista itself will be open to further displacement). Pluralization remains a major tactic in this poem. Rather than offering a homogeneous song of the self, Whitman instead emphasizes the role of difference within that song. In singing this construction Whitman both suggests similarity between himself and others and, at times, insists on radical difference. This play between similarity and difference corresponds to the queries about the relativity of insight that conclude the "Sunday Evening Lectures." The lectures recognize the limits of perspective even as they hope for a deeper insight, and the conflicted poetical becomings of "Song of Myself" express the desire to grasp the vistas of others and so gain a fuller view of reality even as a sense of difference abides between the vista of the other and the vista of the poet-speaker. The becomings of others remain untotalized. This lack of totalization in affirms the difference and the autonomy of the other.

Complementing its exhibition of America's panoramas of efforts and places, the poem's animating persona also becomes others. Section 33 of "Song of Myself" embodies this becoming and its broader situation in an American panorama. At about 160 lines (710–870), it is the longest single section of "Song of Myself." Picking up earlier images from the poem—"Space and Time! now I see it is true, what I guess'd at / What I guess'd when I loaf'd on the grass" (710–11)—it then turns to portraying the physical vistas of the United States.[42] These vistas act as launching points for some of the speaker's most extended becomings of others. Many of these becomings are incidents of suffering, violence, and pain, including a woman mourning her dead husband, the "disdain and calmness of martyrs" (833), the sufferings of an escaped slave, and a soldier's nightmarish recollections of a fort's bombardment.[43] In the midst of those becomings, the persona of "Song of Myself" proclaims, "I do not ask the wounded person how he feels, I myself become the wounded person, / My hurts turn livid upon me as I lean on a cane and observe" (845–46). Instead of posing a difference between himself and a wounded person, he becomes that person, and he heightens the intensity of this becoming by claiming that the (resonantly phrased) "I myself" becomes.[44] However, the following line fuses involvement and distance: even as he suffers these "livid" hurts and thereby feels the pain of the wounded, he also adopts a trope of distance in "lean[ing] on a cane and observ[ing]," which seems an image of reserved—even perhaps genteel—observation. There is both participation and distance, involvement and distinction. Even as this poem offers a story of integration and identification with otherness, the poet-speaker also acknowledges his difference from others.

A similarly conflicted moment occurs earlier in the poem:

> Apart from the pulling and hauling stands what I am,
> Stands amused, complacent, compassionating, idle, unitary,
> Looks down, is erect, or bends an arm on an impalpable certain rest,
> Looking with side-curved head curious what will come next,
> Both in and out of the game and watching and wondering at it. (75–79)

This "what I am" seems to be primarily an observant self, who examines the world without necessarily being caught in its bounds (and bonds). While so much of Whitman seems to exalt the integrated self—the self that takes in and demonstrates the whole sweep of the world—these lines offer a countervailing impulse: an identity apart from the pulling and hauling of the world. This self remains "[b]oth in and out of the game"; it both participates and stands apart. In observing, this self seems to remain somehow sympathetically involved—standing "amused, complacent, compassionating, idle, unitary." By insisting always upon a further understanding, "Song of Myself" suggests the provisionality of any instantaneous conception of the self. The constellation of any set of attachments cannot be total for the poem because it remains always open to revision. This capacity for revision does not nullify preceding attachments, but it does insist that they are not an ultimately sufficient narrative of the self.

The only place where "song of myself" appears in "Song of Myself" affirms the abiding importance of determinate connections between self and others.[45] At the end of an extensive list collating a variety of experiential views—the song of a "pure contralto" (264), immigrants on the wharf (285), the sleeping city (324)—Whitman writes that

> And these tend inward to me, and I tend outward to them,
> And such as it is to be of these more or less I am,
> And of these one and all I weave the song of myself. (327–29)

While proclaiming fusion, these lines also imply distinction. All these tendencies are only "more or less" what the speaker is. Weaving relies on the distinction of the individual threads, which maintain their integrity even as they are brought into a new whole.[46]

As Fichte's egoism is transformed by Schelling's union of the subjective and objective (which is ultimately incorporated by Hegel's union of Spirit and history), Whitman's song of himself reaches beyond the assumed egoism of an isolated self in order to offer an image of the self situated within and articulated through the broader community of the United States (and not merely the United States). He takes on the words of other Americans in singing this song, making it less a solo and more a choral ode. Rejecting Fichte's "all-devouring egoism," Whitman crafts a song of himself that demands a consideration of others. At times denying an easy elision of the self and other, Whitman's poem implicitly recognizes the other *qua* other: the eyes of this other can never be quite the same as the speaker. Pure identity would also be the abolition of otherness. What Herbert Levine has called "styles of union and disunion" permeates much of Whitman's work in *Leaves of Grass,* especially "Song of Myself," which at once joins self and other and asserts a difference between them. Maintaining distinction adds to the richness of this self's experience, but asserting a union in the face of that distinction allows for this richness to be enjoyed. The other is not cast away into some fantastic world of abstraction but is a person experienced in a common spectrum of life. But this play of union and disunion also informs Whitman's portrayal of our own encounters with ourselves: we are at once heterogeneous and unified, singular and disrupted.[47]

Finding a Place for Dialogue

As human contact becomes one way of resolving doubts about reality for Whitman, he often creates nexuses for encounter in his poems. His poems continually invoke some simultaneously vast and personal "you." "Crossing Brooklyn Ferry,"[48] one of his most famous lyrics, offers one such nexus of encounter, and it also models how the course of an overall Whitman poem seeks to find reality within appearance. This poem's turn to sociality also provides another way of looking at the status of particularity in Whitman's work. Philip Fisher finds that "Crossing Brooklyn Ferry" displays the "most remarkable implications of his aesthetics" of abstraction; discounting historical contingency, the poem "depends on Whitman's dazzling arrogance in looking forward generations and even centuries to those who will see the same things, have the same feelings, and look back to him, knowing that he also saw and felt just those things."[49] According to Fisher, the poem hollows out chronological distinctiveness. While "Crossing Brooklyn Ferry" does indeed include assertions of commonality, the aesthetic structure of the work as well as its turn to sociality leave a space for particularity.

In looking at this poem, I would like to foreground M. H. Abrams's definition of the "greater Romantic lyric." Situating "Crossing Brooklyn Ferry" within this convention suggests the importance of particular (historical) location for the poem:

> [Greater Romantic lyrics] present a determinate speaker in a particularized, and usually a localized, outdoor setting, whom we overhear as he carries on, in a fluent vernacular which rises easily to a more formal speech, a sustained colloquy, sometimes with himself or with the outer scene, but more frequently with a silent human auditor, present or absent. The speaker begins with a description of the landscape; an aspect or change of aspect in the landscape evokes a varied but integral process of memory, thought, anticipation, and feeling which remains closely intervolved with the outer scene. In the course of this meditation the lyric speaker achieves an insight, faces up to a tragic loss, comes to a moral decision, or resolves an emotional problem. Often the poem rounds upon itself to end where it began, at the outer scene, but with an altered mood and deepened understanding which is the result of the intervening meditation.[50]

Though Abrams focuses primarily on the greater Romantic lyric as a genre for British Romantic poetry, he also suggests that this generic classification could be applied to "Crossing Brooklyn Ferry," as well. Numerous scholars—including James Dougherty and Kerry McSweeney—have elaborated upon this hint so tantalizingly dropped by Abrams.[51]

As James Dougherty's and M. Wynn Thomas's readings of the poem note,[52] Whitman revises the tradition of the greater Romantic lyric by emphasizing sociality, and this emphasis on sociality affords a way of acknowledging the particularity of another individual. As Dougherty puts it, the speaker of this poem does not "reduce the persons and things he sees to simple projections of his own subjectivity" but instead discovers their "reality . . . through his dialogic relation with them."[53] The "dialogic relation" of "Crossing Brooklyn Ferry" forces the speaker to attend to the reality of those around him. Realizing others in "Crossing Brooklyn Ferry" demands the recognition of them as distinct individuals, with their own worth, dignity, and particularity. Yet this recognition also demands situating this person in a broader narrative that connects person and poet. That very "dialogic relation" affirms the particularity of an individual in light of a greater (democratic) conversation. The poem recognizes particularity even as it asserts the possibility of a greater union.

Jake Adam York locates "Crossing Brooklyn Ferry" in the context of a convention that further underlines the importance of democratic conversation: the public oration.[54] These orations were often delivered in specific settings for specific occasions (such as remarks delivered by Daniel Webster for the laying of the cornerstone at the Bunker Hill monument) and served as a way for their listeners to reflect on the meaning of this specificity. York finds that "Crossing Brooklyn Ferry" has a "double-present structure," in which the act of reading brings together two "horizons of presence": "that of the writer at the time of writing, and that of the reader in the moment of reading."[55] This structure causes the poem itself to be an instrument of "crossing," of uniting the poet and the specific reader. In a parallel to Dougherty's remarks about the dialogic process of "Crossing Brooklyn Ferry," there is something dialogic about York's conception of the public address and the rhetorical structure of the poem. The orations York explores often entail a kind of cognitive dialogue, in which the particulars of place are set into a conversation with a greater context (whether historical, social, etc.). The narrative of a "double-present structure" necessarily presupposes the poem as a place for a dialogic relation between reader and writer. The combination of a dialogic approach to experience (in which experience is interrogated) and a dialogic approach to another person is central to the narrative arc of "Crossing Brooklyn Ferry" (as well as "Song of Myself"), and serves as a key way of honoring particularity within the poem.

According to Abrams, the greater Romantic lyric starts from a determinate location, and "Crossing Brooklyn Ferry" starts from a ferry crossing between Brooklyn and Manhattan in the 1850s United States. Yet here already we have a telling revision. This setting is outdoors, but it is hardly one of pastoral isolation; instead, it takes place within an implicitly urbanized space (a major passage between two major US urban domains). The urban setting hints at Whitman's turn to sociality in this poem (and, implicitly, the role of sociality for his project of realization).

Throughout, this poem includes invocations of commonality and assertions of specificity. "You" becomes a simultaneously vast and determinate pronoun—uniting diverse types even as it calls out for an act of conversation:

Flood-tide below me! I see you face to face!
Clouds of the west—sun there half an hour high—I see you also face to face.

Crowds of men and women attired in the usual costumes, how curious you
  are to me!
On the ferry-boats the hundreds and hundreds that cross, returning home,
  are more curious to me than you suppose,
And you that shall cross from shore to shore years hence are more to me,
  and more in my meditations, than you might suppose. (1–5)

These opening lines suggest assimilation through the ambiguity of the reference for "you": the flood-tide, the clouds, the sun, the crowds of men, the one who supposes in the fourth line (perhaps the reader), and the future crowds who might also make use of the ferry. Five lines provide five different entities addressed by "you." The unifying use of "you" continues throughout the poem. As Whitman asserts an integration of himself and the sweep of world and time, this "you" unifies the sundry objects of experience. Whitman does not simply intervolve himself and the landscape but also interweaves others and the cityscape, and himself and others.

The anaphora in the poem's catalogues is another device for poetic reintegration:[56]

I too many and many a time cross'd the river of old,
Watched the Twelfth-month sea-gulls, saw them high in the air floating
  with motionless wings, oscillating their bodies,
Saw how the glistening yellow lit up parts of their bodies and left the rest in
  strong shadow,
Saw the slow-wheeling circles and the gradual edging toward the south,
Saw the reflection of the summer sky in the water,
Had my eyes dazzled by the shimmering track of beams,
Look'd at the fine centrifugal spokes of light round the shape of my head in
  the sunlit water,
Look'd at the haze on the hills southward and south-westward (27–34)

These lines offer a phenomenal atomization, as different aspects of a bird's flight or the reflection on the water or the landscape are noted. Yet anaphora and the fluid association of these images also lend a cohesiveness to these sights. We move from the sea-gulls to the sun on them to, perhaps, their flight patterns (those "slow-wheeling circles") to the reflection of the sky (the domain of flight) in the water to the dazzling brightness of the sun to the sun's glimmer in the far-off hills (which may also be in the direction of the birds' flight). The anaphora fuses together disparate elements of worldly experience. The language of this section and of many others of "Crossing Brooklyn Ferry" combines the diversity of sights with the unity of seeing.

This tendency toward synthesis is also reflected in the structure of the poem. Throughout, "Crossing Brooklyn Ferry" invokes distance and asserts that distance is a mode of continuity. As the speaker declares, "It avails, time nor place—distance avails not, / I am with you, you men and women of a generation, or ever so many generations hence" (20–21). The specifics of a momentary time or place are acknowledged, embraced, and reached beyond. The third section's listing of the images of the ferry, from the sails of other ships to steamers to the walls of storehouses, provides an extensive elaboration of the specifics of place. The fifth and sixth sections meditate on the specificities of person. At the end of the fifth section, the poetic persona speaks of having "receiv'd identity by [his] body" out of the broader universal "float" (62–63), and those two sections assert commonalities of passions and experiences between the poet and his readers. Whitman portrays the specifics of a landscape and the poetic self in order to set them into conversation with the greater progress of time and space. As he writes later in the poem (in a statement that seems in harmony with York's theory of a double-present structure), "Closer yet I approach you" (86). Even as the poem celebrates distinct entities and identities, it also whispers, *Closer, closer, closer.* That act of growing closer suggests the importance of intimacy between reader and writer, an intimacy that requires the recognition of that other.

As the poem calls for a sense of contact between speaker and reader, it also offers the hope of a transformation of experience. The ecstatic conclusion of "Crossing Brooklyn Ferry" models the arc of the greater Romantic lyric in returning to the surface of appearances in a new light.[57] Far from expressing estrangement from the (historicized) appearances of the world, it instead reflects a new investment in them. The poem calls out to the "tall masts of Manhatta" and "the beautiful hills of Brooklyn" and calls on the "crested and scalloped-edged waves" to "frolic" (103–5). The speaker addresses the flowing world:

Appearances, now or henceforth, indicate what you are,
You necessary film, continue to envelop the soul,
About my body for me, and your body for you, be hung our divinest
 aromas,
Thrive, cities—bring your freight, bring your shows, ample and sufficient
 rivers,
Expand, being than which none else is perhaps more spiritual,
Keep your places, objects than which none else is more lasting. (120–25)

The cry for cities to "bring [their] shows" casts light on how the climax of "Crossing Brooklyn Ferry" revises appearance in pursuit of reality. "Shows" may indicate both theatrical spectacles and the showing of appearance. In *Franklin Evans* and other works, Whitman associates the language of spectacle with unreality, but the climax of "Crossing Brooklyn Ferry" holds out for some testimony beyond the gaudy flash of appearance. In this ecstatic peak, showing phantasms are affirmed as participating in a broader existential sweep.

The title of "Crossing Brooklyn Ferry" itself alludes to the role of mediation. More than a poem about crossing between one shore of America and another shore, it is also about the crossing between the shores of time, subjectivity, and the self. The "you" merges with the "I" to form a "we." All the actual incidents radiate outward to each other—and inward to Whitman's soul—as part of an eternal weave of spirit and flesh. He does not propose leaving the momentary actual behind: the body anchors the great float, the foundry chimneys still smoke, and the river still runs. The rounding upon itself of the greater Romantic lyric affords a narrative pattern for the dynamics of experiential realization: the things of the world are not abnegated but returned to, and that return creates a heightened sense of their reality.

In "Crossing Brooklyn Ferry," the tropes of transparency become, as elsewhere in Whitman, a mode of fellowship. This fellowship may be ever-provisional for Whitman—social dialogue may be a perpetually evolving process. The poem begins with a moment of local perspective: "Flood-tide below me! I see you face to face!" But the course of the poem demonstrates a deepening of this perspective. As the lyric rounds upon itself, it comes to realize the far-reaching possibilities of a local moment of consciousness:

not cut off, atomized, or disintegrated, this perspective instead enters into a communion across space and time. But this communion does not necessarily require the erasure of distinctness. If the poem is to become a place for conversation, that very act of conversation implicitly insists on distinctness. "Crossing Brooklyn Ferry," one of Whitman's great lyrics of fluidity and realization, suggests that the fluid for Whitman also entails the persistence of transparent surface (the material actualities gone through in order to achieve existential flow). As consciousness for Whitman thrives on the enticing provocations of the world, this poem incorporates those worldly provocations, returning to them with a new light of lyrical joy by the end. The realization of "Crossing Brooklyn Ferry" depends on that endless return to beginnings.

An Open-Ended Poetics and Politics

As "Crossing Brooklyn Ferry" holds out the hope for an ever-revised encounter with others and the world, Whitman's poetry more broadly explores the theme of incompleteness, which has significant implications for his work's formal strategies and overarching political vision. The constant flux of worldly life is one of the major reasons for incompleteness in his poetry. Because the world is always changing, new vistas must always be found. Exemplifying this tendency toward incompleteness, the final lines of "Song of Myself" suggest not a set conclusion but a continual cycle of transformation. The speaker declares himself "untranslatable" and "not a bit tamed" (1332). He "depart[s] as the air," spreads his "flesh in eddies," and "bequeath[s]" himself "to the dirt to grow from the grass" he loves (1337–39). Turning to address his readers, the speaker says that they will "hardly know who [he is] or what [he] mean[s]" (1341) and concludes with an invitation to a game of metaphysical tag:

> Failing to fetch me at the first keep encouraged,
> Missing me one place search another,
> I stop somewhere waiting for you. (1344–46)[58]

This "stop" appears as a momentary resting place, where the singular Whitman can be present for his diverse readers over time and space. His readers—being born and dying year after year, decade after decade—are "encouraged" to find continually this person "waiting" for them. This waiting both entails the incidents of time and suggests something that endures beyond these incidents. The poem both stops and does not stop. The lines do end on the page, but the process of the poem continues.

So the speaker of "Song of Myself" always stands ready to wait for his readers, and so "Crossing Brooklyn Ferry" exults in the endlessness of crossing. The turn toward fluidity is in certain ways congenial to the desire to assert the structure of individual experience while also calling for a broader reconciliation. The process of churn allows for distinct moments of experience to be asserted and for distinct individuals to have experience, but it also suggests the later blurring of distinction through the process of change. Whitman often celebrates the process of atoms, combining in one moment to create something but also later recombining into something else. His invocations of "atoms" have at times been taken as representative of a reduction to commonality (in which the uniformity of atoms robs us of individuality).[59] However, atomic churn within Whitman suggests the possibilities of atoms becoming a vehicle for distinctiveness. The experience of the body within many of Whitman's poems seems to be the experience of a sudden union of atoms; the death and decomposition of the body is not the death of these atoms, but merely their movement to another place. The body does not need to wait to die to experience this atomic flow; every breath, every operation of the body, represents a changing of some atoms for some others. Yet the fact that the body is an entity in flux does not nullify the experience of being embodied. Atoms are constantly recombining in Whitman, and those recombinations allow for instants of differentiation. Flow within his verse becomes a way of reconciling distinctiveness (the particular forms) with commonality (the grounding atoms of the distinct object). The realizing vista of *Leaves of Grass* depends precisely on navigating this flow—tracing commonalities and locating differences, searching for metaphysical bases while also celebrating phenomenal performance.

In one of the poems of the 1855 edition of *Leaves of Grass* (which will later be incorporated into "I Sing the Body Electric"), Whitman declares that "all is a procession," the body just as much as anything else. The body, that seemingly solid piece of matter, provides a vista and participates in a broader flow. Near the end of this poem, he situates the body of a woman at auction within a greater nexus of bodies and political questions: "She too is not only herself . . . she is the teeming mother of mothers, / She is the bearer of them that shall grow and be mates to the mothers. / Her daughters or their daughters' daughters . . . who knows who shall mate with them" (105–7).[60] The body becomes an open-ended avenue to future generations and to a meditation on deeper ethical topics. "Who knows who shall mate with them?" Will this woman's daughters be raped by "white" slave owners? Will they be free to marry husbands—"black" or "white"? Will racial barriers persist? Will the legacy of institutionalized slavery be broken? The body, that seemingly solid anchor of our personal identity, the flesh that we wake up with day after day, becomes situated within a greater flux.

The questions arising from this reflection on the woman allude to issues of deep ethical and national importance. Seeing those questions becomes a vehicle for understanding the experiences and potential of that body (how and why flesh itself is an issue for a slave system premised on racial division). The broader flow of questions itself reflects on the particular, helping us to realize new aspects of it. The particularity of this slave's body—like so many other bodies in Whitman—is at once affirmed and gone beyond, and that going beyond allows for a return to the body with a renewed understanding. In this poem the speaker conceives of the body as endlessly expressive: the "expression of the body of a man or woman balks account" (5). So the account of this body remains partial. These lines implicitly juxtapose the accounting of the slave auction—which distills the human body to a single monetary sum—with the accounting of Whitman's poetics of realization. This latter accounting is initiatory rather than totalizing, liberating in its play of questions rather than imprisoning, and expansive rather than reductive.

Another famous instance of accounting in "Song of Myself" underscores the way that interpretive open-endedness can be a way of opening up the possibility of democratic exchange:

> A child said *What is the grass?* fetching it to me with full hands;
> How could I answer the child? I do not know what it is any more than he.
>
> I guess it must be the flag of my disposition, out of hopeful green stuff woven.
>
> Or I guess it is the handkerchief of the Lord,
> A scented gift and remembrancer designedly dropt,
> Bearing the owner's name someway in the corners, that we may see and
> remark and say *Whose?*

Or I guess the grass is itself a child, the produced babe of the vegetation.

Or I guess it is a uniform hieroglyphic,
And it means, Sprouting alike in broad zones and narrow zones,
Growing among black folks as among white,
Kanuck, Tuckahoe, Congressman, Cuff, I give them the same, I receive
them the same.

And now it seems to me the beautiful uncut hair of graves. (99–110)

In this succession of guesses, Whitman offers the grass as an expansive symbol, transcending nineteenth-century racial ("among black folks as among white") and sociopolitical (growing for "Kanuck, Tuckahoe, Congressman, Cuff") barriers. It reaches across time and demonstrates eternal principles: "The smallest sprout shows that there really is no death, / And if ever there was it led forward life, and does not wait at the end to arrest it, / And ceas'd the moment life appear'd" (126–28).

Invoking different groups, the poet-speaker says, "I give them the same, I receive them the same," but that commonness of acceptance does not foreclose the recognition of difference. Indeed, the energy of this catalogue (along with many others) relies precisely on the listing of different meanings for the grass, and this sections shows how, for Whitman, the range of meaning for a symbol can become an avenue for democratic integration and fellowship.[61] In his response to the child's question, the speaker immediately undercuts an initial note of ignorance—"I do not know what it [the grass] is"—with the comparative "any more than he," so the seeming lack of knowledge becomes a claim of (democratic) equality, in which the poet and the inquiring child each have an equal knowledge of the identity of the grass. Rather than strict answers regarding the true being of the grass, the poet-speaker offers guesses, which expand on the associations of the grass—it could be the "flag of [his] disposition," the "handkerchief of the Lord," or the "beautiful uncut hair of graves." As the grass testifies to the endless transitions of life, one meaning for the grass seamlessly transitions into another. The grass connects the speaker's self and the emblems of God, the grave and the promise of new life. The fact that these are "guesses" presents an opportunity for multiplying meanings and expanding a non-constrictive web of possibilities.

The originating source for this moment from "Song of Myself" comes from a question: *"What is the grass?"*[62] Whitman may later carol in this "Song" that "I accept Reality and dare not question it, / Materialism first and last imbuing" (483–84), but he often uses the tactics of questions—of finding the curious—to gain a vista of "Reality." This moment of staring at the grass suggests fundamental parallels between the act of interpretation and that of becoming for Whitman. The act of interpretation complements and compounds the fluctuation of atoms; as atoms perpetually flow, interpretation affords its own fluidity by perpetually going through the objects of the material world or other figures in order to find further meanings. Emerson in "Circles" emphasizes the openness and necessary incompleteness of any interpretation, and Whitman builds on the implicit tendencies of this openness and incompleteness to offer a narrative of democratic and pluralist exchange. This exchange preserves the distinctness of each individual even as it sets this distinctness into a greater context.

Understanding the role of process complements contemporary critical assessments of Whitman's approach to political theory. Commenting on George Kateb's theory of democratic individualism for Whitman, Nancy Rosenblum finds that more attention needs to be paid to the aesthetic form of poetry—what specifically does poetic structure add to an understanding of the way that Whitman's poetry reinforces democratic sentiments (assuming, as Kateb argues, that his poetry does reinforce the democratic)? Rosenblum argues that Whitman's verse in part strengthens democratic feelings through "activat[ing] strong feelings of attraction to democracy . . . by creating a poetic vision of democracy as a spectacle of diversity."[63] For Rosenblum, the attention Whitman lavishes on the diverse scenes of democratic life—parades, work crews, pandering politicians, and the like—creates a celebratory iconography of the democratic. This iconography in turn strengthens the attachments of the reader to the democratic way of life. The affective power of Whitman's creation of a holistic, diverse iconography has been explored by others (including Ken Price in *To Walt Whitman, America*), and the celebratory quality of Whitman's verse could indeed lend affective support to democratic practices.

However, the formal structuring of Whitman's verse can have even more radical implications for a narrative of democracy in his verse. Jason Frank has argued that Whitman offers a poetics and a politics of democratic futurity, of a people yet to be realized. His work seeks, Frank argues, "to provoke and disseminate a democratic sensibility."[64] The narrative of realizing vista casts light on the underlying psychology of this provocative, democratic futurity. Our recognitions of others and of ourselves are always partial, Whitman suggests. That's one of the reasons why "Song of Myself" resists closure: that song is always being revised in light of further experiences and further encounters with others. New experiences (and the encounters with new perspectives) offer moments of alterity that revise our narratives of self and others. Moreover, our understandings of others are themselves partial. Thus, Whitman's poetry often turns to the experiences of others with unanswered questions. That inability to close off our self-understanding and our understandings of others complements (and perhaps causes) our inability to cease inquiring into the character of our *demos* as a whole. The emphasis on incompleteness in Whitman's work suggests that the project of a democratic people is itself always incomplete. In many of his works, Whitman addresses his readers in the hopes of creating an ever-renewed and ever-incomplete polity.

The aesthetic space of Whitman's poetry becomes a place for pondering—and by pondering shaping—that incomplete polity. In a poem such as "Crossing Brooklyn Ferry," the speaker creates a space for a continued negotiation between people. The poem becomes a space of relating to others and of assessing our relationships with others. We can discuss our shared experiences of reading a poem, and a poem can supply a cultural iconography that serves as a vehicle for relation. Considering the details of Whitman's song of himself and of others, we can come to view our relationships with others in a new way. This consideration is necessarily open-ended, incomplete, and open to revision. Moreover, as Kateb and others have found, understanding our relationships with others can in turn give us a vehicle for understanding ourselves in a new light. Our encounters with others can help us understand the potentials of our own selves. This potential expands the vistas for our lives because we understand what we could be. But it also helps us realize the concreteness of our lives—that we are *one* way and not another, if only for a moment.

As "Song of Myself" formally resists poetic closure, the democratic polity prophesized in his verse remains continually unsettled. That lack of stasis requires contingency, not the abolition of it. A self or a polity emptied of all content would be endlessly the same—a blank field as far as the eye could see. Only the persistence of content—the trace of contingency—allows for dynamicism. Whitman's poems offer a democratic narrative that goes beyond strict representation to model instead a dynamic of introspection and conversation that is not limited to the particular objects represented in a poem. Price draws attention to this dynamic in his claim that Whitman believed that "readers and writers, paradoxically, must revise him as they strive to realize themselves and remake America."[65] The open-ended process of revision allows for a continued rewriting of cultural understandings.

This project of endless revision also complements the enterprise of empathy. The concrete instances of empathy in Whitman's poetry are not meant to be confined only to those individuals; instead they offer a prompting to develop certain habits of feeling. Just as the particular enters into a dialogue with a vista, instants of empathy within his verse enter into a dialogue with a broader view of the whole.[66] The expansive polity conjured by Whitman is matched by a project of expansive empathy. The course of *Leaves of Grass* as a whole instructs its readers in the habit of this continually expansive empathy. The individual cases presented in the poetry all come together in a riotous pageant of human existence; each instance demands an understanding and points to a broader constellation of dynamic individuals. The fact that this whole is dynamic demands a continually refreshed accounting of each of the particulars within this whole (including how they relate to each other). Thus, Whitman's poetry models the enterprise of continually sharpening attention—an enterprise with both personal and political implications. The elusive self of "Song of Myself" might model the way we have glimpses of insight into the lives of others, but those insights always need to be constantly renewed.

In declaring himself the "poet of reality" in his early notebooks, Whitman takes on the project of prompting a more intimate engagement with reality. This engagement involves an interrogation of the appearances of the outer world to see how they might be emblems of further spiritual contours. It also involves an act of self-interrogation. The course of a poem encourages the reader to find the possibilities of the self in part through understanding the experiences of others. Finding that reality involves going down into the depths of one's own self and reaching out to one's fellow humans. The textures of his poetry constantly resituate the particular within an ever-shifting panorama. The finding of vista is, like the process of *Leaves of Grass,* endless. It affords at most only a momentary stopping place, one that is itself gone beyond in the endlessly affirming road of Whitman's poetics of realization.

· FOUR ·

Disjunction—Disclosure—Dickinson

While Emerson and Whitman emphasize the poet as the realizer and stress the connections between reality and poetic creation, Emily Dickinson is often more circumspect (if not outright mysterious) in explaining the relationship between her verse and the real. But even if Dickinson does not provide the same copious evidence regarding the real as Whitman and Emerson, we can still situate her verse in conversation with the tradition of the experiential real. Her poetry insists on the dynamic interrogation of experience. Nor does she totally avoid the use of the real in her poetry and other writings. Across her poetic career, the word "real" appears in either the main text or the variants of nine of her poems.[1] "Reality" appears in two of her later poems (according to Franklin's dating, from 1877 and 1884).[2] "Unrealized" appears in one poem, as does "unreality."[3] So a total of thirteen poems mention the real or some variant of the real in some way. This is far from a great number, but, by way of comparison, only seventeen poems mention "circumference," one of the words most commonly associated with Dickinson.[4]

Dickinson's verse draws from the tactics of the experiential real, including the trial of appearance and the role of personal provocation for literature. In 1890's *Poems by Emily Dickinson,* editors Thomas Wentworth Higginson and Mabel Loomis Todd titled one poem "Real." (The following text is the one prepared by Higginson and Todd.)

I like a look of agony,
Because I know it's true;
Men do not sham convulsion,
Nor simulate a throe.

The eyes glaze once, and that is death.
Impossible to feign
The beads upon the forehead
By homely anguish strung.

Higginson and Todd's Dickinson need not be our Dickinson, and the application of the title "Real" to this poem seems to have no authorial intention behind it. But, in light of the nineteenth-century convention of the real as sincere, it is understandable why Higginson and Todd applied this title to the poem. Dickinson's editors seemed to read this poem as an exploration of finding the truth of emotion in appearance. This poem also illuminates some of the broader aims and strategies of her work in relation to appearance.

This poem considers those moments when expression corresponds to the true state of feeling, turning particularly to the true testimony that pain can bring. The truth of suffering was long a topic for the sentimental literature of the antebellum era, and Dickinson, perhaps wryly, replies to this tradition with the easy declaration that she "likes a look of agony" due to its truth.[5] The breezy opening, reminiscent of political slogans almost a century later ("I like Ike"), suggests a glib conviction while also perhaps critiquing the glibness of that conviction. It makes clear the price of the truth bought by this agony: the glaze of eyes and the beads of sweat. As Higginson and Todd suggest by their choice of editorial title, we can find the real in that testimony of suffering—those "beads . . . By homely anguish strung." Moreover, the shift to death in the second stanza presents an immanence that goes beyond questions of sincerity or insincerity; no one wonders whether a corpse is *sincerely* dead.

The central question posed by "Real" is the trial of appearance: What do outer expressions reveal of inner emotion? That trial constitutes a major theme of Dickinson's poetic enterprise. As physical suffering wrings drops of sweat from the afflicted, she so often squeezes appearances to find what we might gain from them. Such a trial of appearance is also the trial of ourselves—what we take for granted, what we cherish, what we hold, and what breaks us. Dickinson reportedly told Higginson, "If I feel physically as if the top of my head were taken off, I know *that* is poetry."[6] Having one's head be blown open can be an agonizing experience, but it can also be an exhilarating one for Dickinson, whose poetry often demands an opening up of the brain.

That potentially self-disruptive trial of appearance situates Dickinson within the tradition of the experiential real and illuminates the way her poetry and elements of that tradition in general have a bearing on the fate of experiential reading. Dickinson shares with Emerson the notion that grasping the real can entail some possible dislocation, with the unrealization of some things (recognizing them as less than real) as the necessary accompaniment of revisionary realization. For Emerson this process of realization can also mean opening up the self to disruption—revising it in response to a new view of experience. Dickinson exaggerates this tendency, making the prospect of realization one of radical ecstasy, in which the self stands outside itself in a moment of alienating revision. Her forays into the real contest the very reality of the self. As part of this interrogation of reality, she will often turn to concepts (such as death and eternity) that push at the limits of conventional apprehension.

Writing a letter to her childhood friend Abiah Root in 1846, Dickinson reflects on the challenges of realizing death: "I cannot realize that the grave will be my last home. . . . I cannot realize that the friends I have seen pass from my sight . . . will not again walk the streets."[7] Jed Deppman understands Dickinson's inability to realize these things as exhibiting a tension between abstractly apprehending a given topic (such as the fact that we are mortal beings) and "seeing or imagining unveiledly that one is going to *die*."[8] Dickinson admits that she can abstractly apprehend that she and her friends will eventually die, but realization requires more than this distant apprehension. Dickinson's many poems about death may be an effort to realize death in that more unveiled sense. These poems often lead to senses of radical otherness and deep confusion, when the resources of meaning are taxed to the greatest extent. This supreme trial of realization is not limited to death, though. For Dickinson, realization can involve an intensity of awareness that strains—if not outright breaks—the self's conceptual resources. Deppman highlights a tension between abstraction and a fuller recognition, a dynamic that drives Dickinson's poems about death. However, this tension also influences the overall course of her poetry, which explores the profound challenges of trying to realize any part of human experience.

For Dickinson, then, the tradition of the experiential real prompts questions about the self's apprehension of both itself and the world around it. Her verse interrogates our ability to realize those concepts that seem so vast that they defy the powers of the self; those defiant concepts can often be grouped under the heading of the sublime (grand heights, the infinite, and so forth). In this interrogation Dickinson's poems become a place for this trial of appearance. They might talk about trying this appearance, but they also perform this trial in the enacted tensions of language.

This trial of appearance connects to possibility, long a popular topic for Dickinson scholarship. Quite understandably, much of this discussion of possibility has attended to the role of indeterminacy in Dickinson's use of materials and form—variants, competing versions of poems, syntactical ambiguities, and so forth. Domhnall Mitchell's *Measures of Possibility,* Sharon Cameron's *Choosing Not Choosing,* and Alexandra Socarides's *Dickinson Unbound* represent some of the range of recent scholarship's interest in the possible. This courting of possibility is intimately intertwined with the task of realization. The variants, syntactical compressions, paradoxes, and imagistic inversions of Dickinson's poetry present a textured surface that provokes us into the interrogation of that surface.

Sometimes, the performance of a Dickinson poem can offer a porthole window into ecstasy, wonder, and the straining self. Virginia Jackson has warned of the limits (and potential dangers) of reducing Dickinson's poetry to the mode of a unified lyric subjectivity, but one can nevertheless see in Dickinson's poetry some provocation toward the trial of subjectivity.[9] Her poems sometimes offer an elaboration of a single existential moment, with all the tensions and gaps inherent in this moment. At times, this moment is turned sideways to expose those tensions and gaps. Her verse simultaneously models the trial of this moment and prompts her readers to see the oblique angles of their own consciousnesses.

Possibility intertwines with realizing trial in her verse; the disruptive opportunity of realization requires finding possibility within seeming certainty, and the complicating textures of her poetry prompt its reader toward the finding of possibility within a poem. This theme of possibility can help situate Dickinson in the context of recent efforts to rehabilitate the experiential aspect of reading, as found in Eve Kosofsky Sedgwick, Marielle Macé, and Jean-Marie Schaeffer. Each of these experiential critics emphasizes the enterprise of reading as the courting of possibility. Moreover, these critics at times turn to reading's exploration of possibility as a way of grounding the enterprise of reading in reality.

Both Macé and Schaeffer argue that we should view reading as a process, connecting reading to life as a whole and to the prospect of possibility. Macé argues that books "bring singular configurations, each implying potential 'paths' to our attention, our perception, and our capacities for action." These paths are "*traced-out* possibilities of existence," and the task of reading is to explore and weigh these possibilities.[10] Drawing from the work of Nietzsche and twentieth-century deconstructionists, Macé argues that stylistics comprise a key component of our lives—our styles help define who we are. Exemplifying certain possibilities of existence, literary works afford an opportunity for devising new styles for our lives and revising existing stylistic strategies: "Reading is a veritable catalyst for the stylization of our mental lives."[11] Like Macé, Schaeffer connects literary reading to the broader course of life: "Reading does not need to be connected a posteriori to life: it is a moment of life, a lived experience as real as any other." He writes that the poem "activates the hermeneutic potentialities of sounds, rhythms, and images, multiplying them through echoes from one stratum to another."[12] The notion of literature as the exploration of possibility and potentiality has clear resonances with Dickinson's own poetic enterprise. In sometimes disorienting ways, her poetry involves the tracing out of possibilities, and reading her work demands the navigation of those generated possibilities.

In her account of "reparative reading," Eve Kosofsky Sedgwick draws attention to the roles of undecidability and readerly discovery—two themes important for Dickinson's relationship to the experiential real. Sedgwick says that the model of "paranoid reading" uses "strong theory" to predetermine the results of a reading, which is supposed to be about "exposing" the hidden imperatives in a work; because the ends are predetermined, paranoid reading offers no hope of literary surprise. She contrasts this paranoid model with reparative reading: "To read from a reparative position is to surrender the knowing, anxious paranoid determination that no horror, however apparently unthinkable, shall ever come to the reader *as new;* to a reparatively positioned reader, it can seem realistic and necessary to experience surprise." Sedgwick elaborates on the consequences of this possibility of surprise. It can create a new inspiration for hope, "often a fracturing, even a traumatic thing to experience." Moreover, the reparative reader must engage in the task of "organiz[ing] the fragments and part-objects she encounters or creates." Part of that process of reorganization means looking back at experience in a new light—"to entertain such profoundly painful, profoundly relieving, ethically crucial possibilities as that the past, in turn, could have happened differently from the way it actually did."[13]

Dickinson is an apt figure for reparative reading. Sedgwick alludes to her poem "'Hope' is the thing with feathers" (Fr311) in an endnote to her discussion of hope for reparative reading.[14] Moreover, Dickinson's work places great value on cultivating the possibility of surprise. The tensions, lacunae, and leaps of her poetry are mechanisms for surprise—for making her poems simultaneously determinate and undecideable. Dickinson's poetry often takes a reparative approach to the real. Reparation holds out the hope of uncertainty and revision, and Dickinson's exploration of the real treads a path of surprise. Moreover, this surprise may demand a reorganization of the self and its experiences. Maurice Lee has suggested that for Dickinson, "epiphanies . . . can be disorienting to the point of self-loss."[15] This point can also apply to her enterprise of realization: in its radical disruption, it can unsettle the very grounding of (narratives of) the self. The next section will examine how Dickinson's poetry of consciousness develops an architecture of continued (reparative) openness. This sets up a discussion of the disorienting thrill of the sublime for Dickinson and an examination of the ways in which she prompts an interrogation of the surface of experience through tracing out (potentially real) possibilities.

Opening Up Consciousness

The disruption of consciousness points to the broader possibility of reparative play in our lives—that we can recast experiences even in the light of seemingly confined and limiting narratives. So often Dickinson's poems offer an experiment of disruption as a way of disclosing experience. This disclosure can grant us a new purchase on experience—reimagining supposed dualities, discovering peninsulas of thought and feeling, and rethinking our responses. Eve Kosofsky Sedgwick finds that reparative reading means "organiz[ing] . . . fragments and part-objects," and the project of consciousness's experiment for Dickinson means continued reorganization. For her the enterprise of realization can mean an ecstasy that alienates the self from its conventional boundaries, and her poetry of "consciousness" offers a demonstration of such self-disruption.

When Dickinson invokes "consciousness," she uses a term with great philosophical charge. By the middle of the nineteenth century, "consciousness" had arisen as a key term for typifying and describing the self, and one of the major themes of eighteenth- and nineteenth-century discussions of consciousness is the notion that it may limit us in its mediation of our apprehension of the world. The limitations of consciousness may include the epistemic and the emotional or affective. While her philosophical predecessors often turn to consciousness as a unifying faculty through its capacity to assimilate instants of experience into a coherent whole (a "self"), Dickinson subverts that idea of conscious unity by suggesting that consciousness can disrupt itself through the act of self-reflection. Dickinson's poetry of consciousness provides both a dramatization of and commentary on the conditions of individual consciousness, including the continuity of personality, the structure of a sense of self, and possible disruptions to this sense of structure or to this personal wholeness. She does not aim to offer a taxonomy of the self according to the conventions of contemporary academic philosophy and instead focuses on the tensions of the lived experience of consciousness. That attention to lived experience highlights one of the ways in which the trial of experience offered by the experiential real demands a return to (and not a flight from) the particular details of living; it is through that focus on lived particularity that a Dickinsonian reader can see what tensions really lie underneath.

In these experiments in subjectivity, she explores both how consciousness can limit us and how it can facilitate its own disruption. Fantasies of escape permeate her poetry of consciousness, as do moments of aperture, when sudden breaks herald the promise of liberty. Though many nineteenth-century discussions of consciousness invoke the language of possession and ownership, Dickinson's poetry of consciousness instead often turns to dispossession; self-reference, which allows consciousness to unify, becomes a tool for interrogating our cognitive assumptions and for surrendering old certainties. In part because Dickinson finds relationality (how we relate to ourselves and to others) to be a major theme for consciousness, her poems of consciousness are inquiries into the limits, tensions, and possible disruptions of relation.

The way Dickinson inverts conventional narratives of conscious captivity (in which the seemingly limiting machinery of consciousness sows the seeds of disruption) reflects the broader way in which her work transforms seeming limits. Dickinson scholars have long expressed interest in the role of captivity (social, gendered, sexual, literary, and so forth), but they have also often suggested that narratives of captivity may be overly simplistic. Vivian

Pollak has observed, for example, that the "freedom from finite designation coexists, within Dickinson's style, with a remarkable vocabulary of physical and mental limitation."[16] Elisa New expresses reservations about seeing Dickinson only as a member of "the contemporary pantheon of incarcerated female poets,"[17] and Sarah Blackwood notes that "consciousness" for Dickinson "engenders both freedom and constraint."[18] Situating Dickinson's poetry of consciousness within a broader philosophical context reveals precisely how close that relationship between freedom and constraint is for her work; the very ways that consciousness limits (through affective remove and the power of association) also afford vehicles for disruption. A similar point could apply to both the experiential real and reparative reading: the attention to particularity (whether a particular object or text) in turn serves as a vehicle for surprising openness.

In this attention to disruption, Dickinson draws from and complicates earlier accounts of consciousness and selfhood. Noah Webster's *American Dictionary of the English Language* (1844), an influential volume for Dickinson, offers the following definition of "self": "*Self* is sometimes used as a noun, noting the individual subject to his own contemplation or action, or noting identity of person. Consciousness makes everyone to be what he calls *self.*"[19] Webster's definition may in part be traced to John Locke's statement about consciousness in his *Essay Concerning Human Understanding:* "By this [consciousness] every one is to himself that which he calls *self.*"[20] Locke plays an important role in the ascent of "consciousness" in English-language philosophy. In the *Essay Concerning Human Understanding,* he defines the "self" as that "conscious thinking thing,—whatever substance made up of, (whether spiritual or material, simple or compounded, it matters not)—which is sensible or conscious of pleasure and pain, capable of happiness or misery, and so is concerned for itself, as far as that consciousness extends."[21] Locke here offers consciousness as the glue that holds together the various impressions of a given self. Like Locke, Webster proposes consciousness as knitting together the self.

Locke uses the structure of a mediating consciousness in order to offer a kind of epistemic limitation. He claims that "the mind knows not things immediately, but only by the intervention of the ideas it has of them."[22] Emerson seems to draw from this Lockean inheritance in his exploration of the claim that "we never go out of ourselves; it is always our own thought that we perceive" (*CW* 1: 202).[23] Perhaps one of the strongest associations of consciousness and captivity in Emerson can be found in "Self-Reliance": "The man is, as it were, clapped into jail by his consciousness" (*CW* 2: 29).[24]

Locke influenced Emerson's and Webster's rhetorics of the self, but Dickinson had many other routes of exposure to the philosophy of subjectivity. The *Atlantic Monthly,* to which her family subscribed, had numerous articles exploring the intellectual history of subjectivity, and, as Jed Deppman has noted, the Dickinson family circle included local professors of philosophy.[25] Thomas Cogswell Upham's *Elements of Mental Philosophy,* a textbook from Dickinson's school days, offers an extended response to Locke's model of consciousness.[26] Upham's work leads readers through a variety of topics about epistemology and the constitution of the self, discussing physical sensation as well as psychological processes. Upham builds on the tendencies of Locke as well as those of Scottish Common Sense writers to explore the ways in which some faculty of consciousness affects our encounter with the outer world and helps structure our senses of ourselves. Upham claims that we are only conscious of the effects of the world upon us—not of the world itself.[27]

Many Romantic writers worried that some faculty of consciousness may pose limits for the intensity of our emotions. Young Werther, one of Goethe's archetypal Romantic heroes, turns to the language of consciousness's limitation on passion: "Whether he [man] is uplifted by joy or engulfed by suffering, is he not stopped in both conditions and brought back to dull, cold consciousness just when he is ready to lose himself in the abundance of the infinite?"[28] Some Romantics worried about the mediating power of consciousness, fearing that this mediation implied some radical separation between ourselves and the other world, but Dickinson at times celebrates (perhaps not with an entirely untarnished trumpet) the potential for a mediating consciousness to free rather than confine. If consciousness plays some mediating role vis-à-vis the "world," the structure of consciousness can potentially provide walls behind which the self can hide from worldly agonies. The potentially estranging walls of consciousness can provide a position from which one can see one's worldly experiences in a new light. The promises of conscious remove are, however, fraught.

"No Rack can torture me" seems at first a poem about the way in which consciousness provides a means of escape from the material fetters of the world, but the course of the poem complicates this narrative of possible liberation:

No Rack can torture me—
My Soul—at Liberty—
Behind this mortal Bone
There knits a bolder One—

You cannot prick with Saw—
Nor pierce with Cimitar—
Two bodies—therefore be—
Bind One—The Other fly—

The Eagle of his Nest
No easier divest—
And gain the Sky
Than mayest Thou—

Except Thyself may be
Thine Enemy—
Captivity is Consciousness—
So's Liberty— (Fr649)

The first two stanzas of this poem seem to offer a somewhat traditional Stoic narrative, in which a person can be tortured, cut, and pierced but still have the ability to escape this torment through contemplative liberation. The seeming unity of the physical person is disrupted ("Two bodies—therefore be") in pursuit of some liberating doubleness, in which soul separates from body. The soul "at Liberty" can escape from the harsh bounds of the world. The rack, saw, and scimitar inflict their pain by tearing the body, by dividing it against itself, but the self can escape from these pains by engaging in its own self-divisions. The pain of these tortures in part occurs through assaulting the physical holism of the body, yet the escape from these pains comes from dissolving the apparent holism of body and soul in order to find the "bolder One" of the soul.[29] This poem thus suggests the capacity of consciousness to disrupt; the narrative of escape enacted in this poem depends on consciousness being able to revise itself.

However, this poem does not necessarily offer the promise of a radical escape from embodiment. Dickinson seems here to offer the soul as a second body in her reference to "Two bodies," suggesting that some trace of embodiment persists. Marianne Noble notes the importance of embodiment for this poem, finding that, like Hamlet's ruminations, "No Rack can torture me" agonizes over the fate of "ourselves" beyond this earthly flesh: "Our bodies give us consciousness, and how can 'we' exist apart from our consciousness? A body in captivity allows for consciousness; a body at liberty allows for consciousness. . . . The 'self' cannot be conscious without the body."[30] While Noble highlights physical embodiment here, this poem might also address figurative embodiment. Consciousness itself can provide a kind of figurative embodiment insofar as it offers an organizing structure for personal identity. Locke, Upham, and Webster speak of consciousness as granting coherence through collecting diverse phenomenal incidents into the unified whole of an "I." Webster's *American Dictionary* finds that the "self" (which is effected by consciousness) involves the "individual subject to his own contemplation or action" and allows for an "identity of person." According to this model of consciousness, being conscious allows one to relate experiences across time and space to oneself and to distinguish between what happens to oneself and to others. This notion of unifying consciousness complements physical embodiment's combination of holism and relationality.[31] That "bolder One" of consciousness "knits" past the bone—bringing together disparate incidences into a single identity, one that can estrange itself from the sufferings of the world.

For Dickinson, that other "body" (the body of consciousness), no matter how far it may go, provides its own limits of embodiment. It can escape, flying with the ease of an eagle, but it is still a determinate something, with its own bounds of awareness and relation. The poem concludes: "Captivity is Consciousness— / So's Liberty." "Consciousness" thus becomes a conflicted faculty, allowing for seeming liberation in thought and awareness but capable of providing its own captivity. The self remains bound within a ring of feelings, whether this ring is constituted by an association through memory, some structure of personal awareness, or some other faculty or tendency. Yet this poem does not entirely nullify the prospects of freedom. The feeling of liberation can be felt within consciousness. Though the self may at times flee to other bounds, the seeming breaking of bonds within this flight can occasion a moment of emancipating joy or other emotional inflections, such as dread or awe.[32] Only being conscious allows the experience of escape, because it permits an awareness of a relation between former captivity and some later new state. The narrative of this poem both celebrates and frustrates escape. It emphasizes interrogation and process, themes of both reparation and the experiential real.

Dickinson's poetry of consciousness also complicates accounts of consciousness as unifying. For some philosophical accounts of consciousness, the unifying activity of consciousness over time provides a foundation for a sense of personal identity. For instance, Locke writes that the "identity of the same man consists . . . in nothing but a participation of the same continued life, by constantly fleeting particles of matter, in succession vitally united to the same organized body."[33] The matter of our body continually shifts, Locke argues, but a sense of "participation in the same continued life" allows us to have a sense of integrity in the face of this fluctuation. Like Locke, Upham attends to the way in which consciousness becomes a mode for personal identity through some kind of "possession, appropriation, or belonging to."[34] Consciousness, for Upham, allows our various sensations and feelings to belong to us.

Rather than "possession, appropriation, or belonging to," Dickinson's poetry of consciousness often emphasizes dispossession, reappropriation, and surrender (sometimes through the language of inflated majesty). In developing this narrative of consciousness as disruptive, Dickinson turns to conscious self-reference—consciousness's ability to reflect upon itself and its ideas—and to the notion of consciousness as a dynamic entity. In this turn she extends and partially subverts some of the underlying principles of earlier philosophical models of consciousness. Both Locke and Upham emphasize a sense of conscious activity, but Dickinson's poems dramatize the manner in which the activity of consciousness can lead not to epistemic coherence but instead to cognitive and affective instabilities. Consciousness may unify through self-reflection, but that very reflective capacity also sows the seeds for consciousness's own disruption.

"Me from Myself—to banish" (Fr709) takes up tropes of the self/identity as embodied residence.[35] Rather than considering the relationship of the soul to exterior objects, though, "Me from Myself—to banish" instead examines the relationship of the self to itself and considers the unavoidable accompaniment entailed by a sense of self-consciousness. This accompaniment reveals the way in which Dickinson takes up the language of consciousness as powerfully possessing even as she suggests some possibly troubling implications for this possession:

Me from Myself—to banish—
Had I Art—
Invincible My Fortress
Unto All Heart—

But since Myself—assault Me—
How have I peace
Except by subjugating
Consciousness?

And since We're Mutual Monarch
How this be
Except by Abdication—
Me—of Me—?

The driving tension of this poem depends on the distinction between some immediate center of awareness and a broader sense of self, a distinction relevant for so many theories of consciousness. This poem, like Werther's passionate cry, also depends on this distinction turning into a kind of friction.[36] Werther exclaims that the limits of consciousness can keep us from the highest apogee of passion. However, rather than focusing on a moment where consciousness strains against some intensity of passion, "Me from Myself—to banish" instead offers an optative narrative about what would happen if the speaker *could* banish "Me from Myself" and, in so doing, break the bounds of consciousness. If this "Me" could stand apart from "Myself," this poem seems to suggest, then one could remove oneself from the attractions of the world. If consciousness could perpetually stand aside from itself, it might dissolve the world's affective bonds with conscious thinking. But the power of "Myself" cannot be so easily broken. The "Myself" becomes a mode of determinate being—not just an identity in the abstract, but a person with corresponding desires, affections, and historical involvements. Within itself, consciousness is not radically isolated but twin-born: a node of instantaneous consciousness (a "me") can critique other parts of itself (a "myself"). The "Me" of this poem might wonder at the possibilities of dissolving itself from the determinate connections with "Myself," but it cannot entirely complete this division.

Self-consciousness allows for a kind of experiential possession, according to Upham, by permitting some node of awareness (some immediate "me") to take ownership of instantaneous sensations and feelings and thereby assign these experiences to some "myself." The connotations of Dickinson's language throughout this poem—the "Mutual Monarch" and references to banishing—draw attention to the might and instability of self-conscious awareness.[37] The "Myself" grants some coherence to the "Me," but, in doing so, it radically limits the power of the "Me" to remake itself *ex nihilo.* Instead, that "Me" is always something rather than nothing (always, that is, a "Myself").

Yet this poem also alludes to dreams of disruption. The "Me" of this poem is not entirely identical to the "Myself." The difference between them suggests the possibility of the "Me," through that very process of self-consciousness, looking inward and criticizing itself. "Me from Myself" hints at the way that we can disrupt our standard patterns of experience through attention to the incidents of experience. In syntactic testament to the powers of disrupting attention, conditionals and questions permeate this poem. The act of posing a conditional implies stepping back from the immediate textures of experience to think about how one might act if a certain condition, or conditions, changed. Asking a question implies an examination of the textures of experience. Both conditionals and questions involve interrogating immediate experience, and that interrogation involves altering or disrupting that immediate experience. That openness of questioning is at the heart of the reparative process, and it also stands as one of the core elements of the tradition of the experiential real: that immediate life can be tried in the hope of some further realization.

Fittingly, these questions are not answered. Just as the speaker of this poem ponders the limits of her ability to free the "Me" from the tyranny of the "Myself," so too do these questions cause her to turn to the limits of her knowledge. The final question of this poem reveals in stark relief some of the poem's underlying tensions, implying that "Abdication" of "Myself" would also be surrendering the ability to view oneself as a coherent "Me." This poem explores the fantasies of breaking the "Myself" free from the "Me," and those fantasies testify to the ability of the "Me" to challenge in some way the conditions of the "Myself."

In "This Consciousness that is aware," Dickinson further meditates on consciousness as a figure of dynamic energy.

This Consciousness that is aware
Of Neighbors and the Sun
Will be the one aware of Death
And that itself alone

Is traversing the interval
Experience between
And most profound experiment
Appointed unto Men—

How adequate unto itself
It's properties shall be
Itself unto itself and None
Shall make discovery—

Adventure most unto itself
The Soul condemned to be—
Attended by a single Hound
It's own identity. (Fr817B)

This poem starts from the self *in concreto,* the deictic *this* offering an immediate specification: "This Consciousness" could be the consciousness of the speaker of the poem, some other individual, or a general kind of consciousness. "This Consciousness" begins with the local and moves progressively to the more abstract or absolute, from neighbors to the sun (still a concrete entity, albeit more distant) to death to consciousness's recognition of its ultimate fate.

This expansion—from local to cosmic transcendental—implies the power of consciousness to move beyond determinate entities, but the poem also suggests the possibility of some kind of endurance of identity in that invocation of the "single Hound." That Hound presents one of the central tensions of "This Consciousness": it might be the soul's hunting companion, but it might also be the hunter itself (while the soul, like a stag, is the prey). In the former sense consciousness assimilates personal experience, allowing a node of a "Me" to gain awareness of exterior and interior impressions. The latter sense, which is strengthened by the soul's "condemn[ation]," suggests a kind of perpetual confinement for the soul in the chase—no matter how far it may run, it still cannot avoid the jaws of identity's hound. This image of identity as the companion and hunter of the soul resonates with philosophical emphases on self-consciousness as a process. As the Hound chases on, self-consciousness continually attends to one's experiences and one's sense of self.

Dickinson closes this poem with an image of consciousness's "Adventure" as an on-going endeavor. As Alexandra Socarides finds that this poem celebrates valuing "process . . . over product," Dickinson's poems of consciousness are so often poems about process.[38] In keeping with Locke, consciousness in her verse also often seems to be a dynamic force that we are unavoidably subject to. As she writes in one poem, "Of Consciousness, her awful mate / The Soul cannot be rid" (Fr1076, 1–2). That fatedness to consciousness is simultaneously a fatedness to the connections drawn by consciousness as well as to the very disruptions of those connections. Indeed, the act of drawing connections in turn allows for the possibility of disruption—only *something* (not *nothing*) can be disrupted, and only the existence of fetters allows for the experience of escape.

Her poems of consciousness offer experimental enactings of the tensions of the consciousness constantly making and unmaking itself. As consciousness troubles its own coherence, so too do Dickinson's poems of consciousness at once stand as poetic wholes and suggest the destabilizing profusions of meaning within. In complement to consciousness's simultaneous making and unmaking, her verse appeals to structures of meaning even as it suggests the disrupting tensions within these structures. We can gain meaning through the interrogation of her verse, but that gaining also entails the loss of old totalized narratives of interpretation. Like consciousness, Dickinson's verse gives and takes—holding and freeing. Dickinson's poems of consciousness highlight the importance of frames of awareness for her poetic project and also illuminate the way that her poetry holds out hope for the challenging of these frames. This hope of challenge is also part of the tradition of the experiential real as well as the project of reparative reading. The dynamic of consciousness's weaving and unweaving holds out the possibility of realization's surprise.

The June Bee's Dance

If consciousness is about process for Dickinson, the erotic and the sublime highlight the task of conscious disruption. As Gary Stonum and Suzanne

Juhasz have shown, the erotic and the sublime intertwine in her work.[39] Dickinson often meditates on the notion of desire deferred, and her approach to the sublime emphasizes moments when the sublime is not quite achieved. In discussing the erotic for Dickinson, I would like to recast the erotic not merely as sexual desire but instead as modeling a play of seeking and absence. The erotic condition of life for Dickinson means that in desiring we both yearn for and lack that object of desire. This lack of fulfillment gives a great charge to life, but it also entails a kind of restlessness and a refusal of satisfaction.

This narrative of desire is implicitly Platonic. In the *Symposium* Socrates argues that we love what we lack—that *eros* is the child of Resourcefulness and Penury.[40] The lineage of *eros* reveals a key characteristic of erotic desire in the Platonic dialogues: it involves the craving to have without the having itself. Dickinson follows in this tradition of conflicted erotic desire. In offering this philosophically themed account of the erotic for Dickinson, I do not mean to efface the importance of sexual accounts of the erotic for her work (as developed by Rebecca Patterson, Juhasz, and others).[41] Indeed, many of critical accounts of sexuality for Dickinson have emphasized precisely these themes. This narrative of the erotic does, though, provide a vehicle for highlighting the tensions embedded in her poetic trials of the real. The task of realization in Dickinson involves the dislocation of the conventional boundaries of the self in order to create a heightened receptivity to experience.

Dickinson's poetry attends to moments of sudden insight, and this attention fuses the material with the transcendental:

A Solemn thing within the Soul
To feel itself get ripe—
And golden hang—while farther up—
The Maker's Ladders stop—
And in the Orchard far below—
You hear a Being—drop—

A wonderful—to feel the sun
Still toiling at the cheek
You thought was finished—
Cool of eye, and critical of Work—
He shifts the stem—a little—
To give your Core—a look—

But solemnest—to know
Your chance in Harvest moves
A little nearer—Every sun
The single—to some lives. (Fr467)

In portraying this moment of existential ripeness, Dickinson seems to be reworking an episode from Genesis: Jacob has a vision in which he "behold[s] the angels of God ascending and descending" a ladder that reaches to the heavens.[42] This poem fuses the sensuous and the spiritual. That "Solemn" moment of soul ripening intertwines with the experience of the sun "toiling at the cheek." The sun itself achieves a double significance, at once glowing on the physical cheek and becoming a grander symbol: "Every sun / The single—to some lives." That "wonderful" instant of ripening can be simultaneously disorienting and thrilling.

At times Dickinson's invocation of reality leads to a meditation on the shocking evasiveness of this reality. Emerson reflects on this theme at various points in his work, and Dickinson sketches out instants where realization is so vast that it resists (and perhaps transcends) the grasping hand. Often, the "real" in Dickinson functions something like Emerson's Nemesis—a vast, indefinite check to any immediate apprehension. One of the four poems Dickinson sent to Thomas Wentworth Higginson when she initiated their correspondence in 1862 ponders not realization but the lack of it:

The nearest Dream recedes—unrealized—
The Heaven we chase—
Like the June Bee—before the School Boy—
Invites the Race—
Stoops—to an easy Clover—
Dips—evades—teazes—deploys—
Then—to the Royal Clouds
Lifts his light Pinnace—
Heedless of the Boy—
Staring—bewildered—at the mocking sky—

Homesick for steadfast Honey—
Ah—the Bee flies not
That brews that rare variety! (Fr304B)

The dance of this June Bee reflects Dickinson's response to the dynamics of realization. Instead of a blithe realization, in which the eager hand securely traps the buzzing vision, Dickinson often emphasizes challenge, dislocation, interrogation, and difference.

In complement to its theme of failed grasping, the poem typographically emphasizes separation, brokenness, and splintering. Dashes set "unrealized" apart from the rest of the very first line, thereby implying both that word's importance and the theme of removal. The myriad dashes in "Dips—evades—teazes—deploys—" at once suggest the dancing evasion of the June Bee (each dash a twist in the bee's whirling flight) and hint at the fracturing entailed in the quest for Dickinsonian realization. The constant sense of loss in hope of gaining, such a prominent theme in Emerson, can be seen in the final stanza of the poem. "Homesick for steadfast Honey" might reflect on that sense of lost certainty that results from the quest for realization; the old certainties of appearance have been denied us, now that we are awakened to the call of some further reality. But this honey is not "steadfast"—at most, we can gain realization by instants, but that hope of realization demands continued trial.

In *Metaphor and Reality* Philip Wheelwright offers a narrative of the effects of reality in harmony with much of Dickinson's poetic project and Emerson's account of Nemesis. Reflecting on the task of living (and thinking) "intensely," Wheelwright concludes his book with an emphasis on the incompleteness of our narratives of reality: "Reality is ultimately problematical, not contingently so; for to grasp and formulate it, even as a set of questions, is to fragmentize it. There is always, in any inquiry, something more than meets the eye, even the inner eye; the permanent possibility of extending one's imaginative awareness has no limits."[43] The June Bee of ultimate reality continually evades and taunts us, according to Dickinson. The sublime realization is too vast to be bound by the fetters of a complacent conscious possession.

A second poem invoking the real and desire unfulfilled elaborates on this tendency:

> Who never wanted—maddest Joy
> Remains to him unknown—
> The Banquet of Abstemiousness
> Defaces that of Wine—

Within it's reach, though yet ungrasped
Desire's perfect Goal—
No nearer—lest the Actual—
Should disenthrall thy soul— (Fr1447)

In the fascicle manuscript of this poem, Dickinson offers four variants for "the Actual": "Reality," "it's penury," "the possible," and "Vicinity."[44] As with many of Dickinson's variants, it is not fully clear what relationship she places between these possibilities. Whatever one's theory for reading variants in Dickinson's work, this set of variants suggests Dickinson's own concern with the difficulties of achieving the object of desire: arriving at the vicinity of one's object could disenthrall the soul, making possible the achievement of this object could be disenthralling, arriving at the reality of this object (that is, its vicinity of being) could disenthrall, and so forth.

This cluster of variants reveals in miniature some of the tensions of realization in Dickinson's work. The actual, reality, penury, possibility, and vicinity join in this manuscript text—and more broadly in Dickinson. The actual can afford an avenue for reality. That reality may become a vista of possibility. Such possibility involves surrendering easy, locked notions, and recognizing the penury of before on behalf of the dazzling opportunities ahead. Revisionary penury demands the persistent readjustment of vicinity, as what seems close may become estranged and the formerly alien becomes a prelude to the further intimacy of possibility.[45]

Just as near dreams may recede unrealized and the "ceaseless Poverty" of existential revision may reveal the prospect of new wealth, so too in this poem does Dickinson ponder the wonderful intoxication of that feast of wanting. The 1896 edition of Dickinson's verse—*Poems: Third Series*—titles this poem "Desire," and this poem explores desire through the dynamic of loss and evasion. As the June Bee dances away from the eager schoolboy's hand, calling him ever onwards, so too does this banquet of denial depend on the lack of grasping. Achievement of a desire might disclose our own hearts and open them to new goals (taking "disenthrall" in the sense of breaking the bonds of thralldom). For Dickinson, however, this achievement is often not an untarnished trophy. Instead, it often entails a sacrifice, a loss of the exquisite intensity of focused desire—at least until a new figure of wondrous wanting is found. Penury becomes within Dickinson a vehicle for new erotic heights. If she means to offer a poetry of possibility,[46] the finding of poverty (absence) can be a first step for the location of further riches.

This theme of disruption in the pursuit of realization connects to the dynamic of the sublime in Dickinson, particularly these two elements: the sense of endless process and the attention to concepts that shatter the assumed conditions of the self. These elements reinforce each other, as the pursuit of endless process can itself shatter conceptions of the self. In *The Dickinson Sublime* Gary Stonum adapts Thomas Weiskel's notion of stages of encounter for the Romantic sublime to Dickinson's poetic enterprise.[47] Stonum claims that the "first or *normative* phrase" is a moment before sublime alterity, when "the subject relies upon what will later be seen as habitual modes of thought and feeling." The second, "*traumatic* phase" is one that "commences with the apprehension of an object, which variously and often simultaneously entices the subject, disrupts his or her conventional modes of consciousness, and challenges the subject's dignity by means of the drastic contrast" revealed between the subject and the attractions of the sublime. In the final, "*reactive* phase," "*sublimation,*" the subject achieves a "new state of consciousness" in which he or she "experiences elevation, empowerment, and a release from traumatic assault."[48] Stonum argues that Dickinson's poetry often achieves its effects through lingering on the "threshold of the reactive [third] stage," denying the reader "the moment of final commitment, sublimation, and identification" usually entailed in the three-step outline of the sublime.[49]

Stonum's narrative of an endlessly deferred sublime illuminates Dickinson's strategies of erotic restlessness. Both Emerson's approach to realization and Dickinson's approach to the sublime rebuke the prospect of finality. Emerson emphasizes the provisionality of any realization by finding that this realization, too, may need to be revised in succeeding moments. Dickinson's rebuke takes a slightly different form: conjuring up some wild vision of absolute transfiguration as a concluding climax to the quest for the absolute, she endlessly defers that vision. She emphasizes the way in which sublime apprehension can break us, shattering old modes of ourselves like clay pots. And the full recognition of the sublime might ultimately evade us.

"He fumbles at your Soul" offers an initial view of the self-revisionary strategies of the sublime for Dickinson:

He fumbles at your Soul
As Players at the Keys—

Before they drop full Music on—
He stuns you by Degrees—

Prepares your brittle substance
For the etherial Blow
By fainter Hammers—further heard—
Then nearer—Then so—slow—

Your Breath—has chance to straighten—
Your Brain—to bubble cool—
Deals One—imperial Thunderbolt—
That peels your naked soul—

When Winds hold Forests in their Paws—
The Firmaments—are still— (Fr477B)

Surveying the various ways in which this poem has been read ("from biographical . . . to structuralist and archetypal to gendered"), Cristanne Miller finds that this poem can also be read as "dramatiz[ing] a moment of anticipation and ambiguous fulfillment."[50] It is precisely that ambiguity of fulfillment that makes this poem a window into the dynamics of erotic deferral for Dickinson. Among the narratives by which this poem might be read, it can be seen as a dramatic performance of the moment leading to (the cusp of) radical realization. This drama is initiated by the conceit of an individual playing at a piano, a conceit that continues in the mention of the "fainter Hammers."

The first ten lines perform and describe the ascent to this realization. The syntax of "Your Breath—has chance to straighten— / Your Brain—to bubble cool— / Deals One—imperial Thunderbolt" suggests a radical fusion. This sense of fusion is achieved through Dickinson's syntactical compression.[51] One might read "Your Brain—to bubble cool—" as "Your Brain—[has chance] to bubble cool—" and further insert the phantom subject of "He" for the verb "Deals"; earlier, in line 5, "He" seems to be the subject of "Prepares your brittle substance," so one might extend the agency of the "He" to "Deals One." However, "Your Brain—to bubble cool— / Deals One" might also be read as "Your Brain—[in order] to bubble cool— / Deals One." Under this latter interpretation, the brain, rather than this "He," deals the thunderbolt. This syntactical ambiguity allows for a blending of grammatical subjects and, in so blending, demonstrates a mix of (affected/affecting) brain and (affecting) He. Does the brain deal this thunderbolt—Is this thunderbolt reflective of the shock registered by the limitations of consciousness?—or does some absolute "He" deliver it? The interior and exterior mingle as distinctions break down. In preparation for the strike of this "imperial Thunderbolt," the poem's language fuses subject and object, means and ends. Diverse forms of agency have merged in the immanence of language. Charging toward the absolute, the poem achieves a sublime concentration.

The poem concludes with a note of disjunction. Rather than continuing the narrative of the struck soul, the final two lines present a sudden imagistic shift: "When Winds hold Forests in their Paws— / The Firmaments—are still." This sense of disjunction arises, in part, from the fact that the final stanza (at eight syllables and six syllables) follows the pattern of the second half of the individual stanzas preceding it (which follow a 6- or 7-6-8-6 pattern). The reader's ear may detect this absence, giving the poem an effect of having leapt over two (invisible) lines.[52] In contrast to the stunning-by-degree of the earlier lines, we now have a sudden jump to the "still[ness]" of the skies. The phantom hands playing at the keys of the earlier lines (implied but never directly stated) have transformed into the "Paws" of the winds. After the thrilling build-up of the playing on the keys, we are left with an awful stillness.

Applying Weiskel/Stonum's categories to this poem's narrative of the almost-sublime reveals how Dickinson complicates the sublime. This "fumbling at the soul" can be seen as the moment of preparation between the first two stages, as the soul is primed for the traumatic rush of the sublime. The "brittle substance" invoked by the poem can easily be read as the "habitual modes of thought and feeling" that the sublime will disrupt. As with many of Dickinson's poems, this one does not offer an easy transition between the second and third stages. Indeed, it seems uncertain whether the concluding lines should be read as a reflection on the moment of climax or perhaps a poetic performance of the "reactive" conclusion of the sublime process.[53] There certainly does seem to be a "release from traumatic assault" at these concluding lines, but "empowerment" of the subject seems an inappropriate word at this turn. If anything, the subject has seemingly been transcended and the cataclysmic experience of the sublime has transformed into an appearance of sublime peace.

Kant's subject-centered account of the sublime in *The Critique of Judgement* has some harmonies with Dickinson's approach to the sublime and highlights some of its tendencies. Both Kant and Dickinson reflect on the way that the sublime can disrupt the subject's perspective.[54] For Kant, the sublime does not reside in an object but is instead found in the internal processes of the experiencing subject.[55] While the beautiful (to which the sublime is contrasted in this *Critique*) is both object-centered and seemingly revealing of natural laws, the sublime instead challenges the subject's apprehension of the orders of the world.[56]

The experience of the sublime brings into focus certain cognitive tensions within the subject. In his discussion of the "mathematical sublime," Kant writes of a sublime feeling arising in response to the limitations of apprehension for the individual and the simultaneous pull of the limitless. Kant offers one sublime process in which the length of a tree might be used to measure mountains, and the height of these mountains could then give one a unit for the measurement of the Earth's diameter, which in turn could provide a unit for the measurement of the solar system, and so on and so on to the greatest scale of the universe—and beyond.[57] This sublime experience does not come from the sheer magnitude of units required to measure something like the Milky Way (indeed, one could offer smaller as well as larger units for such a measurement) but from the "fact that in our progress we arrive at ever yet greater units."[58] The mind can endlessly project itself forward, rendering each object small and great in its turn.

As Kant asserts that the sublime occurs within the processes of an individual subjectivity, Dickinson's poetry of the sublime often takes an interiorizing turn, with the self coiling endlessly upon itself in reflection upon its apprehensions. Dickinson's consideration of the (sublime) whole in the following poem complements Kant's exposition of the mathematical sublime and reveals the ways in which the Dickinson sublime radically challenges conventional standards of apprehension:

> Unto the Whole—how add?
> Has "All" a further Realm—
> Or Utmost an Ulterior?
> Oh, Subsidy of Balm! (Fr1370)

At the outset of this poem, Dickinson takes "the Whole" as some concrete, coherent image and considers the (rational) process of additive extension, but this process of extension also suggests a contradiction: how can more be added to the whole of existence? The whole would seem to embrace the farthest reaches of being, encompassing everything, so addition to this whole causes significant conceptual feedback. The poem's next two lines continue to play with the notion of extending the absolute: could there be a "further Realm" of the all, and a further Utmost for an Ulterior?[59]

Even as Dickinson offers the (stable) figure of the whole, she also considers the process of extending this whole and interrogates our ability to conceptualize an infinite process of extension. The dual question of this poem grants the whole a (perhaps terrifying) vastness, as she considers the notion of a whole that cannot be extended, that embraces and transcends even the furthest reach of her mind. The verse itself becomes pulled between the extremes of an "all" capable of extension and an "all" that embraces the furthest extension: the first case shows the triumph of the process of infinity over a stable notion, and the second offers a concept absorbing all the processes of thought.

This approach to the "all" reveals differences within the processes of conception involved in apprehending the whole. Dickinson uses these differences to bring out the potential of some of the conflicts underlying the modes of cognition and awareness. Throughout her verse, Dickinson turns to various concepts—such as death, ecstasy, the absolute—which offer some challenge to the conventional conceptions of consciousness. In so challenging, these concepts reveal tensions within our apprehension of the world. The following poem's definition of "eternity" reveals this tendency:

As if the Sea should part
And show a further Sea—
And that—a further—and the Three
But a Presumption be—

Of Periods of Seas—
Unvisited of Shores—
Themselves the Verge of Seas to be—
Eternity—is Those— (Fr720)

She conjures a potential vision of eternity as an endless succession of seas, the deepest depths and furthest ranges of each sea only a presentiment of a further one. This exemplifies Kant's model of the mathematical sublime—in which sea is added to sea in a seemingly endless process of extension. The sea itself is already vast and indefinite, but she recasts that figure as relatively concrete compared to an even greater magnitude.

If achieving reality is about disrupting our old apprehensions in order to find some truer depth of being, Dickinson's approach to the sublime shows how radical this prospect of disruption can be—indeed, it might be too radical to anticipate coherently. Her poetry of the sublime considers how profoundly destabilizing epiphanies of realization can be. Creating in her verse a space for the perpetual trial of appearance, Dickinson appeals to the sublime as a totem for this trial. If the experience of the sublime could lead to a self-alienating recognition, the imaginative consideration of this sublime—the attempt to realize it—becomes an exploration of the limits and possibilities of ourselves.

Trials of the Everyday

In making the case for possibility, contemporary proponents of experiential reading at times turn to the imagery of the concrete, as the work of Marielle Macé and Jean-Marie Schaeffer suggests. For instance, Macé offers the distinctive flights of swallows in a Francis Ponge poem as exemplifying different modes of being; reading this poem, she is "suddenly captured by an exterior form, invited to follow its movement and try out, within myself, this style and this particular form of being."[60] Literature can thus offer certain stances of being, which model for the reader certain existential stylistics (to use Macé's framing). However, Macé and Schaeffer draw attention to the way that there can be tensions within a given existential stance, too. Far from presenting a unified whole, individual "traced-out possibilities" in literature can themselves embody certain instabilities. Macé describes the process of reading as follows: "We follow a call, drawn along by the network of tensions implicated in literary sentences, and find ourselves displaced to one place or another on the network."[61] "Tensions" and "displaced" bear important conceptual weights both in this sentence and in Macé's broader argument. A given literary instant reveals its own internal contradictory impulses, and following out those impulses can lead to our own internal displacement—that is, to our instants of self-revision. As Macé writes later, reflecting on reading "allows us to observe the dynamics of individuation in all their instability."[62] Schaeffer also alludes to this potential for readerly revision for poetic reading: "Poetic language puts us into contact with what is at the same time a more elementary and more fundamental understanding of our being in the world: an understanding that takes the form of an affective landscape sculpted by words, but that causes the (re)birth of the reader via a phenomenon of resonance, consonant or dissonant, that is inaccessible to analytic explanation."[63]

Much of this chapter has indicated the way Dickinson suggests those, at times disorienting, tensions of experience. Consciousness undoes its captivity through the process of reflection—just as readerly reflection unsettles the seemingly fixed boundaries of the self. Her poetry of the sublime highlights seemingly divergent impulses. Moreover, the process of many of Dickinson's poems involves taking a moment of (hypothetical) experience and exploring its implications. That moment offers a certain "traced-out possibility" for the reader—whether it's a bird going down a walk (Fr359) or the reflections on a fly-buzz after death (Fr591). However, that moment might also reveal its own instabilities, and reflecting on those tensions becomes a vehicle for the reader to reconsider the textures of his or her own experiences.

"I think To Live—may be a Bliss" (Fr757) offers a voyage into a traced-out possibility of existence. Dickinson thinks about the possibility of living in a manner that soon slides into the realm of fantasy—maybe. This poem highlights the broader enterprise of challenging experiential textures in her verse and the stakes of such challenges for the apprehension of the real.

I think To Live—may be a Bliss
To those who dare to try—
Beyond my limit—to conceive—
My lip—to testify—

I think the Heart I former wore
Could widen—till to me
The Other, like the little Bank
Appear—unto the Sea—

I think the Days—could every one
In Ordination stand—
And Majesty—be easier—
Than an inferior kind—

No numb alarm—lest Difference come—
No Goblin—on the Bloom—
No start in Apprehension's Ear,
No Bankruptcy—no Doom—

But Certainties of Sun—
Midsummer—in the Mind—
A steadfast South—opon the Soul—
Her Polar time—behind—

The Vision—pondered long—
So plausible becomes
That I esteem the fiction—real—
The Real—fictitious seems—

How bountiful the Dream—
What Plenty—it would be
Had all my Life but been Mistake
Just rectified—in Thee (Fr757)

Shira Wolosky finds that this poem parallels in many respects Isaac Watts's "There Is a Land of Pure Delight."[64] However, Dickinson offers a crucial revision of Watts. His hymn speaks of the joys of a paradise beyond this Earth. Her poem invokes the imagery of paradise, yet it perhaps expresses yearning not so much for some later Heaven as for the living of Christian witness. The poem's diction returns again and again to the iconography of conversion: life, testify, heart, former (a key word for any conversion), ordination, soul, mistake (perhaps another key word), rectified, in Thee. In this poem Dickinson sketches a narrative of what it would mean to convert to a Christian life. In such a life the heart opens to divine grace, and the days achieve an ordination—a sublime order under the hand of God. Rather than mortal quibblings about death (the "numb alarm" of final doom) or a sense of life's hollowness (that is, its bankruptcy), that steadfast Christian reaches out to the founding truths of God.[65] The final two lines of this poem ponder how the love of Christ might "rectify" the mistakes of life (particularly that mistake of original sin) and how the act of Christian conversion can grant a renewed life.

This moment of wonder enters a territory of psychological straining. Jed Deppman has cited this as an example of Dickinson's "trying-to-think" (or even "trying-to-believe") poems: such poems show a consciousness pushing at its limits and using all its concentrated energies of thinking in order to try to realize a concept.[66] The repetition of "I think" shows the provisionality and difficulty of this thought experiment, which is perhaps beyond the speaker's "limit to conceive." In the intensity of this trial, the poem writhes between affirmation and denial. The pitch of this poem seems in many respects counterfactual ("if only I could believe and live so"), but the extremes of desire deny an easy dismissal of such a dream.[67]

As a way of compounding the intensity of this confounding trial, Dickinson invokes a vision of the real that blends the real and the fictional:

The Vision—pondered long—
So plausible becomes
That I esteem the fiction—real—
The Real—fictitious seems—

Dickinson seems to propose "the fiction" and "the Real" as contrary alternatives but suggests at such a moment of vision an instant where these oppositions break down.[68] What Dickinson means here by this "Real" remains open to interpretation. For many nineteenth-century Americans, God would be the ultimate reality, so perhaps this is one of the poems of religious doubt in Dickinson: the vision of Christian life seems so alluring that the (hypothetical) "fiction" of God's existence seems real.[69]

But that is not the only way to read the "real" in this poem. If this is a poem about conversion, perhaps the "real" here instead responds to the present historical experience of the speaker, when she cannot commit fully to that vision of Christian conversion. The fiction of this poem—its rhetorical portrayal and imagining of the joys of the steadfast Christian—becomes for the speaker an enterprise of double-edged persuasion: such a poem may entice her with the perceived wonders of religious steadfastness, and the fact that the speaker has composed such a poem suggests that perhaps her heart truly could be opened to conversion. In this poem Dickinson explores one hypothetical stance toward faith. In her life she often expressed a conflicted approach toward faith; her letters as a young woman to Abiah Root suggest a deep interest in religious faith but also impulses of distance from it.[70]

This poem reveals the depth of her efforts to locate a window on possible experience.

This poem thus can be read as an exploration of the act of witnessing, one that depends on one's emotions and one's awareness of these emotions. Reading this poem as an experiment in witnessing suggests the role of witnessing for Dickinson's "real" as well as for Whitman's. The call of reality may within Dickinson cause us to turn within ourselves to examine our own machinery of perspective, but such an internal trial can also disrupt our very enterprise of perspective. Where we stand becomes uncertain, and seeming anchors have the solidity of clouds. The very intensity of this straining against our possible limits creates the opportunity for a new, revisionary testimony.

"I think To Live—may be a Bliss" is not the only place where Dickinson weaves together the discourse of dreaming and reality. Her only poem that includes "Reality" as a nonvariant conflates the two:

Within that little Hive
Such Hints of Honey lay
As made Reality a Dream
And Dreams, Reality— (Fr1633)[71]

In one prose fragment, she claims that no "dreaming can compare with reality, for Reality itself is a dream from which but a portion of Mankind have yet waked and part of us is a not familiar Peninsula."[72] We can in part understand this association of reality and dreaming as a corollary of or at least complement to the destabilization of perspective explored within Dickinson's work: such a destabilization disrupts our old senses of the real. Things that used to seem real acquire the tenuousness of dreams, and perhaps what had seemed far fantasy acquires some echo of truth. The disclosing of Dickinson's verse reorients our sense of what grounds existence.

The fact that "part of us is a not familiar peninsula" could mean that, in venturing into ourselves, we come upon strange territories. Just as Macé portrays reading as the enterprise of exploring the tensions within a given perspective, Dickinson conjures certain experiential instants in order to explore their hidden tensions. The trial of appearance in a Dickinson poem happens through the generation of a cloud of contrasting and complementary resonances within the poem. The instabilities we find within Dickinson suggest a continued trial of appearance and (as the flipside of trying appearance) of our own narratives of apprehension. Trying this appearance can lead to instants of dislocation. Indeed, one aspect of this trial demands dislocation: it requires taking up rote assumptions and turning them around to see what they really might supply.

It is precisely this exploration of tensions that makes Dickinson's work so congenial to Sedgwick's enterprise of reparative reading. Casting light on the tensions of lived experience creates an openness to surprise and wonder—to the hopes of reparative adjustment. Revealing the instabilities of consciousness, the contradictions of the sublime, and other tensions embedded in experience, Dickinson's poems become opportunities for the readerly exploration of self-conceptions and the broader architecture of experience. They thus become an incitement to try the surface of immediate appearance. Dickinson's commitments to some substantive narrative of the real may be opaque at times. But her commitment to the rearticulation of experience seems clear, and her poetry creates opportunities for the interrogation of phenomenal appearance and cognitive assumptions.

In an early poem, Dickinson writes:

We lose—because we win—
Gamblers—recollecting which—
Toss their dice again! (Fr28)

One might say a similar thing about the tradition of the experiential real that Dickinson highlights. We lose a sense of what was formerly real in winning a new sense of the real. Succeeding new insights demand a sacrifice of the totality of old ones. For Emerson, unrealization is the conjoined twin of realization, a theme that Dickinson emphasizes.

A Dickinson poem presents an opportunity for revising our understandings, and every reading is a kind of throwing the dice. We might not know exactly what will turn up, what new realization awaits, and that very uncertainty provides an impetus for reading. Like the dancing June Bee, Dickinson's poetry evades totalized fixity. This evasion forces us to interrogate the textures of our experience of the poem and, more broadly, life itself. Far from effacing the particular, her poetry makes that particular a vista for initiating possibility. The very skeptical eye that Dickinson brings to her poetry often serves as much to enchant as it does to disabuse of glib illusions. The June Bee dance entices and evades us, revealing and baffling. The trials of realization in Dickinson are those instants of intensity that strain the familiar home. We yearn to catch that glorious buzzing bee of high summer, yet the sting may overwhelm: in that wondrous instant of pain and pleasure, our skin breaks and the bite of honey bleeds in, the liquid beads launching upon our forehead.

• FIVE •
Challenging Appearances

The preceding three chapters have examined the stakes of the real and reading for individual nineteenth-century American writers. These chapters have indicated how this appeal to the real involves an interrogation of immediate experience; this interrogation at once goes beyond that immediacy and returns to it in a new light. The particular is, as it were, realized through the encounter with the interrogative eye. While this realization can at times be described in the rhetoric of mastery, that process of realization also demands putting the self into play—cherished assumptions, ideas, and approaches may have to be discarded. Dickinson's verse in particular underscores the coiled possibilities of exhilaration and abnegation in that enterprise of realization.

Drawing attention to the tradition of the experiential real, which tests the surface of appearance in the hopes of finding some greater reality, revises certain elements of literary history. Far from becoming a guiding star only after the Civil War, the real played an important role in orienting antebellum discourse about literature. Recovering a sense of the capaciousness of the real for nineteenth-century Americans in turn affords a vehicle for exploring the literary dynamics of their writings. It now might be helpful to extend this consideration of the way that this dynamic of the real entails a return to particularity. That reflective return to particularity highlights a broader strand of literary practice and helps illuminate the role of the experiential real for the fate of reading in contemporary scholarly debates.

The notion of some nonmaterial real did not begin with antebellum Americans, who tapped into a wider tradition of ideas and lexical associations. Nor did it end with them. In developing their own distinctive literary approaches, American modernist poets draw from the emphases of the real found in the middle of the nineteenth century. As they critique the assumptions and methods of representational Realism, modernist poets sometimes invoke a real that goes beyond the incidents of the actual and advance a theory of poetry that emphasizes the need to re-view the surface of actual objects. The broader course of modernist poetics is a vast and conflicted territory, but in this chapter I offer William Carlos Williams and Hart Crane as providing hints of later, modernist responses to the antebellum traditions of the real.

The tactics of revising particularity involved within the tradition of the experiential real include a return to surface in order to test it for some deeper reality. This process of testing can complicate narratives of transparency in Americanist criticism. In *Surface and Depth* Michael Gilmore notes a pervasive concern with legibility and the penetration of surface in American literature and culture. He argues that "American culture has been preoccupied from its beginnings with the wish, the requirement, to know and to make accessible." According to Gilmore, the interrogation of surface in order to make it legible can become a vehicle for mastery.[1] He closes *Surface and Depth,* for example, with a consideration of the glass paperweight in *1984* as exemplifying the machinery of transparency that makes the oppression of Oceania so terrible and so total.[2] The dialectical interrogation of surface, though, suggests that the effort to find depths through surface can also be initiatory rather than totalizing and freeing rather than imprisoning. For example, Thoreau's simple tests try the surface of any experience, going through that surface to reach out to other things, ideas, and tendencies. This examination sets an entity into a conversation with a broader web of existence and provides an opportunity for new insights.[3] The works of these authors demonstrate how the interrogation of surface can lead to self-reflective and revisionary literary narratives, as conceptual resonance piles atop conceptual resonance. Rather than leading to a single, totalized master narrative, heterogeneous transparency can be the cultivation of pluralities.

Both the revision of particularity and narratives of the experiential real have a bearing on contemporary debates about reading, too. In combining attention to experiential surface with a desire to interrogate that surface in order to see some further reality, the tradition of the experiential real presents a model for certain experiential accounts of reading. Such experiential accounts could simultaneously stress disruptive attention to the surface of the text as well as the effort to interrogate that surface to glimpse some further depths. Indeed, that attention to surface demands interrogation. Within Emerson, attention to daily experience requires a view of deeper principles, which themselves might be informed by these experiential encounters; far from circumscribing the self, drawing correspondences can be a way of disrupting an individual's assumptions and enlivening one's encounter with the things of the world. Applying this dynamic to the experience of reading suggests the possibility of a theoretically-informed eye matching with a formally attentive one.

Returning to Surface: A *Point D'appui*

Many American writers in both the antebellum and modernist periods share a concern with "surface." The enterprise of real transparency involves going through the surface of figures in order to catch a glimpse of the real. The surface is affirmed as an initiatory incident; engagement with this surface is predicated upon setting it in dialogue with something further. The various iterations of this transparency—from Emerson's accumulation of images to Whitman's lyric communions—all rely on some trace of surface, even if this surface is itself disrupted. In one of his last essays on poetry, 1875's "Poetry and Imagination," Emerson emphasizes the importance of the trial of surface for the imaginative enterprise. The realm of the "superficial," fancy merely "relates to surface." Meanwhile, the imagination affirms "a real relation between a thought and some material fact" (*CW* 8: 15). Elsewhere in this essay, Emerson speaks of the liberating interpretive capacities of the imagination. Those "impressions of the imagination" inspire a moment that does not "stay on the surface of the eye or ear, but penetrated to the inward sense, agitates us, and is not forgotten" (*CW* 8: 8). In contrast to "stay[ing] on the surface," the incidents of the imagination penetrate and agitate, suggesting both the crossing of surface and a kind of restlessness. Other antebellum writers also turn to the interrogation of surface.

In the "Where I Lived and What I Lived For" chapter of *Walden,* Thoreau writes that "petty fears and petty pleasures are but the shadow of the reality" (or at least seem that way when we are "unhurried and wise"), and the *Walden* experiment concerns itself with finding some "real" amidst the surfaces of the world, as his conceit of the "Realometer" reveals:

> Let us settle ourselves, and work and wedge our feet downward through the mud and slush of opinion, and prejudice, and tradition, and delusion, and appearance, that alluvion which covers the globe, through Paris and London, through New York and Boston and Concord, through church and state, through poetry and philosophy and religion, till we come to a hard bottom and rocks in place, which we can call *reality,* and say, This is, and no mistake; and then begin, having a *point d'appui,* below freshet and frost and fire, a place where you might found a wall or a state, or set a lamp-post safely, or perhaps a gauge, not a Nilometer, but a Realometer, that future ages might know how deep a freshet of shams and appearances had gathered from time to time. If you stand right fronting and face to face to a fact, you will see the sun glimmer on both its surfaces, as if it were a cimeter, and feel its sweet edge dividing you through the heart and marrow, and so you will happily conclude your mortal career. Be it life or death, we crave only reality. If we are really dying, let us hear the rattle in our throats and feel cold in the extremities; if we are alive, let us go about our business.[4]

The Realometer allows for the distinguishing of the "hard bottom" of "reality" within the flux of appearance. As Emerson speaks of the imagination penetrating surface, Thoreau's paean to the Realometer invokes penetrative imagery in arguing for the need to "wedge ourselves downward" through the muck of appearances. The worldly surfaces to be tried by the Realometer include opinions, delusions, cities, nations, and even great disciplines ("poetry and philosophy and religion"). Understandings of the world, things of the world, and formalizations of approaches to the world thus must themselves be tried in order to find that point d'appui.[5]

We might more broadly think of *Walden* as an experiment toward finding some Realometer and a provocation to its readers to find their own Realometers. Finding that Realometer demands the testing of the surface of appearances. Commenting on Thoreau's use of the figure of Walden Pond, Stanley Cavell claims that the "human imagination is released by fact. Alone, left to its own devices, it will not recover reality, it will not form an edge."[6] For Cavell, Thoreau's encounter with facts (chronicled in *Walden,* his journals, and other works) provides a mechanism for freeing the imagination. Factual encounters disrupt rote assumptions and provide new avenues for intellectual experiment. The project of the Realometer could be viewed as a vehicle for realizing facts—for testing immediate experience in order to find what it really reveals. Reflection on experience is, after all, a key part of the enterprise of gaining facts. A person anaesthetized on an operating table is not directly aware of the facts of the surgeon's art; a blindfolded person cannot perceive the fact of the painting in front of her. Awareness is a key component of any experience with facticity, and Thoreau means in the enterprise of the Realometer to cultivate that awareness. Frederick Garber alludes to the importance of this factual reflection in his claim that Thoreau's "consciousness runs through a series of interlocking mirrors which takes him from the observation of external nature to the deep recesses of the self and then out again."[7] As Garber's metaphor of "interlocking mirrors" implies, the process of pursuing fact leads to the simultaneous interrogation of the outer world and the inner self; only by pursuing the world is the self observed and vice versa.

While *Walden* is in part the narrative of Thoreau's enterprise of testing, it also means to provoke its readers into hefting a Realometer themselves. The original title page of *Walden* underlines this provocative task: "I do not propose to write an ode to dejection, but to brag as lustily as chanticleer in the morning, standing on his roost, if only to wake my neighbors up." Cavell underlines this provocative element of Thoreau's work, writing that "Thoreau learned from Emerson to make sentences that may attract us by their beauty or their curiosity, and at the same time seem to play with our desire for some transformative understanding."[8] While Cavell emphasizes sentences here, a similar point could apply to Thoreau's work on a broader, structural level: it invokes that enterprise of transformative understanding (which might be taken as a rephrasing of the task of a Realometer). Thoreau's chanticleer cries pull us in (their beauty), but they also provoke us (their curiosity). Not only does Thoreau engage in the performative testing of the surface of appearance; he structures *Walden* to incite its own interrogation on the part of readers. *Walden* combines theoretical discussions, lyrical meditations, punning, and acute physical descriptions in order to go about the dialogical business of locating the self in the world. The trial of surface in pursuit of the "real" affords an opportunity to disrupt the linguistic narratives of our lives. Instead of blithely prattling on about economy or valor or friendliness, we can instead ask, *What constitutes real economy or real valor or real friendship?* The details of the world—chronicled so exactingly in Thoreau's journals and woven into *Walden*—provide an impetus for rethinking our stance in the world.

The Realometer's search for some point d'appui involves the perpetual trial of surface, but insights can present their own surfaces. They might be phrased in a certain way, use certain images, depend on certain assumptions, have certain implications, and so forth. This certain conceptual figuration offers a determinate surface, which itself can be tried for a further vision. Walter Benn Michaels has drawn attention to the way that *Walden* simultaneously invokes and unsettles various hierarchies—"between nature and culture, the finite and the infinite, and . . . literal and figurative language."[9] For Michaels, this troubling of hierarchies reflects the broader way that *Walden* both gives and takes away foundational meanings; we search for "hard bottoms" even as these bottoms might be endlessly deferred. The hierarchy of surface and depth—which Thoreau plays with so much in *Walden*—casts light on that dynamic of both unsettling and finding foundations. Thoreau's discussion of the Realometer insists on finding some depth through the surfaces of the world. This impulse is playfully exemplified in "The Pond in Winter," when Thoreau discusses his effort to try the depths of Walden Pond. Using his skills as a surveyor, Thoreau provides a map of Walden, complete with depths at various points, as part of this chapter. Tellingly, though, this survey of depth requires the solidity of surface. Thoreau endeavors to "recover the long lost bottom of Walden Pond . . . before the ice broke up."[10] The surface of the pond provides a "hard bottom," as it were, for the investigation of depths.

This hardness of surface alludes to the enduring trace of particularity in the tradition of the experiential real. Whitman's project of vista, for instance, includes an insistence on the distinctness of the particular even as that particular is seen in light of some grander, realizing vision. The hardness of the pond's surface insists on the endurance of particular experience even in the enterprise of searching for depths. But a further lesson can be taken from it, too (and this has a bearing on the quest for foundations). For Thoreau's enterprise of testing, there are two points d'appui. Real being might indeed offer an existential one (the foundation for being), but immediate particularity offers an experiential one. *Walden*'s simple tests need continually to be reiterated because experience needs to be continually returned to, and each apprehension of or insight into some deeper reality is itself an experience and needs to be refreshed by a new trial. For Thoreau, the hope of the non-experiential viewing of reality is a fundamentally false one; reality is always glimpsed through the avenues of experience, and therefore each realizing glimpse must itself be continually tested.

The new dawn hoped for in *Walden* will be the everyday really seen. This real seeing keeps an eye on the facts, and the edge of life comes from the tempering exchange between external provocation and internal response. Emerson writes in "Poetry and Imagination" that "the world realizes the mind" (*CW* 8: 10), and Thoreau turns to the world with this hope of realization. Though the precise methods of Thoreau may differ from those of Emerson, the enterprise of *Walden* shares a basic premise with much of Emerson's work: the trial of surface in order to find an awakening real. *Walden* remains—perhaps, to be true to itself, must remain—an experiment. The trial is unending, and experiment yields to experiment as the Realometer tries ever anew the surface of ever-shifting appearance.

Inspired in part by Whitman's project of erotic unity, Hart Crane also inherited some dialect of the various, Whitmanian real as well as this deeper desire to test surface.[11] In defending the aesthetic aims of "For the Marriage of Faustus and Helen" and his poetry as a whole in "General Aims and Theories" (1925), Crane explains that he found himself "really building a bridge between so-called classic experience and the many divergent realities of our seething, confused cosmos of today."[12] Crane contrasts his work with the "impressionistic method":

> The impressionist is interesting as far as he goes—but his goal has been reached when he has succeeded in projecting certain selected factual details into his reader's consciousness. He is really not interested in the *causes* (metaphysical) of his materials, their emotional derivations or their utmost spiritual consequences. A kind of retinal registration is enough, along with a certain psychological stimulation. And this is also true of your realist (of the Zola type), and to a certain extent of the classicist, like Horace, Ovid, Pope, etc.
>
> Blake meant these differences when he wrote:
>
> We are led to believe in a lie
> When we see *with* not *through* the eye.
>
> The impressionist creates only with the eye and for the readiest surface of the consciousness, at least relatively so. If the effect has been harmonious or even stimulating, he can stop there, relinquishing entirely to his audience the problematic synthesis of the details into terms of their own personal consciousness.

It is my hope to go *through* the combined materials of the poem, using our "real" world somewhat as a spring-board, and to give the poem *as a whole* an orbit or predetermined direction of its own.[13]

The antebellum concern with surface persists with Crane, as he distinguishes his work from that of the impressionist school that rests content with the "readiest surface of the consciousness." By invoking the Romantic tradition in Blake, he brings into focus a kind of through-ness ("through" suggesting the role of transparency and mediation). The "real" world's springboard allows for a leap of poetic imagination.[14] By attending to the "*causes* (metaphysical)" of his materials or "their emotional derivations or their utmost spiritual consequences," Crane makes his verse a place for revisionary location.

He elaborates on what he terms the "logic of metaphor" in a 1926 letter to *Poetry* editor Harriet Monroe. Crane argues that poetic imagery need not be entirely rationalistic: "In poetry the *rationale* of metaphor belongs to another order of experience than science, and is not to be limited by a scientific and arbitrary code of relationships either in verbal inflections or concepts."[15] He cites a passage from T. S. Eliot—"Every street lamp that I pass beats like a fatalistic drum"—as exemplifying the workings of this logic of metaphor.[16] According to Crane, understanding this image involves delving into the full range of one's own experiences. Those with a "sufficient series of reflections" can "perceive the relationship between a *drum* and a *street lamp—via* the *unmentioned* throbbing of the heart and nerves in a distraught man which *tacitly* creates the reason and 'logic' of the Eliot metaphor." Understanding this metaphor, then, involves a reflection on the elements of one's experiences in order to think about possible resemblances between a drum and a streetlamp. By encouraging such reflection, poetry can help prompt a "field of added consciousness and increased perceptions."[17]

Crane thus emphasizes the importance of poetry prompting a return to experience. The intricate imagery of his poetry can encourage us to reflect on experience in order to navigate the association of meanings within the verse. In his commentary on "For the Marriage of Faustus and Helen" (one of the progenitors of *The Bridge*), Crane poses the cultivation of a mode of ecstasy as one of his goals for this reimagination of experience. In a letter to Gorham Munson, Crane says that "a kind of rhythm and ecstasy" are a "very real thing" to him. Eliot might ignore "certain spiritual events and possibilities as real and powerful now," but Crane instead seeks to defend their abiding power in the modern age.[18] As he writes in a later letter to Louis Untermeyer, Crane holds that "ecstacy and beauty are as possible to the active imagination now as ever," and the course of "Faustus and Helen" aims to show the real viability of both.[19] The poem "starts out from the quotidian, rises to evocation, ecstasy and statement," fusing both the abstract and the everyday.[20] The poem concludes with a proclamation about the ambition of poetry: "Distinctly praise the years, whose volatile / Blamed bleeding hands extend and thresh the height / The imagination spans beyond despair." As John T. Irwin has noted, reaching hands in this poem can function as a figure of aspiration (for instance, reaching toward the idealized Helen), so these lines might embody a union of the ordinary and spiritual craving.[21] Those "blamed bleeding hands" also allude to mortality, and the passage of years might represent a figure of time. But those figures of mortality could also reach toward the "golden, or the shadow of gold hair." Poetry might, then, demonstrate this profound yearning for some apotheosized beauty. Rendering this craving in verse, however, entails a return to the figures of language, which in turn bear the imprint of experience. Indeed, following the course of this imagery involves reflecting not only on one's everyday experiences but also on one's encounter with Crane's poem. This reflection highlights key poetic details (such as the role of hands) that make these lines comprehensible.

This return to surface entails a continuing trial of the particular. Thoreau's Realometer demands a continued interrogation of the concrete instances of everyday living, and Whitman's project of vista demands the ever-fresh grasping of the particular in a perpetually revised context of vision. Crane's remarks about the importance of seeing through the eye show this abiding concern with the trial of particular surface. Moreover, the enterprise of such a trial of surface is not confined merely to the topics discussed in a work; stylistic strategies (as in Whitman's catalogues) can also prompt this trial of the surface of a literary work itself.

Truly Seen: New Beginnings

A theme in this testing of surface is the continued recovery of the initiatory. So often, antebellum Americans speak of how realization disrupts seeming finalities, transforming what at first seemed self-sufficient and ultimate into just another veil of appearance, so a key part of the quest for realization involves exploring how things (or ideas or phenomenal incidents) can provide beginnings. The emphasis on the initiatory has a broader bearing on the encounter with the particular; by disrupting our habitual modes of thinking, particular encounters can initiate new quests of real interrogation. This quest for new beginnings has implications for literary form. In being a spur for the quest for new beginnings, literary works invite continued openness. They might court openness through semiotic proliferation or the sketching out of various dialectics. Perhaps partly as part of this effort to see openness in particularity, antebellum works often suggest their own incompleteness. Whitman's "Song of Myself," for instance, portrays the poem itself as embodying an ongoing process that rebukes the limits set by pages and marks of ink. Dickinson's poetry applies a different tactic; she instead mines her poetry with various instabilities (through variants, syntactical ambiguities, and so forth), creating poems that suggest openness even in their closure.

Thoreau reveals this idea of testing surface in order to render it initiatory in his discussion of "a thousand simple tests":

> We might try our lives by a thousand simple tests; as, for instance, that the same sun which ripens my beans illumines at once a system of earths like ours. If I had remembered this it would have prevented some mistakes. This was not the light in which I hoed them. The stars are the apexes of what wonderful triangles! What distant and different beings in the various mansions of the universe are contemplating the same one at the same moment! Nature and human life are as various as our several constitutions. Who shall say what prospect life offers to another? Could a greater miracle take place than for us to look through each other's eyes for an instant?[22]

The tests invoked in this discussion involve a return to facts that sets them in a further (realizing) context; the simple test reveals the stakes of a phenomenal instant. The first "simple test" that Thoreau poses here entails the recognition of the sun as not exclusive to the Earth but also shining on other planets. This simple test, then, turns to a figure of the natural world (the light of the sun) and reflects on how this single light shines on a diversity of locations—both the earthly beanfield and the far-off spheres.

The light of the sun helps Thoreau locate connections between his field and other physical entities, but it also becomes a means for him to relate himself to other living things. He reiterates this simple test in exclaiming that the "stars are apexes of what wonderful triangles." As he recognizes that the sun's light is not exclusive to his planet, Thoreau now suggests that the sun itself is not exclusive, that it belongs to a wider celestial type (the star). We move from a plurality of planets to a plurality of stars. The transition to triangles effects a shift from the connections of the natural world to those of the personal. Saying that "distant and different beings in the various mansions of the universe" contemplate "the same [star] at the same moment," Thoreau uses the light of a single star as a way of mediating and uniting the "several constitutions" of nature and human lives. The star's "wonderful" reconciliation of diverse lives leads Thoreau to turn to the "miracle" of "look[ing] through each other's eyes for an instant." The passage shifts from a reflection on physical location to a meditation on human perspective.

Rather than resting content with the warm glow of the sun on his face as he labors in the field, Thoreau pushes at that bright surface to see where it might lead: to other planets, to generalized concepts, and to other people. In following this sunny course, he both reinterprets the sun and re-finds his own position. By the end of this simple test of the sunlight, he views himself in a broader conversation with other entities. This conversation does not leave the sunlight behind, however. Instead, attention to that sunlight is crucial for the process of renewed location.

The concluding lines of the passage offer a further iteration of this testing: "Nature and human life are as various as our several constitutions. Who shall say what prospect life offers to another? Could a greater miracle take place than for us to look through each other's eyes for an instant?" After noting the possibility of connection to others through the stars, Thoreau then turns to an assertion of difference. Our lives are so various that he wonders how difficult it truly would be to see the existential prospects of another. This difficulty complicates the narrative of visionary connection sketched out so far in this passage. As Thoreau continues this testing, he returns to his own distinctness as an individual while recognizing the distinctness of so many other individuals, too.

Cavell speaks of the facts "releasing" the human imagination, and this passage reveals this liberation in multiple senses. Thoreau has been freed from a sense of isolation through this testing, as he finds himself in conversation with various entities around him. Moreover, the sun's beams have been liberated from flatness by becoming pathways to other entities. The dialogue between person and place (and person and person, and person and concept) breaks up static unities in order to render them dynamic. Rhetorically, this passage performs this liberation by continually pushing off from one insight to the next.

For Thoreau, Whitman, and others, the testing of surface can in part be initiatory because it leads to pluralities—that surface can combine multiple (sometimes competing) responses. Whitman's project of vista, for instance, synthesizes both attention to individual difference and a call for continued poetic process. This attention to the possibility within surface does not, however, vitiate attention to the particularity of this surface. Indeed, finding that possibility depends on the attention to particularity. Nathaniel Hawthorne's work can be situated within the tradition of the experiential real, and it models the enterprise of finding multiplicity in surface in a way that does not deny the rootedness of the particular. Hawthorne often implies the precariousness or contingency of these moments of realization.

In Hawthorne's notebooks, the real is intimately connected with the experience of indirection and the crowding of possible meanings. This connection suggests that the process of indirection—found in his romances and tales—can be important for finding some "real" for Hawthorne. At one point in his notebooks, he relates the best way to view a landscape: "The best way to get a vivid impression and feeling of a landscape, is to sit down before it and read, or become otherwise absorbed in thought; for then, when your eyes happen to become attracted to the landscape, you seem to catch Nature at unawares, and see her before she has time to change her aspect. The effect lasts but for a single instant, and passes away almost as soon as you are conscious of it; but it is real, for that moment."[23] The "real" of this vision of nature emphasizes less the actuality of the landscape and more the effect it inspires in the individual viewer. This reality is provisional and experiential: it might pass (*for that moment*), but it maintains an authenticity for the experiencing individual. Implicit in Hawthorne's description of this moment is that it occurs through an instant of indirection. He says we might sit down and read a book or think to ourselves or in some way *not* pay total attention to the landscape, and, then, in the moment of realization, you can catch "a glimpse of the face unveiled, which veils itself from every wilful glance. The mystery is revealed, and after a breath or two, becomes just as much a mystery as before."[24]

A scene elsewhere in the notebooks portrays another moment of recognition, one that emphasizes the importance of pluralities: "I have experienced that a landscape and the sky unfold the deepest beauty in a similar way: not when they are gazed at of set purpose, but when the spectator looks suddenly through a vista, among a crowd of other thoughts."[25] If indirection helps that unfolding of beauty, the bustling "crowd of other thoughts" can become a vehicle for dialogic vision. This sight gained through seeing an object through a vista has resonances with Whitman's project of vista in *Leaves of Grass,* which relies on setting the various figures in a vista in conversation with each other.

This theme of transmuting appearance in order to see something further pervades Hawthorne's work. For instance, in "The Old Manse" (the preface to *Mosses from an Old Manse*), Hawthorne conveys how the transmuting effects of a river at certain times cause "each tree and rock, and every blade of grass . . . however unsightly in reality" to assume "ideal beauty in the reflection."[26] Just as the reflection of the river transforms those material objects, so too can the reflection of the writer transfigure the things of the material world. The river that reveals "ideal beauty" in its reflection is a "symbol" of the "infinite spiritual capacity" of the human. The winding narration of "The Old Manse" leads a geographic survey of the lands around the Old Manse that soon becomes a tour of spiritual cravings and history. Episodes of intellectual archeology dot this preface—from the Revolutionary War to old Native American relics. Just as the narrator describes himself as rummaging through old books in the attic, the preface as a whole searches through the immediate appearances of nature in order to find further significances.[27]

In this description of the transformative effects of the river in the preface to *Mosses,* Hawthorne seems to associate reality with the physical, but, as his notebooks indicate, he can also appeal to a more metaphysical reality. The exact condition of reality plays a crucial role in "The Artist of the Beautiful," a story collected in *Mosses.* This tale relates the efforts of the watchmaker Owen Warland to create some work of surpassing beauty and mystery. Critics have had divergent responses to this work, with some seeing it as a satire of Romantic accounts of the artist while others seeing instead a narrative more sympathetic to Romantic transfiguration.[28] Hawthorne's characteristically complex tone provides some evidence for both approaches. While it may poke fun at some Romantic excesses, the tale might also show some sympathy for the transformative hopes of Owen. Elements of the story might indicate that Hawthorne offers Warland something as a stand-in for Hawthorne himself. For instance, characters use "you" throughout most of the story, but, in a few crucial moments, Owen instead uses "thee" and "thou." One of those moments is early on in the tale, when he reflects on his devotion to Annie Hovenden, his former master's daughter: "Annie—dearest Annie—thou shouldst give firmness to my heart and hand, and not shake them thus; for if I strive to put the very spirit of Beauty into form, and give it motion, it is for thy sake alone."[29] This passage echoes the deliberately archaic phrasing that Hawthorne often used in his letters to Sophia Peabody during their courtship and marriage.[30]

Throughout much of "The Artist of the Beautiful," reality and the real are associated with materiality and the practical. Peter Hovenden, the watchmaker Owen used to be apprenticed to, serves as an antagonist. Early on he contrasts Owen's mystical work with the hard labor of the blacksmith: "I know what it is to work in gold, but give me the worker in iron, after all is said and done. He spends his labor upon a reality." Peter reiterates this point, saying that "it is a good and a wholesome thing to depend upon main strength and reality."[31] The blacksmith, Robert Danforth, stands in counterpoint to Owen throughout much of the tale: where the ethereal Owen bends over minute contraptions, Robert Danforth expends his vast muscular energy on creating practical things. While Robert is beloved within the community, Owen is often alienated from it.

Attempting to create something truly beautiful, Owen suffers numerous disappointments, and the tale narrates his successive experiences of inspiration and frustration. Those moments of inspiration are instants where the "real" begins to rise above the physical. Attending to the wondrous chase of butterflies, Owen gains "bright conceptions, which gleamed through his intellectual world, as the butterflies gleamed through the outward atmosphere, and were real to him for the instant, without the toil, and perplexity, and many disappointments, of attempting to make them visible to the sensual eye."[32] That moment where those conceptions become real to Owen resonates with Hawthorne's description of viewing the landscape in a certain way so that it has a real impact for a moment. Both the landscape's revelation and Owen's witness of "bright conceptions" are fragile and momentary.

The end of the story witnesses a collision of two modes of reality. Annie Hovenden and Robert Danforth have married. Owen visits the couple and meets their new child—"a little personage who had come mysteriously out of the infinite, but with something so sturdy and real in his composition that he seemed moulded out of the densest substance which earth could supply." Owen has brought a creation of his own: a mechanical butterfly, an "ideal butterfly . . . realized in all its perfection."[33] In contrast to the child's dense solidity, the butterfly flies through the air with a "delicate gorgeousness." The butterfly baffles the young family, and Annie asks multiple times, "Is it alive?" In the tale's conclusion, the baby boy crushes the butterfly. Annie cries out in horror, but Owen seems untroubled: "He had caught a far other butterfly than this. When the artist rose high enough to achieve the Beautiful, the symbol by which he made it perceptible to mortal senses became of little value in his eyes, while his spirit possessed itself in the enjoyment of the Reality."[34] The final word of this story inverts the earlier uses of "reality" as material; now, "reality" is some realm of spiritual insight, which at last the artist has been raised to. Even though the baby may destroy the butterfly, that physical reality has not utterly destroyed the claims of metaphysical reality.

"Is it alive?" Annie asks. This question might indicate the vitality of art for Hawthorne, but it also suggests the role of open-endedness. The aesthetic layering of Hawthorne's work—its mottling of tones—creates a venue for interpretative testing, for an ever-reinvigorated return to surface. The butterfly is an apt symbol for this endeavor. As Sheldon Liebman has noted, the butterfly serves as a figure for aesthetic accomplishment and the merging of ideal and real in other Romantic works.[35] The butterfly's fragile flight hints at the role of interpretive subtlety (to avoid rudely forcing a narrative) and imaginative heights. In his review of *Mosses from an Old Manse,* Melville hits on the role of the dynamic chase for Hawthorne and other writers: "In this world of lies, Truth is forced to fly like a sacred white doe in the woodlands; and only by cunning glimpses will she reveal herself."[36]

This layering of meaning can also be seen in Hawthorne's longer romances, which present that crowd of thoughts as an opportunity for further revelations. Hawthorne's work has long been known for its use of indirection and ambiguity. In his landmark *Symbolism and American Literature,* Charles Feidelson offers the cultivated ambiguity of Hawthorne and others as anticipating elements of literary modernity. Critics have highlighted other philosophical and political elements of this ambiguity. Drawing from epistemological developments in the nineteenth century, Zachary Turpin finds that Hawthorne offers an "unreliabilist" account of human knowledge (simultaneously engaging in "truth-blurring" and insisting that truth "may still be found").[37] Sacvan Bercovitch has taken this ambiguity to be representative of the tactics of liberalism to enforce a kind of intellectual coercion by a studied preclusion of choice. In an extended reading of the stakes of ambiguity for Hawthorne, Bercovitch finds that Hawthorne's call to perpetual interpretation can ultimately become a mode of confinement. As Bercovitch writes, "To make choices . . . requires us to reject or exclude on the ground that certain meanings are wrong or incompatible or mutually contradictory."[38] Choice requires the rejection of other options, and Hawthorne's deferral of choice in the name of radical ambiguity is ultimately to foreclose that ability to make choices.

However, that cultivation of pluralities might also be read less as a vehicle for nullifying choice and more as a way of granting life to the surface of the text. The proliferation of senses, images, and figures within Hawthorne's stories and romances generates a cloud of resonances. These resonances create a soft haze around any particular figure because the precise meaning of this figure depends on so many shifting variables, and, in instants of clarity, that haze might suddenly fade for a glimpse of something real. However, the profoundness of that clarity depends on the conditions that have created that haze: the endlessly recursive calibration of images.

At the end of *The Scarlet Letter,* Hawthorne writes that Hester Prynne decides to stay in New England: "There was a more real life for Hester Prynne, here, in New England, than in that unknown region where Pearl had found a home. Here had been her sin; here, her sorrow; and here was yet to be her penitence. She had returned, therefore, and resumed,—of her own free will, for not the sternest magistrate of that iron period would have imposed it,—resumed the symbol of which we have related so dark a tale."[39] Bercovitch might read this moment as a sign of her submission to the confines of Puritan society—an instance of how *The Scarlet Letter* "is the story of a stranger who rejoins the community by compromising for principle."[40] And yet the motivation for staying in Puritan New England can be precisely traced to what for her is real, and this sense of the real depends on the particular life of Prynne. "Real life" remains in that place where her sin, sorrow, and penitence reside. Prynne's personal experiences have created a web of associations and meanings that give her life in New England certain emotional and spiritual stakes. Those particular encounters are just what make it possible to find "real life" on the margins of Puritan society. Becovitch notes that making choices requires exclusion, and here Prynne makes the choice to stay in her community, with all the tensions and possibilities embedded in this choice. Even as *The Scarlet Letter* defers insisting on certain set meanings, it also closes on a note of choosing. Prynne chooses *a* society, for all the pluralities inherent in it. The pluralism within a given society may reflect the pluralism within a given text: Hawthorne's subjunctive allegories offer certain contours of possibility. Yet, for all that pluralism, it is also particular. (Only some contours, however vast, are available.)[41]

In a letter to his wife, Sophia, Hawthorne writes of a wish for "something in the intellectual world analogous to the Daguerreotype . . . in the visible—something which should print off our deepest, and subtlest, and delicatest thoughts and feelings as minutely and accurately as the above-mentioned instrument paints the various aspects of Nature."[42] Here, as in his earlier notebook entry about viewing a landscape, Hawthorne invokes the language of delicacy. With the tenderness of butterflies, these various interpretive possibilities light on a given figure, which bears the fantastic weight of all those elusive and contrasting meanings. Hawthorne outlines various interpretations of a figure only to demand that we examine the surface of these interpretations, and part of this examination occurs through putting these surfaces into dialogue with each other. As Thoreau uses the resistance of ice to plumb the depths of Walden Pond, Hawthorne depends on the particular contours of given narrative interpretations even as he suggests the precariousness of such contours.

Melville, too, offers a challenge to surface through a proliferation of meanings, a tactic exemplified in *Moby-Dick.* The white whale in part embodies a sublime and alienating collision of meanings beneath a single surface, and the novel as a whole interrogates surfaces—of language, skin, psyche, literary tradition, and more. The very opening "Etymology" section of the novel offers a listing of the surfaces of language—from Hebrew to Danish to Fijian—of "whale." The figure of the whale is at once refracted through numerous linguistic traditions and made a sublime figure that reaches out dazzlingly past them. The surface of a word is insinuated as partial and thereby in need of further trial. Melville emphasizes this partiality by offering two competing narratives of the development of "whale":

> "WHALE. *** Sw. and Dan. *hval.* This animal is named from roundness or rolling; for in Dan. *hvalt* is arched or vaulted."
>
> *Webster's Dictionary.*

> "WHALE*** It is more immediately from the Dut. and Ger. *Wallen;* A.S. *Walw-ian,* to roll, to wallow."
>
> *Richardson's Dictionary.*[43]

These two narratives might not be entirely contradictory (both, for instance, appeal to rolling), but they suggest somewhat different paths of descent for "whale"—from Swedish and Danish or from Dutch and German, from *hval* or *Wallen.* Granted, there is an overlap between these languages, but the etymological paths differ. This multifaceted derivation of "whale" enters into a dialogue with the listing of words for "whale" in other languages; just as that English "whale" is complicated by history, so too might other words for "whale" also have their own complex histories.

The opening "Etymology" section thus provides the first lesson in reading *Moby-Dick:* the seeming of an immediate surface can reveal hidden complexities. The succeeding "Extracts" section, in providing a "glancing bird's eye view" of the figure of the whale, continues this narrative of surface complication.[44] The sundry extracts pile up in a prismatic tower of meaning. Minute aspects of the whale—as a religious, cultural, literary, social, anatomical (etc.) figure—march before the reader. Especially upon rereading, these fragments call out to each other. The listing of quotations stresses each fragment's incompleteness and its partaking of a vaster dialogue. The two following extracts offer one example of this complication:

> "And pray, sir, what in the world is equal to it?"
>
> *Edmund Burke's reference in Parliament to the Nantucket Whale-Fishery.*

> "Spain—a great whale stranded on the shores of Europe."
>
> *Edmund Burke. (somewhere.)*[45]

Both quotations come from the work of British philosopher-statesman-aesthetician Edmund Burke, yet how different is the "whale" in each of these extracts! According to Melville, the first references something of actual magnitude (the Nantucket whale-fishery), but the second uses "whale" as a metaphor. Politics further complicates this toggling between actual and metaphorical. The first quotation refers to something that is distinctively of the

New World (and is drawn from a parliamentary address calling for conciliation with the American colonies), while the second refers to something that, for nineteenth-century Americans, would be quintessentially Old World (the monarchical, Catholic Spain contrasting with the United States' Protestant republicanism). The dialogue between these two extracts thus offers an international exchange invoking metaphor, empire, modernity, and transatlantic cultural connections. Extract adds to extract, fueling an exponential growth of resonances. By setting the extracts into conversation, Melville hints at the vast depths of possibility within any surface. The whale as a figure is complicated by this compendious array of quotations, and each of these quotations is itself complicated by its dialogue with others. United, the extracts form a web of seemingly infinite variety, which comes under the aegis of the "whale," which organizes these fragments even as it is disrupted by them.

An interrogation of surface, then, offers many opportunities for the reorientation of experience—from beanfields to butterflies, from whales to landscapes. This return to surface allows for the realization of complexity and for the finding of new beginnings. The inspection of what seems can help awaken us to the tensions and possibilities within experience. As Hawthorne's work in particular suggests, that freeing return to surface need not lead to the nullification of particularity: it is within those particular contours of a particular vista that realization occurs.

Reality and Reading

This recasting of particularity highlights one way in which the act of reading can offer a return to experience. In the early nineteenth century, some literary critics (particularly those influenced by the Scottish Common Sense school) held that literature could be a distraction from reality. In part because of the materialist resonances of the "real," popular discourse today often expresses a lingering suspicion regarding the "reality" of literature. It might pass as ivory-tower entertainment, but it otherwise distracts from reality. This assumption obviously has major implications for contemporary debates about education. The purportedly false glamour of literature is contrasted to the hard facts of the physical sciences; the former entertains us, while the latter acquaints us with real facts (and supposedly swells our bank accounts).

Theories of the real for nineteenth-century Americans often involved an appeal to something beyond the physical. What this *something* was could very much be up for debate—whether God or the oversoul or passion or something else. This appeal to some deeper reality partakes of a broader tradition (ranging from Platonism to some traditions of modern-day theism) that locates the foundation of being in something beyond the world of atoms and quarks. In addition to those certain substantive commitments, the "real" has also long been associated with a broader effort to try the immediate presentation of experience (that is, appearance). The quest for the "real" in this sense trial involves the continued return to—and interrogation of—appearance. Appearing and being—the two poles of the line walked by the "real"—remain in an unrelenting dialectic within our experience. What is to us always appears, yet what seems to a given individual is not the sum total of what is. Our experiential encounters with appearance always remind us of its insufficiency, of its openness to challenge, but these encounters also imply its necessity.

The encounter with literature can be one device for this testing. The works of writers in this study prompt us toward such an interrogation of appearance. Emerson, Whitman, Thoreau, and others make clear that one of their aims is to urge us in the direction of "reality," wherever it leads. Later American writers echo this point. In his 1923 verse manifesto *Spring and All,* William Carlos Williams writes, "Imagination is not to avoid reality." Instead, imagination "affirms reality most powerfully."[46] It is not the mere replication of details of the physical world that gives a piece of writing reality. Williams offers a fragmentary discussion of true reality for writing:

> When in the condition of imaginative suspense only will the writing have reality, as explained partially in what precedes—Not to attempt, at that time, to set values on the word being used, according to presupposed measures, but to write down that which happens at that time—
>
> To perfect the ability to record at the moment when the consciousness is enlarged by the sympathies and the unity of understanding which the imagination gives, to practice skill in recording the force moving, then to know it, in the largeness of its proportions—
>
> It is the presence of a
>
> This is not "fit" but a unification of experience[47]

This "condition of imaginative suspense" suggests a vision for the imaginative powers—at their highest pitch—as embodying a tension, in which a variety of competing faculties and perspectives are suspended in a single moment. Williams's sentences themselves perform this suspense, as they at once offer an accumulation of meaning (in the succession of infinitives, for example) and suggest a kind of leaping, fragmentary allusion to other, broader meanings. By this reckoning, the reality of a work of writing depends on some further integration of experience, even if this integration may suggest broader or implicit tensions.

The formal particularity of a work of literature affords a device for interrogating the incidents of experience. Instead of nullifying our concrete experiences, such visionary aspirations toward the real enliven the concrete through nurturing our capacity to reflect. This reflection allows us to find the possibilities of a given concrete instance, to set one occurrence into dialogue with others, and to explore the complexities of our own responses to various events.

Far from a distraction from reality, then, literature can serve as a device to help us realize. It could do so in a number of possible ways. It could help organize appearances into some broader (and potentially provisional) account of reality. It can prompt us to understand the things of the world in a new sense. It can help us challenge our assumptions—to see our premises about human experience with a new, disruptive granularity. As the strategies of Emerson, Whitman, and Dickinson exemplify, reading literature is itself an experience and the place of literature can become a venue for existential trial. The provocation of the literary act can itself be a way of encouraging us to find in experiences new beginnings—to reorient our standard concepts of life and to interrogate them anew. To return to Branka Arsić's distinction between the totalizing gaze and disrupting glance and Elisa New's opposing of the transparent-tending visionary to sight's focus on the incidents of immediate experience: this narrative of the dialogic real suggests a kind of sight that combines the visionary and the seen, or the disruptive possibilities of the glance with the affirming reach of a nondemeaning gaze. Perhaps we can note the green pastures while also keeping an eye toward the Promised Land. Maybe the enterprise of maintaining visionary aspirations and disruptive attention to the everyday is trying to have one's cake and eat it, too. But it might also reflect the deeper complexity of our human condition—that we make our way through both gazing and glancing. The experiential real suggests the possibility of a union of (rather than a war between) visionary aspiration and attention to the heterogeneity of experience.

Emerson's essay "Experience," that great trial of ideas, offers one demonstration of that dialectic between visionary impulses and experiential encounters. In successive stages, it seems to operate under the aegis of various "lords of life"—"Illusion, Temperament, Succession, Surface, Surprise, Reality, Subjectiveness" (*CW* 3: 47). Yet the course of the essay as a whole complicates this narrative taxonomy. In describing the effects of each "lord of life," the essay invokes other lords.[48] For instance, "Dream delivers us to dream, and there is no end to illusion. Life is a train of moods like a string of beads, and as we pass through them they prove to be many-colored lenses which paint the world their own hue, and each shows only what lies in its focus" (*CW* 3: 30). These sentences open the "Temperament" section, but they also use figures of illusion ("no end to illusion"), succession (the string of beads), and perhaps surface (those "many-colored lenses"). The brutal description of Waldo's death earlier in this essay might occur under the aegis of "Illusion," but the passage as a whole fixates on the isolating power of Emersonian subjectivity—the absolute removal of that self from the death of a beloved son. This scene laments the "evanescence and lubricity of all objects," which seems a figure of succession—their slipperiness continually initiates succession. And the description of death includes the devout hope for some encounter with a "reality that will not dodge us" (*CW* 3: 29). These grand, visionary "lords of life" afford a vehicle for making life comprehensible, but explicating individual precise moments (of both the text and life itself) complicates the visionary imperium of each lord—revealing its dependence on, and involvement in, others.

"I am a fragment," Emerson writes, "and this is a fragment of me" (*CW* 3: 47). Fragments of experience can cause swerves that disrupt ascendant vision, but these fragments can also reveal a broader order within them. The fragments of "Experience" (and experience) simultaneously stand in counterpoint to each other and reveal internal conceptual affinities. The course of this essay affirms the distinctive elements of particular moments while also finding that broader conceptual themes (those "lords of life") make such particularity articulate. "Life wears to me a visionary face," Emerson writes near the end of the essay, and the trials of "Experience" can at once check visionary schemes while also prompting new paths of sight. So "the world I converse with in the city and in the farms, is not the world I *think*" (*CW* 3: 48). That "discrepancy" between the two can inspire instants of despair, since such a discrepancy suggests the resistance of the material to ideological transformations and pat visionary narratives. But such a discrepancy also holds out the possibilities of revised understandings—that our worldly encounters can in turn prompt new understandings, that the marbled texture of experience has new riches for us.

Whitman's "Song of Myself" offers an extended demonstration of the attempt to inspect the texture of experience, returning to existential instants while also seeking to see them in a broader panorama. The speaker of the poem makes clear how disruptive those singular moments of experience can be. In section 26 of the "deathbed" version of "Song of Myself," the speaker underlines a turn toward receptivity: "Now I will do nothing but listen" (582).[49] So he listens and chronicles what he hears, as well as the stakes of it—a steam-whistle, the chatter of young people, the swelling song of a soprano. The speaker is transfigured by this "orchestra" (maybe a physical orchestra, maybe the orchestra of existence): "It sails me, I dab with bare feet, they are lick'd by the indolent waves, / I am cut by bitter and angry hail, I lose my breath" (606–7). In saying he seeks "to feel the puzzle of puzzles, / And that we call Being" (609–10), the speaker turns to the experience of touch. Touch, like sight, proves incredibly disruptive. "Is this then a touch?" the speaker asks, "quivering me to a new identity" (619). In one of the most erotically charged portions of "Song of Myself," the poem portrays the experience of touch as an existential wrestling match, with sudden reversals and frantic struggles. The speaker talks of so many "provokers . . . unbuttoning my clothes, holding me by the bare waist" (623–27). He is both exhausted and exhilarated, and the carnival of touch leads to moments that strain his internal coherence:

> I am given up by traitors,
> I talk wildly, I have lost my wits, I and nobody else am the greatest traitor,
> I went there myself first to the headland, my own hands carried me there.
> You villain touch! what are you doing? my breath is tight in its throat,
> Unclench your floodgates, you are too much for me. (637–41)

The bewildering nature of this touch speaks to the ability of sensuous encounters to set us askew. The texture of experience contains worlds within, and the return to that texture can strain our settled apprehensions.

Dickinson alludes to this disruptive strain of experience in "The Brain, within it's Groove":

The Brain, within it's Groove
Runs evenly—and true—
But let a Splinter swerve—
'Twere easier for You—

To put a Current back—
When Floods have slit the Hills—
And scooped a Turnpike for Themselves—
And trodden out the Mills— (Fr563)

That single "Splinter swerve" of experience—whether a moment of insight, a friend's stray remark, or an instantaneous meeting—can break the conventional cognitive habits of our lives. The second stanza of this poem suggests how disruptive such a flood might be, and this poem is in part informed by that tension between the seeming smallness of the splinter (that apparent tininess of a moment of experience) and the radical transformations it can birth.[50]

Works of literature thus discuss and enact how the grain of experience might disrupt our ingrained theoretical narratives. Moreover, the encounter with a work of literature can itself be a vehicle for this dialogue between the quotidian and the visionary. A poem, for instance, can highlight a single, experiential moment and attempt to perform such a moment through the incidents of language, as when Dickinson portrays the strain of trying to realize the sublime. In its performance, a work of literature draws us back to the surface of experience in order to understand both its textures and its depths. This enterprise of realization demands a continued return to the incidents of daily living. The textures of life can serve as a crucial pathway for realizing interrogation, and really paying attention to them disrupts our own glib assumptions. Whitman's example in particular shows that the finding of vista in others need not be an enterprise of degrading instrumentality, in which the other is viewed simply as a vehicle for self-expression. This witnessing of other vistas can be the effort to recognize that other in the fullest extent of his or her humanity. The continued trial of surface ensures that we return to surface again and again.

Surface also has a bearing on questions of reading. In an influential essay Stephen Best and Sharon Marcus outline a distinction between "symptomatic reading" (which seeks to see in texts the symptoms of broader systems or ideologies) and "surface reading" (which seeks to explore the surface of a text). As they phrase it, "A surface is what insists on being looked *at* rather than what we must train ourselves to see *through*."[51] This claim about the importance of surface inspection reflects elements of the broader experiential turn called for by Rita Felski and others, and the narrative of the "real" explored in these pages suggests the possible alliance of *at* and *through:* the enterprise of *seeing through* demands the continued effort of *looking at.* The experiential real demands the continued return to particularity and the textures of experience even as it emphasizes the importance of interrogating them in the hopes of some further (realer) insight.

The tradition of the experiential real attends to the way that the encounter with a work of literature can heighten—not distract from—our appreciation of experience, and attention to the experience of reading might in turn afford a lens for looking at the critical stakes of reading. This dialogue between glance and gaze has also influenced contemporary academic debates about literary reading. One of the promises of various theoretical accounts of reading—whether Freudian, Marxist, feminist, or so forth—has been to show what is *really* going on in a text: its privileging of certain economic, gender, or class interests, for example. New Historicism offered the hope of seeing through a text in order to view it in conversation with various historical trends.[52] Just as various metaphysical accounts of being provide a way of contextualizing the phenomena of experience, a given theoretical approach affords a vehicle for organizing the various phenomenological incidents of a text.

That theoretical gaze can have sometimes an anxious—and sometimes a productive—relation to the experiential act of reading. Pragmatic, experiential accounts of reading often emphasize literary criticism as open-ended and wide-ranging. Eve Kosofsky Sedgwick's call for "reparative reading" emphasizes the ability of reading to surprise and thereby disrupt those theoretical assumptions we might hold prior to encountering a text. Robert Pippin's discussion of "naive reading" contrasts modes of reading that seek to discipline a literary text within some specific theoretical context with a more open-ended mode of reading that allows one to "remain engrossed in the richness of . . . interpretive possibilities."[53] In recent years, Felski's model of "postcritical reading" has become an influential instance of this broader, experientially inflected approach to reading. Fearing that a hermeneutics of suspicion have artificially limited scholarly interpretation, Felski seeks to develop modes of reading that recognize and affirm the range of reasons why we read: "aesthetic pleasure, increased self-understanding, moral reflection, perceptual reinvigoration, ecstatic self-loss, emotional consolation, or heightened sensation—to name just a few."[54] While Felski does not deny the legitimacy of using modes of critique in analyzing literature, she doubts that critique is entirely sufficient as a critical mode.

Stephen Best has suggested that literary criticism "thrives on the distinction between first and second reading, on what is often parsed as absorptive reading versus critical reading, belletristic versus analytic readings." He frames Felski's project as one that seeks a mode of "literary criticism that accounts for rather than dismisses the absorptive aspects of first reading."[55] From an experiential perspective, there are many reasons why critics should *not* dismiss the role of the "absorptive." The intense—at times, far-ranging—encounter with the literary work can give us resources for that project of analysis. The wide experiential spectrum that Felski invokes as part of reading can serve to invigorate and enrich various critical projects. In resisting predetermined critical narratives, the open-ended encounter with and reflection upon a literary work holds out the possibilities of new insights and understandings. Absorptive attention to the textures of a literary work—that "naive" immersion in its details—is a key mode of literary experience and provides new vistas for critical analysis.

Just as it is possible to reconcile the seeing-through gaze with the looking-at glance, critical theory and the disruptive encounter of actual reading can also reinforce each other. Many pragmatic accounts of reading stress the importance of newness and possibility for reading. Sedgwick's narrative of "reparative reading" especially foregrounds this emphasis on the new; one of the benefits of such a reparative encounter with a text is that it has the possibility for surprise. This emphasis on the initiatory in reading—that quest for new readerly beginnings—has parallels with the emphasis on the initiatory found within the tradition of the experiential real. For both pragmatic reading and the experiential real, attention to surface (whether of a poem or a pond) can afford a new beginning of understanding.

Theoretical narratives of a literary work are themselves traced-out possibilities of interpretation, and, just as literature's traced-out possibilities can allow for the enrichment of individual life,[56] so too can a theoretical account of a literary work allow for an enriched understanding of that work. A model of postcritical reading need not be incompatible with the enterprise of theoretical reading—but synthesizing the two requires a double vision. It requires attention both to the disruptive traits of experience and to the purchase that can be gained through that theoretical analysis. Sedgwick has emphasized the importance of surprise for reparative reading, and applying a theoretical concept too rigorously to a work can indeed be reductive and foreclose all possibility of surprise. But that theoretical application can itself also offer surprise. Part of the reason why Theory (with a capital "T") became so influential in the academy in the later portion of the twentieth century was because these diverse theoretical accounts were able to cast light on literary works—on their assumptions, mechanics, contexts, and so forth. Intellectual principles afford one way of making experience articulate, so it should not be too surprising to see such principles be applied to the experience of reading. Moreover, many theoretical critical narratives themselves relied on the close engagement with the details of a text.[57]

Felski has made clear that eliminating all modes of theory is not the aim of postcritical reading; instead, she wishes to supplement these modes with a more capacious approach to literature. More broadly, an experiential account of literature need not call for the ultimate rejection of theory. Instead, it offers a nagging reminder that a given theoretical account is not ultimate—that it can always be refreshed by a return to the details of reading. This seeming irreducibility of literary experience to literary theory may frustrate, but it also liberates, suggesting some richness of life that transcends our surfaces of discursive thinking. Theory can still give us eyes to see—to contemplate and apprehend the world around us—and, though that vision is partial, it is also necessary and potentially delightful. Our experience of reading necessarily involves broader principles, even if that experience might escape reduction to a few totalizing categories and might even complicate these categories.

Reading is in part the coordination of attention. The reader notes symbols, imagery, implications, rhymes, and so forth. In this process the reader begins to calibrate the intellectual and sensual resonances of a work. This calibration is always itself a process and thereby always open to revision.

Theoretical constructs afford one way of organizing these impressions, but these constructs will often fail to account for the whole complexity of the work. (What makes a theoretical construct viable for a work might be less whether it can account for every aspect of the whole of that work and more whether it can account for some aspects.) Literary criticism uses theoretical tools to survey a work of literature, but the actual act of reading often suggests the insufficiency of these tools; other approaches could be taken in addition to the favored mode of a given critic. For the lover of literature (to use erotic language), the experience of the literary work evades in some way even the most complicated theoretical mechanism: the experience of reading of an Emerson essay is very different from even the best reading of an Emerson essay.

The literary factors that cause the insufficiency of any theoretical account also suggest literature's resistance to computational models. Even if one were to create with the most advanced supercomputer a matrix of terms and conceptual variants of these terms (typifying each symbol, each literary aspect, each shading of syntax, etc.) as a way of apprehending a work, this matrix would still fall short of the richness of the individual reading of the work, nor would it contain all possible meaningful variants of understanding for this text.[58] The techniques of quantification and organization inherent in computational models of literature suggest the incompleteness of these models. The items we quantify and the patterns we chart in part depend on our immediate encounter with the text in all its complexity. It is for this reason that any project of "distant reading" (whether this distance is theory or computation) continually needs to be complemented by the act of close reading (that is, the sustained, multivariate attention to a text).

The experiential real offers one narrative of a renewing return to particularity, which has implications for literature as well as the act of literary reading. This tradition highlights the importance of testing appearance and finds that literature can be a vehicle for this testing. This mode of provocation is not simply about memorizing a set of principles; instead, it involves a willingness to enter into a dialogue with a work, to reflect on images and principles, to cultivate responses (emotional and otherwise), and to dwell on the implications of those responses. An Emerson essay offers a labyrinth of resonances that can help transform our understanding of that essay as well as the broader panorama of life. A Dickinson poem reveals the polarities within a moment of experience. The chanticleer warblings of *Walden* prompt an awakening to the textures of our lives. These works urge in the direction of new beginnings, and the act of literary reading can in part be the cultivation of beginnings. The realizing vision sets the particulars of life within some greater perspective, and our encounter with particulars—in and beyond literary texts—at once nurtures and disrupts visionary schemes. The act of reading can awaken us to what waits for us somewhere in the world of experience.

Notes

Introduction

1. H., "Poetry No Fiction," 266. The book's opening epigraphs come from Emerson, *Journals and Miscellaneous Notebooks,* 5: 9, and Shakespeare, *Love's Labour's Lost,* 1.1.1–7.

2. Whitman, *Uncollected Poetry and Prose,* 2: 70, and Emerson, *Collected Works,* 8: 10. Future references taken from *The Collected Works of Ralph Waldo Emerson* will be parenthetically cited in the main body of the text as *CW,* followed by volume number and page number[s].

3. Shortly after the Civil War, American Realists laid claim to the "real" along with a constellation of affiliated concepts: the ordinary, the everyday, the concrete, and the factual. In this book I will use "Realism" (with a capital R) to denote the post–Civil War literary movement. The following are some sources that have been helpful to me in thinking about Realism: Shi, *Facing Facts,* offers an instructive survey of many of the trends of Realist writing in America, which Berthoff, *Ferment of Realism,* and Fishkin, *From Fact to Fiction,* complement. Both Stovall, *American Idealism,* and Menand, *Metaphysical Club,* explore some of the intellectual implications underlying the development of Realism later in the nineteenth century in America. At least since Jane P. Tompkins's *Sensational Designs* and Amy Kaplan's *Social Construction of American Realism,* scholars have shown considerable interest in the role of broader social structures and topics for shaping Realism. As Andrew Lawson suggests in *Downwardly Mobile,* the rise of Realism can also be connected with various social forces (in Lawson's case, economic unrest), and in *Telegraphic Realism* Menke examines how "Realism" as a genre connects with broader developments in the technology of knowledge and communication. Mark Goble's *Beautiful Circuits* continues this exposition of the technological, mediated implications of Realism. Jennifer Fleissner's *Women, Compulsion, and Modernity* examines the role of industrializing modernization and gender narratives for the development of fiction in the later part of the nineteenth century. Marshall Brown, "Logic of Realism," explores some of the broader philosophical-stylistic effects that might link together various

forms of realism. Bell, *Problem of American Realism,* examines some of the literary and cultural difficulties of defining Realism.

4. However, there is a chance that this "alternative tradition" could itself be composed of various, distinct tendencies. Moreover, this alternative tradition has some possible resonances with the conventions of a more actualistic or material real. We might contrast these two traditions (experiential and material) as having different patterns of emphasis rather than being absolute polarities. One of the reasons why I use the term "tradition" in defining these senses of the "real" is because "tradition" carries with it senses of looser association rather than apodictic schematics.

5. This is not the only mode of typology, but it did influence Puritan writing. For instance, John Winthrop in his journal recounts the appearance of a snake at a sermon, which is then killed. Through this figure of the snake, God "discovered somewhat of his mind": the new Puritan commonwealth would face various dangers, but faith would triumph (see Winthrop, *Journal,* 2: 347–48).

6. Pizer, *Documents of American Realism and Naturalism,* 3.

7. Tompkins, *Sensational Designs,* 159.

8. Bell, *Problem of American Realism,* 8.

9. Glazener, *Literature in the Making,* 161.

10. Renker, *Realist Poetics,* 4.

11. Matthiessen, *American Renaissance,* 105–6.

12. Howe, *Making the American Self,* 203.

13. Packer, *Emerson's Fall,* 159–60.

14. Tompkins, *Sensational Designs,* 152.

15. Renker, *Realist Poetics,* 6.

16. *Realist Poetics in American Culture, 1866–1900* is the culmination of Renker's revelatory work on this topic.

17. As Emerson proclaims in the kenotic apotheosis of the transparent eyeball, "I am the lover of uncontained and immortal beauty" (*CW* 1: 10).

18. Philip Rahv's dualism of "paleface" and "redskin," for instance, seems informed by this presumption. Rahv argues that the palefaces who dominated in the nineteenth century tend "toward a refined estrangement from reality" and created artistic works that "remain abstract for the reason that they fall short on evidence drawn from the material and sensuous world" ("Paleface and Redskin," 252–53). While the redskin remains intimately involved with the conditions of the everyday from Rahv's perspective, the paleface (and this essay seems to count Emily Dickinson, Nathaniel Hawthorne, and Herman Melville among the palefaces) abstracts from reality in some pursuit of transcendence. Emerson is not mentioned, but he would seem to be part of that "thin, solemn, semi-clerical culture of Boston and Concord" that Rahv identifies as the seat of paleface-dom (251). Rahv seems to identify Whitman as belonging with the redskins. Rahv's dichotomy might not be without its infelicities, but some critics have found some persistent relevance in his work. See, for example, Pinsker, "Philip Rahv's 'Paleface and Redskin.'"

19. New, *The Line's Eye,* 9.

20. New, *The Line's Eye,* 15.
21. New, *The Line's Eye,* 9.
22. New, *The Line's Eye,* 15.
23. Arsić, *On Leaving,* 71.
24. Arsić, *On Leaving,* 72.
25. New, *The Line's Eye,* 10.
26. Lee Rust Brown, *The Emerson Museum,* 46.
27. "Silhouetting"—a term proposed by Marshall Brown for interpreting later nineteenth-century Realism—illuminates some of the stakes of this model of transparency. The discourse of transparency is obviously somewhat removed from that of the silhouette (which is often *not* transparent), but both metaphors reveal some dialectic between fore and ground. Brown bases realism on a "silhouetting effect," where "dramatic action emerges from a static background that gives it context and representative significance" ("Logic of Realism," 231). As Brown explains, "We consider a piece of writing to be realistic . . . whenever and insofar as we perceive ordered silhouetting or embedding effects" (238). I might adapt Brown's language of silhouetting to emphasize the way that the experiential real often makes use of play between fore and ground. Something is called "real" when it is viewed as connected to a greater account of being (which acts as a "background" for the viewing of this particular). How it is connected will vary depending on the details of the particular and one's greater account of reality, but many uses of the real operate in relation to some (perhaps implicit) background of being. For instance, one might call a soul "real" when it is seen in the context of some reality that includes the existence of metaphysical personhood. One might call a mirage "unreal" in the context of a sense of a reality that includes physical atoms—and not perceptual figments of the brain. Adding another dialectical layer is the fact that one's own particular encounters might also revise one's understanding of the greater account of reality. For instance, a young child might not think that physical reality included a place of perpetual cold and snow until he saw a picture of Antarctica.
28. Cady, *Light of Common Day,* 5.
29. Cady, *Light of Common Day,* 20.
30. Disruption has long been a topic of interest for Americanists, though it has rarely been located in the context of the real. Stanley Cavell's path-breaking work on Emerson and Thoreau draws attention to the role of what he terms "aversive thinking," one suggesting both a personal and a political nonconformity; throughout his collected essays on Emerson, Cavell notes the disruptive qualities of Emerson. The broader aversive tradition in Emerson—explored in chapter 2—is heavily invested in the question of disruption. The fact that a major collection on Whitman in the 1990s should be titled *Breaking Bounds* also suggests the importance of disruption for Whitman studies. We might find a similar interest in explorations of personal disruption in Dickinson. Cameron's work in *Lyric Time* and *Choosing Not Choosing* explores some of the possibilities of disruption in Dickinson, as does Gary Stonum's *The Dickinson Sublime.*

31. For example, Stanley Cavell's pioneering readings in Emerson—collected in *Emerson's Transcendental Etudes*—depend on the interpretation of literary form and the exposition of the philosophical implications of the details of literary form. The qualities of literary and philosophical provisionality emphasized by Cavell have had a large influence on later readings of Emerson. Sharon Cameron's reading in "impersonality" in Emerson depends on the methodology of abandonment in his works, partially gleaned through attention to literary textures; see *Impersonality*. Branka Arsić's *On Leaving* builds on this morphology of abandonment precisely through an attention to the performance of Emerson's prose and a theoretical explication of the implications of this formal performance. Nor is this formalist revival limited to Emerson. Helen Vendler's much-praised *Dickinson* also spends a considerable amount of time engaged in the formal analysis of Dickinson's work, and Cristanne Miller's *Reading in Time* offers a historically informed reading of the formal qualities of Dickinson's verse. As Theo Davis aptly notes, many politically informed narratives of American literature make use of the tactics of close reading; see *Formalism, Experience*, 17–19.

32. As Moretti writes in "More Conjectures," "We have a lot to learn from the methods of the social and of the natural sciences" (*Distant Reading*, 118).

33. Moretti's *Distant Reading* offers a helpful survey of his thoughts on distant reading, of which *Graphs, Maps, and Trees* offers an early iteration. Earhart and Jewell's *American Literature Scholar in the Digital Age* considers some of the strategies of digital humanities for Americanists and their theoretical implications. Brian Connolly raises doubts about some of the assumptions of computational analysis in "Against Accumulation." The March 2000 special issue of *MLQ* ("Reading for Form") has an intriguing range of perspectives on the enterprise of (close) reading.

34. See Moretti, *Distant Reading*, 71–85.

35. The enterprise of counting clues in fiction might not be considered as the most distant of distant readings (it only relies on a survey of about twenty stories), but it still moves in the direction of distance and computational analysis (albeit an analysis aided by human readers).

36. However, the value of literary criticism is not only as a propaedeutic to computational analysis. While such analysis does raise interesting points, it seems to serve more as a complement to—rather than Darwinian successor of—the practice of meditating on a work and its details in depth.

37. Sedgwick, "Paranoid Reading and Reparative Reading," 146.

38. Matthew Flaherty has suggested that postcritical reading currently lacks "a canon—a tradition of texts distinctly amenable to promoting the attitudes of reflective evaluation championed by scholars in the recent phenomenological turn" ("Expressive Realism," 140). He has offered selected nineteenth-century realist novelists (such as Jane Austen, George Eliot, and Henry James) as potential candidates for a postcritical "canon" centered around "expressive realism." It seems to me that a vast range of texts might be amenable to this enterprise of "reflective evaluation," and the poetry explored in this study can be situated in conversation with the postcritical.

39. See especially Felski, *Limits of Critique,* 52–84.

40. Felski, *Limits of Critique,* 84.

41. Felski, *Limits of Critique,* 176. Felski's discussion of the broadness of the act of reading has resonances with claims about ornamentation in antebellum writing recently advanced by Theo Davis in *Ornamental Aesthetics.* Drawing from Heidegger, Davis argues that Thoreau, Dickinson, and Whitman are informed by an aesthetics of ornamentation that does not view the purpose of literature to be purely representational. Instead, such an aesthetics advances a view of literature "as a way of connecting and relating to life" (29). My narrative of the real in part focuses on that enterprise of nurturing living connection and relation through reading.

1. Real Excavations

1. Martin's *The Instructed Vision* remains a helpful study of the role of Scottish Common Sense writers for American literature. Charvat claims that "the chief influences on the mind of the American critic were Scotch criticism and Scotch philosophy" (*Origins of American Critical Thought,* 36). Davis's *Formalism, Experience, and the Making of American Literature* uses Scottish Common Sense writings on aesthetics and perception as a way of explicating how antebellum American writers turned to categories of experience. Howe finds political and cultural similarities between American Revolutionaries and Enlightened Scots: both "advocat[ed] an enlargement of the political arena through union" (the union of the American colonies for the Americans and the union of Scotland and England for the Scots) and were "socially conservative but economically progressive" and "concerned with the cultivation of the self" (*Making the American Self,* 57–58). Howe's *The Unitarian Conscience* also explicates some of the influence of Scottish thinkers on the philosophical development of the United States. *The Cambridge Companion to the Scottish Enlightenment* (edited by Alexander Broadie) offers a helpful survey of the Scottish Enlightenment (including the Common Sense thinkers).

2. Frisbie, *Miscellaneous Writings,* 16. This address was excerpted and praised in various publications, including the *North American Review* ("Professor Frisbie's Inaugural Address," *North America Review* 6 [January 1818]: 224–41).

3. Frisbie, *Miscellaneous Writings,* 18, 21, 19–20.

4. Martin, *The Instructed Vision* (62–74), has an extensive discussion of (and excerpting from) Gray's address. Martin finds this "the most thorough and searching analysis I have discovered from the point of view of one whose philosophic credo was Common Sense philosophy" (64). Like Martin, I would like to use Gray's remarks as drawing from a Common Sense view, though I would like to emphasize somewhat different aspects of them.

5. Gray, "Female Education," 93.

6. Gray, "Female Education," 94–95.

7. Gray, "Female Education," 96.

8. Martin, *The Instructed Vision,* 70.

9. Gray, "Female Education," 95.

10. Gray, "Female Education," 94–95.

11. Martin, *The Instructed Vision,* 69.

12. Austen, *Persuasion,* 108.

13. Regarding religious texts, Gray finds that they are even truer than secular nonfiction. He finds the Bible, for instance, to be the "only absolutely true history that was ever written" ("Female Education," 94).

14. Gray, "Female Education," 96–97.

15. "Poetry and Reality," 3.

16. Dennie, "Miscellany," 209.

17. Rowson, *Charlotte Temple,* 5.

18. Williams, *Keywords,* 258. (The "existing and nonexisting" and "being and seeming" are my phrases—not Williams's.)

19. Independent existence is a major theme in approaches to the real.

20. The beginning of this definition includes uses of the word from 1440, 1570, and 1598 in which the "precise sense [of the real] is uncertain."

21. It should be noted, however, that *res* itself has a considerable range of meaning. The *Oxford Latin Dictionary* also offers a number of other definitions other than "thing," including "fact," "condition," "advantage," "world," "universe," "power," "valour," and "exploit."

22. Locke, *Essay,* 2: 303.

23. See Locke, *Essay,* 2: 304–24.

24. See Locke, *Essay,* 2: 26–29. Complicating the matter, Locke says that "substances" demonstrate this separation of "real" and "nominal" essences. However, for "simple ideas and modes" the "real" and "nominal" essences are the same. For instance, "a figure including a space between three lines" is both the real and the nominal essence of a triangle (28–29).

25. The "Plato" entry in the *Stanford Encyclopedia of Philosophy* outlines this standard interpretation—and possible challenges to it.

26. Plato, *Phaedrus* (Nehamas and Woodruff trans.), 36–37.

27. Plato, *Phaedrus* (Nehamas and Woodruff trans.), 37.

28. Etienne Gilson considers the difficulties of translating "ὄντως ὂν" from Greek. He notes that this is often translated as "really real," which he finds an acceptable translation (even if he has some misgivings about it). As he finds "beingly being" too awkward a phrase, he says that this term could also be translated as "reality." See Gilson, *Being and Some Philosophers,* 10.

29. Plato, *Phaedrus,* vol. 3 of *The Works of Plato,* trans. Taylor and Sydenham, 326. In "Poetry and Imagination" Emerson calls Taylor "a better man of imagination, a better poet . . . and a better feeder to a poet, than any man from Milton to Wordsworth" (*CW* 8: 69).

30. Reid, *Essays on the Intellectual Powers of Man,* 472. In *The Cambridge Companion to Thomas Reid,* Benjamin W. Redekop notes that Reid's work was taught at Harvard (and other places) throughout much of the nineteenth century (see 330–31).

31. Cassin, *Dictionary of Untranslatables,* 879. Courtine also finds that the original use of "realitas" was distinct from the adjective *realis* (a likely forerunner to "real").

32. Cassin, *Dictionary of Untranslatables,* 882.

33. Urbas, *Emerson's Metaphysics,* 9.

34. See Kuklick, *History of Philosophy in America,* 58–94.

35. Ripley, *Philosophical Miscellanies,* 33.

36. Philip Gura's *American Transcendentalism* explores the range of transcendentalist influences.

37. Brownson, "Two Articles from the *Princeton Review,*" 272.

38. Frothingham, *Transcendentalism in New England,* 181. As he writes in the preface to this work, he "was once a pure Transcendentalist"; his "ardor may have cooled," and "later studies and meditations may have commended to him other ideas and methods," but he "has enough of his former faith to enable him to do it [transcendentalism] justice" (viii).

39. Brownson, "The Community System," 130. He differs with these Realists in their finding that such Ideas could be known without individuals and exist without them.

40. Emerson, *Complete Sermons,* 1: 55.

41. Miles Orvell describes the phrase "the real thing" as "at once concrete (thing), abstract (real), and etymologically redundant (res=thing)" (*The Real Thing,* xvi).

42. For Trilling on the etymology of sincerity, see *Sincerity and Authenticity,* 12–25. The *OED*'s first citation of real as "sincere" is from a 1597 essay by Francis Bacon.

43. See Orvell's *The Real Thing,* which discusses the cultural history of the rise of "authenticity" in America.

44. This statement was part of the tagline for the MTV show "The Real World," which ran for decades.

45. Thoreau, *Walden,* 96.

46. Along these lines, consider the distinction posed by Roy Harvey Pearce when he writes that "Emerson's real world" would "have perhaps [been] called . . . the world of appearance" by Emerson (*Continuity of American Poetry,* 153). It seems that in this case, Pearce's "real world" is the world of hard actualities.

47. William Wells Brown, *Clotel,* 100.

48. Much of the fourth chapter of *Clotel* comes from Lydia Maria Child's story "The Quadroons" (1833): the quote "Her high poetic nature regarded the reality, rather than the semblance of things" is found directly in Child's work (*Clotel,* 276–77).

49. Brown, *Clotel,* 174.

50. "Appearances and Realities," 151.

51. "Perversion of Scripture Language," 101.

52. James Walker, "Associations for Benevolent Purposes," 245. *History of the Harvard Church at Charlestown* (Boston: 1879) notes Walker's contributions to the *Christian Examiner* (see 204).

53. Dickinson, *Letters of Emily Dickinson,* 3: 731.

54. Coleridge, *Biographia Literaria,* 1: 261. This passage from the *Biographia* draws from Friedrich Wilhelm Joseph von Schelling's writings; see the editor's footnotes to Coleridge, *Biographia Literaria,* 1: 261–63.

55. Coleridge, *Biographia Literaria,* 1: 263.

56. Coleridge, *Aids to Reflection,* 284.

57. Brownson, "The Community System," 129.

58. Lowell, *Complete Writings,* 2: 151.

59. Brackets in original.

60. Brackets in the original. Some of these definitions and citations are borrowed from Samuel Johnson's *Dictionary of the English Language.* For "real," Webster's fourth definition is Johnson's first. (The citation is an abbreviated version of Johnson's.) Webster's fifth definition (on property) seems a slightly expanded version of Johnson's third. Johnson's second definition of "real" is: "Not fictitious; not imaginary; true; genuine." Webster's first, second, and third definitions share aspects of that earlier definition. For "reality," Webster's second definition is a copy of Johnson's second definition; the citation is a shorter version of the same quotation Johnson uses from Milton. Johnson's first definition of "reality" is "truth; verity; what is, not what merely seems," and its citation is a longer version of the (slightly mangled) quote from Addison that Webster uses. There are differences between their definitions here, but both emphasize reality in contrast to appearance.

61. For many Scottish Common Sense theorists, even "unreal" literature could have some value or serve some purpose, but others were willing to use the "unreality" of novels as a reason for rendering them suspect.

62. Kames, *Essays on the Principles of Morality and Natural Religion,* 17.

63. Brownson, "Synthetic Philosophy" V, 54.

64. Hobbes, *Leviathan,* 23.

65. Brownson, "Synthetic Philosophy" V, 54.

66. Brownson, "Synthetic Philosophy" V, 53.

67. The identity of "H."—the author of this essay—remains unknown to me. This essay had a rather extended and somewhat bizarre life in the nineteenth century. It was anthologized in *The Family Treasury of Western Literature, Science and Art,* ed. Jethro Jackson (Cincinnati: Applegate and Co, 1854). Oberlin undergraduate Clarence J. Chase borrows heavily from this essay in an article published in the *Oberlin Review* in 1876 titled "Poetry and Religion."

68. H., "Poetry No Fiction," 265.

69. H., "Poetry No Fiction," 266.

70. H., "Poetry No Fiction," 265.

71. H., "Poetry No Fiction," 266.

72. H., "Poetry No Fiction," 268.

73. After all, questions of form are in part questions of seeming.

74. Thoreau, *Walden,* 101.

75. Thoreau, *Walden,* 90.

76. Sarah Josepha Hale—author of what we now know as "Mary Had a Little Lamb"—was editor of the magazine during this period, though she did not sign her name to this column.

77. "Editor's Table," *Lady's Book* 16 (March 1838): 143–44.

78. "Editor's Table," *Lady's Book* 16 (April 1838): 191.

2. The Drops of Summer Rain

1. Poirier, *Poetry and Pragmatism,* 10.

2. See Cameron, "The Way of Life by Abandonment," 3–40.

3. Paul, *Emerson's Angle of Vision,* 25.

4. See Urbas, *Emerson's Metaphysics* and "'Bi-Polar Emerson.'"

5. In *Emerson and Self-Reliance,* Kateb emphasizes the importance of this receptivity for Emerson.

6. Emerson, *Complete Sermons,* 1: 55.

7. Urbas notes that many Americans were deeply dissatisfied with Kant's response to Locke and Hume; see Urbas, *Emerson's Metaphysics,* 2–10.

8. Cole, *Mary Moody Emerson,* offers an instructive survey of some of Emerson's influences, including his aunt.

9. In *The Emerson Museum,* Lee Rust Brown has a very instructive reading of this passage (246–47).

10. Emerson, *Early Lectures,* 296. Hereafter parenthetically cited as *EL.*

11. The notion of spontaneous self-determination rises as an important concept in German philosophy in the aftermath of Kant, and Emerson offers a variation on this tradition in his positing of a spontaneous and self-determining soul free of social convention. Terry Pinkard's *German Philosophy 1760–1860* uses the figure of spontaneity as a thread for his narrative of German philosophy.

12. Brown, *The Emerson Museum,* 248.

13. Kateb, *Emerson and Self-Reliance,* 49.

14. Kateb discusses "seeing . . . one's own social experiences or activities through retrospection, and seeing . . . the world at large through honest perception completed or enhanced by retrospection" (*Emerson and Self-Reliance,* 49). This is not to say retrospection does not play a role—Emerson's compositional strategies show how much he depends on the process of retrospection in order to achieve a realizing effect.

15. Paul, *Emerson's Angle of Vision,* 130–31.

16. *Letters of Ralph Waldo Emerson,* 1: 425.

17. As Coleridge in the *Biographia Literaria* identifies idealism and realism, Emerson identifies real affinities and ideal affinities.

18. This essay, as well as much of *Letters and Social Aims* as a whole, draws from Emerson's earlier writings, including some reaching back as far as the 1840s. See the "Textual Introduction" of the *Collected Works* edition of *Letters and Social Aims* for a discussion of some of the compositional sources for this essay (*CW* 8: cclix–cclxii). In part due to Emerson's cognitive "descent" in the 1870s, much of this essay and the

rest of *Letters and Social Aims* was revised and organized by Ellen Tucker Emerson, Emerson's daughter, and James Elliot Cabot. (For a history of this collaboration, see *CW* 8: xix–cclxxiv.)

19. This same essay also tells us that poetry is "the expression of a sound mind speaking after the ideal, and not after the apparent" (*CW* 8: 14). This repetitive revision, with its similar organization of clauses and its substitution of "ideal" for "real," suggests that for Emerson as well as his two collaborators, there was a significant connection between the ideal and the real.

20. Mariotti, "Emerson and the 'Disagreeable Particulars' of Slavery," 306.

21. Cameron, "Way of Life by Abandonment," 18.

22. Though Emerson does not explicitly declare that this child is the emblem for or representative of a poet, the fact that this child's poem is prefixed to "The Poet" suggests some relationship between the two—as does the fact that the child sees "pairing rhymes" (10).

23. Waggoner, *Emerson as Poet,* 144.

24. Waggoner finds that those "winds of remembering" echo "this do in remembrance of me" and notes other religious parallels in this poem (*Emerson as Poet,* 143–44).

25. And I do wish to emphasize the limitation implicit in "at times." Other parts of Emerson seem sometimes to celebrate forgetting as a vehicle for renewal and new growth (see, for example, "Circles").

26. Emerson, *Journals and Miscellaneous Notebooks,* 5: 20.

27. Emerson, *Journals and Miscellaneous Notebooks,* 5: 275.

28. Vision and tropes of the visual appear throughout the book. The original 1836 epigraph, a quotation attributed to Plotinus, references the visual: "Nature is but an image or imitation of wisdom" (see *CW* 1: 1). The prefatory poem to the volume added by Emerson in 1849 speaks of the "eye read[ing] omens where it goes" (line 3). The fourth sentence of the introduction invokes the iconography of vision: "The foregoing generations beheld God and nature face to face; we, through their eyes" (*CW* 1: 8). Emerson declares that "to speak truly, few adult persons can see nature" (*CW* 1: 9).

29. Cornel West, *American Evasion of Philosophy,* 25.

30. The Greek *theoreo* (I see, view, or behold) and *theoria* (a seeing or beholding) emphasize sight—not elaborate theoretical constructs, as in Einstein's theory of relativity or Thorstein Veblen's *The Theory of the Leisure Class.*

31. Windolph, *Emerson's Nonlinear Nature,* 15.

32. Duquette, "Making an Example," 352.

33. Douglass, "Self-Made Men," 547–48.

34. This can even be seen in the at-times conflicted exemplification of persons in his work. In *English Traits* Emerson sometimes appeals to notable people in order to exemplify some traits of Englishness. But this turn to exemplification can complicate efforts to reduce a person to a rote example. For example, Emerson recounts multiple encounters with William Wordsworth (at the beginning and end of the book). At times

the narrative seeks to reduce Wordsworth to a mere example, saying that he "made the impression of a narrow and very English mind" (*CW* 5: 12) or that he showed "that complacency which never deserts a true-born Englishman" (*CW* 5: 166). However, other moments of these encounters reveal a more complex portrait. When Wordsworth recites some of his poetry for the young Emerson in the garden, the "recitation was so unlooked for and surprising" that Emerson says his first impulse was to laugh, but then he recognizes the true force of the seen: "I saw that he was right and I was wrong, and gladly gave myself up to hear" (*CW* 5: 11). Rather than merely being fodder for predetermined narratives, this encounter with personal particularity can disrupt.

35. It is in this section that Emerson says that the "perception of real affinities between events, (that is to say, of *ideal* affinities, for those only are real,) enables the poet thus to make free with the most imposing forms and phenomena of the world" (*CW* 1: 33).

36. In a penetrating reading of the "Idealism" section of *Nature,* John Michael emphasizes a more pessimistic or at least agonistic theme. As he puts it, in *Nature* "Emerson does not recount the triumphant assimilation of exterior by interior in the apotheosis of the self. He recapitulates an anxious battle in the crack between nature and spirit" (*Emerson and Skepticism,* 68). In my own discussion of "Idealism" and *Nature,* I might not foreground anxiety; however, Michaels's assertion of the resistance to assimilation in *Nature* might find some harmony with my own account of the way this work embodies a persistence of dialogue that undercuts some totalizing, homogenizing assimilation.

37. The salience of the distinction between "reason" and "understanding" is appropriated from Kant (who uses both terms in a somewhat different way).

38. Packer, *Emerson's Fall,* 159–60.

39. For instance, philosophy, poetry, religion, science, and nature itself are all devices leading to idealism.

40. The "Melody, Rhyme, and Form" section of "Poetry and Imagination" comments further on the role of meter and rhyme for Emerson's theory of poetics (*CW* 8: 24–30). Here, Emerson also has an interest in revising and extending narratives of these poetic terms. Rhyme becomes a kind of mirroring similarity in this essay. Shadows, he writes, offer us "finer rhymes," and funeral processions "where all wear black," soldiers in uniforms, and matching outfits in a "bridal company" are other examples of rhyme (*CW* 8: 24). He defines "real rhymes" as "the correspondence of parts in nature,—acid and alkali, body and mind, man and maid, character and history, action and reaction" (*CW* 8: 26). Far from simply being aural resonance, rhyme in "Poetry and Imagination" suggests the complementary features of existence.

41. In "Poetry and Imagination," Emerson says that "metre begins with pulse-beat" (*CW* 8: 24), which further hints at the union between meter and "Merlin I."

42. Gelpi draws attention to some of the physical imagery of union in the first part of "Merlin II" and notes that Emerson "catalogues the senses" in these opening lines (*The Tenth Muse,* 88–89). This intensity of physical imagery further distinguishes the first stanza from the second, heightening a sense of complementarity.

43. Interestingly, Emerson himself left out "Merlin II" from 1876's *Selected Poems,* a fact that causes some puzzlement for Edward Waldo Emerson in editing the volume of poems for *The Complete Works* in 1904: "The second part of 'Merlin' was omitted . . . which is surprising, for it well expressed his idea of correspondence, universal rhyme and harmony in nature, and compensation in life" (*Complete Works* 9: 422). Emerson's son, at least, saw "Merlin II" as part of a broader "Merlin" and not as a separate poem. (This is not to suggest, of course, that Edward Waldo Emerson should be taken as the definitive voice on his father's works.)

44. The essay is broken down into sections for each of the lords of life this work explores: illusion, temperament, succession, surface, surprise, reality, and subjectivity. Those readings that center "Experience" as a work of mourning—such as Sharon Cameron, "Representing Grief," and Julie Ellison, "Tears for Emerson"—rely on this passage as a key point of evidence. Jonathan Bishop wonders at the "dreadful" candor of Emerson in this passage (*Emerson on the Soul,* 198). Barbara Packer in part defends Emerson's approach in this passage from Bishop's (and others') criticisms; see *Emerson's Fall,* 165–70.

45. Additionally, in some of his later works (such as "Poetry and Imagination"), Emerson invokes the real in more hopeful terms.

46. Emerson, *Journals and Miscellaneous Notebooks,* 5: 30. In "The Poet" Emerson offers variants on trinitarian discourse in his outlining of "three children" for the universe with various sets of names: "cause, operation, and effect" or "Jove, Pluto, or Neptune" or "the Father, the Spirit, or the Son" or—in the phrasing Emerson will use in "The Poet"—"the Knower, the Doer, and the Sayer" (*CW* 3: 5). The poet assumes the mantle of the sayer.

47. Kateb, *Emerson and Self-Reliance,* 49.

48. New, *The Regenerate Lyric,* 41. See also pages 40–53 for New's fuller critique of Emerson's "unnervingly undistinguished" poems.

49. The "affinities" of Emerson's approach to poetry thus can be seen in the strategies of this essay.

50. Causation is a theme throughout Urbas's *Emerson's Metaphysics.* As he puts it at one point, "Emerson's lifelong doctrines may thus be resolved back into the core principle of reality: causation" (165).

51. Arsić, *On Leaving,* 173.

52. *Topical Notebooks of Ralph Waldo Emerson,* 2: 118. I am indebted to Anita Patterson for drawing this passage to my attention. Emerson did not read Hafez in depth until 1846, so much of his work was written without the direct influence of the Persian poet. However, he might have been indirectly influenced by Goethe's response to Hafez. Robert D. Richardson writes of Emerson's purchase of a translation of Hafez and its influence on his work in 1846 and after in *Emerson: Mind on Fire* (423–28). Goethe was deeply influenced by Hammer-Purgstall's translation (his 1819/27 *West-Eastern Divan* was shaped by his reading of this translation), and Emerson read thoroughly in Goethe. Hafez's relationship to Emerson has generated increased scholarly interest over the past few decades. Wai Chee Dimock's *Through*

Other Continents offers an extended meditation on the Goethe-Emerson-Hafez relationship (see 23–51). Paul Kane, in "Emerson and Hafiz," examines some of the poetic connections between the two writers. As Kane notes, Emerson remarked on the role of wine for Hafez. Written in 1846, "Bacchus," which focuses on a liberating transformation of wine, was influenced by his reading of Hafez.

3. In and Out of the Game with Walt Whitman

1. David E. Shi offers a standard claim in finding Whitman to be a "ferry linking antebellum romanticism to later nineteenth-century realism" (*Facing Facts,* 33); Whitman is "the most potent catalyst for change in nineteenth-century American culture" by "rooting romantic idealism in an affection for everyday realities" (*Facing Facts,* 29). In his influential *Ferment of Realism,* Walter Berthoff argues that "Whitman above all others sanctified for the younger writers who had opened their ears to him the general program of realism—the rendering of things as they actually appear, and in the language of natural feeling, the familiar dialects of a nation of free men" (9). In *From Fact to Fiction,* Shelley Fisher Fishkin draws parallels between Whitman's "journalistic" style and that of later writers such as Howells and Twain.

2. Whitman, *Poetry and Prose,* 8.

3. Philip Fisher, "Democratic Social Space," 70.

4. Dimock, *Residues of Justice,* 114.

5. Its limits help make it an individual by distinguishing it from others. At the same time, though, he also resists these limits through the vista-finding enterprise.

6. See Kateb's *The Inner Ocean* for a discussion of this theme.

7. The text quoted here follows that of the "deathbed" edition of *Leaves of Grass,* as found in the textual variorum (*Leaves of Grass* 2: 273–89).

8. Nussbaum, *Political Emotions,* 209.

9. The exact date of this notebook—the "Talbot Wilson" notebook—is contested. Many sources date it to 1847 (because of one page bearing that date). Floyd Stovall offers an alternative dating for these lines in "Dating Whitman's Earliest Notebooks," arguing that, though one page of the notebook is dated 1847, the lines themselves were written at least after 1853. In *Collage of Myself* Matt Miller surveys the complexities of dating this notebook and offers evidence for a date closer to 1854 (see 2–8). The controversies over the date of this fragment do not too much trouble my argument here: the proponents of various dates believe that these lines represent a key point in Whitman's development.

10. Whitman, *Uncollected Poetry and Prose,* 2: 69–70. The brackets, which are in the Holloway text, indicate that these lines are crossed out in the original notebook manuscript. Holloway's text differs slightly from that of the *Collected Writing*'s version of the notebooks (see *Collected Writings of Walt Whitman: Notebooks and Unpublished Prose Manuscripts,* 1: 69). Riddled with cross-outs and overwriting, the original manuscript text of the notebooks is hard to make out at times. But "I am the

poet of reality" is scrawled out clearly across the page. Hereafter, citations from the notebooks will be cited as *Notebooks.*

11. Whitman is not alone in declaring himself to be a "poet of reality." In an 1856 review of *Leaves of Grass* in the *North American Review,* Edward Everett Hale says that one "reads and enjoys the freshness, simplicity, and reality of what he reads, just as the tired man, lying on the hill-side in summer, enjoys the leaves of grass around him,—enjoys the shadow,—enjoys the flecks of sunshine,—not for what they 'suggest to him,' but for what they are" (275). Later in this review, while praising the variety of life that Whitman has incorporated into *Leaves of Grass,* Hale says that these "little thumb-nail sketches of life . . . strike us as real,—so real that we wonder how they came on paper" (277).

12. Whitman also keeps these lines in another early draft of "Song of Myself," when he writes: "I am the poet of Reality / And I say the stars are not echoes, / And I say that space is not an apparition; / But all things seen or demonstrated are so" (*Notes and Fragments,* 18). Unless otherwise mentioned, all citations from Whitman's poetry will come from the text of the "deathbed" edition of *Leaves of Grass.* For the text of "Song of Myself," see *Leaves of Grass,* 1: 1–83.

13. See *Leaves of Grass,* 2: 377–78.

14. See *Leaves of Grass,* 2: 561.

15. See *Leaves of Grass,* 2: 404.

16. Whitman, *Franklin Evans,* 33.

17. Whitman, *Uncollected Poetry and Prose,* 2: 93. (A variant of the text can be found in *Notebooks,* 1: 455.) Holloway dates this notebook to around 1860. With a similar interest in the distinction between showing and being, Elizabeth Barrett Browning's *Aurora Leigh* at one point offers the claim that "Art's the witness of what Is / Behind the show" (Book 7, 834–35).

18. Whitman, *Poetry and Prose,* 18.

19. See *Leaves of Grass,* 1: 265–72.

20. Whitman, *Poetry and Prose,* 14.

21. Dimock, *Residues of Justice,* 115.

22. In *Residues of Justice* Dimock situates Whitman in the broader tradition of thinkers such as Kant and John Rawls, who often conceive of the core of the self in this more abstracted way. She notes, for instance, how Rawls in the first edition of *A Theory of Justice* often seeks to cut off the self from its personal traits in order to ward off the specter of luck (102–6).

23. Dimock, *Residues of Justice,* 116–17.

24. Dimock, *Residues of Justice,* 117.

25. Harris, *E Pluribus Unum,* 71.

26. Grossman, "Poetics of Union," 67. In his narrative of Whitman's "song," Grossman finds that there are some tensions in this project.

27. Whitman, *Poetry and Prose,* 24–25.

28. Belknap, *The List,* 99.

29. Belknap, *The List,* 74.

30. Michael West, *Transcendental Wordplay*, 385.

31. Michael West, *Transcendental Wordplay*, 385.

32. Other people are very likely in this factory with the "Yankee girl," but their presence goes unmentioned.

33. One sees a similar move toward representation in the very next line, as the "paving-man leans on his two-handed rammer, the reporter's lead flies swiftly over the note-book, the sign-painter is lettering with blue and gold" (296). All the individuals in this line are engaged in a type of inscription, whether laying down pavement, lead, or paint. Recognizing the form of writing (of putting marks down with an implement) provides a way of organizing this line.

34. The lines themselves do not seem to tell us directly whether this moment is before or after the wedding, but the combination of details suggests that the setting is most likely before.

35. Bailey, *Walt Whitman*, 175.

36. Max Cavitch in *American Elegy* offers an extended reading of this poem within the context of elegy (see 233–93). The political reading of this poem in Erkkila's *Whitman: Political Poet* attends to the topics of reconciliation and the representative (227–37).

37. David Reynolds offers some comments on the relationship of these philosophers to Whitman in *Walt Whitman's America* (253–54) and emphasizes the importance of Hegel (especially for the later Whitman, 480–81). For an extended consideration of Whitman's relation to Schelling, see Scholnick, "'The Original Eye.'" Kant, Fichte, Schelling, and Hegel make an appearance in Whitman's later poem "The Base of All Metaphysics." Some passages can have an earliest date based on the publication dates from which Whitman quotes in these lectures. He incorporates passages from Hedge's *Prose Writers of Germany*, the *Encyclopedia Britannica*, and Gostwick's *German Literature*. Both Eleanor and Stovall identify the sources of some of these quotations; their identifications are later included in *The Collected Writings*. Whitman also cites *Democratic Vistas* in a later passage (*Notebooks* 6: 2017), which dates that passage as from at least 1871. The editors of *The Collected Writings* find "very plausibl[e]" Richard Bucke's claim that these lectures date from the late 1860s or early 1870s. Controversies about this text include more than its dates of composition. The text that appears in *Notebooks and Unpublished Manuscripts* follows the transcription of Richard Bucke; the editors of these *Notebooks* believed that the original manuscript was lost (*Notebooks* 6: 2009). This manuscript has since been revealed to be bound in the Harry Ransom Center at the University of Texas at Austin. In 2001 Gary Wihl published a transcription of this manuscript in "The Manuscript of Walt Whitman's 'Sunday Evening Lectures.'" Noting a difference between the order of the manuscript pages and that of Bucke's original published version, Wihl argues against Bucke's ordering of the sections, finding that it entailed some logical flaws and gaps. Paul Benton in "Elbert Hubbard's Manuscript Muddle" argues that the bound ordering of the manuscript pages may have been haphazard and finds the manuscript's ordering to suffer from a lack of coherence; he instead locates more editorial authority in Bucke.

38. When one considers this description, it is perhaps not surprising that scholars have long been interested in some connection between Whitman and Hegel. Gay Wilson Allen's *Solitary Singer* also suggests the relevance of Hegel for the later Whitman.

39. This is from the 1860 edition of *Leaves of Grass,* in the "Calamus" cluster; see pages 230–31 in Schmidgall's *Walt Whitman: Selected Poems.*

40. Kateb, *The Inner Ocean,* 246.

41. Salska, *Walt Whitman and Emily Dickinson,* 68.

42. This "loaf[ing] on the grass" alludes to the famous fifth section, where the speaker loafs with his soul on the grass, and this succession of guesses also calls to mind the interpretation of the "grass" earlier in the poem.

43. That martial theme continues in section 34 with a portrayal of the slaughter of soldiers and section 35's narration of a naval battle.

44. Earlier in this poem Whitman declares that the "Me myself" (74) is separate from the "pulling and hauling" of the world (75). At the very outset of "Song of Myself," Whitman proclaims, "I celebrate myself, and sing myself" (1).

45. The line "And of these one and all I weave the song of myself" first appears in the 1881–82 edition of *Leaves of Grass,* which is also the first edition to title this poem "Song of Myself." The 1855 edition titles this poem "Leaves of Grass" (if it gives it a title at all); the 1856 edition titles it "Poem of Walt Whitman, an American"; and later editions prior to 1881–82 title it "Walt Whitman." Earlier editions of this poem end this section with some variant on (as the 1855 text reads) "And such as it is to be of these more or less I am" before moving on to the next line, "I am of old and young, of the foolish as much as the wise." Thus, this line's inclusion can be tied to what is now known as the title of perhaps Whitman's most famous poem.

46. In *Whitman's Drama of Consensus,* Kerry Larson writes that the dynamics of Whitman's poetry of the assimilating self "no more imply the forfeiture of other selves . . . than the loss of his own" (xv).

47. See Levine, "Union and Disunion in 'Song of Myself.'"

48. See *Leaves of Grass,* 1: 217–25.

49. Fisher, "Democratic Social Space," 68.

50. Abrams, *The Correspondent Breeze,* 76–77.

51. See Dougherty, *Walt Whitman and the Citizen's Eye,* and McSweeney, *Language of the Senses.*

52. See Dougherty's *Walt Whitman and the Citizen's Eye* and Thomas's *Lunar Light of Whitman's Poetry.* Moreover, many readings of this poem have also viewed it as a poem of process, if not a poem of crisis. Dougherty and McSweeney both consider this approach. See also Gilbert, "From Anxiety to Power."

53. Dougherty, *Walt Whitman and the Citizen's Eye,* 154. In this discussion Dougherty builds on the work of E. Fred Carlisle in *The Uncertain Self.*

54. See York, *Architecture of Address,* 15–78.

55. York, *Architecture of Address,* 49.

56. Gilbert, "From Anxiety to Power," focuses on the turn to sight in this poem as a sign of a loss of power, when the speaker becomes "enslaved by the literality

of the eye" (349). Citing Wordsworth's claim that the eye is "the most despotic of our senses," Gilbert locates Whitman's approach to tradition within a greater Romantic agony over sight. While it is possible that the literality can become a form of enslavement for Whitman, the search for a vista can also be a means of liberation. Dougherty's *Walt Whitman and the Citizen's Eye* associates the tropes of sight with a civic negotiation.

57. In *Poets Thinking,* Helen Vendler highlights this broader strand in Whitman's poetry in her discussion of the role of reprise for his verse: "Looking at the function of reprise, we see that this poem ["Sparkles from the Wheel"] enacts the revision wrought by intense poetic thinking upon a perceptual scene that streams in through sight and hearing" (48). Vendler notes the way that formal reprise in Whitman's verse is representative of the broader way his poetry seeks to return to the things of the world in a new light.

58. In the 1855 edition no period concludes the poem, which further emphasizes the endlessness of the process of (what we now know as) "Song of Myself."

59. Fisher, for instance, finds that the "deepest account of that unity was atomistic and uniform" ("Democratic Social Space" 67).

60. The text of these lines comes from the 1855 edition as shown in Schmidgall's *Walt Whitman: Selected Poems* (see 89–95).

61. See also Betsy Erkkila's reflections on the grass as an egalitarian figure in *Whitman: Political Poet* (98–99).

62. An originating source in a textual sense is also the following passage from Isaiah: "All flesh *is* grass, and all the goodliness thereof *is* as the flower of the field: The grass withereth, the flower fadeth: because the spirit of the Lord bloweth upon it: surely the people *is* grass. The grass withereth, the flower fadeth, but the word of our God shall stand forever" (40: 6–8). Whitman takes up Isaiah's portrayal of the grass as a figure of mutability and also of commonality.

63. Rosenblum, "Strange Attractors," 56.

64. Frank, "Aesthetic Democracy," 414.

65. Price, *To Walt Whitman, America,* 8.

66. This has some parallels with Martha Nussbaum's claim of the need "to construct a *bridge* from the vividly imagined single case to the impartial principle by challenging the imagination, reminding people that a predicament to which they respond in a single vividly described case is actually far broader" (*Political Emotions,* 157).

4. Disjunction—Disclosure—Dickinson

1. Those poems are as follows: "One Year ago—jots what?" (Fr301); "A Prison gets to be a friend" (Fr456); "'Twas Love—not me" (Fr562); "Her sweet Weight on my Heart a Night" (Fr611); "I think To Live—may be a Bliss" (Fr757); "Fitter to see Him, I may be" (Fr834); "I'd rather recollect a Setting" (Fr1366); "You cannot make Remembrance grow" (Fr1536); and "And with what body do they come?" (Fr1537). Unless otherwise mentioned, all citations from Dickinson's verse will be from *The*

Poems of Emily Dickinson, edited by R. W. Franklin. "Fr" followed by the poem number in Franklin's edition will identify each poem. All citations from Dickinson's manuscripts will be from Franklin's facsimile, *The Manuscript Books of Emily Dickinson.*

2. "Who never wanted—maddest Joy" (Fr1447) and "Within that little Hive" (Fr1633), respectively.

3. "The nearest Dream recedes—unrealized" (Fr304) and "A Doubt if it be Us" (Fr903), respectively.

4. If we add the two poems in which Dickinson uses the word "really"—"Will there really be a 'Morning'?" (Fr148) and "Make me a picture of the sun" (Fr239)—this brings the count of Dickinson poems using "real" and affiliated words to fifteen, which is only two fewer than her poems of circumference. The *Emily Dickinson Lexicon* was a very helpful resource for tabulating the uses of "real" and its variants as well as "circumference."

5. Some significant recent studies discussing sentimentalism and suffering include Cheryl Walker's *The Nightingale's Burden,* Jane Tompkins's *Sensational Designs,* and Marianne Noble's *Masochistic Pleasures of Sentimental Literature.*

6. Dickinson, *L*342a. Citations from Dickinson's letters come from *The Letters of Emily Dickinson;* letters will be cited by *L* followed by the letter's number.

7. Dickinson, *L*10.

8. Deppman, *Trying to Think with Emily Dickinson,* 57. It is at least a supremely telling coincidence here that, in speaking about Dickinson's inability to *realize,* Deppman should say that this breakdown of realization is the inability to see or imagine "unveiledly" that oneself will die. For Whitman the realizing poet tears away the veils of the world—as the persona of "Song of Myself" declares, "I remove the veil" (line 517)—and Deppman argues that the breakdown of realization is also the inability to see/imagine without veils. For these two writers a century and a half apart, reality and the removing of veils are associated. This is a sign perhaps of the way that contemporary discourse still registers that sense of "reality" as going through (occluding) surface.

9. See Virginia Jackson's *Dickinson's Misery* for a historical and theoretical exploration of the norms of the lyric.

10. Macé, "Ways of Reading," 216.

11. Macé, "Ways of Reading," 223.

12. Schaeffer, "Literary Studies and Literary Experience," 281.

13. Sedgwick, "Paranoid Reading and Reparative Reading," 146.

14. See Sedgwick, "Paranoid Reading and Reparative Reading," 151n4.

15. Lee, *Uncertain Chances,* 175.

16. Pollak, *Dickinson: Anxiety of Gender,* 106.

17. New, *The Regenerate Lyric,* 151. Though she finds these "madwoman in the attic theories" both "persuasive" and "compelling," New suggests also that their "self-sufficiency and self-consistency insure . . . their parochialism" (153). New wishes to complicate the relationship between freedom and captivity in Dickinson by situating her in a religious context.

18. Blackwood, "'The Inner Brand,'" 56.

19. For more on dictionaries and Dickinson, see Benvenuto, "Words within Words."

20. Locke, *Essay,* 1: 449.

21. Locke, *Essay,* 1: 458–59.

22. Locke, *Essay,* 1: 228.

23. Emerson attributes this claim to the French thinker Etienne Bonnot de Condillac.

24. Although he demonstrates his awareness of the tradition of consciousness as limiting, there are also numerous narratives of possible liberation in Emerson's writings.

25. E. Miller Budick helpfully draws attention to some of the philosophically themed essays published in magazines subscribed to by the Dickinsons such as the *Atlantic* and *Harper's New Monthly Magazine* (*Emily Dickinson,* 23). Budick summarizes these essays as exploring "such topics as the mind's perception of reality, the existence of God, the origins of the universe, the relationship between image and idea, and the outlines of moral science" (23). The article on Leibniz in the June 1858 issue of the *Atlantic,* for example, offers a spirited survey of theories of epistemology and metaphysics from the Greeks to the nineteenth century: particular attention is paid to the shift to psychology (or, as the author calls it, "Noology") in Locke and the implications of this shift for our capacity to know the world. For the Dickinson family's philosophical acquaintances, see Deppman, *Trying to Think with Emily Dickinson,* 75–108, esp. 81–85.

26. In a letter to her childhood friend Abiah Root in 1845, Dickinson mentions "Mental Philosophy" as one of her "four studies" (*L*6), implying that Dickinson may have been exposed to Upham's work when she was a student. Kearns finds that the *Elements* were studied at both Amherst Academy and Mount Holyoke Female Seminary ("Emily Dickinson," 18–19). See also Melanie Hubbard, *Emily Dickinson,* 52–77, on Dickinson's relationship to various theories of epistemology.

27. Upham, *Elements of Mental Philosophy,* 137–38.

28. Goethe, *Sorrows of Young Werther,* 102.

29. Even the rack uses the holism of the body in order to inflict the pain of stretching.

30. Noble, "Dickinson on Perception and Consciousness," 205.

31. The holism of physical embodiment involves connecting the diverse parts of the flesh into a single body, and the distinction between one body and others can be seen as a kind of relationality.

32. Thomas Wentworth Higginson and Mabel Loomis Todd titled this poem "Emancipation" in 1890's *Poems by Emily Dickinson.*

33. Locke, *Essay,* 1: 444. Elsewhere in his *Essay* Lock writes that "person" means "a thinking, intelligent being, that has reason and reflection and can consider itself as itself, the same thinking thing, in different times and places; which it does only by that consciousness which is inseparable from thinking, and, as it seems to me, essential to

it" (1: 448–49). This self-referential awareness allows us to yoke together our various thoughts, sensations, and perceptions across time and across space, and this yoking renders a sense of personhood, according to Locke.

34. Upham, *Elements,* 136–37.

35. In "The Soul selects," Dickinson speaks of the soul as having (or as residing in a place that has) a gate and a mat. The rhetoric of location permeates Dickinson's poems about consciousness. "Too little way the House must lie" (Fr902) finds that every "Consciousness must emigrate / And lose it's neighbor once" (7–8). Other poems discussing location (and often residence) and identity include "A Prison gets to be a friend" (Fr456) and "It was a grave—yet bore no Stone" (Fr852).

36. Dickinson's use of the trope of the fortress for portraying the self has echoes with John Donne's sonnet "Batter My Heart, Three-Person'd God." Just as Dickinson's poems of the self suggest the possibility of disruption, Donne's verse often presents the self as experimental and at play—craving moments of spiritual disruption.

37. Dickinson appeals to the language of majesty in discussing consciousness in "I'm ceded—I've stopped being Their's" (Fr353), which contrasts childhood baptism with the gaining of adult identity and in many ways identifies growing consciousness with increased power. The speaker describes how, in her baptism, she was "Crowned—Crowing—on [her] Father's breast— / A half unconscious Queen" (15–16). Rather than her unconscious weakness as an infant, the speaker as an adult chooses "just a Crown" (20), celebrating the power of her conscious will and awareness.

38. Socarides, *Dickinson Unbound,* 116.

39. See Stonum, *The Dickinson Sublime,* and Juhasz, *The Undiscovered Continent.*

40. See Plato, *Symposium,* 48–49.

41. For more on Dickinson and the sexually erotic, see Patterson's *Riddle of Emily Dickinson,* Pollack's *Dickinson: Anxiety of Gender,* Juhasz's *The Undiscovered Continent* and "Amplitude of Queer Desire," and Smith's *Rowing in Eden.*

42. Genesis 28: 12.

43. Wheelwright, *Metaphor and Reality,* 172.

44. When it was published as "Desire" in 1896's *Poems by Emily Dickinson,* third series, the poem used "reality" in the main text.

45. Suggestively, in both "Who never wanted—maddest Joy" and "A Prison gets to be a friend" (Fr456), words of location are proposed as variants for the real ("vicinity" in the former, and "close" and "near" in the latter).

46. See "I dwell in Possibility" (Fr466).

47. See Stonum's *The Dickinson Sublime* and Weiskel's *The Romantic Sublime.* Alfrey's "Against Calvary" and Deppman's *Trying to Think with Emily Dickinson* offer other discussions of the sublime for Dickinson. The former considers Dickinson's rhetoric of the sublime within the context of the Christian conversion narrative, while the latter explores the way in which the figure of death can invoke the sublime for Dickinson. "He fumbles at your Soul" can be read within a religious context, in which the "He" is God. Death often seems to stand as some radical limit

for Dickinson, and her approach to the sublime often considers the challenges of limitations and the absolute.

48. Stonum, *The Dickinson Sublime,* 69.

49. Stonum, *The Dickinson Sublime,* 141. Stonum offers a number of reasons for Dickinson's emphasis on hinging trauma, including her concern with mastery and submission (and the relationship between reader and writer) and her approach to the use of language (129–41).

50. Miller, *Emily Dickinson,* 114–15.

51. For a general discussion of some of the stakes and methods of Dickinson's compression of language, see Miller's *Emily Dickinson* (24–44). Budick's *Emily Dickinson and the Life of Language* also examines some of the implications of Dickinson's literary compressions.

52. A version of the poem sent to Sue Dickinson heightens this sense of disjunction—the only stanza break in the poem occurs before the concluding couplet; see 477A. (Adding further to the dramatic texture of the manuscript, the front side of the version sent to Sue ends with the invocation of the thunderbolt, creating a clear division before and after the striking of the thunderbolt.)

53. Though one might also consider the peeling of the soul to be the poem's proper climax. These final two lines could then be understood as a sort of postcoital sublimation, a climax transformed.

54. Kant's own approach to the sublime is influential for both Weiskel and Stonum. In his four-part "Dickinson-Kant" series (published over a four-year period in *Dickinson Studies*—see numbers 60, 64, 67, and 74 of this journal), Frederick L. Morey explores some of the relationship between Kant and Dickinson. The third part, "The Beautiful and the Sublime," particularly attends to aspects of Dickinson's approach to the (Kantian) sublime. See also Deppman's *Trying to Think with Emily Dickinson.*

55. Kant, *Critique of Judgement,* 83.

56. Kant, *Critique of Judgement,* 83–84.

57. Kant, *Critique of Judgement,* 95.

58. Kant, *Critique of Judgement,* 95. In his discussion of the mathematical sublime, Kant speaks of the challenge of units and comparison for the apprehension of the sublime. Defining the sublime as the "absolutely great," as "great beyond comparison" (86), Kant hits on a problem for the use of measuring units: this "beyond comparison" vitiates any attempt to offer a unit-based measurement of the sublime. The measurement *via* units itself necessarily compares this sublime to these units (estimating the length of the Milky Way by however many thousands of light years). We cannot, according to this Kantian notion, estimate the greatness of a sublime, which transcends all comparisons and stands as an absolute, through taking its unitary measure.

59. Michael Theune in "'One and One Are One'" analyzes the way in which this poem, among others, can be understood in the light of Dickinson's interest in mathematics. Stonum also draws attention to Dickinson's use of mathematics (*The*

Dickinson Sublime, 133–34). Stonum argues that often, for Dickinson, "mathematical terms and operations represent a means by which the self constructs, controls, organizes, and takes possession of experience" and "calculation works to ensure that objects and experiences do not elude our mental grasp" (133), but this poem seems instead to show Dickinson's use of the language of mathematics as a way of unsettling experience and setting into contrast some of the tendencies of our "mental grasp." Our calculations can render objects paradoxical and figures of alienation.

60. Macé, "Ways of Reading" 214.

61. Macé, "Ways of Reading," 216.

62. Macé, "Ways of Reading," 219.

63. Schaeffer, "Literary Studies and Literary Experience," 281.

64. See Wolosky, "Rhetoric or Not," 229–32, for a discussion of this poem and its connection to Watts.

65. And, of course, for many nineteenth-century Americans, God was the ultimate reality.

66. Deppman, *Trying to Think with Emily Dickinson*, 92–93.

67. Shira Wolosky's discussion of this poem in *The Cambridge History of American Literature* emphasizes this counterfactual sense (454–56). Wolosky writes that in this poem Dickinson "appeal[s] to the faith that she has just denied" (456).

68. She offers "Truth" as a variant for "Real" in line 24, suggesting some possible alliance of the true and the real.

69. This "(hypothetical) 'fiction'" refers to the perspective of the poem—not my own.

70. In January 1846 she wrote to Root that "I was almost persuaded to be a christian" and that "I never enjoyed such perfect peace and happiness as the short time in which I felt I had found my savior." However, she then says this sentiment weakened and that she "cared less for religion than ever" (*L*10). In a letter from September of that year, Dickinson writes that she has "not yet made [her] peace with God" (*L*13).

71. "Within that little Hive" occurs at the end of a letter to Elizabeth Holland (*L*890). In this letter Dickinson grieves at the death of Otis P. Lord and includes a postscript asserting that Lavinia had told Dickinson in great detail the events of her visit with Elizabeth Holland.

72. Dickinson, *Letters*, 3: 911.

5. Challenging Appearances

1. Though Gilmore finds that this drive to render surfaces transparent and to achieve "ocular mastery" through legibility can be found in much American writing and thinking, he also notes that various works of "elite literature"—such as *The Scarlet Letter* or *Moby-Dick*—have a more ambiguous position regarding legibility: these works "tended at once to embrace the knowledge wish and to check the urge to 'strike through the mask'" (*Surface and Depth*, ix–xi). For a discussion of surface for Thoreau, Melville, and Hawthorne, see *Surface and Depth*, 79–99.

2. Gilmore, *Surface and Depth,* 183–84.

3. I am not in total disagreement with Gilmore on this topic. His assertions that the works of Thoreau, Melville, and Hawthorne often emphasize radical privacy, mystery, and impenetrable surfaces are persuasive. But I would add that the moments of going through surface in their works need not be instances of ocular tyranny but instead further vehicles to cultivate diversity. And the attempt to see through surfaces can, rather than dispiriting us, lead us to further mysteries.

4. Thoreau, *Walden,* 98.

5. My thinking about the role of the point d'appui and *Walden*'s approaches to "hard bottoms" is indebted to the analyses of Stanley Cavell in *Senses of Walden* and Walter Benn Michaels in "*Walden*'s False Bottoms."

6. Cavell, *Senses of Walden,* 75.

7. Garber, *Thoreau's Redemptive Imagination,* 28.

8. Cavell, *Philosophy the Day after Tomorrow,* 220.

9. Michaels, "*Walden*'s False Bottoms," 145.

10. Thoreau, *Walden,* 285.

11. As Crane wrote in a letter to William Wright, he "run[s] joyfully towards . . . Whitman" (*Complete Poems and Selected Letters,* 254). In his 1930 essay "Modern Poetry," Crane writes that the "most typical and valid expression of the American *psychosis* seems to me still to be found in Whitman. . . . He, better than any other, was able to coordinate those forces in America which seem most intractable, fusing them into a universal vision which takes on additional significance as time goes on" (172–73). In another letter to Wright, he also declares Dickinson's poems to be an "enthusiasm" (473). See also Crane's "To Emily Dickinson."

12. Crane, *Complete Poems and Selected Letters,* 160.

13. Crane, *Complete Poems and Selected Letters,* 162–63.

14. Crane's use of quotation marks around "real" might indicate that, for him, true reality might be more than what is conventionally assumed to be materially "real."

15. Crane, *Complete Poems and Selected Letters,* 167.

16. The excerpt from Eliot comes from "Rhapsody on a Windy Night."

17. Crane, *Complete Poems and Selected Letters,* 167–68.

18. Crane, *Complete Poems and Selected Letters,* 308.

19. Crane, *Complete Poems and Selected Letters,* 310.

20. This is from a letter to Waldo Frank; Crane, *Complete Poems and Selected Letters,* 316.

21. See Irwin, *Hart Crane's Poetry,* 342.

22. Thoreau, *Walden,* 10.

23. Hawthorne, *The American Notebooks, CE* 8: 485–86. All citations from Hawthorne's work come from the *Centenary Edition,* cited as *CE,* followed by the volume number and page number[s].

24. Hawthorne, *The American Notebooks, CE* 8: 485–86.

25. Hawthorne, *The French and Italian Notebooks, CE* 14: 91.

26. Hawthorne, *Mosses from an Old Manse, CE* 10: 7.

27. Hawthorne, *Mosses from an Old Manse, CE* 10: 18–21, describes the narrator going through books. Peter James West finds that for Hawthorne, "reality" is "always invoked as an implicit challenge to the consensual meaning reality contains outside the romantic view of things" (*Arbiters of Reality,* 79). West thus suggests the way that the enterprise of finding reality can lead to the enterprise of dislocation or at least disruption for Hawthorne.

28. Frederick Newberry offers a survey of critical responses to this story in "'The Artist of the Beautiful'" (especially 78–79).

29. Hawthorne, *Mosses from an Old Manse, CE* 10: 452.

30. Though Hawthorne will often use archaic language, such an overt tone switch at a pivotal moment when the artist reflects on his beloved might indicate this broader parallel between Owen and Hawthorne. For instance, "thou" and "thee" permeate his letters to Sophia in April 1840 (see *Letters, CE* 15: 434–55). Examining Hawthorne's pattern of correspondence reveals how sharp this rhetorical demarcation can be. In an October 4, 1840, letter to Sophia, he adopts a very formal and archaic phrasing (see *Letters, CE* 15: 494–96), but his October 12 letter to Longfellow is very casual and uses "you" (*Letters, CE* 15: 497).

31. Hawthorne, *Mosses from an Old Manse, CE* 10: 449.

32. Hawthorne, *Mosses from an Old Manse, CE* 10: 458.

33. Hawthorne, *Mosses from an Old Manse, CE* 10: 468–70.

34. Hawthorne, *Mosses from an Old Manse, CE* 10: 475.

35. Liebman, "Hawthorne's Romanticism," 93–94. Coleridge, for instance, appeals to such "air-sylphs" in *Biographia Literaria.*

36. Melville, "Hawthorne and His Mosses," 244.

37. Turpin, "Hawthorne the Unreliabilist," 500.

38. Bercovitch, *Office of the Scarlet Letter,* 21–22.

39. Hawthorne, *The Scarlet Letter, CE* 1: 262–63.

40. Bercovitch, *Office of the Scarlet Letter,* 30.

41. This particularity of possibility may be one reason why Evan Carton found that the "the tension between overdetermination and indeterminacy . . . informs *The Scarlet Letter*" (*Rhetoric of American Romance,* 193). Hawthorne simultaneously determines a figure and a set of figures, but the play between these determined figures creates a (particular) space of indeterminacy.

42. Hawthorne, *Letters, CE* 15: 384.

43. Melville, *Moby-Dick,* xv. Michael Gilmore says that the "Etymology" and "Extracts" sections suggest how "virtually every form of written discourse . . . will be mobilized to help us understand the whale" (*Surface and Depth,* 48). As Gilmore notes, this enterprise of understanding may be frustrated. That very proliferation of discourses can serve not to lock the whale into some limited category of comprehension; instead, that vastness of discourse can itself make the whale seem more vast, multifaceted, and heterogeneous.

44. Melville, *Moby-Dick,* xvii.

45. Melville, *Moby-Dick,* xxiii.

46. William Carlos Williams, *Imaginations,* 149.

47. William Carlos Williams, *Imaginations,* 120.

48. For more on the involvement of the "lords of life," see Finan, "'The Lords of Life.'"

49. See *Leaves of Grass,* 1: 1–83.

50. Whitman's poem "This Compost" enacts the way that moments of experience can cause a reevaluation of life. The speaker reflects on dead carcasses and comes to see in them emblems of new life by the end of the poem.

51. Best and Marcus, "Surface Reading," 9.

52. Many practitioners of poststructuralism and deconstruction might be interested in challenging some conventional notions of reality, but their enterprise of undoing certain narrative assumptions can be viewed as an extension of the broader testing of appearance toward which many invocations of the real urge us.

53. See Pippin, "In Defense of Naive Reading."

54. Felski, *Limits of Critique,* 188.

55. Best, "*La Foi Postcritique,* on Second Thought," 337–38.

56. See Macé, "Ways of Reading," 216.

57. Jane Gallop develops the role of close reading for theory in "Historicization of Literary Studies."

58. At least in the present, no supercomputer has been able to equal the human ability to forge meaning from the aesthetic encounter.

Bibliography

Abrams, M. H. *The Correspondent Breeze.* New York: Norton, 1984.

———. *A Glossary of Literary Terms.* New York: Holt, Rinehart, and Winston, 1988.

———. *Natural Supernaturalism: Tradition and Revolution in Romantic Literature.* New York: Norton, 1971.

Adams, Richard P. "Whitman's 'Lilacs' and the Tradition of Pastoral Elegy." *PMLA* 72.3 (1957): 479–87.

Alfrey, Shawn. "Against Calvary." *Emily Dickinson Journal* 7.2 (1998): 48–64.

Allen, Gay Wilson. *The Solitary Singer: A Critical Biography of Walt Whitman.* New York: New York University Press, 1967.

Anderson, Douglas. *Philosophy Americana.* New York: Fordham University Press, 2006.

"Appearances and Realities," *Literary American* 3.7 (August 25, 1849): 151.

Arsić, Branka. *On Leaving.* Cambridge, MA: Harvard University Press, 2010.

Arsić, Branka, and Cary Wolfe, eds. *The Other Emerson.* Minneapolis: University of Minnesota Press, 2010.

Austen, Jane. *Persuasion.* Vol. 6 of *The Cambridge Edition of the Works of Jane Austen.* Edited by Janet Todd and Antje Blank. Cambridge: Cambridge University Press, 2006.

Bailey, John. *Walt Whitman.* New York: Macmillan, 1926.

Banzer, Judith. "'Compound Manner': Emily Dickinson and the Metaphysical Poets." *American Literature* 32.4 (1961): 417–33.

Barrish, Phillip. *American Literary Realism, Critical Theory, and Intellectual Prestige, 1880–1995.* New York: Cambridge University Press, 2001.

Beiser, Frederick C. *German Idealism: The Struggle Against Subjectivism, 1781–1801.* Cambridge, MA: Harvard University Press, 2002.

Belknap, Robert E. *The List: The Uses and Pleasures of Cataloging.* New Haven, CT: Yale University Press, 2004.

Bell, Michael Davitt. *The Development of American Romance.* Chicago: University of Chicago Press, 1980.

——. *The Problem of American Realism: Studies in the Cultural History of a Literary Idea.* Chicago: University of Chicago Press, 1993.

Benfey, Christopher. *A Summer of Hummingbirds.* New York: Random House, 2008.

Benton, Paul. "Elbert Hubbard's Manuscript Muddle: Restoring Whitman's 'Sunday Evening Lectures' on Metaphysics." *Walt Whitman Quarterly Review* 21: 65–79.

Benvenuto, Richard. "Words within Words: Dickinson's Use of the Dictionary." *ESQ: A Journal of the American Renaissance* 29 (1983): 46–55.

Bercovitch, Sacvan. *The Office of the Scarlet Letter.* Baltimore: Johns Hopkins University Press, 1981.

Berkeley, George. *Berkeley's Philosophical Writings.* Edited by David M. Armstrong. New York: Collier, 1965.

Berthoff, Warner. *The Ferment of Realism, 1884–1919.* Chapel Hill: University of North Carolina Press, 1965.

Best, Stephen. "*La Foi Postcritique,* on Second Thought." *PMLA* 132.2 (2017): 337–43.

Best, Stephen, and Sharon Marcus. "Surface Reading: An Introduction." *Representations* 108.1 (2009): 1–21.

Bishop, Jonathan. *Emerson on the Soul.* Cambridge: Harvard University Press, 1964.

Blackwood, Sarah. "'The Inner Brand': Emily Dickinson, Portraiture, and the Narrative of Liberal Interiority." *Emily Dickinson Journal* 14.2 (2005): 48–59.

Blair, Hugh. *Lectures on Rhetoric and Belles Lettres.* New York: Robinson and Franklin, 1838.

Blake, William. *The Complete Poetry and Prose of William Blake.* Edited by David V. Erdman. Berkeley: University of California Press, 1982.

Bloom, Harold. *Agon: Towards a Theory of Revisionism.* New York: Oxford University Press, 1982.

——. *The Ringers in the Tower: Studies in Romanticism.* Chicago: University of Chicago Press, 1971.

Booth, Wayne C. *The Rhetoric of Fiction.* Chicago: University of Chicago Press, 1961.

Bowron, Bernard R. "Realism in America." *Comparative Literature* 3.3 (1951): 268–85.

Broadie, Alexander, ed. *The Cambridge Companion to the Scottish Enlightenment.* Cambridge: Cambridge University Press, 2003.

Brown, Lee Rust. *The Emerson Museum: Practical Romanticism and the Pursuit of the Whole.* Cambridge: Harvard University Press, 1997.

Brown, Marshall. "The Logic of Realism: A Hegelian Approach." *PMLA* 96.2 (1981): 224–41.

Brown, William Wells. *Clotel.* Edited by Robert S. Levine. Boston: Bedford/St. Martin's, 2000.

Browning, Elizabeth Barrett. *Aurora Leigh.* Edited by Margaret Reynolds. New York: Norton, 1996.

Brownson, Orestes A. "The Community System." *United States Magazine and Democratic Review* 12 (February 1843): 129–44.

———. "History of Philosophy." *Brownson's Quarterly Review* 1.2 (April 1844): 137–74.

———. "Synthetic Philosophy" V. *United States Magazine and Democratic Review* 12 (January 1843): 38–55.

———. "Synthetic Philosophy." *United States Magazine and Democratic Review* 12 (March 1843), 241–54.

———. "Two Articles from the *Princeton Review.*" *Boston Quarterly Review* 3 (1840): 265–323.

Budick, E. Miller. *Emily Dickinson and the Life of Language: A Study in Symbolic Poetics.* Baton Rouge: Louisiana State University Press, 1985.

———. *Engendering Romance.* New Haven, CT: Yale University Press, 1994.

Buell, Lawrence. *Emerson.* Cambridge, MA: Harvard University Press, 2003.

———. *Literary Transcendentalism: Style and Vision in the American Renaissance.* Ithaca, NY: Cornell University Press, 1973.

Burke, Kenneth. *Language as Symbolic Action: Essays on Life, Literature, and Method.* Berkeley: University of California Press, 1966.

Cady, Edwin H. *The Light of Common Day.* Bloomington: Indiana University Press, 1971.

Cameron, Sharon. *Choosing Not Choosing: Emily Dickinson's Fascicles.* Chicago: University of Chicago Press, 1992.

———. *Impersonality: Seven Essays.* Chicago: University of Chicago Press, 2007.

———. *Lyric Time: Emily Dickinson and the Limits of Genre.* Baltimore: Johns Hopkins University Press, 1979.

———. "Representing Grief: Emerson's 'Experience.'" *Representations* 15 (Summer 1986): 15–41.

———. "The Way of Life by Abandonment." In *The Other Emerson,* edited by Branca Arsić and Cary Wolfe, 3–40. Minneapolis: University of Minnesota Press, 2010.

Capper, Charles. *Margaret Fuller: An American Romantic Life.* New York: Oxford University Press, 1992.

Capps, Jack L. *Emily Dickinson's Reading, 1836–1886.* Cambridge: Harvard University Press, 1966.

Carlisle, E. Fred. *The Uncertain Self: Whitman's Drama of Identity.* East Lansing: Michigan State University Press, 1973.

Carton, Evan. *The Rhetoric of American Romance.* Baltimore: Johns Hopkins University Press, 1985.

Cavell, Stanley. *Emerson's Transcendental Etudes.* Edited by David Justin Hodge. Stanford: Stanford University Press, 2003.

———. *In Quest of the Ordinary: Lines of Skepticism and Romanticism.* Chicago: University of Chicago Press, 1988.

———. *The New Yet Unapproachable America: Essays after Emerson after Wittgenstein.* Albuquerque, NM: Living Batch Press, 1989.

———. *Philosophy the Day after Tomorrow.* Cambridge, MA: Harvard University Press, 2006.

———. *Senses of Walden.* Chicago: University of Chicago Press, 1981.

Cavitch, Max. *American Elegy.* Minneapolis: University of Minnesota Press, 2007.

Chai, Leon. *The Romantic Foundations of the American Renaissance.* Ithaca, NY: Cornell University Press, 1987.

Chambers, Robert, ed. *Cyclopedia of English Literature.* Boston: Gould, Kendall, and Lincoln, 1847.

Chapman, John Jay. "Emerson, Sixty Years After." *Atlantic Monthly* 79 (January 1897): 27–41.

Charvat, William. *The Origins of American Critical Thought.* New York: Russell and Russell, 1968.

Chase, Clarence J. "Poetry and Religion." *Oberlin Review* 3 (March 8, 1876): 15–18.

Cheyfitz, Eric. *The Trans-Parent: Sexual Politics in the Language of Emerson.* Baltimore: Johns Hopkins University Press, 1981.

Cole, Phyllis. *Mary Moody Emerson and the Origins of Transcendentalism: A Family History.* New York: Oxford University Press, 1998.

Cole, Rachel. "The Reality Effect." *Yale Journal of Criticism* 18.1 (2005): 67–86.

Coleridge, Samuel Taylor. *Aids to Reflection.* Edited by Henry Nelson Coleridge. Port Washington, NY: Kennikat Press, 1971.

———. *Biographia Literaria.* Edited by James Engell and W. Jackson Bate. 2 vols. Princeton, NJ: Princeton University Press, 1983.

Connolly, Brian. "Against Accumulation." *J19: Journal of Nineteenth-Century Americanists* 2.1 (2014): 172–79.

Crane, Hart. *Complete Poems and Selected Letters.* Edited by Langdon Hammer. New York: Library of America, 2006.

Cudworth, Ralph. *The True Intellectual System of the Universe.* London: Thomas Tegg, 1845.

Cull, Ryan. "Beyond the Cheated Eye: Dickinson's Lyric Sociality." *Nineteenth-Century Literature* 65.1 (2010): 38–64.

Davis, Theo. *Formalism, Experience, and the Making of American Literature in the Nineteenth Century.* Cambridge: Cambridge University Press, 2007.

———. *Ornamental Aesthetics.* New York: Oxford University Press, 2016.

Dennie, Joseph [Oliver Oldschool, pseud.]. "Miscellany." *Port Folio* 3.14 (April 4, 1807): 209–10.

Deppman, Jed. "Dickinson, Death, and the Sublime." *Emily Dickinson Journal* 9.1 (2000): 1–20.

———. *Trying to Think with Emily Dickinson.* Amherst: University of Massachusetts Press, 2008.

Descartes, Rene. *The Philosophical Works of Descartes.* 2 vols. Translated by Elizabeth S. Haldane and G. R. T. Ross. Cambridge: Cambridge University Press, 1968.

Dickinson, Emily. *The Letters of Emily Dickinson.* 3 vols. Edited by Thomas H. Johnson. Cambridge, MA: Harvard University Press, 1958.

———. *The Manuscript Books of Emily Dickinson.* 2 vols. Edited by R. W. Franklin. Cambridge, MA: Harvard University Press, 1981.

———. *Poems by Emily Dickinson.* Edited by Mabel Loomis Todd and Thomas Wentworth Higginson. Boston: Roberts Brothers, 1890.

———. *Poems by Emily Dickinson.* Third Series. Edited by Mabel Loomis Todd. Boston: Roberts Brothers, 1896.

———. *The Poems of Emily Dickinson: Variorum Edition.* 3 vols. Edited by R. W. Franklin. Cambridge, MA: Harvard University Press, 1998.

Cassin, Barbara, et al., eds. *Dictionary of Untranslatables.* Princeton, NJ: Princeton University Press, 2014.

Dimock, Wai Chee. *Residues of Justice.* Berkeley: University of California Press, 1996.

———. *Through Other Continents.* Princeton, NJ: Princeton University Press, 2006.

Dougherty, James. *Walt Whitman and the Citizen's Eye.* Baton Rouge: Louisiana State University Press, 1993.

Douglass, Frederick. "Self-Made Men." In Vol. 5, *The Frederick Douglass Papers,* edited by John W. Blassingame and John R. McKivigan, 545–75. New Haven: Yale University Press, 1992.

Dryden, Edgar. *The Form of American Romance.* Baltimore: Johns Hopkins University Press, 1988.

Duquette, Elizabeth. "Making an Example: American Literature as Philosophy." In *The Oxford Handbook of Nineteenth-Century American Literature,* edited by Russ Castronovo, 343–57. New York: Oxford University Press, 2012.

Earhart, Amy E., and Andrew Jewell, eds. *The American Literature Scholar in the Digital Age.* Ann Arbor: University of Michigan Press, 2010.

Eberwein, Jane. *Emily Dickinson: Strategies of Limitation.* Amherst: University of Massachusetts Press, 1985.

"Editor's Table." *Lady's Book* 16 (March 1838): 143–44.

"Editor's Table." *Lady's Book* 16 (April 1838): 190–91.

Edmundson, Mark. "'Lilacs': Whitman's American Elegy." *Nineteenth-Century Literature* 44 (1990): 465–91.

Eleanor, Mary. "Hedge's Prose Writers of Germany as a Source of Whitman's Knowledge of German Philosophy." *Modern Language Notes* 61.6 (1946): 381–88.

Eliot, T. S. *Collected Poems, 1909–62.* New York: Harcourt, Brace & World, 1963.

Ellison, Julie. *Emerson's Romantic Style.* Princeton, NJ: Princeton University Press, 1984.

———. "Tears for Emerson." In *The Cambridge Companion to Ralph Waldo Emerson,* edited by Joel Porte and Saundra Morris, 140–61. Cambridge: Cambridge University Press, 1999.

Emerson, Ralph Waldo. *The Collected Works of Ralph Waldo Emerson.* 10 vols. Edited by Robert E. Spiller et al. Cambridge, MA: Harvard University Press, 1971–2013.

———. *The Complete Sermons of Ralph Waldo Emerson.* Vol. 1. Edited by Albert J. von Frank. Columbia: University of Missouri Press, 1989.

———. *The Complete Works of Ralph Waldo Emerson.* Boston: Houghton Mifflin, 1903–4.

——. *The Early Lectures of Ralph Waldo Emerson.* Vol. 2. Edited by Stephen E. Whicher et al. Cambridge, MA: Harvard University Press, 1964.

——. *The Journals and Miscellaneous Notebooks of Ralph Waldo Emerson.* 16 vols. Edited by William Gilman et al. Cambridge, MA: Harvard University Press, 1960–82.

——. *The Letters of Ralph Waldo Emerson.* Edited by Ralph L. Rusk. New York: Columbia University Press, 1964.

——. *The Poetry Notebooks of Ralph Waldo Emerson.* Edited by Ralph H. Orth et al. Columbia: University of Missouri Press, 1986.

——. *The Topical Notebooks of Ralph Waldo Emerson.* Vol. 2. Edited by Ronald A. Bosco. Columbia: University of Missouri Press, 1993.

Emsley, Sarah. "Was Emily Dickinson a Metaphysical Poet?" *Canadian Review of American Studies* 33:3 (2003): 249–65.

Erkkila, Betsy. *Whitman: The Political Poet.* New York: Oxford University Press, 1989.

Feidelson, Charles. *Symbolism and American Literature.* Chicago: University of Chicago Press, 1953.

Felski, Rita. *The Limits of Critique.* Chicago: University of Chicago Press, 2015.

Finan, E. Thomas. "'The Lords of Life': Fractals, Recursivity, and 'Experience.'" *Philosophy and Rhetoric* 41.1 (2012): 65–88.

Fisher, Philip. "Democratic Social Space." *Representations* 24 (1988): 60–101.

Fishkin, Shelley Fisher. *From Fact to Fiction: Journalism and Imaginative Writing in America.* Baltimore: Johns Hopkins University Press, 1985.

Flaherty, Matthew. "Expressive Realism and the Phenomenological Turn: A Canon for Postcritical Literary Studies." *Poetics Today* 40.1 (2019): 136–58.

Fleissner, Jennifer. *Women, Compulsion, and Modernity.* Chicago: University of Chicago Press, 2004.

Fox, Thomas Bayley. "The Reality of Fiction." *Christian Examiner* 75 (July, September, and November 1863): 176–85.

Frank, Jason. "Aesthetic Democracy." *Review of Politics* 69.3 (2007): 402–30.

Freedman, Linda. *Emily Dickinson and the Religious Imagination.* New York: Cambridge University Press, 2011.

Frisbie, Levi. *A Collection of the Miscellaneous Writings of Professor Frisbie with Some Notices of His Life and Character.* Edited by Andrews Norton. Boston: Cummings and Hillard, 1823.

Frothingham, Octavius Brooks. *Transcendentalism in New England: A History.* New York: Harper Torchbooks, 1959.

Fuller, Margaret. *Woman in the Nineteenth Century.* New York: Greeley and McElrath, 1845.

Fuller, Randall. *Emerson's Ghosts.* New York: Oxford University Press, 2007.

Gallop, Jane. *Around 1981.* New York: Routledge, 1992.

——. "The Historicization of Literary Studies and the Fate of Close Reading." In *Profession 2007,* 181–86. New York: MLA, 2007.

Garber, Frederick. *Thoreau's Redemptive Imagination.* New York: New York University Press, 1977.

Gelpi, Albert. *The Tenth Muse: The Psyche of the American Poet.* Cambridge: Cambridge University Press, 1991.

Gilbert, Roger. "From Anxiety to Power: Grammar and Crisis in 'Crossing Brooklyn Ferry.'" *Nineteenth-Century Literature* 42.3 (1987): 339–61.

Gilmore, Michael T. *Surface and Depth: The Quest for Legibility in American Culture.* Oxford: Oxford University Press, 2003.

Gilson, Etienne. *Being and Some Philosophers.* 2nd ed. Toronto: Pontifical Institute of Medieval Studies, 1952.

Glazener, Nancy. *Literature in the Making: A History of U.S. Literary Culture in the Long Nineteenth Century.* New York: Oxford University Press, 2015.

Goble, Mark. *Beautiful Circuits.* New York: Columbia University Press, 2010.

Goethe, Johann Wolfgang von. *Die Leiden des jungen Werthers.* Munich: Deutscher Taschenbuch Verlag, 1997.

———. *The Sorrows of Young Werther and Selected Writings.* Translated by Catherine Hutter. New York: Signet Classic, 1982.

Goodale, Dale. "Some of Walt Whitman's Borrowings." *American Literature* 10.2 (1938): 202–13.

Gray, James. "Female Education." *The Port Folio* 4 (July 1810): 84–120.

Greenwald, Elissa. *Realism and the Romance: Nathaniel Hawthorne, Henry James, and American Fiction.* Ann Arbor, MI: UMI Research Press, 1989.

Grossman, Allen. "The Poetics of Union in Whitman and Lincoln." In *The Long Schoolroom,* 58–84. Ann Arbor: University of Michigan Press, 1997.

Grossman, Jay. *Reconstituting the American Renaissance: Emerson, Whitman, and the Politics of Representation.* Durham, NC: Duke University Press, 2003.

Gura, Philip F. *American Transcendentalism.* New York: Hill and Wang, 2007.

Gura, Philip F., and Joel Myerson, eds. *Critical Essays on American Transcendentalism.* Boston: G. K. Hall and Co., 1982.

Gustafson, Thomas. *Representative Words: Politics, Literature, and the American Language, 1776–1865.* Cambridge: Cambridge University Press, 1992.

H. "Poetry No Fiction." *New-England Magazine* 4 (April 1833): 265–71.

Hale, Edward Everett. Review of *Leaves of Grass. North American Review* 82 (January 1856): 275–77.

Harris, W. C. *E Pluribus Unum.* Iowa City: University of Iowa Press, 2005.

Harris, William T. "The Dialectic Unity in Emerson's Prose." *Journal of Speculative Philosophy* 18 (1884): 195–202.

Hawthorne, Nathaniel. *The Centenary Edition of the Works of Nathaniel Hawthorne.* 22 vols. Edited by William Charvat et al. Columbus: Ohio State University Press, 1962–97.

Hedge, Frederick Henry. *Prose Writers of Germany.* Philadelphia: Carey and Hart, 1848.

Hegel, G. W. F. *Phenomenology of Spirit.* Translated by A. V. Miller. Oxford: Oxford University Press, 1977.

Herz, Judith Scherer. "Under the Sign of Donne." *Criticism* 43.1 (Winter 2001): 29–58.

Hobbes, Thomas. *Leviathan, Or the Matter, Forme and Power of a Commonwealth Ecclesiasticall and Civil.* Edited by Michael Oakshott. New York: Simon and Schuster, 1997.

Hopkins, Vivian C. *Spires of Form: A Study of Emerson's Aesthetic Theory.* New York: Russell & Russell, 1965.

Howe, Daniel Walker. *Making the American Self: Jonathan Edwards to Abraham Lincoln.* Cambridge: Harvard University Press, 1997.

———. *The Unitarian Conscience: Harvard Moral Philosophy, 1805–1861.* Cambridge, MA: Harvard University Press, 1970.

Howe, Susan. *My Emily Dickinson.* Berkeley, CA: North Atlantic Books, 1985.

Hubbard, Melanie. *Emily Dickinson: Poetics in Context.* New York: Cambridge University Press, 2020.

Hume, David. *A Treatise of Human Nature.* Edited by David Fate Norton and Mary J. Norton. Oxford: Oxford University Press, 2002.

Irwin, John T. *American Hieroglyphics: The Symbol of Egyptian Hieroglyphics in the American Renaissance.* New Haven, CT: Yale University Press, 1980.

———. *Hart Crane's Poetry.* Baltimore: Johns Hopkins University Press, 2011.

Jackson, Jethro, ed. *The Family Treasury of Western Literature, Science and Art.* Cincinnati: Applegate and Co, 1854.

Jackson, Virginia. *Dickinson's Misery: A Theory of Lyric Reading.* Princeton, NJ: Princeton University Press, 2005.

Jacobson, David. *Emerson's Pragmatic Vision.* University Park: Pennsylvania State University Press, 1993.

Jakobson, Roman. "On Realism in Art." In *Readings in Russian Poetics,* edited by Ladislav Matejka and Krystyna Pomorska, 38–46. Cambridge, MA: MIT University Press, 1971.

Johnson, Greg. *Emily Dickinson: Perception and the Poet's Quest.* Tuscaloosa: University of Alabama Press, 1985.

Juhasz, Suzanne. "The Amplitude of Queer Desire in Dickinson's Erotic Language." *Emily Dickinson Journal* 14.2 (2005): 24–33.

———. *The Undiscovered Continent.* Indianapolis: University of Indiana Press, 1983.

Kames, Lord (Henry Home). *Essays on the Principles of Morality and Natural Religion.* Edited by Mary Catherine Moran. Indianapolis: Liberty Fund, 2005.

Kane, Paul. "Emerson and Hafiz: The Figure of the Religious Poet." *Religion and Literature* 41.1 (2009): 111–39.

Kant, Immanuel. *Critique of Judgement.* Translated by J. H. Bernard. New York: Hafner, 1951.

———. *Critique of Pure Reason.* Translated and edited by Paul Guyer and Allen M. Wood. Cambridge: Cambridge University Press, 1998.

Kaplan, Amy. *The Social Construction of American Realism.* Chicago: University of Chicago Press, 1988.

Kaplan, Justin. *Walt Whitman: A Life.* New York: Simon and Schuster, 1980.

Kateb, George. *Emerson and Self-Reliance.* Thousand Oaks, CA: Sage Publications, 1995.

———. *The Inner Ocean.* Ithaca, NY: Cornell University Press, 1992.

Kearns, Michael. "Emily Dickinson: Anatomist of the Mind." In *Emily Dickinson and Philosophy,* edited by Jed Deppman, Marianne Noble, and Gary Lee Stonum, 13–29. Cambridge: Cambridge University Press, 2013.

Knapp, Steven, and Walter Benn Michaels. "Against Theory." *Critical Inquiry* 8.4 (1982): 723–42.

Kuklick, Bruce. *Churchmen and Philosophers: From Jonathan Edwards to John Dewey.* New Haven, CT: Yale University Press, 1985.

———. *A History of Philosophy in America, 1720–2000.* New York: Oxford University Press, 2001.

———. *The Rise of American Philosophy, Cambridge, Massachusetts, 1860–1930.* New Haven, CT: Yale University Press, 1977.

Larson, Kerry. *Whitman's Drama of Consensus.* Chicago: University of Chicago Press, 1989.

Lawson, Andrew. *Downwardly Mobile.* New York: Oxford University Press, 2012.

Lee, Maurice. *Uncertain Chances.* New York: Oxford University Press, 2012.

Levine, Herbert. "Union and Disunion in 'Song of Myself.'" *American Literature* 59.4 (December 1987): 570–89.

Liebman, Sheldon W. "Hawthorne's Romanticism: 'The Artist of the Beautiful.'" *ESQ* 22 (1976): 85–95.

Locke, John. *An Essay Concerning Human Understanding.* 2 vols. New York: Dover, 1959.

Longfellow, Henry Wadsworth. *The Complete Poetical Works of Henry Wadsworth Longfellow.* Edited by Horace E. Scudder. Boston: Houghton Mifflin, 1893.

Lovejoy, A. O. *Essays in the History of Ideas.* New York: George Braziller, 1955.

Loving, Jerome. *Emerson, Whitman, and the American Muse.* Chapel Hill: University of North Carolina Press, 1982.

———. *Walt Whitman: The Song of Himself.* Berkeley: University of California Press, 1999.

Lowell, James Russell. *The Complete Writings of James Russell Lowell.* Boston: Houghton, Mifflin, 1904.

Macé, Marielle. "Ways of Reading, Modes of Being." Translated by Marlon Jones. *New Literary History* 44.2 (Spring 2013): 213–29.

Manning, Susan. *The Puritan-Provincial Vision: Scottish and American Literature in the Nineteenth Century.* Cambridge: Cambridge University Press, 1990.

Mariotti, Shannon L. "Emerson and the 'Disagreeable Particulars' of Slavery." In *A Political Companion to Ralph Waldo Emerson,* edited by Alan M. Levine and Daniel S. Malachuk, 305–40. Lexington: University Press of Kentucky, 2011.

Martin, Terence. *The Instructed Vision.* Bloomington: Indiana University Press, 1961.
Matthiessen, F. O. *American Renaissance.* New York: Oxford University Press, 1941.
May, Henry F. *The Enlightenment in America.* New York: Oxford University Press, 1976.
McGann, Jerome. *The Romantic Ideology.* Chicago: University of Chicago Press, 1983.
McSweeney, Kerry. *The Language of the Senses.* Montreal: McGill-Queen's University Press, 1998.
Melville, Herman. "Hawthorne and His Mosses." In *The Writings of Herman Melville,* vol. 9, *Piazza Tales and Other Prose Pieces, 1839–1860,* edited by Harrison Hayford et al., 239–54. Evanston, IL: Northwestern University Press and the Newberry Library, 1987.
———. *Moby-Dick.* Vol. 6 of *The Writings of Herman Melville,* edited by Harrison Hayford, Hershel Parker, and G. Thomas Tanselle. Evanston, IL: Northwestern University Press and the Newberry Library, 1988.
Menand, Louis. *The Metaphysical Club.* New York: Farrar, Straus and Giroux, 2001.
Menke, Richard. *Telegraphic Realism.* Stanford, CA: Stanford University Press, 2008.
Michael, John. *Emerson and Skepticism: The Cipher of the World.* Baltimore: Johns Hopkins University Press, 1988.
Michaels, Walter Benn. "*Walden*'s False Bottoms." *Glyph* 1 (1977): 132–49.
Michaels, Walter Benn, and Donald E. Pease, eds. *The American Renaissance Reconsidered.* Baltimore: Johns Hopkins University Press, 1985.
Miller, Cristanne. *Emily Dickinson: A Poet's Grammar.* Cambridge, MA: Harvard University Press, 1987.
———. *Reading in Time: Emily Dickinson in the Nineteenth Century.* Amherst: University of Massachusetts Press, 2012.
Miller, Matt. *Collage of Myself: Walt Whitman and the Making of* Leaves of Grass. Lincoln: University of Nebraska Press, 2010.
Mitchell, Domhnall. *Measures of Possibility: Emily Dickinson's Manuscripts.* Amherst: University of Massachusetts Press, 2005.
Moon, Michael. *Disseminating Whitman: Revision and Corporeality in* Leaves of Grass. Cambridge, MA: Harvard University Press, 1991.
Moretti, Franco. *Distant Reading.* London: Verso, 2013.
———. *Graphs, Maps, and Trees.* London: Verso, 2005.
Myerson, Joel, ed. *The Historical Guide to Ralph Waldo Emerson.* Oxford: Oxford University Press, 2000.
New, Elisa. *The Line's Eye.* Cambridge, MA: Harvard University Press, 1998.
———. *The Regenerate Lyric: Theology and Innovation in American Poetry.* Cambridge: Cambridge University Press, 1993.
Newberry, Frederick. "'The Artist of the Beautiful': Crossing the Transcendent Divide in Hawthorne's Fiction." *Nineteenth-Century Literature* 50.1 (1995): 78–96.
Noble, Marianne. "Dickinson on Perception and Consciousness: A Dialogue with Maurice Merleau-Ponty." In *Emily Dickinson and Philosophy,* edited by Jed

Deppman, Marianne Noble, and Gary Lee Stonum, 188–206. Cambridge: Cambridge University Press, 2013.
———. *The Masochistic Pleasures of Sentimental Literature.* Princeton, NJ: Princeton University Press, 2000.
Nussbaum, Martha. *Political Emotions.* Cambridge, MA: Harvard University Press, 2013.
Orvell, Miles. *The Real Thing: Imitation and Authenticity in American Culture, 1880–1940.* Chapel Hill: University of North Carolina Press, 1989.
Packer, Barbara L. *Emerson's Fall: A New Interpretation of the Major Essays.* New York: Continuum, 1982.
Patterson, Rebecca. *The Riddle of Emily Dickinson.* Boston: Houghton Mifflin, 1951.
Paul, Sherman. *Emerson's Angle of Vision.* Cambridge, MA: Harvard University Press, 1952.
Pearce, Roy Harvey. *The Continuity of American Poetry.* Princeton, NJ: Princeton University Press, 1961.
"Perversion of Scripture Language." *Christian Examiner* 2 (March and April 1825): 98–103.
Petrino, Elizabeth. *Emily Dickinson and Her Contemporaries.* Hanover, NH: University Press of New England, 1998.
Pinkard, Terry. *German Philosophy 1760–1860: The Legacy of Idealism.* Cambridge: Cambridge University Press, 2002.
Pinsker, Sanford. "Philip Rahv's 'Paleface and Redskin'—Fifty Years Later." *Georgia Review* 43.3 (1989): 477–89.
Pippin, Robert. "In Defense of Naive Reading." *New York Times,* October 10, 2010. https://opinionator.blogs.nytimes.com/2010/10/10/in-defense-of-naive-reading.
Pizer, Donald, ed. *Documents of American Realism and Naturalism.* Carbondale: Southern Illinois University Press, 1998.
Plato. *Euthyphro, Apology, Crito, Phaedo, Phaedrus.* Translated by Harold North Fowler. Cambridge: Harvard University Press, 1999.
———. *Phaedrus.* Translated by Alexander Nehamas and Paul Woodruff. Indianapolis: Hackett, 1995.
———. *Phaedrus.* Vol. 3 of *The Works of Plato.* Translated by Thomas Taylor and Floyer Sydenham. London: R. Wilks, 1804.
———. *Republic: Books 6–10.* Translated by Paul Shorey. Cambridge, MA: Harvard University Press, 2000.
———. *Symposium.* Translated by Alexander Nehamas and Paul Woodruff. Indianapolis: Hackett, 1989.
"Poetry and Reality." *Boston Olive Branch* 15.30 (July 27, 1850): 3.
Poirier, Richard. *Poetry and Pragmatism.* Cambridge, MA: Harvard University Press, 1992.
———. *A World Elsewhere.* New York: Oxford University Press, 1966.
Pollak, Vivian R. *Dickinson: The Anxiety of Gender.* Ithaca, NY: Cornell University Press, 1984.

Porte, Joel. *Consciousness and Culture: Emerson and Thoreau Reviewed.* New Haven, CT: Yale University Press, 2004.

Porte, Joel, and Saundra Morris, eds. *The Cambridge Companion to Ralph Waldo Emerson.* Cambridge: Cambridge University Press, 1999.

Porter, David T. *Dickinson, The Modern Idiom.* Cambridge, MA: Harvard University Press, 1981.

Price, Kenneth M. *To Walt Whitman, America.* Chapel Hill: University of North Carolina Press, 2004.

Rahv, Philip. "Paleface and Redskin." *Kenyon Review* 1.3 (Summer 1939): 251–56.

Redding, Patrick. "Whitman Unbound: Democracy and Poetic Form, 1912–31." *New Literary History* 41.3 (Summer 2010): 669–90.

Redekop, Benjamin W. "Reid's Influence in Britain, Germany, France, and America." In *The Cambridge Companion to Thomas Reid,* edited by Terence Cuneo and Rene van Woudenberg, 313–40. New York: Cambridge University Press, 2004.

Reid, Thomas. *Essays on the Intellectual Powers of Man.* 5th ed. Edited by James Walker. Boston: Phillips, Sampson, and Co., 1854.

———. *An Inquiry into the Human Mind.* Edited by Timothy Duggan. Chicago: University of Chicago Press, 1970.

Renker, Elizabeth. *Realist Poetics in American Culture, 1866–1900.* New York: Oxford University Press, 2018.

Reynolds, David S. *Beneath the American Renaissance: The Subversive Imagination in the Age of Emerson and Melville.* New York: Knopf, 1988.

———. *Walt Whitman.* Oxford: Oxford University Press, 2005.

———. *Walt Whitman's America: A Cultural Biography.* New York: Knopf, 1995.

Richardson, Robert D. *Emerson: The Mind on Fire.* Berkeley: University of California Press, 1995.

Ripley, George. *Philosophical Miscellanies: Translated from the French of Cousin, Jouffroy, and B. Constant.* Boston: Hilliard, Gray, and Co., 1838.

Rosenblum, Nancy. "Strange Attractors." In *A Political Companion to Walt Whitman,* edited by John E. Seery, 47–58. Lexington: University of Kentucky Press, 2011.

Rowson, Susana. *Charlotte Temple.* Edited by Cathy N. Davidson. New York: Oxford University Press, 1986.

Salska, Agnieszka. *Walt Whitman and Emily Dickinson: Poetry of the Central Consciousness.* Philadelphia: University of Pennsylvania Press, 1985.

Sanchez-Eppler, Karen. *Touching Liberty.* Berkeley: University of California Press, 1993.

Schaeffer, Jean-Marie. "Literary Studies and Literary Experience." Translated by Kathleen Antonioli. *New Literary History* 44.2 (Spring 2013): 267–83.

Schelling, F. W. J. *System of Transcendental Idealism.* Translated by Peter Heath. Charlottesville: University Press of Virginia, 1978.

Scholnick, Robert. "'The Original Eye': Whitman, Schelling, and the Return to Origins." *Walt Whitman Quarterly Review* 11 (Spring 1994): 174–99.

Sedgwick, Eve Kosofsky. "Paranoid Reading and Reparative Reading, Or, You're So Paranoid You Probably Think This Essay Is about You." In *Touching Feeling: Affect, Pedagogy, Performativity*, 123–51. Durham, NC: Duke University Press, 2003.

Shakespeare, William. *Love's Labour's Lost.* Edited by H. R. Woudhuysen. London: Arden Shakespeare, 1998.

Shi, David E. *Facing Facts: Realism in American Thought and Culture, 1850–1920.* New York: Oxford University Press, 1995.

Short, Bryan Collier. "Emily Dickinson and the Origins of Language." *Emily Dickinson Journal* 9.2 (Fall 2000): 109–19.

Smith, Martha Nell. *Rowing in Eden.* Austin: University of Texas Press, 1992.

Socarides, Alexandra. *Dickinson Unbound: Paper, Process, Poetics.* New York: Oxford University Press, 2012.

Stern, J. P. *On Realism.* London: Routledge, 1973.

Stewart, Dugald. *The Collected Words of Dugald Stewart.* Edited by William Hamilton. Edinburgh: Thomas Constable and Co., 1854–60.

———. *Elements of the Philosophy of the Human Mind.* Edited by Francis Bowen. Boston: James Monroe and Co., 1859.

Stonum, Gary Lee. *The Dickinson Sublime.* Madison: University of Wisconsin Press, 1990.

Stovall, Floyd. *American Idealism.* Port Washington, NY: Kennikat Press, 1965.

———. "Dating Whitman's Earliest Notebooks." *Studies in Bibliography* 24 (1971): 197–204.

———. "Notes on Whitman's Reading." *American Literature* 26.3 (1954): 337–62.

Sundquist, Eric J., ed. *American Realism: New Essays.* Baltimore: Johns Hopkins University Press, 1982.

Thayer, William Roscoe. "The Bases of Fiction." *Open Court* 4 (July 17, 1890): 2383–88.

———. "The Fallacies of Realism." *Open Court* 4 (July 3, 1890): 2361–64.

———. "Realism." MS AM 1081 2210, Houghton Library, Harvard University.

———. "The Scientific Method in Fiction." *Open Court* 4 (June 26, 1890): 2347–50.

Theune, Michael. "'One and One Are One' . . . and Two: An Inquiry into Dickinson's Use of Mathematical Signs." *Emily Dickinson Journal* 10.1 (2001): 99–116.

Thomas, M. Wynn. *The Lunar Light of Whitman's Poetry.* Cambridge, MA: Harvard University Press, 1987.

Thoreau, Henry David. *Walden. The Writings of Henry D. Thoreau.* Edited by J. Lyndon Shanley. Princeton, NJ: Princeton University Press, 1971.

———. *The Writings of Henry D. Thoreau: Journal Volume 2: 1842–1848.* Edited by Robert Sattelmeyer. Princeton, NJ: Princeton University Press, 1984.

———. *The Writings of Henry D. Thoreau: Journal Volume 3: 1848–1851.* Edited by Robert Sattelmeyer, Mark R. Patterson, and William Rossi. Princeton, NJ: Princeton University Press, 1990.

Tompkins, Jane P. *Sensational Designs: The Cultural Work of American Fiction, 1790–1860.* New York: Oxford University Press, 1985.

Trilling, Lionel. *Sincerity and Authenticity.* Cambridge, MA: Harvard University Press, 1971.

Trowbridge, John Townsend. "Reminiscences of Walt Whitman." *Atlantic Monthly* 89.2 (February 1902): 163–75.

Turpin, Zachary. "Hawthorne the Unreliabilist: His Epistemology in 'The Custom-House' and Other Prefaces." *ESQ* 60.4 (2014): 487–520.

Upham, Thomas Coggswell. *Elements of Mental Philosophy.* New York: Harper and Brothers, 1842.

Urbas, Joseph. "'Bi-Polar Emerson': Nominalist *and* Realist." *Pluralist* 8 (Summer 2013): 78–105.

———. *Emerson's Metaphysics.* New York: Lexington Books, 2016.

Van Leer, David. *Emerson's Epistemology: The Argument of the Essays.* Cambridge: Cambridge University Press, 1986.

Vendler, Helen. *Dickinson.* Cambridge, MA: Harvard University Press, 2010.

———. *Poets Thinking: Pope, Whitman, Dickinson, Yeats.* Cambridge, MA: Harvard University Press, 2006.

Waggoner, Hyatt. *Emerson as Poet.* Princeton, NJ: Princeton University Press, 1974.

Walker, Cheryl. *The Nightingale's Burden: Women Poets and American Culture before 1900.* Bloomington: Indiana University Press, 1982.

Walker, James. "Associations for Benevolent Purposes." *Christian Examiner* 2 (July and August 1825): 241–52.

Webster, Noah. *An American Dictionary of the English Language.* 2 vols. New York: S. Converse, 1828.

———. *An American Dictionary of the English Language.* 2 vols. Amherst, MA: J., S., and C. Adams, 1844.

Weiskel, Thomas. *The Romantic Sublime: Studies in the Structure and Psychology of Transcendence.* Baltimore: Johns Hopkins University Press, 1976.

West, Cornel. *The American Evasion of Philosophy.* Madison: University of Wisconsin Press, 1989.

West, Michael. *Transcendental Wordplay: America's Romantic Punsters and the Search for the Language of Nature.* Athens: Ohio University Press, 2000.

West, Peter James. *The Arbiters of Reality: Hawthorne, Melville, and the Rise of Mass Information Culture.* Columbus: Ohio State University Press, 2008.

Wheelwright, Philip Ellis. *Metaphor and Reality.* Bloomington: Indiana University Press, 1973.

Whicher, Stephen E. *Freedom and Fate: An Inner Life of Ralph Waldo Emerson.* Philadelphia: University of Pennsylvania Press, 1953.

Whitman, Walt. *The Collected Writings of Walt Whitman: Notebooks and Unpublished Prose Manuscripts.* 6 vols. Edited by Edward F. Grier. New York: New York University Press, 1984.

———. *Franklin Evans.* Edited by Christopher Castiglia and Glenn Hendler. Durham, NC: Duke University Press, 2007.

———. *Leaves of Grass: A Textual Variorum of the Printed Poems.* 3 vols. Edited by Sculley Bradley, Harold W. Blodgett, Arthur Golden, and William White. New York: New York University Press, 1980.

———. *Notes and Fragments.* Edited by Richard Maurice Bucke. [n.p.]

———. *Poetry and Prose.* Edited by Justin Kaplan. New York: Library of America, 1996.

———. *Prose Works 1892.* 2 vols. Edited by Floyd Stovall. New York: New York University Press, 1963–64.

———. *Selected Poems 1855–1892.* Edited by Gary Schmidgall. New York: St. Martin's Press, 1999.

———. *The Uncollected Poetry and Prose of Walt Whitman.* 2 vols. Edited by Emory Holloway. New York: Peter Smith, 1921, 1932.

Wihl, Gary. "The Manuscript of Walt Whitman's 'Sunday Evening Lectures.'" *Walt Whitman Quarterly Review* 18 (2001): 107–33.

Williams, Raymond. *Keywords.* Rev. ed. New York: Oxford University Press, 1985.

Williams, William Carlos. *Imaginations.* Edited by Webster Schott. New York: New Directions, 1970.

Wilson, Eric. *Emerson's Sublime Science.* New York: St. Martin's Press, 1999.

Windolph, Christopher. *Emerson's Nonlinear Nature.* Columbia: University of Missouri Press, 2007.

Winthrop, John. *Winthrop's Journal, "History of New England," 1630–1649.* Edited by James Kendall Hosmer. 2 vols. New York: Charles Scribner's Sons, 1908.

Wittgenstein, Ludwig. *The Blue and Brown Books.* 2nd ed. New York: Harper, 1960.

Wolosky, Shira. *Emily Dickinson: A Voice of War.* New Haven, CT: Yale University Press, 1985.

———. "Emily Dickinson: The Violence of the Imagination." In *The Cambridge History of American Literature,* vol. 4, edited by Sacvan Bercovitch, 427–80. New York: Cambridge University Press, 2004.

———. "Rhetoric or Not." *New England Quarterly* 61.2 (1988): 214–32.

Wordsworth, William. *Lyrical Ballads, and Other Poems, 1797–1800.* Edited by James Butler and Karen Green. Ithaca, NY: Cornell University Press, 1992.

Yoder, R. A. *Emerson and the Orphic Poet in America.* Berkeley: University of California Press, 1978.

York, Jake Adam. *The Architecture of Address.* New York: Routledge, 2005.

Index